THE
CHESHIRE
MOON

ALSO BY ROBERT FERRIGNO

The Horse Latitudes

THE
CHESHIRE
MOON

ROBERT FERRIGNO

William Morrow and Company, Inc. · New York

It is the policy of William Morrow and Company, Inc., and its imprints and affiliates, recognizing the importance of preserving what has been written, to print the books we publish on acid-free paper, and we exert our best efforts to that end.

Library of Congress Cataloging-in-Publication Data

Ferrigno, Robert.
    The Cheshire moon / by Robert Ferrigno.
       p.   cm.
    ISBN 0-688-10314-6
    I. Title.
PS3556.E7259C48 1993
813'.54—dc20

92-22573
CIP

Printed in the United States of America

First Edition

1 2 3 4 5 6 7 8 9 10

BOOK DESIGN BY LINEY LI

To the Hillside Comets #13
and to Ruthie,
The girl who loved him

Acknowledgments

My thanks to Liza Dawson, Sandra Dijkstra,
William Ungerman, Bonnie Kaplan, Mark Michaelson, and
most of all, to Jody

He came back too soon. He knew it the night he flew in, watching from the window of the jumbo jet as it began its descent into LAX, the Cheshire moon hanging over the Pacific, an ominous smile above the waves.

Katie was the one who named the Cheshire moon, pointing it out to him late one night on their way back from getting soft ice cream on Second Street. She was just six years old then, up past her bedtime, fresh from Alice in Wonderland and the White Rabbit—she rode on his shoulders, giggling, holding on to his hair.

He heard her cry out, her fingers tearing at him, then she was cowering from the crescent moon peeking through the palm fronds, begging him to make the mean cat stop looking at them like that. Make him go *away*, Daddy.

It took him a few minutes to get it, but she was right. The moon was in the waning phase of the lunar cycle—it happened every month, but a few times a year, like tonight, that bleak curve of moon was horizontal, a perfect Cheshire grin across the sky. For six days that cold smile would get thinner and sharper as it approached the utter darkness of the new moon. Like it couldn't wait for the lights to go out.

He had lifted Katie off his shoulders, cuddled her to his chest. Her heart fluttered against him as he tried to reassure her, telling her it was a special smile from the nice Cheshire Cat who lived out there among the stars.

"No, Daddy," she insisted, "he's *not* nice." Her face was so serious he didn't even try to change her mind, just held her close. He heard a rustling in the palms as he walked and glanced behind him, feeling foolish as he hurried his steps, carrying her home under that knowing smirk.

The jet dropped down, turning away from the moon as it dipped its wings over Los Angeles—he saw the HOLLYWOOD sign floodlit against the distant hills, the letters so tilted it looked like a different alphabet.

They came in low, and he pressed himself against the window, following the stream of headlights winding down the coast—Hermosa Beach, Redondo Beach, San Pedro, and there was Long Beach, Belmont Shore . . . home.

He spotted the *Queen Mary* parked in Long Beach Harbor, its three-stack profile stark against the wharf, just as the 11 P.M. fireworks display started from the rear deck. He held his breath as the Roman candles lit the sky, blooms of green and red stars, fading from sight.

It was all so beautiful he didn't want to land, knowing things couldn't get better, they could only get worse.

Chapter 1

Jen Takamura walked around the Jeep, a camera bag slung over her shoulder, one finger idly running over the scratched camouflage paint job. You'd have thought she was listening to music the way her nails danced across the dents, clear polish on steel.

Quinn sat in the driver's seat, enjoying the rhythm of her movements as she sauntered past—the sway of her shiny bobbed hair, the rustle of the black miniskirt along her thighs, crushed silk on smooth skin. A necklace of silver bones bounced against her sweater. Even her red cowboy boots had chains that snaked across her arch with every step—snick-snick-snick. Tough enough, no doubt about it. He found himself tapping his foot in time with her.

Jen caught him staring, looked right back at him, her eyes the same green color as that Japanese horseradish served with sushi, sweet one moment, fiery the next.

She turned those hot green eyes on the jacked-up 4x4 Jeep, surveyed the heavy-duty bumpers and screened fog lights, the chopped-off roof and padded crash bar. "This thing is *so* macho, Quinn," she mocked, shaking her head in disbelief, "I feel like I'm swimming in testosterone."

"Just keep your mouth closed, you don't want to swallow any," he laughed, and she laughed back with those ripe lips. He extended his hand to help her in, but she smacked it aside, pulled herself up into the passenger seat in one fluid movement. He waited until she was buckled in before peeling out of the *SLAP* magazine parking lot and down Century Boulevard.

SLAP was a snide, trendy monthly known for its insider political profiles and gritty photojournalism, celebrity exposés and holographic liquor ads. One critic described it as "the schiz-oid offspring resulting from the rape of *Vanity Fair* by the *National Enquirer,* attack journalism with a manicure."

Quinn had been writing for *SLAP* for five months, but this was the first time they had worked together. Not that he hadn't noticed Jen before. He had spotted her his first day, watching Jen argue with the photo chief on the other side of the cafeteria. She must have won the argument, because she got the next three cover assignments.

Last month she had done a six-page centerspread on pre-teen gangsters—"Locoboys"—formal portraits in black-and-white, each of the subjects posed with his favorite gun. She had spent two weeks on her own in the worst barrio in the city; her assistant, a two-hundred pound intern from USC, had fled the first day and refused to return.

Quinn pinned the pages next to his desk at home, fasci-nated with the sad, deadly children, and the young woman who had faced them down with only her cool self-confidence. He still remembered what that felt like. An attitude like that could get you killed. Or somebody right next to you.

A year ago he had been an investigative reporter for the *Times-Herald,* as hard-core as she was, trolling biker bars and the city morgue for information, comparing tattoos with speed-freaks who couldn't remember having front teeth. Keeping bad company. No more. *No más.*

These days he played it safe. Last issue he had interviewed haberdashers who outfitted Madonna impersonators. The ac-companying photo showed nine dumpy old men, each wearing glossy red lipstick and a beauty mark. One of them sent Quinn a 44-DD gold-lamé brassiere afterward—"For you, gratis." He hung it on the rabbit ears of his TV. It seemed to improve the reception.

Quinn ran a hand through his long dark hair, raked it straight back, suddenly angry and not sure why. He gunned the Jeep forward. He was thirty-seven years old, tall and still solid, his face all nose and jaw, more predatory than pretty. Tonight he wore tight jeans, scuffed engineer boots, and a yellow happy-face T-shirt with the sleeves rolled up.

"I almost forgot," said Jen, raising her voice. "They were

paging you over the intercom when I left the office. Somebody named Andy called for you—I think he was having an anxiety attack."

"Yeah, that's him," he said, slowing slightly. Andy was a high-strung hustler in his late twenties, a former Cal Tech whiz kid who specialized in heavily discounted status toys: in-dash CD players and portable fax machines, Rolexes and Guccis and Mont Blancs. All new and in their original containers. Just don't ask for a receipt. He was probably sitting in some fast-food joint right now, someplace that offered unlimited coffee refills, sitting there with a gym bag full of cash on his lap, knees bouncing as he watched the door. "He had the new receptionist in tears," Jen said. "He kept saying he had to talk with you. A matter of, and I quote here, 'fucking life and fucking death.' "

"It's *always* life and death with Andy. I'll call him later."

Jen shrugged.

Porsches and BMWs roared out of the underground garages of the surrounding highrises, darting onto Century Boulevard, jockeying for position. It was early Friday evening in the entertainment district, account executives and production supervisors abandoning their offices for other roosts, playing chicken, too busy jabbering on their car phones to bother using turn signals.

"Napitano recruited you himself, didn't he?" asked Jen. The wind whipped her hair. "That's what I heard. He did the same thing to me. Called me up at this apartment I was staying at in Paris. Three A.M. He just starts in like we're old friends, offering me anything I wanted. I don't even know how he got the number." She shook her head.

Antonin Napitano was the publisher of *SLAP*, a former Roman tabloid mogul, enormously wealthy, a pink, pudgy little man with exquisite taste in art and a soft, dirty laugh.

Quinn had to force himself to relax his grip on the steering wheel.

It was raining in Corpus Christi the night that Napitano called and introduced himself, the storm coming in off the Gulf, hitting the tile roof as the phone rang.

Quinn had been lying low in Texas after the minimart killing, hiding out from himself more than anyone else. He worked a double shift throwing up cheap houses for oil riggers, swinging a thirty-two-ounce hammer from dawn to dark, so tired afterward he couldn't even remember his dreams.

The night Napitano called, Quinn was listening to the thunder, still in his work clothes, thinking how it wasn't really that late in California, and maybe Katie would still be up. Sometimes he called just so they could sing the theme from *Gilligan's Island* together, Katie dropping her voice, rasping, "for a six-hour-cruise." He was reaching for the phone when it rang. He never did learn how Napitano found him, but he recognized the man's name immediately.

"I know *all* about you too," Napitano had cooed, his voice buttery. "You've done nothing to be ashamed of—a vast ambition is often sloppy, that is of no consequence. Better your grand bloody failure than the niggling mistakes of lesser men. We are much alike, you and I." He sighed, the sound so drawn out that Quinn thought they'd been disconnected. "Come work for me, dear boy," purred Napitano. "These moral pygmies who condemn us . . . Come home—together we will fuck their teeth out." Quinn flew back the next day. He told himself it was because he missed Katie.

"I didn't get this assignment until twenty minutes ago," Jen said, fiddling around in her camera bag, checking lenses. "All I heard was 'Musclemen for Jesus' and knew it had to be one of your ideas."

Quinn grinned. He was a light-heavyweight with an easy laugh and biceps the size of Indian River grapefruit. You'd think he had forever with that smile, but when it faded, the years crashed back around him.

"They're called 'the Samson Squad,' " he said, "three macho evangelicals who minister to wayward youth by tearing phone books in half. These guys combine iridescent bodysuits and hair extensions with smoke machines, strobe lights, and psalms. Very professional. Very Deutschland—"

"Very *Vegas*."

A powder-blue Rolls Corniche veered over from the next lane but Quinn cut the Rolls off at the freeway onramp, ignoring the driver's outraged beeps and finger-flip.

Jen put both feet up on the bare-metal dash, bracing herself as they entered the freeway. Her skirt slid toward her hips as he punched it toward the fast lane.

Quinn slammed on the brakes, downshifting, grinding into first. Traffic was stopped as far as he could see. An accident somewhere ahead, an overturned tractor-trailer, or maybe a jumper from one of the overpasses. Drivers around them were shutting off their engines, settling in with paperbacks, reapplying mascara, calling to postpone their dinner reservations. The next exit was two miles away.

An L.A. County ambulance raced down the shoulder past them, an undulating wail echoing in its wake. He hated that sound—it was like a woman screaming in pain.

"Quinn? I *asked* if you could finish the Samson article by the day after tomorrow," said Jen. "I have an early color deadline. Are you okay?"

He blotted sweat from his forehead, not answering. The line of cars stretched into the distance, all of them going nowhere. Waiting for the ambulances to finish. He checked his rearview, revved the engine, redlined it, then cranked the steering wheel hard left and let out the clutch. The Jeep bumped across the rocky median and thudded directly into the hedge dividing the freeways.

Jen yelped, hanging on with one hand, holding her camera bag in place with the other.

He rocked the Jeep back and forth, shifting from first to reverse and back into first, suddenly floored it. The lugged offroad tires spun for a moment on the flattened vegetation, then the Jeep lurched and roared over and through the bushes, spraying crushed flowers in its wake. He entered the opposite freeway, cut across four lanes and took the first offramp.

"Don't give me that look," he said as they continued west on surface streets. "It'll grow back." He checked for police cars in his rearview, spotted a yellow oleander blossom caught on the driver's side windshield wiper. "This is Southern California," he said, plucking the flower free and handing it to her, "the land of infinite renewal. *Everything* grows back."

He saw a phone booth, thought of calling Andy just in case, but they were already running late.

Jen saw him eye the phone booth. "This Andy character

offered the receptionist a microwave oven if she'd tell him where you were. I was tempted to turn you in myself."

He glanced over at her, then went back to squinting into the setting sun, the sky streaked with red and orange. "I didn't figure you for the domestic type." Out of the corner of his eye, he could see Jen smiling, tickling her cheek with the oleander blossom. The flower looked on fire in the light.

Chapter 2

Andy needed a gun. Something big enough to bring down a dinosaur. He made it a point to stay away from hardware; getting busted with a piece, in addition to his usual stock, could be the difference between parole and hard time. Besides, violence was for subnormals. He glanced down at his blood-splattered high-tops. He needed a gun.

The girl ahead of him dropped her change onto the concrete, coins rolling everywhere. She giggled, bending over to pick them up. Bennington watched her tube top and cutoffs playing peekaboo with her fat. Andy watched the street instead, checking out every car that passed. The girl staggered past him, still giggling. She smelled of peppermint schnapps.

Bennington nodded at him from the cashier's cage of the CHEAPGAS self-serve station. "Handy-Andy, my man," he said, "this ain't your delivery day." Caution glazed his eyes, thicker than the bulletproof glass between them.

"I need—" Andy jerked around. A white-haired gent in a plaid suit had come up behind him to wait in line. Andy glanced at Bennington, then back to the old man, then back to Bennington.

Bennington cocked his head, waiting, his high cheekbones like polished black hardwood. He sat on a stool in the booth, a slender sixteen-year-old surrounded by displays of pine-tree car deodorizers and cigarettes, a signed photo of Don King taped next to the cash register.

Andy fished out a twenty-dollar bill, shoved it into the cash drawer. "I'll be back for my change."

Andy jammed the gas-pump nozzle into the tank of his

Dodge van, felt the hose jerk as he squeezed the handle. The CHEAPGAS station was on the corner of Bolsa and Edwards in Westminster, right off the freeway. He methodically scanned the busy street as the pump chimed away, shielding his body with the van. It was Friday night, everyone had a date. The man he was worried about would be driving by himself.

He had called Quinn's office three times, left a couple of messages on his home answering machine—where *was* he? Andy slouched against the van, knobby knees and elbows poking out from his baggy shorts and sweatshirt. He felt like he was made of Pic-up-Stix.

He could see his own reflection in the gas pump as the numbers rolled past, a headdress of dark blond dreadlocks framing serious, intelligent features. His eyes were too large for his face. Quinn said he looked like an endangered species caught in the headlights.

He glanced over at Bennington, saw him staring back at him through the glass.

It wasn't really glass, of course, but a sandwich of high-density acrylic. Soon to be obsolete. The latest issue of the *Polymer Research Quarterly* had described a new armored plastic based on a protein that golden-orb spiders used to make their webs. Andy could still see the molecular arrangement in his mind—fucking awesome simplicity. *PRQ* reported that the new material was ten times stronger than acrylic; within three years a bulletproof plastic would be on the market that was no thicker than windowpane. If he got out of this alive, Andy was going to have his whole house done over.

What the hell was Bennington looking at? Andy glanced at his shoes. He should have changed at his place while he had the chance, but he hadn't noticed the blood. It wasn't like he didn't have boxes of high-tops stacked to the ceiling, 322 pairs of last year's model, strictly swap-meet material now—everybody wanted sneakers that pumped up or slam-dunked by themselves.

At the next service island over, the girl with the tube top and cutoffs stood filling a battered Datsun. She dropped the gas nozzle on the concrete, picked it up, and struggled to replace it on the pump, finally gave up and left it dangling.

Andy watched her stagger into the Datsun and wanted to

brain her with a tire iron. He hated drunk drivers, seeing in their sloppiness the foreshadowing of his own random death. He was going to die behind the wheel, according to Ginger, who read Tarot cards. "Don't worry, hon," she said, "I'm always wrong."

He had breezed through the first two years at Cal Tech before dropping out, too smart to need to graduate. He was a rational positivist who subscribed to forty-seven international science journals and balanced his checkbook in his head . . . but he knew Ginger was right.

Andy imagined a drunk racing the wrong way down I-5 slamming into him, cars tumbling end over end, fire everywhere. Or an earthquake collapsing a freeway overpass on top of him. Maybe something as simple as a leak in the van's exhaust system . . .

Where the fuck was Quinn?

Gasoline gushed out the van's full gas tank and onto his shoes. He could see Bennington laughing silently as he hung back the nozzle and walked over.

"You get me some more of them Dunhill lighters?" said Bennington.

Andy shook his head, checking the street.

"Gold Dunhills," said Bennington. "They's pussy magnets, certain. You got 'em, I can move 'em."

"I need to buy a gun," said Andy. "Now."

Bennington stared at him. "We ain't allowed to carry. Company policy." He rapped the thick glass with a shiny knuckle. "Don't need to, neither."

"What you need doesn't matter," said Andy. "You got a gun or not?"

Bennington scowled, then thought about it, considering the possibilities. He beckoned Andy closer, nodding at the floor of the booth. He pulled up his pant leg a few inches so Andy could see a small blued-steel pistol held against his ankle by a frayed Ace bandage.

"How much?" said Andy.

Bennington's watery eyes glimmered, a feral intelligence rising to the surface. "You retiring or running? Either way, you're gone, right?"

"How much, dude?"

Bennington beckoned him closer, the pistol now nestled in his smooth palm so only Andy could see. "Little ol' .380 auto, eight in the clip, one in the chamber. Hollow points. Nobody be messin' with Smith and Wesson," he singsonged, "on special tonight for only . . . seven-fifty."

The only sound was the neon lights sputtering overhead.

"I like this here little-bitty gun." Bennington shrugged. "I got a personal attachment. You gots to pay for that. Sides, it's your own fault, *dude,* for not dealing no guns."

Andy dipped into a pocket and came out with an inch of fifties, folded in half and secured with a rubber band. He peeled off the bills, keeping the roll half-hidden. The money drawer slid out and he tossed the bills in, heard it slam shut with a heavy metallic thud.

Bennington scooped up the money, counted it twice.

"Pass it over," said Andy. He glanced over his shoulder. "I want to get out of here."

Bennington counted it again, looked up at him.

"Come on!"

Bennington watched him through the thick glass, expressionless, cold undersea eyes staring back from the depths of the aquarium as Andy beat against the glass.

Chapter 3

Hulking phys. ed. majors in Samson Squad! T-shirts and stone-washed jeans handled traffic control outside the Pure Light Temple, yelling at each other as they haphazardly waved cars into position, making a mess of it.

The temple was a glass-and-steel cathedral overlooking the Huntington Beach oil fields, an immaculate crystal shard ringed with searchlights. The people inside were visible through the translucent walls, diffuse, bodies moving with the organized randomness of the hive. It reminded Quinn of the mother ship in *Close Encounters*.

Quinn and Jen flashed their press cards at the bored security guards, passed folding tables piled high with Samson Squad videotapes, audiotapes, and Tough-Enough-for-God? paperbacks. Posters of the Samsons lined the walls, the three longhairs in full flex, their expressions orgasmic with endorphins.

The darkened auditorium was packed, the crowd surging to the thunderous music, all bass and feedback, an apocalyptic storm so loud that Quinn and Jen had to shout to hear each other. Red and yellow spotlights played across the eager faces of the audience, caught the gloved fists raised high, Bibles pumping in time to the beat.

Quinn looked around, trying to get his bearings, but Jen headed right into the seething shadows, working her way through sideways, snapping away with one of the three cameras that dangled around her neck. Quinn lowered his shoulder and forced his way through, following the white flashing of her strobe, a marker buoy in that warm young sea.

19

The Samsons were onstage, heads tilted in prayer, hair hanging past their shoulders. The star-spangled jumpsuits bulged with sheets of lumpy muscle, their sharecropper faces stolid as axheads.

Quinn felt himself jostled, glimpsed black leather jackets and spandex, letter sweaters and the sharp gleam of stainless-steel orthodontic braces—a thousand perfect smiles in the making. A flat-chested girl in a red bustier stumbled past; he counted eleven snaps on the back before she was swallowed up. "Hollywood High meets the Jesus Posse," he scribbled in his notebook.

The stage lights blazed on, the backdrop behind the Samsons ablaze with blue light—a forty-foot airbrushed Jesus on the cross. This wasn't the Prince-of-Peace Jesus, however, this was a pissed-off Jesus, an angry longhair in a loincloth, with washboard abdominals and rippling pectorals, every muscle in his outstretched arms clearly defined. He looked like he was about to pull the nails from his hands with his teeth.

The tallest Samson stood in front of the microphone, hands on his hips—he would be Ironman, the former pro wrestler known for his Killer-Claw Deathgrip and using his championship belt to whip opponents and referees alike.

"You got *TROUBLE*?" Ironman bellowed, the cords in his neck bulging out like he'd swallowed a blowfish. "Parent trouble? Job trouble? Boy trouble, girl trouble? Well, *PUNCH OUT* your troubles with the blessed fist of Jesus, and I'm here to tell you, the Samson Squad *IS* that fist!"

The crowd whooped.

"A lot of preachers tell you to forgive and forget," said Ironman. "Pencilneck Christianity!" he spit. "The Devil hears that crap and he licks his chops. The Devil loves to mess with pencilneck Christians, likes to cut their tires, trip them at the goal line. . . . Well, the Samson Squad doesn't turn the other cheek to the Devil—we kick his flabby *ASS!*"

The crowd cheered and clapped, waved back and forth like a field of wheat in a strong wind.

Quinn squeezed his way closer to the stage, the air getting thicker the closer he got, a ripe melange of sweat and leather, Lovesoft body mist, and sensimilla. A kid in a studded vest lurched into him, mumbled an apology, and offered him a joint.

Quinn waved him off, pushing forward, always forward, still looking for Jen.

Ironman was at center stage, flanked by the other two Samsons, who held bouquets of baseball bats in their hands, boxes of bats behind them. "Jesus is no punk!" shouted Ironman. "And neither is the Samson Squad!" He flung back his long hair and the girls squealed.

Ironman hung on to the microphone, face contorted, voice crackling and overamplified. He grabbed a bat, banged it on the floor. "This is a hickory-wood Louisville Slugger, José Canseco autograph model," he said as the other Samsons beat on the stage, keeping a steady tattoo rhythm. "Hickory's hard," Ironman whispered into the mike, "harder than any of your problems." He nodded, and the other two Samsons snapped a bat over their knee like chopsticks, tossed the pieces aside as the crowd gasped.

"Give Jesus a big hand!" shouted Ironman, and the crowd applauded. "Give it up for Jesus! He can bust your problems just that easy." Ironman strutted back and forth, chest out, swinging a Louisville Slugger, mighty Casey belting one out of the ballpark for the Messiah. "You say you're not popular?" He thumped the stage, barely missing the outstretched hands that clutched at him. "You say you're flunking algebra?" Wham! "You think nobody'll ever ask you *out*?" Wham! "Ask Jesus *in*, and see what happens."

Quinn spotted Jen at the edge of the stage, calmly shooting the crowd, the eager faces transfixed by Ironman.

"Look at Joseph here," shouted Ironman, indicating the Samson on his left. "Joseph was molested as a child, repeatedly raped by his stepfather, sodomized like an animal." Joseph hung his head, looking uncomfortable. "When he was fourteen years old, a shotgun blast blew off a piece of his skull—"

"What piece?" someone shouted.

"His brain tissue was exposed to the light of day," Ironman continued as though he hadn't heard. "The doctors thought he'd die, or at least be paralyzed." Ironman held up a pair of handcuffs for the crowd to see.

"You gonna spank him?" The same voice from the edge of the stage, a kid with a blue mohawk wearing a Megadeth T-shirt. "Little bondage action?"

"These are police handcuffs, twenty-gauge forged steel." Ironman slapped them on Joseph's wrists, jerked them roughly to show they were locked. "Without the power of Jesus, Joseph would be helpless, bound and delivered, just like Samson among the Philistines."

The lights dimmed, a single spotlight on Joseph's fleshy chest and huge arms, his eyes dull as mushrooms. He was a star-spangled side of beef in the spotlight, straining against the handcuffs.

"You were used like a beast of the field," Ironman exhorted him, "used like a dumb brute." Sweat ran down Joseph's face as he struggled with the cuffs. "You weren't expected to ever speak again"—Ironman shook his head—"so brain-damaged they didn't think you would be able to experience the joy of marital relations—"

"Show him your *dick,* Jo-Jo!"

Ironman kicked the kid with the mohawk in the side of the head, knocked him into the swarm of hands.

"HEY!" Quinn shouted angrily.

"The doctors gave up on you," rasped Ironman, moving back into the spotlight, "but not *Jesus.*"

The music stopped. Joseph raised the handcuffs over his head, closed his eyes, groaning, then lurched forward as the handcuffs tore apart. The audience raised their flaming Bics in the cool darkness of the glass auditorium.

Quinn saw Jen stick her camera close to a girl who was weeping with joy in the flickering light, her whole body shuddering. Jen caught the tears and mascara running down her cheeks, the black motel Bible hugged against her chest.

"Are you ready for Jesus?" bellowed Ironman, wrapping his hands with Ace bandages. The road crew drove forklifts loaded with ice blocks onstage, wheeling them into a wall five feet high. "I'm not talking about that turn-the-other-cheek Jesus!" Ironman roared as he placed both hands on the wall. "That lovey-dovey Jesus don't cut it on the late, great planet Earth, people. What we got here's a Texas grudge match between the kick-butt Jesus and the Devil, winner-take-all for the championship belt."

Red smoke poured from the fog machines, flooded the stage, as the strobe lights danced.

A skinny boy clawed his way onstage, reached down and pulled others up to join him, girls clambering onto the apron. Bouncers charged from the wings, body-blocking the kids as the crowd surged forward. A dozen hands grabbed a terrified bouncer, pulled him down, his SECURITY T-shirt torn to pieces as he disappeared into the churning horde.

Ironman stood oblivious, concentrating, taking slow deep breaths, his every movement digitally disassembled, awful in its strobe-lit clarity.

Quinn saw Jen leaning over the stage, trying to get a better angle. A security guard grabbed her arm and she smiled at him, took his picture, whispered something to him. The guard looked around, then hooked a hand in her belt and held her up for her shot.

Ironman reared back and karate-chopped the blocks of ice, drove the edge of his hand through the top layers as the crowd gasped. "Break through!" he roared, hair flying, frozen splinters thrown everywhere. "Break through!"

A collective gasp bounced off the cold glass walls of the temple.

Ironman attacked the ice in a frenzy, hair flying, great frozen chunks falling everywhere. His fists punched through the ice, spraying the first five rows, chopping away until the wall was breached and broken. He stood over the shattered blocks, wobbling, giving thanks in a hoarse mumble. Melted ice dripped from his taped hands, dripped red in the klieg lights.

Chapter 4

O

Quinn stopped at a phone booth along Jefferson Boulevard as they drove to Jen's apartment, but it wasn't working. He'd try Andy again from her place.

Jen was examining one of her cameras, tilting it in the glare of the streetlight, as he climbed back into the Jeep. "The Samsons were interesting," she said, not looking up, "but the *real* story was the kids in the audience. That whitebread suburban desperation—"

Quinn turned the ignition. "I know what the story is," he said tightly.

"Sure you do." Jen dabbed at the 85mm lens with a tiny wad of tissue, cleaning crusted cherry Coke that someone had accidentally sloshed on her. She exhaled on the lens, continuing her efforts.

He ground the gears, glancing over at her, but Jen's face was obscured by the camera, and he couldn't tell if she was smiling.

It was after 10 P.M. on a Friday and Venice was still going strong, the sidewalks of the beach town buzzing with random energy—punks looking for the party, silicone-perfect secretaries trolling for a SAG card. Unemployed young professionals talked too loudly about tomorrow's interview, swigging bottled water they kept refilled from the tap. Bleary-eyed USC fratboys in madras Bermudas and brown penny-loafers lurched into the street without any thought of traffic, convinced of their golden potential.

At a Stop sign, Quinn watched an emaciated man stalk a waddling pigeon who kept three steps ahead of him. Last sum-

mer, a group of movie stars in new denim clothes had led
swarms of homeless to Venice while the TV news cameras
rolled. The stars helped build packing-crate shanties on the
beach, then left for Malibu. The pigeon fluttered out of the
stalking man's grasp as the Jeep Dopplered past, its barely muffled engine noise bouncing off the old brick buildings.

Jen lived on the third floor of a blue stucco building with
sagging front steps flanked by a pair of concrete lions. One of
the lions was missing his head. Like everything and everyone
in Venice, the neighborhood was in a state of transition: A
golden angel trumpeted from the roof of the Mormon temple
across the street, two blocks away the new condos were layered
with gang graffiti, the writing so dense it was like trying to read
a newspaper under water.

She unlocked the door. "Come on in." She led him into
the living room, flipping on lights. Quinn glimpsed a tangled
unmade bed through an open door, flowery red sheets and
fluffy pillows in the soft light. She saw his expression. "Don't
get any big ideas," she said, "I've got a darkroom set up in
there."

"So you're not going to be changing into something more
comfortable?"

"I should have tonight's film developed and proof sheets
in an hour," she said patiently. "I want you to stick around to
see them so we can talk about the direction of your story. If
my shots turn out the way I think they will, the crowd portraits are going to be a lot stronger than the show onstage. I
saw you interviewing some kids, so you shouldn't have any
problem—"

"Why don't you write the story too? Save me time."

The bedroom door closed behind her.

The living room was devoid of furniture, strewn with
empty film canisters, plastic dry-cleaning bags, and wispy lingerie. He picked up a pure white G-string, spun it around his
index finger, and let it fly. Stacks of magazines lay on the wood
parquet floor, tottering piles of *Spin, Headbanger, Details,* the
Italian *Vogue, Harper's Bazaar, Elle.* Pages from the magazines
were pushpinned to the walls, Axl Rose's leering tattoos going
one-on-one with pouting ingenues in Blackglama chic.

A half-dozen potato plants sprouted in water-filled jelly jars on the kitchen windowsill, the tubers pierced by toothpicks to hold them in position. They were perfect for someone who liked plants but didn't have a set schedule: She could leave for a two-week shoot and they would just keep growing.

Taped to one wall was a male Hot Buns calendar, three months behind. Quinn riffed through the calendar, but there wasn't a date marked or circled in the whole year. It was as if nothing had happened and nothing was anticipated. Maybe Mr. March was all she needed.

The refrigerator overflowed with apples and oranges and cherries, bottles of juice, bunches of carrots and celery, stacked cartons of yogurt. He worked his way through the bottles without making a sound, picked out a quart of raspberry kefir and gave it a shake. He took a long drink straight from the carton, replaced it, and strolled back into the living room.

"Where's the phone?" he called to the closed bedroom door. No answer. "Jen?" He shrugged and went into the bathroom.

He turned on the tap, splashed cold water on his face, put a cold washcloth against his throbbing ear. The shower curtain was clear plastic, with a shadowy knife-wielding Norman Bates superimposed. He checked behind it, just in case. One ladies' razor. A couple of dark hairs curled against the drain. He picked one up. It was thick and black—hers. French soap and French shampoo.

A glance toward the door, and he shrugged and opened the medicine cabinet. The cabinet contained a tube of number 25 sunblock, eight different shades of lipstick, hypo-allergenic eyeliner and mascara. No contact-lens paraphernalia; maybe those green eyes were real. Tom's natural toothpaste, dental floss, a large bottle of generic aspirin, allergy pills, and a prescription bottle of yellow capsules. Xanax fifty milligrams. That was a relief. Fifty milligrams was like lemon Pez. He had worked with one photographer who popped 250 milligrams of Thorazine for lunch and washed it down with a Coors. Jen just got the jitters once in a while.

Quinn knew about the jitters. He never closed the door in a phone booth. He never slept over. He looked. He listened.

And when he got the chance, *like now,* he improved his odds. What you didn't know about people could kill you. And you never knew enough. Oh yeah, he knew all about the jitters.

He had gone through Jen's clips in the photo morgue the day after he first saw her, then bribed Melanie in Personnel with a Dove Bar. While he read Jen's file, Melanie gobbled down the ice cream. "You want to really know about that one," she clucked, scraping her horsey teeth along the wooden stick to get the last bit of chocolate, "you best ask the big I-talian boy on the loading dock."

Jen had an incredible portfolio. For the last five years, she had freelanced all over the world; her credits ranged from Palestinian refugee camps to high-contrast fashion layouts to grainy close-ups of the Paris after-hours club scene. She had also done a series on innocent victims of drive-by shootings and portraits of crack babies staring out from clear plastic incubators, IV lines running from the wrists and feet. If she only needed fifty milligrams of Xanax to put herself to sleep after *that,* she was a brick.

What the hell. He turned the water in the sink back on, stood on the toilet, and checked the top cabinet. It was an old habit—you get an opportunity, you take advantage. You push your luck. Sometimes you push it too far.

She had nice thick towels. No monogram. A couple of hotel rip-offs. He never knew a photographer who didn't steal towels. Next to the towels was a half-full vial of golden love oil. He unscrewed the top and sniffed. Apricot. It smelled like dessert. Beside the oil stood a slim pink vibrator. He resisted the impulse to switch it on and see if the batteries were charged.

The bathroom door swung open and Jen walked in, stopped halfway, blinking.

He almost dropped the love oil. "I locked the door," he said, like that would make it better.

"The lock doesn't work." If emeralds could burn, they'd leave hot embers that looked like her eyes. "You want to check my dresser drawers?" she said, her boot tapping on the tile floor. "Maybe the bed? I've got some wild things under the mattress."

He carefully put the love oil back. "I was curious. I just wanted to know you better."

"Well," she said evenly, "now we both know each other better."

As he started down from the toilet, she gave him a push, knocked him toward the bathtub. He grabbed the shower curtain as he fell, tore it off its hooks, snap-snap-snap. He banged his head on the bottom of the tub, saw Anthony Perkins floating down toward him like a murderous butterfly.

He groaned, pushed aside the curtain, his legs still outside the tub. When he turned, Jen was sitting on the toilet, skirt hiked, white lace panties ringing her ankles.

"You didn't have to bother snooping, you know," she said, "you could have asked. I grew up sharing a bedroom with two brothers and a sister—I lost my sense of modesty a long time ago." She languidly scratched the back of her knee. "My name is Jen Takamura," she recited in her husky voice. "I'm a Japanese-American female. My father was born at the Minidoka Relocation Camp in southeastern Idaho. Twenty below zero during the winter and outdoor privies. My mother is half white and remarried. I'm twenty-four years old, single, and a high school dropout. I speak four languages. Mensa member since age thirteen—I don't attend meetings, but I still get the local newsletter." Her pee hit the water.

Quinn averted his eyes, stared at the faucet dripping slowly into the tub, then back at her.

"I have a five-inch shrapnel scar along my hip," she said. "Beirut."

He leaned forward, watching the faucet drip.

"I vote in every election," she continued, her voice edged with condescension, "even the primaries. I do pro bono work for Greenpeace and NOW. At home, I'm an ovo-lacto vegetarian—no meat, no fish, no poultry. On the job, I eat whatever comes my way." She was still peeing.

The back of his head hurt where he had hit the tub. He pulled himself halfway up, trying to get some leverage on the slick porcelain, but couldn't get any farther.

"I use a diaphragm," she said, "but whoever's playing the part of the boyfriend uses a rubber, or he doesn't play at all. When there's no one suitable, I solo with the love oil and Mr. Ed. Usually, I have a better time with Mr. Ed." She wiped, pulling up her panties as she stood. Her hands were on her hips now. "I change my own flat tires, do my own taxes, and carry my own camera equipment. There's more, but I figure that's enough for now."

He rubbed his nose, smelled apricots on his fingers, and felt himself blush.

She started to smile, puckered her lips instead. "I have a phone in the darkroom. The receptionist at the magazine just called here looking for you. That guy Andy keeps calling and calling—he's gone from pleading to threatening to flat-out hysterical."

"May I use your phone?"

"*May* you? What a gentleman." She walked out, shaking her head.

Chapter 5

Quinn parked midway down the hill overlooking Second Street, and sat there watching Burgerama's cool blue neon, feeling foolish for his caution.

Andy had answered Quinn's return call on the first ring. "I'm in megatrouble, dude, Panic City," he said, voice fading—probably using one of those portable cellulars he was peddling a few weeks ago—"Meet me at the usual spot, and pronto Tonto. Please?"

Panic City? Andy had never lived anywhere else. Still, there had been . . . something in Andy's voice, even coming through that scratchy portable phone. They had known each other five years, and Andy had called scared before, convinced he was about to be busted or ripped off. Tonight was different. It sounded like his teeth were chattering.

Burgerama was a gleaming oasis in Belmont Shore, a reconstructed fifties-style hamburger joint with glass-brick walls and soft deco curves, carhops on roller skates and a prop cherry-red Ford roadster parked out front. Everything strictly decorative and open twenty-four hours a day. It was Andy's favorite restaurant.

Belmont Shore was an affluent beachfront enclave just south of Los Angeles, with high turnover and the collective memory of a meatgrinder. Palm trees lined the streets. The Goodyear Blimp floated serenely overhead. Second Street, the business strip, was eight blocks of Hawaiian shaved ice and investment diamonds, Rollerblade rentals and gourmet takeout. A European lingerie salon replaced a pizza parlor, a heavy-metal boutique pushed out a video store—only their creditors noticed.

Ambition ran through the Shore like an underground pow-
erline, pulsing with success and failure, devoid of value judgments. You could walk into the most expensive restaurant
without a tie, without socks even, but the banks wouldn't make
change unless you had an account with them. Andy said he did
more business in the Shore than anyplace on the Coast.

Quinn crossed Second Street and made a slow circuit of
Burgerama, staying to the edge of the surrounding parking lot,
dodging the carhops in their V-neck sweaters and short pleated
skirts. He checked the patio first. Nothing. Just fashionably
blank couples with spiked hair and sunglasses. At the very back
of the lot, he spotted Andy's empty van straddling two spaces.

There he was. Andy stepped out of the men's room, wiping
his hands on his paisley skateboarder shorts. Quinn watched
him move along the row of pay phones, flicking the coin returns
as he walked to the patio. He sat at the far table, hunched over,
head in his hands so that his blond dreadlocks grazed the ta-
bletop.

The patio was walled off from the street by thick safety
glass, but left open to the sky. A bubbletop Wurlitzer squatted
in one corner, its Bakelite plastic softly lit with pinks and blues.
Nat King Cole crooned "Mona Lisa" while the bug-zappers
crackled overhead.

Andy jerked upright, stared right at him through the glass,
his fear suddenly turning to relief. By the time Quinn was seated
opposite him, Andy was shaking again, his watery eyes checking
and rechecking the door. He dragged a hand through his ropes
of hair, and Quinn half expected clumps to come out.

"I called the magazine for hours," Andy said. "They didn't
know how to get in touch with you." He shook his head in
amazement. "No portable cellular, not even a beeper—Jesus,
Quinn, this is the nineties. *Access*, dude, reach out and fucking
touch someone." Andy had that old arrogance again, and Quinn
thought for a moment things were fine. Then his face fell and
he bent back over the table, tearing a napkin into smaller and
smaller pieces. Sad confetti.

The interior of the restaurant was decorated with disconnected bump-'em cars and peeling carousel horses, rusty Wonder Bread and Coca-Cola signs—a world of happy, pink-
cheeked families on their way to innocent refreshment. Burg-

erama was calculated kitsch, designed by an architectural firm in Laguna Beach that specialized in Eisenhower-era serenity, alluring and artificial as the maraschino cherries atop the sundaes.

"I've been going through the periodic table in my head," said Andy, eyes downcast as he started on another napkin. "You know, Hydrogen, Helium, Lithium . . . I do that sometimes. Anyway, I get to Osmium and I can't remember what comes next. It's either Iridium or Platinum, but I'm not sure." He stared at the bits of paper piled in front of him. "I was a fucking National Science Finalist my senior year, and I am *losing* it."

"Yeah, well, I was captain of the debate team, and I haven't won an argument in years, so—"

"I walked into something bad this afternoon," interrupted Andy. He started on another napkin. "A murder." His voice was barely audible. Quinn noticed dried blood on the right sleeve of Andy's sweatshirt. "The movies have it all wrong," said Andy, his hair swinging back and forth, hiding his face.

"Who died?" said Quinn.

"His name is Tod. You don't know him." Andy blew the bits of napkin off the table, watched them flutter to the floor. "Tod was a customer. We were in Chess Club at Cal Tech before I dropped out. He got expelled a couple of semesters later for cheating on an astrophysics exam, but he was flunking anyway. Now he's . . . he *was* a hotshot executive assistant to that TV talk-show babe, you know the one . . . Big Beautiful Woman type . . . married to that old cowboy actor?"

"Sissy Mizell? *Straight Talk with Sissy?*"

"Yeah, that's her," said Andy. "The white Oprah."

They faced each other like looking into a camera, speaking in a syrupy southern drawl: "I'm Sissy Mizell, y'all, and I'm no expert, but I got sense and this is what I think."

Andy laughed so hard he had to wipe his eyes. It wasn't that funny. "I used to think Tod was a flunky, but Sissy just gave him a promotion—mondo bucks and he's allowed to make suggestions to her, even prepares some of her questions. You know that thing they do with the opening of the show? Where the camera zooms in on one person, tighter and tighter, until all you see are a pair of clapping hands? That was Tod's idea." Andy jerked around, held up his coffee cup to a freckly waitress with henna-red hair. "Little coffee here, miss? Sometime this geological era?"

She walked right past him, balancing a tray of vanilla malts, a cute girl in a poodle skirt, pink angora sweater, and saddle shoes. Any minute now Archie and Veronica were going to show up and invite everybody to a sock hop.

"Last week, me and Tod are watching basketball on one of those forty-inch Mitsubishis I had on special a while ago. He lives in this waterfront house in Naples. His grandmother owns it but she's shacked with her boyfriend at LeisureWorld, the two of them Alzheimersed out, hooked up to oxygen tanks like a couple of Martians . . . Anyway"—Andy shrugged—"we're watching the Lakers—Tod's nuts for hoops—and I tell him he's wasting money paying for cable, I can sell him a satellite dish and it's free forever. Tod says the local zoning regulations won't allow them. Supposed to be an eyesore, so—"

"Is there a point to this?"

The redheaded waitress reappeared. "You need something?" She smiled at Quinn. Quinn winked back, said he needed a vacation and some new friends, but he'd settle for one of her fine thick malts. She giggled and Quinn smelled sweet onions. She glared at Andy. "You going to order?"

Andy looked at Quinn, who nodded wearily. "Maybe I will have a little something," Andy said, like he was considering the idea for the first time. "Give me a large fresh orange juice, no pulp, and a . . . Lumberjack Breakfast, eggs easy. And extra sausage!" he called to her retreating back.

"I'm glad the terror hasn't hurt your appetite."

"So I tell Tod not to worry about zoning," said Andy, oblivious, "I've got these new dishes look just like patio umbrellas. Three different stripe patterns—for an extra hundred bucks I can custom-order a Cinzano knockoff that would fool the pope. Five hundred dollars, which is less than half retail, if you're interested?"

Quinn just stared at him.

"Okay." Andy shrugged. "My point is, I should have just dropped the dish off. I didn't *have* to install it for Tod, but customer satisfaction means a lot to me."

"Oh yeah, you're a people person."

"Make jokes. So, this afternoon, I show up and Tod's all

stressed out, keeps asking how long is it going to take . . . ?
Fucking pinhead, I should have split."

The waitress brought Quinn his malt, leaned over him. He
felt her angora, soft and warm, brush his cheek. She poured
coffee for Andy without looking at him, slid over his Lumberjack Special, and left.

Quinn heard the rustle of silk and whirled around, thinking
it was Jen. Which made no sense. Hoping it was Jen. Which
made even less sense. He rubbed the knot at the back of his
head, and smiled to himself.

"So I'm working outside on the patio, aligning the unit,"
continued Andy, "Tod's watching some college game. Fucker's
got the curtains pulled, so I'm not tempted to ask him for a
Pepsi with a slice of lemon, and maybe some of those jumbo
prawns he keeps stashed in the freezer, cheap bastard. . . . A
couple hours later, I come back inside, and Tod's crashed on
the recliner. I could hardly see him, the only light in the living
room is from the TV. I tossed him the remote and told him to
see if he can pull in HBO, but he didn't say anything. So I
leaned over to wake him, and . . . and"—Andy licked his lips—
"and there's all this . . . stuff pouring out of him. I-I stepped
in it. . . . It's on my shoes. I can't get it off."

"Take it easy."

"I hate the soft sciences," said Andy, "biology, zoology,
anatomy. . . ." His hand moved independently of him, punc-
tured his over-easy eggs with the fork, the yolks oozing from
the perforations. "We're so ugly inside," he whispered, eyes
shimmering, "all of us, Julia Roberts, Michelle Pfeiffer, it
doesn't matter, we're filled with greasy slop. . . . Jesus, man, we
look like fucking SpaghettiOs inside."

Quinn's grip gently enclosed Andy's scrawny upper arm.

Andy pulled away, unable to meet Quinn's gaze. "I'm not
like you," he said. "Hey, you know me. . . . I don't do well under
pressure."

One of the carhops leaned against a Mustang, laughing.
As she straightened, she stopped suddenly. Quinn couldn't see
what she was looking at.

Andy saw Quinn's expression. "You said it was okay here,
right?" he said. His eyes darted back and forth like they were
trapped in his face. "This is a public place, right?"

Quinn didn't bother answering. If Andy wanted to believe that bad things only happened in private, in the dark, let him. He walked over to the jukebox, lip-synching to Chuck Berry while he checked out the parking lot. Just a well-groomed couple in matching green leather jackets sitting on their restored Harley hogs. Très chic. A giant bucket of chicken slowly revolving above the Kentucky Colonel outlet across the street. He tried to get the carhop's attention, but she continued on her rounds.

"What's wrong?" Andy asked as he returned.

"Nothing."

Andy pushed his plate away, the food untouched. "So, I'm standing there, looking at Tod . . . and I . . . hear the toilet flush. Funny the things that can scare you. . . . Next thing, this huge fucker comes walking out of Tod's bedroom, zipping up his pants, which is not that easy because he's wearing pink surgical gloves. This old guy is total monstro, got this crewcut makes his head look like a giant pumpkin. He didn't even notice me at first, and that was all I needed. I mean I am *out* of there, dude, I am through the sliding doors, over the fence and gone."

"Did you call the cops?"

Andy snorted. "Tod's a good customer, but the guy with the crewcut doesn't know me. Fuck Chess Club. I go back to my crib and play some Nintendo, and . . ." He tore open three packets of sugar, his hands shaking so badly that he spilled most of it trying to pour it into his coffee.

"What did you forget?"

"You figured that out, huh? You're smarter than you look." Andy's hands skimmed the table, his fingers dancing across the counter, playing piano. "How that little girl of yours?" His fingers pounded out fortissimo. "She still taking lessons? You should get her a real piano, that upright is dogshit."

"I bought it from you."

"Yeah . . . well, you could do better."

"What did you leave behind, Andy?"

"Just my address." Andy's laugh was bitter. "I actually won something, hit one of those lottery scratchers for two dollars. They got this bonus deal where you write your address on the back of the ticket, and when you turn it in, you get entered for the Big Spin. That's a ten-million-dollar payout, minimum. So

I fill it out, used my real address too, figured maybe my luck was finally changing." He moistened a fingertip, touched it to the spilled sugar, and put it in his mouth. "Oh, it's changing all right, it's changing from bad to terminal. So now the ticket with my address is in my parka, and the parka is at Tod's, and the big guy probably found it and is coming to get me. My luck, he kills me, and two weeks later I hit the Big Spin."

"I don't think you have a problem," said Quinn. "A guy murders somebody, he doesn't stick around checking pockets."

"Easy for you to say."

"He's long gone. Don't worry."

"You didn't see him ambling out of the bathroom. This fucker wasn't in any hurry—he didn't even try to chase me. I drove by with my lights off, and he's standing on the front porch, scratching his belly, watching me go."

"Any chance he could read your license plate?"

"No way. It was dark and I keep a light coat of mud on it."

"Go to the cops. Tell them what you saw."

"I can't," insisted Andy. "They'll have too many questions, and once they start they don't let go. I got a house full of merchandise— *You* talk to them. Call that cop pal of yours . . . Morales. Tell him whatever you have to, just get into Tod's house and see if the lottery ticket's still in my jacket. It's a green nylon surf parka." He lifted his sweatshirt, showed two cellular phones tucked into his pants. "Make sure you call my personal number. I'm not taking business calls until this thing is settled."

"What an opportunity. I get to pick up the check and be an accessory to a homicide, all in the same night."

"Let your conscience be your guide, dude, but I need to know if it's safe for me to go home. I'm out in the cold here. You know what that's like."

Quinn hadn't touched his vanilla malt. It was gloppy and sickly sweet but he drank it anyway, watching Andy's lower lip tremble. "Why would somebody kill Tod?" he said at last.

"How should I know?"

"Was he into drugs?"

Andy shrugged. "I don't think so, but you know me—that's not my area of expertise."

"You said he was always watching sports. Did he put bets down? Serious money?"

"Why else would anybody watch a bunch of overpaid ectomorphs? You going to help me or not?"

"Maybe Tod was into his bookie a little too deep. The guy you described, the way he reacted, not being rattled . . . he could have been a pro." Quinn nodded, thinking. "You said Tod was jumpy when you showed up to install the satellite dish . . . was he expecting somebody?"

"I figured he had some babe coming over later," said Andy. "Tod got laid more than fucking JFK." He glanced around. "Help me, Quinn. You're the only one I can ask."

Quinn nodded. "I'll call Morales. You've got twenty-four hours to take care of business, then you turn yourself in and sit down with a sketch artist and work up a composite of the killer. I'll go down to the station with you if you want. I don't know about the lottery ticket. I'll do what I can."

"Deal." Andy wiped his eyes and grinned. "You had me going." He bobbed his head at Quinn. "I just want to put this behind me. Let me tell you, walking in on Tod like that was the worst thing that ever happened to me. Total bummer." His hands were shaking again. "I should have known something was going to happen when I hit that two-dollar lotto," he moaned. "I'll tell you, if it was possible to buy luck, I'd pay fucking retail."

"No you wouldn't. You'd try to corner the market, then jack up the price."

"True." Andy cleared his throat, wiped his eyes with a napkin. "Look at that." He nodded at the mural on the near wall, an idealized vision of Southern California in the fifties—clear blue sky and eight-foot surf, wooden station wagons loaded with longboards, clean blond kids heading out for the endless summer. "It's a lie," he said, "all of it."

"Tell me something I don't know," said Quinn.

Chapter 6

The white Saab Turbo was parked in front of Rachel's house again, the second time this week his ex-wife's new boyfriend had come over for dinner and stayed after dessert.

Quinn had run Mr. Saab Turbo's license plate through the DMV, then used that information to check out his credit history. Tynan DeWitt, age forty-three, brown hair, hazel eyes, never married, lived at the same address in Newport Beach for the last eighteen years. Commercial real estate developer. Homeowner. No moving violations. No bounced checks. Even repaid his student loan. Rachel had learned her lesson.

He had kept his promise to Andy, calling Morales first at the police station, then trying him at home. Quinn was sure he had awakened him, but you couldn't tell from Esteban's voice. He always sounded on duty. Quinn gave him Andy's description of the man with the crewcut, but didn't mention the lottery ticket. Time enough for that later.

It was after midnight—this late he was the only one out, the large houses silent and dark, the clipped lawns dotted with ARMED RESPONSE signs. Not a pink flamingo or a dandelion in sight. He had walked straight up the hill from Burgerama into Belmont Heights, the faint click of his boots on the sidewalk a private tap dance in the stillness. He twanged the Saab's antenna as he passed.

He met Rachel ten years ago at a party given by the publisher of the paper—Quinn was the only reporter invited, flush with his first Pulitzer nomination, drunk for the first time on good champagne. Rachel was an art professor at the university

39

who said he had the freest laugh she ever heard. They were married six weeks later.

Rachel had picked out their house, used her inheritance for the down payment. People in the Heights played squash, never tennis. Their dogs were AKC obedience-trained, one-on-one; their kids had to settle for a spot on the Montessori school waiting list. He liked the house, but he always thought a neighborhood committee was going to show up someday and ask him to move.

He and Rachel had been divorced for over two years now, but they were still friends, still neighbors—she and Katie lived in the main house, while he camped out in the guest cottage out back. Their settlement called for the property to be sold and split, but the market had slowed and sales kept falling through escrow and neither of them were in a hurry. Rachel said it was good for Katie to have him nearby. He knew just how Katie felt.

Quinn hurried around back, stood looking up at Katie's room on the second floor for a moment, then swung himself up into the big elm tree, pulling himself easily through the familiar branches and onto the platform of two-by-fours next to her open window. They were going to make a real treehouse someday.

Katie's bed was right next to the window, the room lit by the Wonder Woman lamp on her nightstand. A gift from him on her last birthday; she said it was "juvenile," but kept it anyway. Most of her stuffed animals had been put away, replaced with fossil fish and an ant farm and a plastic anatomical model of the Visible Woman. She still slept with the bespectacled White Rabbit tucked under her arm. I'm late, I'm late, I'm late. He wondered how long that would last. She was eight years old, slipping away from him by the moment.

Katie's curly brown hair floated on the pillow, soft as foam on the sea. One small hand flopped out of the covers. She had Rachel's artistic hands. He smiled at her snoring.

The branch creaked as he shifted on the platform, leaned out, and rested his arms on the windowsill, bridging the space between them.

When he worked for the newspaper, he'd come home in

the middle of the night and kneel beside Katie's crib, just watching her sleep, so close he could feel her breath on his cheek. After Groggins . . . after that, Quinn watched her from the elm tree, not wanting to get too near, afraid his own nightmares would somehow intrude on her dreams.

He was still an investigative journalist the first time he met Groggins, a small-time thief charged with raping and murdering two Long Beach State University coeds. The bodies had been dumped in the boat channel, so there was no physical evidence to tie Groggins to the crime, but the D.A. was talking gas chamber—he had an eyewitness.

Halfway through the trial, Quinn was tipped that the eyewitness was a police snitch, a crackhead stamped "Property of Detective Nate Odom," the cop who made the bust. Three days before closing arguments, Quinn broke the story that Odom's witness was passed out in a rockhouse at the time he testified that he saw Groggins running from student housing.

The jury found Groggins innocent, and his public defender stood outside the courthouse, gave a peptalk about the Bill of Rights, and announced she was taking offers for screen rights. ABC-TV mentioned the case on its evening broadcast, and the newspaper nominated Quinn for his second Pulitzer.

A month after the verdict, Quinn's editor rushed over to his desk, said Groggins was holding a clerk hostage in a minimart and demanding to talk to Quinn.

The Long Beach SWAT team had the minimart surrounded when Quinn arrived, local TV helicopters circling overhead. The cops were holding back, giving him a chance to defuse the situation, sensitive to the negative PR possibilities. Quinn had walked through the police line, hearing his name whispered, the officers and camera crews parting like he was Charlton Heston. He was so hot he glowed.

"Hey, pardner," Groggins greeted him as he walked into the minimart. "You want some jalapeño beef jerky? My treat." He kept the pistol pressed against the back of the clerk's neck. She was a doughy black woman with terrified eyes behind her thick glasses. "It's okay, Doreen," Quinn reassured her, reading her nametag, the three of them caught in the glare of the camera lights outside.

"You're too smart for this," Quinn said to Groggins. "These cops would love an excuse to waste you, and they don't like me either—why make them happy?" He held open the door.

Groggins edged past him, still using the woman as a shield. He glanced at the phalanx of cameras and microphones. "You got a comb I can borrow?"

"Let Doreen go," Quinn said. "What are you looking at here, armed robbery? That's chickenshit. You'll spend a year pumping iron at county, come out looking better than you went in. Don't make it worse."

Groggins spat. "Oh, I'm long past armed robbery, pardner. I just wanted you to hear it from me direct. Professional courtesy like." His eyes were flat and gray as river rocks. Quinn felt cold. "I did some bad shit to my landlady this morning," said Groggins. "She was fun"—he licked his lips—"but the college girls were better."

Quinn stared at Doreen, her eyes so big there wasn't room in her face for anything else. He heard the gun go off as he reached for her, her shattered glasses flying through his fingers. All Quinn remembered after that was the sound of ambulances screaming.

Katie turned on her side, stretched, and opened her eyes. She stared at him for a few seconds before he registered. "Daddy," she yawned, not surprised.

Daddy. She must still be half-asleep. When she was awake she called him "Quinn." He liked "Daddy" a lot better.

She sat up on one elbow, blinking. "Are you sleeping inside tonight?"

"I'm making waffles tomorrow morning," he said. "I hope you're hungry."

She wasn't distracted. "Are you?"

"Not tonight."

She sighed.

"I've got my own house now, you know that. You can see me any time you want. Just look out your window."

"After you sleep inside, Mommy sings the whole next day."

"Shhh. It's late."

She rubbed her eyes with her fists. "Mommy says I can buy a microscope with my allowance if I save up." She yawned again, eyes drooping, and laid her head back on the pillow.

"That's good." Quinn pulled the covers up under her chin. She suddenly jerked upright.

He turned around to see what she was staring at.

The Cheshire moon peeked through the tree, a leering grin hiding among the falling leaves.

She buried her head in the pillow.

The smile was full tonight, perfectly positioned, an arc of dirty yellow light in the night. The smile would get thinner and thinner over the next week—even when it disappeared, it would still be out there waiting. You didn't need a child's imagination to see what was coming.

Quinn reached through the window and began stroking her hair. "It's okay, honey," he lied.

She looked up from the pillow. "That bad cat's going to hurt you," she whispered.

"No chance." He winked at her, his hand on her shoulder.

She glared at the moon, took the nasty smile straight on. "I hate him, Daddy." She had his stubborn eyes.

"Shhh."

She scooted closer to the window, closer to him, cuddling her tattered White Rabbit.

He pulled the covers around her, humming a song they made up when she was small and afraid of shadows in her room. He watched her fight sleep, eyes slowly closing as she gave in.

The wind stirred the branches around him, and he zipped up his jacket against the chill.

You find out who your friends are when you get your face on the nightly news. The convenience-store killing had led every broadcast, both local and national, Quinn's grief caught by the cameras as the anchor intoned that the landlady and the clerk would still be alive if "an overzealous reporter" hadn't gotten Groggins acquitted of a prior murder charge. Quinn had come to the same conclusion all on his own.

The district attorney demanded his source. California had a press-shield law, but the editor of the paper suggested he cooperate for the good of the community. And for their subscribers, who were canceling by the thousands. Quinn didn't feel very cooperative. He had walked into the editor's fifth-floor office, tore the framed copy of the First Amendment off the wall, and smashed it across the desk. They decided he didn't work there anymore.

Rachel never wavered. They were already divorced, but she insisted on going out to dinner at all their favorite restaurants. She held his hand at the table, and refused to lower her voice. It reminded him why he had fallen in love with her, made him wish he still felt that way.

Rachel didn't surprise him, but Andy did. He showed up with a paper bag filled with cash, fake I.D., and a moderately warm open airline ticket. The ticket would take him anywhere in the continental United States, far from the district attorney's press conferences. The money would allow him to make his child-support payments until he returned. The money was a loan, of course, prime rate plus one point—better than BankAmerica, dude. Pay it back whenever.

Katie cried out and he jerked, almost fell. "It's okay."

Doreen, the clerk at the minimart, had a daughter too. A two-year-old she was raising by herself—that's why she worked afternoons at the minimart, so she could spend mornings with her little girl. Nights she went to school. Her sister was taking care of the child now.

"Daddy's here," he said, rubbing Katie's back. He wondered if Doreen's little girl woke up in the middle of the night, crying, wondered if the sister could hear her when she did.

Andy was afraid of the dark too. And spiders. And the IRS. And now a big man with a crewcut.

Quinn had kept his promise to Andy—let the cops deal with the murder. There was no reason for him to get involved. He almost had himself convinced.

Quinn checked his watch. Nearly midnight. Morales and the homicide team should have arrived at the scene . . . Tod's house. The familiarity of the man's name was incongruous. They had never met, but a connection had been established, a trail of blood from Tod to Andy to Quinn. He didn't like it— he preferred more distance between himself and the dead. He looked again at Katie, then started down the tree. Tod's address was in his pocket. He had checked.

A wind rose, sent wisps of cloud across that grinning moon . . . spiderwebs on the smile.

Chapter 7

Sissy checked her watch. Almost midnight. Liston should have called by now to let her know everything had gone smoothly at Tod's. She didn't expect Tod to call; it would have been nice, but she didn't expect it. He was probably still a little embarrassed.

"You call that applause?" Tommy Jay shook his head. He looked in pain. "I've seen harbor seals do better than that, folks, and they're working for fish heads. I know it's late, but come on, you people are going home with complimentary love toys!" A ripple of laughter worked through the studio audience. "Like this," said Tommy Jay, really whacking his hands together. "Try it."

The crowd applauded briskly.

"There you go," Tommy Jay beamed. "We appreciate you people coming out for this late-night edition of *Straight Talk*—"

Sissy turned off the sound in her dressing room, picked up the phone, dialed her private line. No messages. She tapped her front teeth with a fingernail, thinking. Liston should have called. He was eager but unreliable—weren't they all? She was tempted to phone Tod . . . no, let him stew.

The studio audience looked fine, a blend of not-too-young and not-too-old, dressed mostly name-brand, urban chic. Just enough ahead of her demographic to make the viewers feel like they were in good company, not so well-off as to make them feel inferior.

Market research said she had a younger, more hip audience than Donahue, a more affluent and educated one than Oprah or Sally Jessy, and only slightly less salacious than Geraldo.

Smart and nasty. Sissy had personally Okayed the promo for today's show: a handsome man in a business suit on his knees with his hands handcuffed behind him, a ball-gag in his mouth. Tagline: "Honey, I'm home!"

She leaned back in her chair and closed her eyes as Alexandra started doing her makeup, the soft ermine brush sweeping up her cheeks, delicately applying blusher to her creamy white skin.

She mentally reviewed the prep sheet that the line-producer had handed in for today's show: brief profiles of the guests, background on the subject, and provocative quotes from experts in the field. The producer worked up a rough time schedule for the show, but Sissy ran the clock, preferring her own gut instinct to set the pace.

The brush caressed her jawline, dipped down to her throat. Sissy didn't need much makeup; she was almost forty and her face was smooth and taut, with just a hint of crow's-feet. She had always stayed out of the sun, and being a big girl helped. She tapped two fingers under her plump chin, pleased with herself.

"Sissy?" Alan's voice was hesitant. "Sissy?"

She waved Alexandra back, slowly opened her eyes.

Alan shifted from one foot to the other; the talent coordinator was a balding man with wire-rim glasses and suspenders. "Reverend Chitman won't go on," he said.

"Look at me when you talk," said Sissy. She checked her watch. "What's wrong with the preacher?"

Alan blinked behind his thick lenses. "He says he wasn't told that there was going to be a prostitute on the program."

Sissy snapped her fingers and Alan dived for the telephone, handed it to her and punched the green-room button. "Put him on," she said to the assistant who answered. "Reverend," she said sweetly, "what's this I hear about y'all refusing to do my show?" She nodded. "Well, honey, I know that, but if you don't come on, I'll have to tell the folks why you canceled, and it's going to look like you're scared of a silly little whore, pardon my French. What with all that stuff about Jimmy Swaggart, people are going to think you got something to hide. I know," she said, "but that's the way it's going to look. Five minutes, Reverend, make a decision. Fine, you pray on it. Bye."

Sissy kept the phone. "Control room," she snapped, and

Alan hit the yellow button. "Carol, this is me," she said. "Tell Camera B, I want close-ups of the preacher ready to cue whenever the hooker is talking. I'm looking for nervous feet and hands, sweaty forehead, you name it." She tossed the phone back to Alan and lay back in her chair.

Alexandra finished up her makeup. Sissy checked the results in the mirror, then dismissed her. Sissy insisted on doing her lipstick herself, appreciating her wanton mouth, the full lips, sensual and infinitely expressive. She carefully outlined the contours, put on a light gloss, blotted, and added another coat. She puckered for her reflection.

On the wall next to the mirror was a framed snapshot of a slender girl of fifteen, with flyaway blond hair and a faded polka-dot dress from Goodwill. Raylene Mae Mizell. Sissy. Standing there with his arm around her was Talbert Jones, her first husband, who was twenty years older and drove a Rebel oil truck.

They had been married an hour when the picture was taken. She was six months pregnant but you could hardly see her belly. Talbert had bad skin and liked to caw like a rooster when he finished doing that thing inside of her, but he had a black Pontiac Firebird and she had needed to get out of her daddy's house. A week after the ceremony at the justice of the peace she lost the baby, and Talbert started hitting her for using big words.

Sissy had taken the snapshot with her as she worked her way up from Vicksburg to Birmingham to Atlanta to Chicago and now Los Angeles. She had gained eighty pounds since that picture was taken, her hair was longer and darker, but if you looked close, you could see that even back then she had smart eyes, too smart to settle for a piece of the pie—she wanted all of it.

Marcos poked his head in the door and she waved him in. He hummed as he combed out her thick strawberry-blond hair, his hips swiveling slightly as he worked.

Sissy glanced at the monitor. Tommy Jay was getting the three sections of the audience to compete against each other in applauding on cue. He stood with his ear cupped, listening intently before declaring it a dead tie. The cameras panned the crowd and Sissy grimaced.

Camera C showed a fat woman in a muumuu with a swap-meet frosted-blond wig. The woman was near the back of the center section, but letting her in was inexcusable. She was every fat joke come home to roost. Why didn't they give her a bag of jelly doughnuts to complete the picture?

Sissy picked up the phone, got Carol in the control room back on the line. The page who had passed the woman in the muumuu was fired. Now. If any of the camera people showed the cow on-screen during the show, *Carol* was fired.

Marcos clucked sympathetically as she spoke. He put the brush down and began to massage her temples, whispering that tension was bad for her follicles. She closed her eyes as his fingers made tiny circles.

Her watch alarm beeped and Sissy was out of the chair and down the hall, plucking tissue paper from her neckline, tossing it in her wake. A last look in the full-length mirror offstage as she heard Tommy Jay ask, "Are you ready for some straight talk?" The crowd cheered, then screamed as Sissy pushed through the curtains.

She pirouetted for the audience as their applause rolled off the walls of the studio, a deafening wave. She laughed and fluffed out her hair playfully, waved to the regulars in the front row. She wore a bulky pink sweater and full-cut shorts that came right to the edge of her slightly dimpled knees. The sweater's scoop neck revealed just a hint of her rounded white cleavage.

"I want to thank Tommy Jay for that introduction, and I want to thank each of you for coming to this special midnight presentation. As you know, we usually do our show live in the morning, but we're taping a couple weeks' worth so my husband, John—"

The audience burst into spontaneous applause.

"Thank you." She blushed. "I know y'all love John as much as I do. Well, once I get these shows done, he and I are going to take a vacation, a second honeymoon. I'm also real busy getting ready for my first-ever prime-time special. I'm turning forty in a week"—she mock-screamed—"and I thought I'd have a few friends over to the ranch to help me celebrate. Don't you forget to watch, now, or I'm going back to selling cosmetics door-to-door."

The audience cheered even louder.

"So you folks at home, get comfortable, cause we've got a real juicy show today: 'Hookers' Love Secrets.' So put your feet up and let the dishes soak, this next hour could save your marriage." She looked right into Camera A and promised to be back "soon as the network gets done trying to sell you something."

The floor director gave her the "cut" sign and the red light on camera A blinked off. Sissy waved once more to the audience, then walked back to the large overstuffed sofa at center stage, the sofa flanked by two wing-back chairs. She sat regally erect on the sofa, her arms draped over the back, filling one whole side.

Alexandra and Marcos scurried over; the makeup buff fluttered over her cheeks like butterfly wings, while Marcos plucked at her hair with a rat-tail comb.

"More hairspray, Marcos," Sissy ordered, her eyes shut so Alexandra could give her lashes a final lift. "Damnit, you never use enough hairspray." She could hear the gentle whooshing of the camera hydraulics as the operators moved into position, the murmur of the audience, then the floor director's countdown: "Ten, nine, eight, seven, six . . ." Alexandra and Marcos rushed off, Marcos grabbing a chocolate from the candy dish on the coffee table. "And three, and two, and one . . ." Sissy opened her eyes and smiled into the camera.

"What do hookers know that you don't?" she asked. The tip of her tongue poked out of the corner of her mouth. "Maybe what they know could put the fire back into your sheets? Today, we're going to get some straight talk from these ladies of the evening, so get out your pencils and paper, you might want to take notes."

The projection screen directly behind her lit with a red neon light as the Jimi Hendrix song "Foxy Lady!" began, sending a tickle up her spine. A page led her three guests onstage while the tape rolled.

She checked the monitor: images of women in hot pants flagging down cars along the Sunset Strip, blowing kisses, the flashing porno palaces of Forty-second Street, then the mirrored ceiling of a swanky apartment and Jane Fonda as Bree Daniels in *Klute* staring with a knowing depravity. As the images dissolved into each other, statistics crawled across the screen: Eighty-three percent of the men who regularly patronize prostitutes are married; 89 percent of the customers characterize the sex as "very satisfying" compared to 73 percent of married men who characterize sex with their spouse as "very satisfying."

The projection screen dimmed and Sissy took the cue.

"I'd like you to give a warm 'down-home' welcome to Francine Tousey," she said, indicating the slim, fresh-scrubbed young woman in the cheerleader outfit sitting on the sofa next to her. "For eight years Francine was a five-hundred-dollar-a-night call girl in New York. Five hundred? Whoa, girl. Francine wants you and the IRS to know that she is now retired and working on a book." Applause. You'd have thought she discovered a cure for leukemia. Francine inclined her head, plucked at her pleated plaid skirt. "On my left"—Sissy looked at the woman in the wing chair—"is Dr. Alice Tigard, Ph.D., and certified sexol—"

"A-leece," said the woman on her left. She had short, bristly hair and a sallow, unhealthy complexion.

"What?" said Sissy. She took in the woman's black leather jodhpurs and motorcycle jacket like she was looking into a microscope.

"A-leece," the woman repeated, "not Alice."

Sissy rolled her eyes at the audience. "Dr. Tigard's a certified sexologist, so I guess she can call herself anything she wants. This good-lookin' gentleman on my right," she said, winking, "probably has a few names he'd like to call you both. I'd like to introduce the Reverend Robert Chitman, from the Bethany Assembly of Christ."

"Thank you, Sissy," boomed the awkward man with the black suit and bright yellow bow tie. His voice seemed bigger than he was.

"Now that we're all acquainted," said Sissy, reaching down to the candy dish and popping a chocolate into her mouth, "let's get down to the nitty-gritty. Alice—I'm never gonna get that right—Dr. Tigard"—she chomped happily away—"isn't it true that men will have sex with warm mud, but what they're willing to pay for is oral sex?"

"Absolutely," said Dr. Tigard, as she watched Sissy chew.

"Head jobs are the bread-and-butter of the business,"

agreed Francine, tucking one of her saddle shoes under her. "I can say 'head job' on TV, can't I?"

The audience applauded.

Reverend Chitman swallowed.

"What I want to know is why do these husbands have to go out for oral sex?" said Sissy. "Why aren't they staying home for it? What's wrong with home cookin'?"

"Many women are uncomfortable about oral sex," said Dr. Tigard, toying with the zipper of her motorcycle jacket. "My studies have shown—"

"Sissy," said Francine, "it's not just that wives won't do it, it's that a lot of them just aren't very good at it."

"That's where a trained sexologist can—" said Dr. Tigard.

"That's where a trained hooker—" said Francine.

"Sissy, I think we're missing the point," said Reverend Chitman. "Men seek prostitutes, not because they desire perversion, but because they lack intimacy with God."

Dr. Tigard looked at Francine, who looked at Sissy.

"With all due respect, Reverend," said Sissy, "are you saying that there's no oral sex in heaven?"

Reverend Chitman glared at her, spots of color in his cheeks. He kept both feet flat on the floor.

"If he thinks that," Francine said to Sissy, "he doesn't know what heaven is."

Sissy was going to call Tod after the show. Definitely.

The second segment featured a latex-and-leather fashion show, and a film clip of sex toys sold in public vending machines on the streets of Tokyo. A phone-sex operator gave tips on how to bring your mate to fulfillment by talking dirty, and managed to do it without using any four-letter words, although the producer used the delay switch on "Split me with your hot salami." It was a judgment call.

The ex-hooker and Reverend Chitman sniped at each other throughout the show, Francine accusing him of trying to look up her skirt at one point—"and I'm not wearing underwear!" The butch sexologist talked statistics and ended up arguing with everybody. Sissy had fun, pointing out inconsistencies in each guest's point of view, pretending to be shocked, then interested, by various orgasmic suggestions.

The pages raced through the audience, fielding questions

with their wireless mikes—Sissy had learned early in her career that women loved to talk to handsome young men in blue blazers and tight pants.

She got the wrap-up signal from the floor director and interrupted Dr. Tigard in midsentence. "Thanks, Doc, for those words of wisdom." Sissy stood and walked to the front of the stage. She could feel the audience leaning forward.

"I think we've all learned something from today's show," said Sissy, nodding at her three guests, "but I think we could use a little . . . straight talk." The whole front row yelped their approval. She paced back and forth, feeding off the audience's anticipation.

"I'm Sissy Mizell," she intoned—the audience applauded—"I'm no expert, y'all"—the applause was louder—"but I got sense, and this is what I think." The audience stamped their feet, egging her on.

"Girl"—Sissy wagged a finger at Francine—"you may have given up the business, but you still act the part. I think you look right cute in that little-bitty cheerleader getup, but a grown man who's running up his MasterCard bopping somebody pretending to be the prom queen who wouldn't sit next to him in French class is one sick puppy. You got a brain, Francine, and a real talent for sales. So, get yourself some serious clothes and take some business classes. You can do better."

The audience howled their agreement.

She pointed at Dr. Tigard. "Lady, you got a fancy-pants college degree and an attitude problem to go with it. Find some M.D. to remove the pole from your butt and you'll be better off. Maybe you can arrange a trade of services. Most of the doctors I met could use a little help in the love department." She turned to the audience as Dr. Tigard stalked off the set. "Am I right, y'all?"

The audience stomped their feet.

"Reverend, I got great respect for God and I think of myself as a Christian lady, but let me tell you, if the good Lord didn't want us to have all that nekkid fun, he wouldn't have given us the equipment he did."

The crowd whooped and hollered as the Reverend dropped his gaze into his lap.

"I say forget all these electrical appliances and rubber G-string outfits," said Sissy. "Who needs 'em? You folks want to heat up your bedroom, *I'll* tell you what to do. When you get home from work, go run yourself a bubble bath. Leave the kids with a neighbor, trade afternoons if you want to, but get them out of the house for the evening. Then light a couple of those strawberry-scented candles and give yourself a good soak in the tub. You'll come out feeling like the queen of Sheba, and when your man comes home, you make him feel like the king of the world!"

The audience cheered.

She stared directly into the camera. "I been married to my husband, John, for five years now, and I want to tell you, things are better—"

The applause was so loud she saw the sound man take off his headset. Sissy turned around as John Stratton pushed through the curtain, took off his pearl-white cowboy hat, and waved it at the cheering crowd. He walked over to Sissy, picked her up like she was a doll, and swung her into his arms.

Someone in the audience shouted out, "Stratton for Governor!" and the cry was picked up, rolling from one side of the studio to the other, the crowd whooping and hollering, all giddy with the sound of themselves.

She was crying so hard she could hardly see, nuzzling his seamed neck, saying, "John, darn you, John, you didn't tell me you were coming, darn you, John, I love you."

"I love you too, babe," he said, holding her lightly in his strong arms as the applause rolled around them.

Forget Tod. For tonight anyway.

Chapter 8

A Long Beach police car was double-parked in front of 327 Villa Rio, the two uniforms slouched against the stairway to the house, smoking. The white cop must have been telling the black cop a joke, laughing, grabbing his crotch. They didn't even notice Quinn until he stepped over the drooping yellow crime-scene tape.

"Hey, dipshit!" shouted the skinny white cop, straightening up, Adam's apple bobbing. "Can't you read?"

Quinn straddled the yellow ribbon. "Morales is expecting me," he said, not moving.

The black cop stared at Quinn. "I know this monkey." He flicked his cigarette butt at Quinn's head.

Quinn batted it away with the back of his hand. Later, motherfucker. "Why don't you go get Sergeant Morales?"

"It's Lieutenant Morales," Morales said softly, standing in the doorway, a short, bull-necked detective with dark, pugnacious eyes. He glanced at the two uniforms. They took a few steps down.

"I was just about to get you, sir," said the white cop.

Morales ignored him, watching Quinn instead, unhurried and expressionless. They had known each other for almost ten years now, since Morales had joined the force, and every time they met, he sized Quinn up like they were meeting for the first time.

The Long Beach PD had the worst arrest record of any major city in the state of California, and one of the highest rates of job-related disability pensions. Outmanned and outgunned, Quinn had seen the department attract too many rookies who squeaked through the academy, too many transfers from Newport Beach and Beverly Hills, aging bullies who complained about red tape and carried their sap gloves in plain sight.

Then there was Morales. Morales was the only Long Beach cop Quinn had ever met who didn't smoke, didn't curse, and wouldn't allow reporters or anyone else to buy him lunch. Before every court appearance, even a shoplifting case, he would duck into a courthouse bathroom to shave and brush back his thinning hair. Now a plainclothes detective, he wore no flashy jewelry or bright colors, no handcuff tie tack or American flag lapel pin; he dressed corporate and conservative. Tonight he wore a blue suit, creases sharp, Windsor knot in his tie. It didn't fool Quinn, not for an instant. Not anymore.

Quinn had seen Morales take on a beefy redneck narc who called him "an uppity little beaner" one day in the near-empty squadroom. Morales took off his badge, then punched the guy so hard against the wall that the plaster cracked, continuing to hit him with fists and knees until the narc begged him to stop. Morales pinned his badge back on and looked over at Quinn, the only reporter in the room. "You feel that, Detective?" Quinn had asked innocently. "I think we had an earthquake, five-point-seven at least." Morales almost managed to hide his smile.

"What's *he* doing here, sir?" said the black cop, glaring at Quinn. "He's on the wrong side. You know that."

"Pritchard," Morales sighed, "do not try to figure out what I know. You'll pull a muscle." He crooked a finger at Quinn and walked back into the house.

Morales waited for him in the hallway, impassive, surrounded by framed photographs—that must be Tod smiling from all those snapshots, a smug, good-looking preppy who couldn't keep his eyes off himself.

Tod in a red Porsche, Tod with Sissy Mizell at some awards banquet, Tod at a party on a yacht, standing next to that soap-opera star with all the facelifts. Pretty people holding champagne glasses to the camera, endless fun on the blue-blue sea. How nice to be a winner.

"I knew you would call, sooner or later," said Morales. He had a broad Olmec face, with full lips and a flat nose, his skin brown and smooth as a razor strop. The people in the photographs looked insubstantial beside him, pale ghosts blown to dust. "Before I even picked up the phone tonight, I told Linda it would be you."

"I've been back in town for a while," said Quinn. "I was going to call sooner, say hello, but . . . you know how it is."

Morales squeezed the knot in his tie. "I heard you went to live with your brother in Corpus Christi after what Groggins did. Sounds like an easy life: Gulf shrimp, cold beer. Maybe you should have stayed?"

"It was time to come home."

"Perhaps," said Morales. "For the record, I am allowing you into an active crime scene only because you are cooperating with my investigation. So look, but don't touch."

"Hey, I've been to the ballet before, Esteban."

" 'Esteban.' " Morales savored his name. "I don't hear that so much anymore."

"That's right. '*Lieutenant*,'" Quinn said, turning the idea over in his mind. "Congratulations. It must have been an easy call for the department—Odom gets eighty-sixed for running that snitch, and there you were, all polished up and ready to move up the food chain. Ten years you'll be chief of detectives."

Morales picked an invisible bit of lint off his jacket. "Five."

They stood on the edge of the sunken living room, side by side, just looking. Quinn could see the whole room from this position—he was in no hurry to walk in further.

The paintings were straight—Gorman's stolid Navaho portraits staring at the gaudy LeRoy Neiman racing sloops on the opposite wall. A couple of months of *Sports Illustrated* and *GQ* lay stacked on the coffee table, the pillows fanned out neatly on the light green sofa. Wet bar, three stools. A butter-colored leather recliner faced the TV, tilted back. It was an innocent room until you noticed the blue fingerprint powder covering all the shiny surfaces.

Andy's dirty, fluorescent-green surf parka hung from the row of hooks next to the sliding glass doors. It looked out of place in that Playboy-After-Dark living room. The glass doors were open to the waterfront; Quinn could hear the slop-slop sound of the waves against the dock.

"You said Tod . . ."—Morales checked his notes—"Tod Bullock was a TV star?"

"No, I said he worked for one. Sissy Mizell. She has a talk show, *Straight Talk*. He was one of her producers."

"I'll give the lady a call tomorrow," said Morales, "it's one A.M, too late to be giving her bad news. Your . . . source, the friend of the deceased, he witnessed the killing?"

"His name is Andy Prefontaine. He didn't see it go down, but he saw who did it. He promised to come in and talk—Saturday night or Sunday morning. Twenty-four hours. He'll work with you; you can put out a composite of the killer for the Monday morning news."

Morales rolled his right shoe from side to side, checking the shine. "Why didn't Andy call us, play the part of the good citizen? He have some warrants outstanding?"

"No. I don't think so, anyway."

"You don't think so. But maybe." Morales tugged on one of his thick earlobes. "He dealing?"

"Not dope. Strictly lifestyle accessories." Quinn waved at the big-screen TV, the stacked audio components, the art on the walls. "Andy told me once that he considered himself a 'discounter of the American Dream.' "

"It doesn't come discounted," Morales said softly, his eyes so black you couldn't tell where his pupils began. "So Andy deals. That explains why he didn't call the police. What I don't understand is why he called you."

Quinn hesitated. "I think he was afraid you were going to tag him with the murder—he left prints all over, and the shooter wore gloves. What Andy wants is for me to take an interest in the case, maybe look over your shoulder, keep you honest." Morales's jaw thrust out and Quinn spread his hands in resignation. "What can I say? He trusts me."

"Do you trust him?"

"I trust him when he tells me he didn't murder Tod. Did you put out that preliminary description? Big white guy, two hundred fifty pounds plus, late forties to early fifties, crewcut."

"That narrows it down"—Morales glowered—"half the men on the force fit that— What?" he glanced over to the hallway.

A sour-faced man in a baggy brown suit stood there, the knees of his trousers stained with fingerprint powder. He was a sagging, middle-aged bruiser, lumpy as an old sofa, with a brown-stubble haircut. "I heard voices," he said to Morales. "You want to check the bedroom?"

"See what I mean?" Morales said to Quinn, then turned back to the sour-faced man. "Draveki, where were you this afternoon? Can you account for your whereabouts at the time of the homicide?"

Draveki looked from Morales to Quinn and back again. "You jerking me off, Lieutenant?"

"Finish out the bedroom," said Morales. "I'll check it later. And make sure you toss around plenty of fingerprint powder," Morales called after him. "TV crews should be here by dawn, and I want to make sure the taxpayers feel like they're getting their money's worth."

Draveki belched and kept going.

"*That's* your forensics guy?" asked Quinn. The technicians who specialized in physical evidence—fingerprints, ballistics, spectographic, and fiber analysis—were usually quiet and meticulous, more scientists than cops.

Morales shook his head. "Draveki is a homicide detective who works under me. The whole PD had their budget cut a few months ago, and Forensics was already understaffed. On a Friday night, they've got their hands full with drive-bys and domestics, so we do what we can to help."

"What's Draveki mad at you for?"

"He was on duty tonight, so by rights I should have turned your call over to him and gone back to sleep. Can't blame him for being annoyed. A killing in a classy neighborhood is a juicy plum, but you know me"—Morales almost smiled—"I don't like to share."

Quinn stared at the forty-inch Mitsubishi. The set had a great picture, just like Andy said. A grinning guy in a plaid jacket held up a crystal decanter like it was the Holy Grail. "Did one of your team change the channel?" Quinn asked suddenly. "Andy said Tod was watching basketball—that's Channel Eleven."

Morales considered it. "I didn't. Draveki wouldn't either."

The sound of heavy wings echoed off the canals out back— one of the big gray pelicans splashing down. Chow time.

"Come on," said Morales, "time to get your feet wet."

Quinn hesitated, then stepped down into the living room,

following Morales to the recliner. He had to fight the impulse to turn his eyes away.

Tod may have started the day pretty, but he wasn't pretty anymore. He lay on the recliner in a white terry-cloth robe, barefoot, his delicate features contorted, mouth clamped shut. The back of his skull was blown out, a sliver of bone spiking his head to the recliner. The white robe was soaked with red. What had Andy said? . . . SpaghettiOs. Tod looked like somebody had spilled a plateful of pasta down the front of him.

Quinn sat heavily on the ottoman, put his head between his knees. He brushed against Tod's toes and shuddered.

Morales laughed. "Oh yes, you've been to the ballet before."

"Give me a minute here." Quinn stared at the rug, trying to swallow. "I'm a little out of practice."

"You said you wanted to look over my shoulder," said Morales. "Here's your chance." He took off his jacket, folded it, draped it over the sofa, then clipped his necktie down so it didn't dangle loose. "Come on up here, would you?" he said, rolling up his sleeves. He put one hand on Tod's chin, braced the other against the nose, and slowly pried the clenched mouth open. There were faint popping sounds.

Quinn moaned.

"Early rigor," Morales said, grunting from the exertion. "Another couple of hours we'd need a breaker bar to get in here. Why don't you tell me where your pal Andy is? If he's innocent he's got nothing to worry about."

"I left him at Burgerama, but he's gone by now. I don't know where he lives. I *don't*—word of honor—he moves around."

Morales leaned on Tod's lower jaw with both hands. "Grab the penlight out of my breast pocket," he gasped. "Do it, will you? Shine the light in his mouth."

Quinn held the tiny flashlight tighter, his hand slippery with sweat.

"See," said Morales, "the front teeth have been snapped off, the bullet entering at the rear of the palate, blowing out the brain stem. Death would have been instantaneous. There was also at least four, perhaps five, shots fired at close range into the chest. Someone was very angry. Or very conscientious."

Quinn tried to breathe through his mouth. "Andy said the

guy with the crewcut strolled out of the bedroom like he owned the place. He must have . . . done this, then gone in and taken a leisurely piss."

"Steady!" said Morales, peering in so close that he could have begun mouth-to-mouth on Tod. "Move the light over! Look. There's powder burns to the soft tissue, but no residue on the front teeth. So the teeth weren't damaged by the blast, but from the gun barrel being thrust into the mouth. Did Andy have a temper? Maybe when somebody was late in paying their bill for the American Dream?"

Quinn shook his head.

Morales stood up. Tod's jaws snapped together with a crunch.

Quinn wiped his forehead. "We didn't need to do that," he said quietly. "You could have just asked me."

"You don't tell me everything you know," said Morales. He walked to the wet bar, washed his hands in the stainless-steel sink. "Even when I ask, you keep a little something for yourself. Why do you think that is?"

"Hey, Lieutenant?" Draveki stood in the hallway, a silly grin on his grizzled face. "You got to see what's in this guy's closet. It's a crack-up."

Morales shook his hands dry. He buttoned his cuffs, slipped on his jacket, checking himself in the mirror.

"Hey, civvie," Draveki said to Quinn, "don't puke on my crime scene, okay?" He looked at Morales and they both laughed.

Quinn watched them disappear into the bedroom. He hurried to Andy's parka, slipped his hand into the right pocket. Empty. He almost pushed his fingers through the lining searching for the lottery ticket. No ticket in the left either, just a couple of Certs. His heart was beating so loudly he thought someone was knocking on the front door.

"There's nothing in that ratty jacket," said Morales from the hall. "I checked it already. Anyone could tell it doesn't belong in this house."

"I need to make a call." Quinn looked around for a phone, spotted one next to the couch. "Did you pull prints off this one already?"

"First thing."

"Lieutenant! You coming?" called Draveki.

"Andy left a lottery ticket in the pocket," Quinn said, propping the receiver against his ear. "He wrote his address on it."

"Give me his phone number," said Morales, "I'll call him."

"Sure, but it won't do you any good. It's a mobile, billed to a P.O. box."

"Go ahead then, but let me talk to him when he answers."

Quinn punched in the number. "Andy was afraid the guy with the crewcut would find the ticket and know where he lives," he said as the phone rang. "I thought he was paranoid." No answer. He must have dialed the business number by mistake. He tried again, making sure to call Andy's personal line. The number rang and rang and rang. Quinn glanced over at Tod's body sprawled on the recliner and let it keep ringing.

Chapter 9

"Don't get up," Liston said to Andy as the phone beeped. "I've got it." He shook when he laughed, driving Andy's Dodge van south on the 405 freeway, both portables safely tucked into his jacket.

Andy squirmed in the passenger seat as the phone beeped away, his seat belt cinched so tight he could hardly breathe, the release button twisted underneath.

Liston filled the silky blue jogging suit—he looked even bigger now than in Tod's living room, overflowing the bucket seat, his head almost touching the roof liner. Tufts of red and gray hairs sprouted from his thick, powerful neck, more gray hairs than red. He guided the van through traffic using just the heel of one huge hand, a silly grin on his face. He reminded Andy of a rhinoceros on vacation.

"Don't look so glum, chum," Liston said as the phone finally stopped, "they'll call back if it's important."

"I'm hungry," said Andy.

"Pleased to meet you. My name is Emory Roy Liston. I played some football, but that was before your time." He lightly punched Andy in the shoulder, his small eyes gleaming in the oncoming headlights.

"Why don't we stop for something to eat . . . Mr. Liston? You like chorizo burritos? Smothered in cheese? I know a place. Ninety-nine cents." Cadmium, Indium, Tin, Antimony . . .

Liston picked up a thick twist of Andy's blond hair, tickled the end of his own nose with it. "You remind me of Shirley Temple with all these curls. 'On the good ship *Lollypop,*'" he sang in a high falsetto.

Strontium, Yttrium, Zirconium . . . Zirconium . . . Andy

trembled, bit the inside of his cheek to stop himself from screaming.

Liston grinned and ran a hand over his own brush cut. "Who am I to talk, right?" he said. "Forty-seven years old and I'm wearing a varsity crewcut."

"L-Looks excellent, dude. Totally excellent."

Liston chuckled, throwing his head back as though it tickled. "You're taking this a lot better than Tod, if you don't mind my saying. Boy, did he ever flunk the gut-check—'please-please-please.' I hate that. Look at you; I mean, *you're* up shit creek too, no paddle, canoe's leaking, but you're not slobbering all over the place, begging for mercy."

Andy glanced over, saw blood splattered across Liston's jogging suit in the glare of the oncoming headlights. Liston had grabbed him in the Burgerama parking lot, coming out of nowhere as he got into the van. One punch in the side had knocked all the fight out of him. He vaguely remembered being cradled against a broad chest that smelled like a butcher's apron, and Andy had to bite his cheek again to stop from screaming and slobbering and begging for mercy and all the other things that Liston hated.

"You really surprised me at Tod's place," Liston said ruefully. "I didn't know where you'd come from. You're a real jackrabbit too—you ever run track?"

"Misunderstandings happen, man, it's all part of business. No hard feelings."

"You're comfortable, aren't you? I know the belt's tight, but it's for your own protection. I slam on the brakes"—he pumped the brakes for emphasis—"you go right through the windshield."

"If you were going to kill me, you'd have done it already, right?"

"You almost got away from me," said Liston as he watched a police car pass on the opposite freeway. He held the van at the legal limit, nothing more, nothing less. "Here's your lottery ticket," he said, tucking it into Andy's front pocket, "wouldn't want to gyp you. I 'bout croaked when I saw your address— we're almost neighbors. I live right down from the Penguin's Frozen Yogurt. You ever try their fresh raspberry topping? They use whole berries, no pieces."

Andy stared at him.

"I *just* missed you back at your house, saw you pulling away when I made my left off Electric Avenue. Had to run a couple of lights to keep up, must have red-dogged you for three hours—when you stopped at the CHEAPGAS, I was filling up at the Shell station right across the street. Let me give you a word of advice: Don't use that junk unleaded, you're just asking for trouble."

"I never saw you behind me. I looked too."

"You pretty near lost me at the traffic circle on Pacific Coast Highway. If that sourdough-bread truck hadn't cut you off, you'd have gotten clean away."

"I'm glad you caught up with me," said Andy, "it gives us a chance to straighten things out. There's no problem worth dying for, that's for sure."

Liston fiddled with the knobs of the radio as he drove, jabbed the buttons in quick succession, his fingers pink and powdery through the surgical gloves. Every one of Andy's presets brought in a classical station, a soaring Bach cantata, a graceful Mozart waltz. Liston snorted. "How can you stand to listen to that?"

"Those burritos, man . . . you're really missing a chance—"

"Don't get me started on missed opportunities," growled Liston as he stared through the windshield, watching the red taillights pull away from them. "I'm the expert on that."

Liston signaled his lane change and checked the blind spot before he made a move. "That guy you were talking to at the hamburger joint," he said lightly, "good-sized fella—I bet you gave him an earful, huh?"

"No way."

Liston's smile was distant and dreamy. "I saw you two going at it, a couple of regular chatterboxes. You didn't even touch your food. Yeah, I bet you told him plenty"

"His name is Quinn. I don't even know his last name. He's just a guy looking for a deal, like everybody else. I'm kind of a niche broker—you want it, I can get it."

Liston thought that over. "Quinn. I like the way you came right out with his name, not making me ask. I'd like us to be able to talk, you and me, not have any secrets." The phone started beeping again, and Liston's face hardened, an ugly flush mottling the leathery skin. "That thing's starting to piss me off. Is that your buddy Quinn checking up on you? Making sure you got home safe and sound?"

"I'm in business," Andy's voice cracked, trying to head things off, "I've got customers who need me. Customer service is the key to survival in the nineties."

Liston took a deep breath, let it slowly out. The two of them listened to the road hum for over a mile before Liston spoke. "I got a problem with negative energy," he said at last. "It's a chemical imbalance, I think, too much sugar in my diet. Sissy had a show all about it. You'd be amazed what you can learn from TV." He played with the radio dial, angry at the static, then shook his head in delight as Aretha Franklin pounded out the speakers. "Now we're talking"—he rocked in time to the beat—"*that's* music."

Andy's clothes were sticking to him. He opened the vent, felt the night air rush against his bare legs. The van's side windows were smoked glass, muting the lights of the nearby gas stations and industrial parks. Easy access was crucial to success in a freeway-intensive environment like Southern California.

They passed a couple kissing in a Toyota pickup. Andy tried to get their attention, but their faces were hidden in each other's necks.

"I like reggae and soul best," said Liston, "busted hearts and broken dreams. Back when I was drinking, all I could stand was country: Hank Williams, the pappy not the junior, Patsy Cline, Tammy Wynette . . . but I don't drink anymore." He sang along with Aretha, voice booming and off-key, "If you want a do-right woman, you got to be a do-right, all-night man . . ."

"I got a pretty radical system here"—Andy nodded at the cassette deck—"forty-five RMS watts per channel, minimal harmonic distortion, eight times oversampling on the CD. I could make you a deal on a similar unit if you're interested. State-of-the-art Sony. I guarantee you'll hear notes you never heard before. Hey, I'll even install it for you. No charge."

"No charge? That's a temptation, sure enough." Liston's laugh sounded like gravel in a bucket. He turned up the music.

"I don't know about that guarantee, though," he had to shout, "you might be a kind of fly-by-night guy. What if you're not around to back up your work?"

The Toyota pickup had drifted over toward their lane, the couple still going at it.

"You're no good, heartbreaker, you're a liar and a cheat," sang Aretha, the accusation bouncing off the smoky windows, filling the dark interior, every inch of it. Andy beat his fists against the glass, calling out to the pickup. He moved like he was under water.

"I don't think they heard you," said Liston, "can't really blame them; they're preoccupied and, like the ad says, this baby's built ram-tough." He pounded on the thickly padded dash. "Feel that? Solid, clear down to the whitewalls. Made in the U.S. of A." He ran a hand through his graying crewcut. "I got nothing against foreign cars, but they're not right for us big old boys, no way." He smacked his belly proudly, beaming, head bobbing to the music.

The Toyota drifted back across the lane.

"We're not in competition," said Andy. "You're . . . who you are, and I'm a businessman. I'm heavy into buy-and-sell, not right-and-wrong, if you get my drift. So, if we have a problem here, I'd like to make it right by you. You're a red-meat kind of guy, am I right?"

"Right as rain," Liston beamed. He gently punched Andy in the shoulder, smiled as he squirmed against the seatbelt.

"Let me make you a present," said Andy. "I got a couple of fifty-pound cases of aged Kobe steaks in cold storage. Kobe's like this totally outrageous meat comes from these Japanese cows, you know, the ones that get fed beer four or five times a day, Suntory or Asahi or whatever. Awesome meat, dude, makes Kansas City fillets seem like Birkenstocks. Let me lay them on you. No hard feelings."

Liston flipped his turn signal, took the airport exit. "Well, kid"—he grinned—"I *am* a man with a healthy appetite." His eyes were red points in the light from the speedometer, his smile a ghost reflection floating in the windshield.

Chapter 10

"Check these out, Lieutenant." Draveki clomped into the living room holding up a handful of magazines.

"*Tinseltown Confidential,* April 1959, *Gossip,* May 1963 . . ." He grinned as he riffed the pages for Morales. "Look how all the naked starlets got black tape on their titties. Big titties too, you don't see that so much anymore—they like little ones today."

Morales took one of the magazines, a thoughtful expression on his face.

"Geez, this brings back memories," said Draveki, his dull gray skin brighter somehow, "My old man used to keep his collection in the garage when I was kid—best sex I ever had was with those *T-Town Confidentials* . . ." He wiped his mouth with the back of his hand. "There's a couple of boxes of them in the closet: *T-Town, Silver Screen Scandals* . . . all from the fifties and sixties. Classics." He noticed Quinn sitting on the couch with the phone pressed to his ear. "What the fuck's wrong with the civvie? He looks like his dog got run over."

Morales held up the magazine to Quinn. "What do you make of this?"

"How do I know?" Quinn said, still listening to Andy's phone ring. "Research, probably—that's what producers do. All the talk shows run Golden Age of Hollywood stories, where-are-they now pieces. You can get ideas from those old gossip magazines."

Draveki tapped an autographed photo of Sissy on the set of her show. "*That's* who the stiff worked for? Sissy? *Straight*

Talk with Sissy?" He gave a low whistle. "Holy shit, Lieutenant, I thought he was just a fan."

"You watch her show?" asked Morales.

"Every day." Draveki scratched himself as he ambled back toward the bedroom. "I got hooked when I was working day shift. There's that TV in the break room, and we'd all check her out, didn't matter what she was talking about. I don't care if you're into fat broads or not, that's the hottest woman on the tube."

Quinn could see Morales and Draveki talking, but his attention was focused on the phone in his hand, ringing away in his ear. Andy said he'd stick close; he was probably driving around in circles, afraid to stop. There were plenty of dead spots along the coast, places where a cellular phone signal couldn't get through. . . .

"Still no answer?" said Morales.

Or maybe the man with the crewcut had caught up with Andy. Quinn got the number of Burgerama from information. The manager who answered said there hadn't been any trouble this evening. What did he know. Something was wrong.

"Did I mention that Draveki found about a quarter-ounce of cocaine in Tod's room?" asked Morales. "Hidden in a pair of rolled-up socks in the dresser. If dope is supposed to make people so creative, why don't users come up with better stash spots?"

"I don't know about Tod, but Andy doesn't mess with dope." There was something between the cushions of the sofa. Quinn slid his fingers down, pulled out a small electronic notebook, a Filofax knockoff with a memory chip. The notebook was hardly bigger than a pocket calculator, one of the cheap solar-powered models Andy had given away for presents last Christmas. He flipped it on, but the battery had run down.

Morales stood in the doorway, watching the yachts tied along the canal, their outlines bobbing in the moonlight. "Maybe you made an error in judgment about Andy," he said, his voice husky from the damp salt air. "These things happen. You get blinded by friendship and you don't see the obvious."

Quinn wanted to tell him about the notebook, hand it over and let him take care of it, but something in Morales's tone made him wait.

Morales kept his back to Quinn. "The house is tidy, you can see that. Nothing missing, nothing apparent, anyway. No forced entry, no sign of a struggle—Tod died with his feet up, so forget a botched burglary or a visit from the local psycho. No, whoever killed Tod got invited inside."

"Did you canvass the neighbors?" said Quinn. "The guy with the crewcut was huge, wearing a dark running suit . . . Andy said this guy stood out on the front porch and watched him drive away. It was barely dark, *somebody* should have seen him."

"Nobody did. Not so far, anyway—I'll get a couple of uniforms to check in the morning." He took a deep breath. "Naples is nice—before I made detective, I used to moonlight as a security officer for the neighborhood association. They supplied a newer cruiser than the city. Kept it cleaner too. Twenty dollars an hour to roust Hispanic kids on bicycles, black kids selling candy door-to-door." He shook his head.

"Andy said Tod gambled on basketball. Andy said when he showed up that afternoon, Tod was nervous, like a guy who needed a win. Maybe Tod had a bet down on the game. Maybe he needed to win. The guy with the crewcut could have been a headbreaker sent by Tod's bookie."

"Who are you trying to convince?" said Morales, turning around to face him. "Your friend Andy tells you a story and you suspend reason, as well as caution." He shook his head at Quinn's gullibility. "What if there was no man with a crewcut?" Morales explained patiently. "Perhaps Andy was afraid the *police* would find his address in the parka. Maybe Andy killed Tod, and in his haste to get away, he forgot his jacket. Now, for the life of him, he can't remember what he left in it. So he calls a friend. Someone he can trust—that's what you said, yes?"

"I don't—"

"Would you have handed me Andy's address if the lottery ticket had been there?" said Morales. "I don't think so. You would have given him twenty-four hours, and twenty-four hours is long enough to come up with an alibi, long enough to cash in some assets and leave the country. No, you wouldn't tell me because deep down you don't respect authority. You think you know better."

Quinn glanced toward the recliner, saw Tod's arm flopped

over the side. "I wouldn't protect someone I thought did this."

"You wouldn't *know* he had done it," said Morales. The wind rustled his suit but he was solid as an anchor. "You'd think it was a man with a crewcut. A man who no one saw, who left no fingerprints. The only one who left fingerprints at the scene was your friend Andy."

"What are you trying to do, Esteban?" Quinn tried to hold back his anger. "You want to have the case solved before morning roll call? You trying for a new department record?" He picked up the phone, jabbed in Andy's number again. "Why would Andy even need to ask me? Why didn't he just drive back here and get his jacket himself?"

"The neighbors might have reported hearing gunshots," Morales said calmly. "They didn't, but Andy wouldn't know that. In any case, he wouldn't have been in any hurry to get back here and check for himself. Let me tell you something, no matter what you've seen on television, the killer almost *never* returns to the scene of the crime."

There was still no answer. If the man with the crewcut had snatched Andy at Burgerama, he must have seen Andy and Quinn talking. He looked down and saw his hands trembling, just the way Andy's had a couple of hours ago, shaking too much to eat a free meal.

Morales fingered the thick drapes that framed the door. "I patrolled Naples for three years and this is the first time I've been inside one of these beautiful houses." He examined the drapery fabric, rubbed it between his fingers. "Linda would like these—she has a taste for fine things." His face was a smooth mahogany mask that betrayed no emotion.

Quinn slid the notebook into the pocket of his pants.

Morales looked up. "Andy will call you when he wants to talk. You tell him the preliminary investigation suggests an impulsive act, no premeditation. Seven years, max. He should come in before somebody gets hurt."

"Andy would sell his mother's kidneys if the price was right, but he didn't kill anybody. He's not the violent type."

Morales sighed, a long, drawn-out sound so tender that Quinn felt the sadness himself. "Ah, my friend, there is no such animal, believe me."

Chapter 11

"Call me old-fashioned, but I think a guy makes a deal, he's got to live up to it," said Liston. He turned off Lakewood Boulevard and onto a service road behind the Long Beach Airport, the van kicking up dust. "I don't think that's too much to ask." Liston drove using only the parking lights, leaning forward, his bulbous nose almost touching the glass—Andy thought of him again as a rhino in a blue jogging suit, charging through the night.

"Tod made a deal," said Liston. The van skidded into the weeds, and he steered back onto the narrow road, bushes scraping the sides. "Then, after he gets paid," he said, raising his voice to be heard as they bounced over potholes, "he gets cute." He turned off the radio, still wearing his pink surgical gloves, letting the van coast to a stop next to the chain-link fence that overlooked the runway. "You're not like that, are you?" Rows of yellow landing lights blinked toward the distant terminal.

"No way," said Andy.

Liston played with the control buttons on the console—he rolled down both windows but kept the doors locked. The bucket seat tilted back, the electric motor whining as it labored to support his weight. When he was comfortable, he switched off the engine.

In the sudden silence, Andy could hear the hum of crickets crackling around them. He stared straight ahead through the windshield, the freeway in the distance streaming with headlights.

"What happened between you and Tod is none of my business," said Andy, trying to keep his voice steady. "I don't make moral judgments."

Liston glanced at him, looked back at the runway lights blinking toward the horizon. "I come here once in a while and just sit, watch the planes come in."

"You going to kill me, dude?"

"What?"

"You heard me."

"Don't ask so many questions, you're getting yourself worked up about nothing."

"I want to know." Andy leaned forward, waiting, then cried out as the big man turned to him, seeing the ponderous calm on his face, the utter certainty.

Liston patted Andy's bare knee. "No way around it, pal. It's not going to happen right away, if that helps any. I'll give you plenty of notice. We have to talk first."

Andy shivered against the seatbelt. "This thing's cutting into me," he said.

Liston reached over and released the belt. "Don't get any ideas," he warned, "I was All-American in 1960. Linebacker. Played pro-ball for about thirty-seven minutes, but that's a whole other story." He grinned and Andy could see him in a stretched-out letter sweater on every other page of the yearbook. "God, I was something then—curly red hair, all my own teeth, muscles out to here."

"I've got a hundred-fifty-two thousand dollars stashed away—"

"Keep it," said Liston. "I signed with the Chicago Bears for a hundred thousand. That was real money in those days. Didn't do me any good at all. I never played ball for the money—I played for the sound of the crowd cheering a solid hit, for the grunt and pain and pure glory of it all. Glory doesn't last, though. Glory's gone by the time the people in the stands get to the parking lot, stepping on their programs with your face on the cover and deciding what to eat for dinner. Ask them a week later what the score was and they don't remember. *Nothing* lasts. Once you understand that, really understand it, you won't mind so much what has to happen here tonight."

Andy shifted slightly in his seat.

"I take these night courses," said Liston, " 'World History,' 'World Literature,' anything with 'World' in the title—I haven't got time for the small stuff. Let me ask you something; I'm in the middle of World Religion, and I was raised a deep-water Baptist, but I'll tell you, this Hinduism thing really makes sense. What do you think? You believe in reincarnation?"

Andy punched him in the face, pummeled his chest. Liston made no move to defend himself, watching Andy with a bemused expression, as though the blows were the beating of birds' wings. Andy stopped at last, exhausted, his arms hanging limp.

Liston dabbed at his lips with a Kleenex, tucked the tissue into his pants pocket. He looked at Andy. "You can't be too careful these days. They have these tests now . . . lab techs can run a DNA spectrum on a blood sample that's as good as fingerprints." He shook his head.

"I'm not sorry, fucker," Andy panted, "I'm not."

"No reason to be. Hey, you didn't go quietly; I respect that. What are you, a hundred fifty pounds? My lunchbox weighs more than that." Liston's belly bounced with laughter; oh yeah, he was a big, jolly killer.

Andy could smell clover in the fields nearby, fresh grass and a clean breeze. He wished he had something big and heavy to hit Liston with.

"I got into it three years ago with a guy about your size," said Liston, "little fella, said he was a black belt. Busted my nose with one of those sneaky-pete roundhouse kicks. Cracked some ribs. Crushed a testicle too, and that hurt something awful, let me tell you, but it didn't stop me. I'm a determined individual. I got one ball, but he's *still* on dialysis." He smiled. His face was the color of raw hamburger. "My philosophy is let a guy take his best shot, then you can do whatever you want to him. Fair's fair."

"I'm not going to the cops."

"Cops aren't so bad; I was a cop myself for a while. Too much paperwork." He shook his head at the memory, turned, and leaned close. "Look, let's be mature people with each other, no bullshit. I can't let you go, you know it as well as I do. Once you accept that, you'll see that the smartest thing you can do is make sure checkout's quick and painless." He clapped his hands and Andy jumped. "Good night, Irene, that's the best deal you're going to get from me. Quick and painless."

The crickets had quieted with Liston's hand-clap. They started up again.

"Maybe you've got a high pain threshold," said Liston, "but I doubt it. People think they're tough, but usually they take the easy way out. When you get your teeth drilled, you ask the dentist for novocaine, right? Right. You take the easy way. I can make things easy for you, but one hand washes the other. Right?"

Andy nodded.

"I guess you knew Tod pretty well?"

"Not . . . not really."

An airplane screamed overhead and Andy flinched, started to shake as the plane bounced onto the nearby runway and taxied toward the terminal.

"I like watching planes land," said Liston, "because you just know that everybody on board gives this big sigh of relief— ahhhhhh—once those wheels hit the deck, even the ones that say they're not afraid to fly. Yeah, getting back safe, that's a good feeling." He glanced at Andy and the angry flush crept up his neck again, rose to his cheeks, a nebula of broken capillaries. "You try to run away," he said slowly, "I'll chase you down and tear off your ears. I'm not as fast as I was, but I'll catch you and rip them right off your head. You wouldn't believe the sound that makes. I hate that sound."

Andy took his hand from the door handle.

"Tod must have told you what he was up to. People in show business like to brag. It's only natural."

"He said he got a big promotion—producer, with his own office, maybe a percentage on reruns. Big deal, he still expected free installation. Everybody wants a bargain."

"He was Sissy's personal assistant," confided Liston. "Can you imagine that? You'd think that would be enough, but some people are never satisfied. More, more, more. Do you consider yourself a greedy person?"

"No. I think everybody's got their price, that's all."

Liston tugged gently on a lock of Andy's hair. "You have nice soft hair. What kind of conditioner do you use?"

Andy didn't answer. He could feel Liston's steamy heat through his clothes as the man moved closer, tried to push him away as Liston's hand worked through his scalp.

"Sissy is a real lady," said Liston, "and if you knew me, you'd know what a compliment that is. Last year, I was a guest on her show, one of those where-are-they-now hours, but she didn't treat me second-string. She put me up in a big hotel, stretch limo to drive me around in, the whole nine yards. Made me feel important—I haven't felt like that for a long time. A woman like her . . . someone like Tod comes along, he's going to use her. I couldn't abide that."

"That's between you and Tod," said Andy. "Not me."

"Tod's dead." Liston pressed his thumb against Andy's right temple. "There's just you and me now." He gradually increased the pressure. "You young guys, you want ice cream with sprinkles and a cherry on top, and you don't want to pay for it. . . ."

"I don't know what you're talking about," said Andy. He tried to twist away, but Liston cupped his head with one hand while digging in with the other thumb.

"I went out of my way for Tod," Liston said, breathing heavily, "I treated him like an adult and he tried to cheat me. Cheat Sissy. He was supposed to hand them over—not some of them, all *six* of them. Tod just sat there, saying there wasn't any more. 'Please don't hurt me,' " he mimicked, " 'please!' "

"You're hurting me," said Andy, still struggling. "That *hurts*!"

The telephone beeped and Liston let him go. "That your friend from the hamburger joint again?" said Liston, panting with excitement. "Is that Quinn?"

Andy's hands were on his knees, fingers playing the opening bars to the Beethoven piece he had taught to Quinn's kid. Nice to sit on a piano bench next to a little girl who thought you were wonderful and funny and smart.

"He's real persistent," said Liston as the phone beeped away. "You must have told him plenty. 'Dabba-dabba-dabba, said the monkey to the chimp,' " he singsonged. "You talk about me?"

"He ordered an espresso maker. I got a special this month."

"He parked a couple of blocks from the burger shop. What do you think he was worried about?"

"I'm no mind reader, dude."

"He moves on the balls of his feet, that one," said Liston,

"like a running back. I watched him. Maybe he and I'll play together sometime." His face was shiny in the dim light. "You think he'd like that?"

"Knock yourself out."

"I really made a mess at Tod's place," said Liston, "but whose fault is that, huh? I gave him a chance, but he took me for granted, just like you."

"I don't know what Tod did," said Andy. "I didn't hear anything; I was outside with my headphones on. What are you picking on me for? It's not fair!"

"I'll tell you about fair," said Liston. "First play of my pro career, I return the kickoff ninety-seven yards for a touchdown. Look it up, it's in the record book. I run back another one before the half, and nobody even gets a hand on me. Crowd's going nuts, high fives all around, and I am at the center, the very heart of things. Let me tell you, once you're there, really *there,* nothing else ever measures up."

"Look—"

"Third quarter . . ." Liston ground his teeth. "Third quarter, I get whip-tackled by this old-timer for New York, blow out my knee, and I'm gone for the whole season. Next year I come back, but I'm not the same." He turned to Andy. "I was never right after that one hit. Never. One hit and it was all over." The capillaries in his cheeks glowed in the runway landing lights. "I've been looking to even things up ever since," he whispered.

Andy blinked back tears.

"You give me the one that Tod held back," said Liston. "It's not going to do you any good."

"Tod didn't give me anything."

"Did you turn it over to your friend Quinn last night? Is that it, you're protecting him?"

"Do I look like a hero?"

"Tell me where it is, and I'll give you a head start," said Liston. "What have you got to lose? I'll open the door and let you run for it. Me with a bum leg and all." Liston held up his right hand in a V. "Scout's honor."

"It's in my safety-deposit box. I can't fool you, man, soon as the bank opens on Monday I'll get it for you. You can wait outside for me. I won't try to ditch you—I don't want to spend the rest of my life looking over my shoulder. Take it, I don't want any trouble."

"That's a relief," said Liston. "I believe you, but just to ease my mind, what are we talking about?"

The crickets were louder. "You know . . . I don't have to spell it out for you."

"That's okay, spell it out for me."

"Dope. Tod . . . skimmed off some dope."

"Wrong answer."

"Dope was part of it, but mostly it was pictures . . . he had secret . . . diagrams of the keel of that racing yacht they're getting ready for the America's Cup. . . . It's a new design—he said they've got divers patrolling the marina, and guards posted, but he—he got pictures and was going to sell them. . . . Sailing and basketball, that's all Tod talked about, and how you gonna cheat at basketball?"

Liston shrugged. "Maybe you don't know anything. You can still do me a favor, though, and maybe I can do you one." He was drowned out by the whine of another jet landing down the runway. "I need you to kill yourself," he shouted over the roar of the engines.

Andy stared at him.

"I know, I know, it's a lot to ask," he said playfully, "but it's not such a bad deal." He pulled out the pistol Andy had seen back at Tod's. "If you use this, the cops will have their case made, and I can go on to other things. Look, I can blow your brains out, but it's hard to get the angle just right so it looks natural. It would be better if you cooperated."

"Why don't you let me blow *your* brains out? I'm good with angles."

Liston punched him lightly in the arm. "Blow my brains out, that's rich. But let's be logical. You're not getting out of this alive anyway. I can make it easy or I can break every bone in your body—snap, crackle, pop. Then I'll toss you onto the tarmac, and watch you try to crawl away before the next plane comes in. They'll have to scrape you off the landing gear. The cops'll write you up as Tod's killer just so they don't have to look at what's left. It's your call, but if you want things ugly, I got to get to it. The sun'll be up in a few hours and I have to hike out of here."

Andy hugged himself, rocking in his seat. Paper cuts were agony, and a hangnail could spoil his whole day. He'd never get away. "The gun," he said in a voice he didn't recognize, "will it hurt?"

"Naaaa." Liston emptied the gun, handed him the revolver and bullets. "Here, you load it. I need your prints."

The bullets slid smoothly into the chambers. Andy's hands didn't shake at all. It was amazing. He snapped the cylinder back, felt Liston's surgical gloves brush his hand as the man took the gun from him.

"Get out," said Liston. "We got to switch places. You first."

The ground was spongy, the weeds crunching underfoot. Andy felt like he was floating high above the van, looking down on a skinny man in shorts and a sleeveless sweatshirt, sliding behind the wheel. He could see right through himself.

"What are you, a wiseguy?" said Liston from the passenger seat, as Andy held out his left hand. "You're right-handed, I noticed that at the burger joint. That's just the kind of thing those forensics guys look for. You're trying to fuck me up—I knew I liked you." He grinned, handed Andy the gun, cupping Andy's hand on the butt. "No more funny stuff now," he cautioned, "that would send me over the edge. Neither of us want that."

"No," said Andy. He couldn't tell where his voice was coming from. Definitely not from his throat. The driver's seat was hot from Liston's body.

"Take your time," said Liston. "I could pull the trigger for you, but it's better you do it yourself. Be your own boss. Am I talking too much? You want me to shut up?"

"It doesn't matter." Andy could feel Liston's hand wrapped around his own on the gun. It was like they were holding hands. Andy slowly brought the gun to his temple, flinched at the coldness of the metal against his skin.

"Don't rush it," said Liston. "Let it rest against your head until you're completely relaxed. That way they know you did it yourself."

"I'm scared."

"I believe in reincarnation myself," Liston soothed, "and I'm not the kind of guy who reads his horoscope—the stars could give a shit about us, but reincarnation is different. It's *fair,* just like you wanted. The rules of the game have to be fair or the game doesn't make sense. You understand, I know you do. I can't believe that God wouldn't give us a second chance, a chance to make up for all we missed the first time. People make mistakes, they get lost, they get hurt, and it's too late. Reincarnation means we get to come back and try again. Let me tell you, kid, next time around, I'm going to the Super Bowl."

Andy closed his eyes, slipped his finger against the trigger. Maybe next time around he'd graduate from Cal Tech, get a Ph.D., maybe next time around he'd win a Nobel Prize.

He was going to die behind the wheel, just like Ginger's Tarot cards predicted. She finally got one right. There went her perfect record.

"What's so funny?" said Liston.

"Everything," said Andy. "Everything is funny."

The crickets were louder now, the sound undulating across the field, an intricate symphony of need. His hearing was so acute at that moment that he could discern each individual voice within the pattern. His finger tightened on the trigger. He didn't even hear the gun go off, he was paying such close attention to the music.

Chapter 12

Quinn peeked his head out of Rachel's kitchen, listening for his phone to ring. No sound from the cottage. It was Saturday morning, almost ten, and Andy still hadn't called, still wasn't answering. The phone had rung once—he had jumped for it—but it was Jen, saying her deadline had been moved forward again and she was driving over to show him the proof sheets. Yes, ma'am.

Last night Quinn had gotten halfway home from Tod's, then turned around and drove back to confront Morales one more time. "Okay," he had said, "if Andy killed Tod, why isn't he answering his phone? He's got to know it's me calling—why doesn't he care anymore if he left his address behind?"

Morales didn't seem surprised to see him again. "Simple," he said, staring at a photograph of a sleek racing yacht, Tod standing at the wheel, one of those stupid caps on his head. "He sent you here because he wasn't sure if the lottery ticket was in his jacket. It wasn't. He found it someplace else. Now, he's got plenty of time to create an alibi; he doesn't need to talk to you." Then Morales looked at him, concerned. "If you're going to have such intelligent friends," he had said, "you must become a better judge of character."

Bull's-eye. Dead center, Esteban. Lieutenant.

Quinn spent the rest of the night sitting on his front porch, replaying his conversations with Andy and Morales, going back and forth. . . . He yawned, went back into the kitchen, and checked on the waffles.

It had been over two years since the divorce, but every Saturday they had family breakfast, he and Rachel alternating cooking. She usually prepared quiche or crepes almondine or frittata with melon balls. He made pecan waffles and the Velveeta 'n' hot dog omelets that Katie liked.

He tore open the package of low-fat kosher franks that Rachel insisted on—she wasn't religious, she just read labels. The carving knife rocked back and forth as he chopped pecans.

Katie stood on tiptoes, watching him work, a wiry eight-year-old in denim overalls and red high heels with rhinestone bows. One hand clutched Quinn's pant leg for support as she snagged a pink frankfurter, and waved it at him. "This looks like a doggy's penis," she announced.

Quinn almost cut off his thumb. "Uh-huh," he said, trying not to make a big deal about it—probably scar her for life, or lead her into a career in veterinary medicine. "Well, sort of, honey."

Rachel sat at the white-pine kitchen table reading the paper, a tall, willowy woman with dark brown hair she wore in a thick braid on weekends. She had strong, handsome features and a serious mouth that made her look older than she was. This morning she wore faded jeans and a blue cotton shirt with the sleeves rolled past her elbows. Saturday was green-thumb day, her favorite day of the week.

Through the big bay window he could see the lush yard, plants everywhere. Rachel refused to hire a gardener. Quinn heard her every morning, singing to the flowers as she watered them. She had a lousy voice, but he liked to listen to her anyway.

The morning haze was just beginning to burn off. It was going to take a while for the electronic notebook he had found at Tod's to recharge in the weak sunlight. A little earlier he had checked it, but the battery was still low—he only scrolled halfway through the calendar before it ran down. The most recent entry was over a month ago, which must have been when Tod lost it down the sofa.

He should have turned the notebook over to the police—removing evidence from a crime scene was a serious offense. Morales was right, he didn't have respect for authority.

Quinn peeled a waffle off the waffle iron, juggled it into the warm oven, and poured fresh batter. He shook more pecans onto the cutting board. "Another five minutes," he called, glancing out the door again.

Katie clip-clopped off to get some more crayons and paper, legs wobbling in the red high heels, the frankfurter wiggling in her hand.

"I don't like your new boyfriend giving Katie presents," said Quinn. "Particularly those shoes. She's growing up fast enough already."

"How did you get the bump on your head?" Rachel didn't look up from the newspaper.

He absently rubbed the spot where he banged his head on the edge of Jen's bathtub. Rachel didn't miss a thing. "I . . . slipped in the bathroom."

Rachel's glance was somewhere between jealous and patronizing. "I bet." Since the divorce, she imagined him constantly on the prowl. She was wrong. "I saw you sitting on the porch this morning," said Rachel, "must have been five A.M. I got up to start my yoga exercises and there you were, dirty and exhausted and looking sick to your stomach. It was as though we were still married."

"Ha-ha. Next time you see Mr. Saab Turbo, tell him that was my parking spot he was in last night."

"Not anymore."

"That's not what I meant." Quinn walked to the kitchen door and listened, his cheeks burning.

Rachel looked over her paper at him. "Are you in trouble?"

Again? She didn't need to say it, he knew what she meant. "I've been trying to get in touch with Andy," he said.

"Check the jail," Rachel said, tossing her long braid. "What are you doing calling him? I thought you were through with that sort of thing."

"He needs my help."

"I don't doubt it."

Katie stood in the doorway, both hands filled with crayons. "Who needs help?"

"No one, Katherine," said Rachel.

"The man who played the piano at your birthday last year," said Quinn.

"The man with Raggedy-Andy hair," pronounced Katie. "But it was a week *after* my birthday. Remember? You missed my party 'cause you were working far away." She hummed the opening bars. "*Für Elise,* Daddy. Raggedy Andy played beautifully. Can he come to my party this year? Please? I could show him how good I play the *Minute Waltz.*"

"How 'well,' " corrected Rachel.

"That'd be nice," said Quinn, setting the table. Rachel had put fresh flowers as a centerpiece, those big red ones that didn't have a smell.

Rachel slowly turned the pages of the magazine. Her nails were perfectly shaped, flecks of yellow and blue paint caught in the cuticles. She was an art professor at the university, head of department as of last semester. In her spare time she painted portraits, children mostly. First she photographed them at play, then worked from the photos. He loved her work: The paintings were wistful and evocative and absolutely true. She had given him a small pastel of Katie for Christmas last year that tore at his heart every time he looked at it.

She was talented, but Belmont Shore was one of the few places affluent enough for an artist like her to flourish. Owning one of her paintings was more than a status thing—the rising stars in real estate and finance, who didn't have time to play with their kids, could spend seven thousand dollars on a painting that never asked to go to Seaworld. She was booked three years in advance.

"Why don't you put away your coloring until after breakfast, and go wash your hands?" Quinn said to Katie as he laid out the utensils. After she scampered off, he turned to Rachel. "There was a murder last night in Naples," he said softly. "Andy was involved. I checked out the scene with Morales . . ." He looked away for a moment, cleared his throat. "I may have gotten in over my head. . . ."

Rachel laid the paper down, taking time to carefully fold it before she spoke. "I thought you had decided not to do that kind of work anymore. Those people . . . the things they do. . . ." She shook her head, worried about him.

"I didn't go looking for trouble," Quinn said, pouring the last of the batter. Steam poured out of the waffle iron. "I thought Andy needed help . . . You heard Katie, she still remembers that Beethoven thing he taught her. He didn't have to do that."

"You said he charged you twenty dollars."

"Well, he did. But still . . ." They were both laughing.

"Raggedy Andy put ten dollars in my piggy bank." Katie was back in the doorway, clutching Baby Seal. "I saw him when he didn't think anyone was looking."

"Are you sure he wasn't *taking* money?" said Rachel.

The doorbell rang at the same moment he heard his phone. He rushed for his porch. When he came back the waffle was just starting to burn, smoke curling from the edges of the waffle iron. He opened it up and started jabbing at it with a fork, scattering blackened crumbs onto the floor.

"Quinn's not just a nosy ex-husband and all-around father," said Rachel, "he's also a gourmet cook."

He looked up and saw Jen standing next to Rachel, the two of them laughing. He had forgotten she was coming by.

"I didn't realize the address you gave me was for out back," said Jen. "I brought the proof sheets."

Rachel saw his face. "What's wrong?"

"That was Morales on the phone," Quinn said. He took the waffles from the warming oven, scooped omelet onto plates, moving mechanically, grabbing strawberry preserves and maple syrup from the refrigerator, making too much noise. He poured milk for Katie, kissed her nose. "I'm sorry, honey, but I've got to leave. We'll play later."

"I'm coming with you," said Jen.

"Quinn?" said Rachel.

"I've got to go see Andy." He kissed Rachel on the cheek. "Sorry." As he ran out the door he wondered if Rachel would think he was apologizing for leaving in the middle of breakfast, or for kissing her.

Chapter 13

Liston needed a long hot shower to wash off last night. Sissy was going to be so mad at him.

He cranked up Aretha on the stereo, loud enough that he could hear the music even with the shower full-on. He wasn't worried about the neighbors complaining. He stepped into the steam, stood there with his eyes closed, hands spread against the tile, the spray blasting his skin as he swayed to the bluesy beat—"R-E-S-P-E-C-T." Oh yeah, baby-baby-baby.

He soaped his face carefully, making small circles with his fingertips, the warm lather lifting free the tiny particles of gunpowder that clogged his pores. He had gotten dirty at the airport with Andy. Even with the windows down in the van, there was always a back discharge from a gunshot, an invisible cloud that left traces behind. He thought of it as a dying exhalation, a funeral pyre launching the soul.

That was nice. It sounded like something from one of the poetry books he read for the World Literature class at adult education. He tried to imagine what Stenkowsky and Jeffries and the rest of the Bears' offensive line would say if they heard that fancy talk from him. Most of them wouldn't even know what the word "pyre" meant. Football didn't lend itself to poetry—you think too hard receiving a kickoff you were going to fumble, sure as shit. Pure instinct, that's how you make the pros.

He saw himself again in the locker room at halftime, the room filled with steam from the showers, sweaty pads and bloody towels piled on the concrete floor, hairy bodies sprawled everywhere. He emerged from the mist, naked and raw, howling with delight, and the sound bounced off the walls—Jeffries picked it up, then Nichols and Stenkowsky, until the whole team was bellowing, red-faced, all knuckles and muscle and touch-down fever.

Then, suddenly it was over and done with, as final as the end of the dinosaurs.

It was the first game of the season, a beautiful crisp fall afternoon. He smelled burning leaves on his way to Soldier Field and knew he was going to be unstoppable. For three quarters he had the crowd on their feet every time he touched the ball. On that last kickoff he had watched the football slowly turning end over end, his senses so acute he could see the laces on the pigskin. He grabbed it in full stride, hip-faked the Giants' fastest man, and was gone, spinning off hits, heading for day-light and then . . . he heard his leg snap before he felt the pain, wondered who was screaming. They carried him off the field in a goddamned wimpy-ass golf cart, the crowd so silent he thought he had died.

The bar of Ivory crumpled in his angry fist. He looked at the crumpled chunks of soap, uncomprehending for a moment, then went back to washing himself with the biggest piece.

He worked his fingers through the thick reddish-blond hair covering his belly, slopped balsam conditioner into his hand, rubbing it down his shaggy thighs until he was sleek and shiny as a seal. He ran his hands through his crewcut as he continued his shuffling dance in the hot spray—rub-a-dub-dub, Aretha.

Black powder grains speckled the white tub—he carefully hosed them down the drain, even cleaned the underside of the plug. It was a futile gesture; there were probably threads of carpeting from Tod's place stuck to the floormats of Liston's car, skin and hair samples from Liston left behind in Andy's van. If the cops wanted you bad enough, if they spent the money and the overtime, even these microscopic, invisible nothings could send a man to the gas chamber. You could only do so much to protect yourself—wear gloves and disposable clothes, don't beat off in the dishtowels or spit on the dining-room table. Lisbon wiped down the tub anyway. He did what he could.

He dried himself off with a rough towel—easy on that right knee!—rubbing so that his pale skin flushed, billows of blood rolling toward the surface. Chumming the waters. I'm a poet, but don't know it, he thought, drying his feet, they're long-fellows.

He threw on some talc, slipped into the purple silk robe with "Bangkok" stitched on the back over a grinning appliqué Buddha. He knotted the robe loosely, so his legs had room, then checked his lip in the mirror: It was swollen double where Andy had smacked him. He shook his head in amazement at the courage of the little guy. R-E-S-P-E-C-T.

Liston cleared the steamy bathroom mirror with his hands. The swollen lip made him look like his old self after a good scrimmage. He wanted to kiss his reflection, he was so grateful. Yeah, the kid had taken it like a grown-up.

Tod was a whole other story. Sissy was going to flip when she heard. Probably blame Liston. Maybe it *was* his fault . . . he should have slapped Tod around a little, hurt him some, just enough for him to get the message. It was hard to be patient with somebody you hated that bad . . . anyway, if Tod had played straight, he'd still have the best job in the world. Now, he was closed casket all the way.

Liston had never killed anybody before. If he had known he'd enjoy it so much, he'd have started sooner.

The robe swished against his legs as he walked to the kitchen. He opened the refrigerator, took a large Ziploc bag of crushed ice out of the freezer, and a thirty-two-ounce bottle of diet grape soda off the shelf. He shook out ten aspirins from the economy-size bottle, washed them down with a swallow of soda. The diet pop left an aftertaste, but he was watching his weight these days.

He started out of the kitchen, came back, and grabbed the bag of sour-cream potato chips off the counter. What the heck. One step at a time, he thought as he limped toward the living room.

His knee hurt from all the walking this morning. It had been miles from the airport to a bus stop. He could have called a cab, but taxidrivers remembered a 5 A.M. fare. His car was where he left it, two blocks from Burgerama. He had made sure not to park on the side of the street designated for sweeping. The last thing he needed was a ticket.

The blue corduroy easychair was in the exact center of the room, the chair equally distant from the front door, the refrigerator, and the TV. It had been thirty years since he played linebacker, but Liston still went for position.

The chair was oversized and heavy-duty, with a double-thick oak frame, reinforced with steel straps. He had bought the chair for five thousand dollars in 1971, when five thousand dollars would buy a new Buick. The chair's corduroy fabric had been replaced six times, and the wood groaned as he settled in, but it was still solid. He put his knee up, draped the icebag over it.

Bright ceramic floral arrangements from the Cable Shopping Club filled the room—shiny red and blue bouquets covering the dining room table and chairs, some of them even shoved under the desk. Once he started buying things through the club it was hard to stop. Everyone was so excited to take your call, shouting and hooting in the background—and like June Delany, his favorite CSC hostess, said, these hand-painted flowers never died.

The bag of chips crackled as he tore it open, spraying crumbs everywhere. He listened to the morning sounds in the neighborhood: bicycles riding past, cars starting, the keening voices of the women next door. They'd be hanging out clothes in the backyard, four or five of them in their bright dresses and straw hats, pinning up cloth diapers and talking a language he couldn't understand—Vietnamese, Cambodian, Laotian, whatever. They sounded cheerful. He was tempted to take a night class, just so he could know what they were talking about.

His house was on a dead-end street in Seal Beach, a quiet, middle-class town just south of Belmont Shore, bounded by freeways and a naval weapons station. Seal Beach was separated from the rest of affluent Orange County by a scraggly bird sanctuary, a sandy wetlands awash in toxic effluent from the nearby military base. He had bought this house and a couple of rental units nearby because the price was right and he liked the mix of retirees and recent immigrants, the well-behaved families where nobody talked back, and Mom stayed home while Dad went to work.

People minded their own business in Seal Beach. Live and let live. He felt bad about Andy—they had been neighbors, almost, might have rolled their shopping carts right past each other in the cereal/crackers/cookies aisle at Von's and never known it.

The TV was nestled in a black wrought-iron wall unit that he bought in Tijuana—a real bargain, considering the workmanship. It weighed over four hundred pounds; he had carried it in by himself, almost taking out the doorjamb when he stumbled. The shelves were filled with trophies: Southeast Conference Player of the Year—1958, 1959, 1960, Most Tackles, Most Sacks, an eight-by-ten picture of him at the All-American banquet shaking hands with Mike Ditka, signed and dated game balls from the 1959 North-South game and the 1960 Orange Bowl, each in an individual glass container.

He polished his trophies every week with a soft cloth, taking his time, buffing every curve and surface. Bodies were fragile things; his own was scarred and battered beyond repair, but his trophies were inviolate pieces of history that would remain long after he was gone.

Interspersed among the awards was his collection of European bisque figurines, jolly trolls and en-pointe ballerinas, playful shepherds and Rapunzel, Rapunzel, let down your hair. Right above the TV was "Hansel," a rare piece, circa 1922, a bisque boy in lederhosen, with tousled blond hair and lively blue eyes. There was a hairline crack in the base—you could hardly tell it was there unless you knew where to look.

Bits of potato chip drifted down across his robe as he chewed, staring at Hansel, oblivious to the mess. He had been looking for the matching "Gretel" for years.

Along the bottom of the wall unit were a couple hundred videotapes, neatly catalogued, alphabetically arranged—every NFL playoff game and Super Bowl, every John Madden roast and highlights video. Every *Straight Talk with Sissy!* since he had caught her first show three years ago.

He drank from the bottle of grape soda, threw his knee over the arm of the chair, and flipped on the TV with the remote.

"Toot-toot! I've got megabargains today, folks!" gushed Marlis, as she put layered slices of Wonder bread and Velveeta into the Dekasonic sandwich maker, retail, $80, the Cable Shopping Club price, $36.75. Marlis hosted the weekend morning shift, talking a mile a minute, like she could hardly wait to hear what she had to say.

Thirty-six seventy-five was a good deal for a double sandwich maker. He had bought the identical model from the club last month for forty-one dollars, and it worked great. Marlis had already sold 345 Dekasonics this segment, 346, 347, 348. "We're having fun!" she chirped. "Toot-toot!"

Liston got up and went to the bathroom. When he came back, Marlis was holding up a Vanna doll, every golden polyester hair on the doll's head sparkling in the light.

"Vanna is eleven inches tall," Marlis said, "and for just nineteen ninety-five, she comes with either a red-dot dress or silver-dot dress, plus accessories: a brush, a comb, and high heels, and as you can see, she looks just like the *real* Vanna!"

Vanna was too skinny. You could cut yourself on a woman like that.

"The Vanna doll is almost interchangeable with Barbie,"— Marlis winked—"and you know what old Barbie dolls are selling for, don't you?" Marlis fanned herself with her hand. "Buy two, people. One for the kids to play with, and one to put aside for their college education."

Barbie was too skinny. All of them, just skin and bones. He looked at the bottle of grape soda in his hand, hurled it into the kitchen, ashamed of himself. Diet soda—he patted his belly. What did he have to worry about? Purple droplets floated through the sunlit kitchen, a garish chemical prism. No calories, no nothing. Make you hate yourself for having some heft. He heard the bottle fizzing, out of sight—it sounded like a time bomb.

Sissy didn't diet. She was ripe as a Georgia peach, full-figured, with no excuses and nothing to hide. Size 16, she had bragged on her show devoted to summer fashions, "sweet 16," she had said, modeling a pale lilac swimsuit for the camera.

He envied Sissy's unchecked appetite, her consuming pleasure—he wanted to watch her devour a roast chicken using just her hands, wanted to hear the bird's joints pop and see the juice run down her wrists. What would she do when she found out that Tod was dead? There would be nothing to stop her fury, her rage would tear right through him. He was breathing so hard his chest hurt.

On the Cable Shopping Club, Marlis suddenly announced a special offer available only to club members.

Liston picked up the phone next to the easychair, his finger poised.

Marlis showed off a dozen long-stemmed roses, either white for friendship or red for love, for a members-only price of $19.95. But hurry, our supply is lim—

Liston speed-dialed the club's 800-number, got through on the fourth attempt. He punched in his nine-digit club number, ordered four, no five, dozen red roses sent to the TV studio where Sissy taped her show. "Red," he repeated so the operator would make no mistake. He told her to write, "Please forgive me" on the card. No name.

He hoped Sissy would be careful of the thorns when she unwrapped them. Her skin was so delicate that even the leaves would scratch.

Chapter 14

"**I**s that Andy?" Jen said quietly. He hadn't heard that gentleness in her voice before, and he was grateful.

"Sort of. Yes. Shit." Quinn was exhausted. His back ached from sitting up all night waiting for Andy to call, and now . . . "That's him."

"I'm sorry," she said.

Andy slumped over the wheel of his van, face hidden from the morning light as though he were asleep. His scalp was blown out on one side of his head, dreadlocks dangling loosely, barely attached. Quinn could see dried blood on the tall grass around the door, a spray of rust on the bright green blades.

A couple of patrol cars were positioned near the van, uniformed officers standing around drinking coffee with a half-dozen reporters and photographers well outside the taped-off site.

Morales beckoned to Quinn and Jen, indicated to the uniforms that they be allowed to cross the tape. He looked freshly showered, a dark gray suit draped perfectly over his stocky frame. Morales watched them approach, his expression somber, his smooth brown cheeks pitted with tiny red acne scars, a fine scrollwork visible in the direct sunlight.

"I thought we had an understanding," said Quinn.

"You act tired," he said to Quinn. "Didn't you eat your Wheaties?" He inclined his head to Jen, eyed her outfit—a man's black shirt, blousy black workout pants tucked into black cowboy boots. "Who's your accomplice?"

Jen reached out and shook his hand. "Jen Takamura. I'm a photographer at *SLAP*."

They walked through the high weeds toward the van—grasshoppers fluttered up with every step, whirling around their legs. Morales and Jen ignored the insects, but Quinn cursed, smacked them aside with the back of his hand until he stopped himself.

His frustration was so pervasive that he noticed it only in such small actions. This morning he had broken his favorite coffee mug—it just shattered in his grip. His left thumbnail was chewed down until it hurt. Now, he was mad at grasshoppers.

It started last night when he stepped into Tod's living room, saw what was left of that young, confident smile in the photographs. Someone blew his heart apart, then shoved a gun down his throat—Quinn kept asking himself what Tod could have possibly done to deserve that. No wonder Andy had been terrified.

Quinn turned at the braying laughter from the uniforms—saw the crew from a local cable TV station swarming around Detective Draveki, the youthful on-air reporter reading from his notes. Draveki spit into the Styrofoam cup in his hand after every question. He needed a shave.

"You told me on the phone that I could take a look at Andy before the circus arrived," Quinn said to Morales.

"Me, I like the circus," Morales said, "I thought everyone did." He jabbed a thumb at Andy. "Airport security noticed him around seven A.M.—they're supposed to do a circuit of the perimeter every couple of hours, but after midnight they mostly coop up out of sight, smoke a joint, watch the planes land. I was at Sissy's place when I got the call. Drove right over."

They were close enough that Quinn could see a blue-green fly crawling over Andy's ear. What was left of it. The back of Quinn's neck itched—he started to scratch it but stopped himself.

"You probably can't tell," said Morales, "but he looks good compared to most I see. The side where the bullet exited is a mess, but his face is . . . peaceful."

"You could have fooled me."

"Do you mind, Lieutenant?" asked Jen. "I'd like to get some close-ups. I'll be careful not to touch anything."

"Be my guest."

Quinn watched Jen circle the van. The blue-green fly

buzzed against the inside of the windshield, hitting it again and again. "You going to put out an all-points for the man with the crewcut? I'll go over everything Andy told me, come up with the best description I can." The fly kept at it, banging against the glass. "He probably didn't leave any prints in the car either, but this guy had to have walked out from here, so you could do some foot casts or maybe Forensics can come up with a hair sample—"

Morales patted him on the shoulder. "Foot casts? That's funny. You see any nice wet mud around here? Forget hair samples or skin samples, there were lookie-loos all over this place before we got here."

A baggage handler from the airport drove up in an empty cart, turned off the engine, and watched them through the chain-link fence that separated the runway from the access road. After a minute he pulled a paper bag from under the seat and started eating a sandwich.

Morales shook his head. "See what I mean?"

"So what *do* you have?" said Quinn.

"We have a .357 in the deceased's hand," Morales said evenly, "unregistered, same caliber as the Naples homicide last night. Ballistics is checking it out." He held up one of Andy's hands, a claw in a clear plastic baggy, the fingers smudged with ink. Hard to imagine those hands gliding over piano keys. "Preliminary fingerprint match with those on Tod's glass doors. I'm having them run a paraffin test too, but it's academic—we've got a wrap here."

Quinn turned and looked at Morales. "What does that mean?"

"I think your pal Andy saved the city the cost of a trial. I wish more of the bad guys were that considerate." Morales smiled but didn't show his teeth. An old habit. Quinn remembered what they looked like before he got them capped.

"Last night you thought Andy murdered Tod. Now you think he drove out here afterward and killed *himself*? That's what you're trying to sell?"

Morales shrugged. "We found over eleven thousand dollars cash on him, so that pretty much rules out the mysterious hitman with the crewcut. I never knew a hitter yet who'd leave that kind of money behind. Oh yeah, one more thing—the lottery ticket he sent you to Tod's for? We found it in his pocket, just like I told you. Half of it anyway."

"Half?"

"He must have thrown the other half away. Little joke of his, once he knew he wasn't going to get to spend it."

"You don't believe any of this," said Quinn. He could hear that fat fly buzzing against the windshield, but he didn't take his eyes off Morales. "You don't expect me to believe it either."

Jen had wandered back to them, listening.

"Come over here," said Morales. The three of them clustered around the door, leaning against the open window. Morales reached in and grabbed a handful of Andy's hair, tilted his head toward them. "Forget the powder burns. See this? The way the bone's shattered? See how the impact made a nice tight circle? That's what we call a starburst wound—you get an entrance wound like that when a bullet's fired from point-blank range, right *there*." He pressed his forefinger against the side of Quinn's head. "See. You flinched, Quinn. It's a natural reaction. You shoot somebody, even if they don't see it coming, they flinch at the last second, and you get a completely different kind of wound. You only see a starburst in a suicide, when the guy cuddles that gun like it was his mama."

"Andy didn't kill himself," said Quinn. "He had company. Did you check the seat position? How about the rear view mirror? Andy said the guy with the crewcut was huge. If he drove Andy out here, he might have forgotten to change them back when they switched places."

"I know my job, Quinn. Everything's where it's supposed to be."

"Lieutenant?" said Jen. "Excuse me, but the grass around the passenger-side door is bent down. It looks like somebody got out that side. I'm sure you checked—"

Morales nodded. "I saw that too, miss. First thing. Problem is the site wasn't clean when we got here—Airport Security was standing around taking Polaroids of each other like they secured Fort Apache."

Quinn stayed close to Andy, staring into the van, while Morales and Jen went around to the other side. Morales opened the door so she could get some interior shots.

"Esteban, do me a favor," said Quinn. "Put on the radio."

"You bored?" Morales shrugged, then turned the key in the ignition. He hit the On button and Michael Jackson sang his latest hit, the sound rich and full through Andy's top-of-the-line speaker system.

"That's not Andy's station," Quinn said, trying to hold back his excitement. "Go ahead. Press his presets. Go on."

Morales's finger hit each of the buttons in succession. Every one was a classical station. He went through the presets again, just to make sure. "Interesting."

"Andy wasn't alone in this van when the gun went off," said Quinn. "The same guy who changed the channel on Tod's TV left Andy's radio on a soul station. This guy just can't keep his hands to himself."

"Maybe Andy just wanted to hear some good music—" Morales's head swiveled as the double-axle Channel 6 ActionNews van roared up the access road in a cloud of dust. "I'll take the radio into consideration," he said. "I've got to go."

Nancy Tyler-Tuck, roving anchor for Channel 6, stepped out of the van, waved to Morales, and checked her makeup in the side mirror. She was a prim blonde with a helmet hairdo and no sense of humor. Channel 6—"We LOVE L.A.!"—was the highest-rated station in the Southern California market.

Morales straightened his tie as Nancy Tyler-Tuck spoke intently into her microphone, then inclined it toward him. Morales nodded sagely before answering, like she had asked him the most intelligent question imaginable.

The Trashman stood almost at Nancy Tyler-Tuck's elbow, taking photographs of the interview, ignoring her requests that he stop. In fact, he enjoyed her discomfort. Trashman was a beaky, hyperkinetic freelancer who raced from disaster to divorce court with equal enthusiasm—a photo of Nancy Tyler-Tuck looking uncharacteristically frazzled was an easy sale.

People magazine had run one of Trashman's photos for their feature about the killing at the minimart. It was quite a shot, full-page color—Quinn dazed, his face splashed with blood; Groggins was behind him, sheepish, hands raised in surrender.

"You're right about the radio," said Jen. She came over and stood next to him, the two of them looking in on Andy.

"What? I'm sorry . . ."

"People are very loyal about their music," said Jen. "Somebody who's going to kill themselves doesn't decide to check out the other end of the dial at the last moment. Andy would have wanted to hear something familiar when he pulled the trigger. I know I would."

"He came to me for help last night . . . made me promise . . ." The collar of Andy's Cal Tech sweatshirt was crusted with blood. "I told him he was paranoid," Quinn whispered.

"It's not your fault."

He watched the breeze lift one of Andy's curls.

A plane screamed overhead but neither of them moved.

Andy must have been snatched right after he and Quinn talked at Burgerama. Quinn remembered the startled look on the carhop's face as something or someone beyond the parking lot caught her attention.

The man with the crewcut had watched the two of them sitting on the patio, waited while Andy begged for help, hands shaking, waited until Quinn left—he must have been very sure of himself. It was the crewcut man's certainty, his implacable calm, that had terrified Andy as much as anything, the way he had casually stood on Tod's front porch, right under the light, watching Andy drive off.

Quinn felt fear in his throat like a small cold flower, growing by the moment. He could barely breathe around it—a death orchid passed from Tod to Andy and now to him. He took one last look at Andy, wondering what his friend had said before he put the gun to his head. Did you give me up, Andy? And how did you ever manage to pull the trigger without flinching?

Quinn was going to have to tell Morales about the carhop—maybe she could corroborate Andy's description of the killer.

He found himself checking the faces of the reporters and photographers milling around, paying particular attention to the ones he didn't recognize. He stared through the chain-link fence at the baggage handler sitting with his feet up in the empty baggage cart. The man stared back, stolidly chewing an apple, his head obscured by a floppy cap and protective earphones.

Quinn felt the world getting smaller, contracting, people being pushed together until you couldn't tell who was who.

Jen put her hand on his upper arm, the warmth flooding through him.

They walked in silence back through the high weeds, their shoulders brushing with every step.

Chapter 15

The image of Quinn standing next to Morales floated up from the developer as Jen gently rocked the photographic tray, the contrast deepening until she yanked the eight-by-ten out and slid it into the stopbath. The hiss of the acid stopbath neutralizing the base developer always made her smile.

Jen moved back and forth between the trays in the small darkroom she had set up in her apartment, a graceful dance without music under the red safelight. She had curtained off half of the bedroom with black plastic, running in water from the master bathroom. It seemed luxurious—during the last coup in Haiti, she had set up a functioning darkroom in a hotel closet in downtown Port-au-Prince.

She took three eight-by-tens out of the water bath and hung them on the string with clothespins—a clothesline of images, different shots of the van, the bloody weeds . . . and Quinn.

It wasn't her fault he had such good strong features. Portraits were her specialty—nothing told a tale like the human face. She had started out in fashion photography, but clothes didn't interest her. Even her combat photography emphasized the warriors more than the war—she found the blank, reptilian gaze of an Iraqi tank general more menacing than the weapons under his command.

She bent over a close-up of Quinn peering into the van, noting the pain crinkling the edges of his eyes, but his mouth holding firm as he looked at what was left of his friend. Tenacity was the most attractive quality in a man. Seeing it in him had been a pleasant surprise.

There were plenty of stories about Quinn—everyone at

SLAP knew what had happened at the minimart, how Groggins had asked for Quinn so he could murder the clerk right in front of him. There were accusations afterward that Quinn had used stolen police files to get Groggins acquitted the first time. The *Columbia Journalism Report* had used him as the lead in their cover story on "Outlaw Journalists, Danger to the Profession?" Quinn never responded to the criticism. She would have. She would have come out swinging, insisting that the best journalists were all outlaws. She would have shown them the proof.

Instead, Quinn had disappeared for almost a year before showing up at *SLAP*. She heard he was researching a book on the Mafia. She heard he had a complete breakdown, recovering slowly at a private sanitarium in the Bahamas. The Mafia, maybe. The sanitarium, never. She couldn't imagine him staying still that long.

She changed the lens of the enlarger to F3.5, gave the next print a thirty-four-second exposure, watching the second hand of the timer sweep toward zero. She liked seeing the increments of time glide past with such perfect regularity. It was the precision of photography that attracted her, the interplay of light and shadow, black and white, and every gray-tone in between. With a camera she could freeze action, capture movement, and take it home with her. In the darkroom she could distill the most subtle and fleeting emotions, controlling them through definite mathematical ratios.

Quinn's face swam up through the developer solution, his expression a mix of anger and sadness. Morales loomed at the edge of the frame. While Quinn seemed to vibrate with barely restrained energy, Morales was pure mass, an immovable object.

Her fingers slid over the photo, lightly rubbing Quinn's face, the heat of her finger tips activating the developer, bringing out details. It was a wild, stubborn face—she imagined it flushed with passion, nostrils flared. . . . She looked at her fingertips idly caressing his powerful chinline, quickly dropped it in the stop. That's all she needed.

She had some plain shots of the van that needed to be developed. There were already plenty of Quinn strung up on the line, edges curling in the red light.

Andy lay over the wheel of the van, head canted to one side, a trickle of dried blood running down one ear. What a waste. Morales said Andy looked peaceful—it must be a matter of perspective. She had covered wars and religious atrocities and backyard arguments. The dead never looked peaceful.

The phone rang and she grabbed it, tucked it against her neck as she worked.

"Jen? You sound odd."

"I'm fine, Mother. I'm in the darkroom."

"Where else would you be on a lovely Saturday afternoon? Jen dear, we really need a decision from you about Aspen."

"I'm not going to be able to make it, Mother." Jen slipped another negative into the enlarger. "I'm in the middle of three different projects right now. Did you get the copy of Italian *Vogue* I sent you? They ran five pages from my skinhead portfolio—"

"Your pictures were very nice. That's not what we're discussing, though. I'm *very* disappointed that you've chosen not to join your stepfather and me at the mountain. Your brothers and sister have already committed themselves. I've booked you a room of your own."

"You had no right to do that. I told you weeks ago that I was too busy."

"I was sure you'd reconsider once you had an opportunity to think more clearly." Jen thought she could hear her mother tapping her foot on the marble floor of her living room. "Obviously you're intent on insulting your stepfather, and his generosity. Someday perhaps you'll think of pleasing someone other than yourself."

"I doubt it, Mother."

"Don't you *dare* use that sarcastic tone with me. I'm glad your father didn't live to hear such rudeness from your lips. We were married seventeen years and that man never raised his voice to me."

Jen closed her eyes for a moment, then continued rocking the photographic tray. She could see her parents in their formal portraits: her father awkward in a rented tuxedo that was too big for him, his eyes tender. He held himself stiffly erect, but was still shorter than her mother, the beautiful, austere Mrs. Takamura, half-white and full-time . . . lady. Jen had her father's brains, his strong, practical hands and fine golden skin, his ability to fix things, from a broken dishwasher to a broken heart. She had her mother's cool green eyes, her assaying glance.

Her father had left school at fourteen, gave up his dreams to help support his family. He should have been an electrical engineer, worn a spotless white labcoat—instead he owned a small appliance-repair shop, and never made enough money. Jen was his favorite child—he took her with him to work, gave her a soldering gun for her tenth birthday. He died before her eleventh.

Mrs. Takamura never made the same mistake twice. She married for love the first time, the next time she married for money. Mrs. Takamura . . . now, Mrs. Bigelow.

"I am waiting for an apology, young lady."

Young lady. The print in the developer was a wide-angle shot of the van with the passenger-side door open so you could see the cramped position Andy was in. She reached down and help it up, tilting the print back and forth, squinting in the dim light. There was . . . *something* in the doorframe of the van. She checked the negative with a magnifying look. It wasn't a dust spot. She cranked the enlarger higher, blowing up that section of the negative. Eighteen-second exposure.

"I am still waiting."

"Could we not do this, Mother? Please? Just this once? I love you, I don't want to quarrel."

"If your father was alive, he'd *demand* that you apologize to me." She was definitely tapping her foot.

"Mother, my father never demanded anything in his life and it's a good thing for you that he didn't." The receiver buzzed in her ear. She closed her eyes, seeing the pained expression on her father's face when she and her mother used to fight. It had been a long war. Now that he was gone there was no reason to make peace.

She wiped tears from her eyes, glad that no one could see her. In the developer tray, the enlarged image of the doorframe had coalesced—the other half of Andy's lottery ticket was stuck in the door. An impossible reach for a man who died in the driver's seat. She called Quinn's number. She didn't have to look it up.

Chapter 16

"**Y**ou want to get that, *mi cielo?*"

Morales rustled the speech he was writing for the Kiwanas Sunday breakfast club, showing his annoyance. Here it was almost dinnertime Saturday, and he was still working on it.

Linda clattered whatever it was she was burning in the kitchen to show *she* was too busy to answer the goddamned motherfucking door.

"Okay." He straightened his tie, just in case it was a news crew wanting to do a follow-up, then opened the door.

Quinn stood on the welcome mat. He was wearing the same clothes he had on this morning: black pants, boots, and that silly-ass happy-face T-shirt to show off his build. His eyes were so angry that Morales thought Quinn was going to take a swing at him.

"Who is it, *guapo?*"

"Hey, Linda," called Quinn, staring at Morales. His voice was chipper, but his eyes stayed hot.

"Quinn? Is that you?" She came out of the kitchen waving at the smoke, crossed the room, and embraced Quinn. She had on the eighty-dollar Guess? jeans that were too fucking tight in the can, and whatever was on the end of that fork in her hand looked like it should go directly into the garbage disposal.

"Girl, you look *great*," said Quinn.

Linda patted her straight blond hair with the black roots. "You're going to stay for dinner, aren't you?"

Quinn wrinkled his nose at the smell and laughed. Then he kissed her hand—her *hand,* give me a fucking break—and said, "Come on now, that's assault with a deadly weapon, and we've got a cop on the scene."

She punched him on the arm.

David and Alex looked up from Super Mario Brothers, then went back to their video game, beep-beep-beeping, their mouths slack as junkies in the flickering light.

"Thanks for the offer, Linda," said Quinn, "but I need to talk to the lieutenant."

Morales steered Quinn out the door. "Back in a minute," he called over his shoulder. He patted his pockets for a cigarette, caught himself.

Morales hadn't smoked since he graduated from the academy, hadn't used profanity or spoken Spanish except in the line of duty. He kept a lid on himself, kept it tight—it was the only way to get ahead. Ever since Quinn's call last night he had craved a Marlboro, tasted them at the back of his throat. Next he'd be ordering fucking chorizo burritos delivered to his desk at the station. Maybe a couple of bottles of Inca Cola too.

"You lied to me," said Quinn when they got to the sidewalk.

"Let's keep walking." Morales smoothed back his hair, then waved to Jameson across the street who was watering his driveway, the runoff trickling down the gutters. Jameson waved back with the hose, got his loafers wet. He was an insurance salesman, strictly corporate accounts; Linda said according to his wife, Jameson pulled down over $150,000 last year. Asshole still couldn't keep his shoes dry.

Windward Estates was a gated development—no security bars, no graffiti. The houses came with tiled entryways, beamed ceilings, and built-in trash compactors. He and Linda had moved in two years ago, bought the cheapest model, and still had to take out a second mortgage and drain his pension plan to do it. Linda said they were stretched too thin, but he told her it would be fine. Their first night there, they made love like on their honeymoon—the boys' rooms were on the other side of the house, and Linda made the noises that drove his prick crazy.

"I saw the news conference," said Quinn. "I almost put my foot through the set. This morning you stood next to Andy's van and told me you were going to keep the case open. I turn on the news this afternoon and there you are with all that brass—case closed and the citizens can sleep well tonight. Fuck you, and your badge, Esteban. Andy didn't kill Tod, and he *sure* didn't kill himself."

Quinn was the only reporter Morales had ever liked. Most of them were ass-kissers, or bleeding hearts who hadn't been in a fight since third grade and thought people were basically good. Quinn knew better.

"I told you I'd keep the case open until I got more evidence," Morales said, not raising his voice. "We got it. The ballistics—"

"Did you even talk to the carhop at Burgerama?" said Quinn.

"She said she heard somebody out near the garbage bin, but she didn't see anything. They get transients—"

"It was *him*."

"The ballistics report came in right after lunch," said Morales. "I made them rush it because I knew how concerned you were—there was a positive match with the gun that killed Tod. Nobody's prints on it but Andy's. The paraffin test was positive too—black powder grains embedded in his right hand. So Andy fired the shot that blew his brains out. That's evidence enough for the chief."

"Did anyone ask why Andy wouldn't take his chances in court even if he *was* guilty?" Quinn said. "The average time served for murder in this state is seven years." He was trying to keep his voice as unemotional as Morales's, but he needed more practice. It had taken Morales a lot of practice. "Anyone at the press conference wonder why he drove to the middle of nowhere to kill himself?"

"It's settled."

"It's not settled. Jen found the other half of Andy's lottery ticket. Have your evidence team open the passenger door of the van and check the frame. It's there."

Morales shrugged.

"Don't you get it?" Quinn looked in pain. "Andy tore the ticket and left half in the doorframe *deliberately*. To let us know that he was sitting in the passenger seat. He wasn't alone that night at the airport."

Morales was so intent on what Quinn had just said that he didn't hear Addison across the street. There was no telling how long he had been calling. "Steve!" yelled Addison. "Got a minute?" He pushed a fertilizer-spreader across his brown lawn toward them, gray dust billowing in his wake. Addison was a dermatologist who introduced himself as "Dr. Addison," and loved to stand around after work in flip-flops and plaid shorts, leaning on a rake.

Growing up, Morales had spent every weekend and summer working with his father at places just like Windward Estates, cutting, clipping, weeding. Addison's Bermuda hybrid definitely didn't need weekly applications of that manganese-based fertilizer he was using.

Addison nodded at Quinn and turned to Morales. "The wife said she saw you on the news. You get paid extra for that?"

"No."

"Too bad. Anyway, I need some advice about this darned lawn of mine. You have a great little yard, so green and full . . . maybe you could tell me your secret."

"Wish I could help you, Howard, but lawns aren't my area of expertise. Linda has a Japanese man come around every month."

Quinn waited until they walked out of earshot. "Steve? You meet ol' Howard at a Tupperware party?"

"We don't save Linda's cooking."

Their shared laughter helped. He and Quinn just walked for a while, taking a spin around the block, the breeze cool and clean. Dinner was cooking all over the neighborhood: lemon chicken, salmon, pot roast. Sometimes he missed the familiar smells of his childhood—the pungent mole sauce his mother made, the smoky sweetness of roasted goat from the Jamaican family next door.

His sons were growing up thinking Mexican food was the Anglo shit they served at Taco Bell. It was a trade-off—David and Alex could play in their front yard here and not worry about catching a stray round from a drive-by. Except they spent most of their time playing Nintendo.

At the end of the street, he and Quinn stopped to watch the kids racing radio-controlled cars around the cul-de-sac, the sound like angry hornets.

"So Andy's radio being turned to a station he never listened to, that doesn't count?" said Quinn. "The ticket doesn't count . . . none of that matters?"

"You don't understand," said Morales, watching the little cars hurtle around and around. "There is a . . . momentum to law enforcement. Once the brass goes public with a case, you don't embarrass them by issuing a correction: Sorry, we blew it. It's going to take something definitive to reopen the case— not lottery tickets, or the wrong music on the radio."

"You owe me, Esteban," Quinn said it so softly that Morales thought for a moment it was his own heart speaking, the way it did sometimes when he needed to go to St. Ignacio's for confession. He let his heart talk all it wanted, but he never listened to it. He didn't go to confession either.

"I should have been suspicious when you let me pay for coffee that time," said Quinn. "You never did that before. You used to say it was unethical."

"It is unethical." Morales resisted the impulse to shove his hands into the front pockets of his suit—he wanted to protect the crease.

Morales remembered that lunch. They had sat in a booth at the back, their heads bent close, and he had told Quinn that Detective Nate Odom was using jailhouse snitches to make his tough cases, and now one of those snitches had fingered Groggins for the murder of the two coeds. The snitch was lying. Quinn had almost spilled his coffee, he was so excited. Morales had said he couldn't go to Internal Affairs—breaking the code of silence would sink his career right along with Odom's. Morales hadn't even remembered Quinn picking up the bill for lunch until he mentioned it now. Funny the things you forget.

"You were right about the snitch," said Quinn, watching the little remote-controlled cars bounce off the curb. "I checked it out—he *was* lying. Just like you said." His face fell. "That didn't mean that Groggins was innocent."

"Who would have figured it?" Morales said. "Groggins was a small-timer, nothing on his rap sheet but a bunch of pled-down priors, no history of violence. You were doing your job. That's what we were both doing."

"The clerk at the minimart, the one Groggins murdered, she was doing her job too. . . ." Quinn swallowed. "Her name was Doreen. She had a daughter. She lived with her in a studio apartment on Atlantic, right off Hill—"

"I grew up around there, don't tell me—"

"The little girl's name was LaToya. Because Doreen loved the Jacksons. Her mother said Doreen had every one of their albums." Quinn wiped his eyes, angry at the tears. "Her mother lives in Carson. I spent an afternoon with her looking at photo albums." He cleared his throat. "She kept bringing me coffee and these little cakes with the creme filling . . . I don't know what they're called." Quinn shook his head. "She felt sorry for *me.* Can you imagine that?"

The buzzing of the remote-controlled cars bounced off the bones in Morales's skull, an insistent whine that couldn't quite drown out the sound of Quinn's voice.

"I'm scared," Quinn said quietly. "Andy and I were together a couple of hours before he was killed—I think this guy with the crewcut saw us talking. Maybe he thinks Andy told me something."

"Did he?"

"No. But the guy with the crewcut doesn't know that. You've seen what he does to people . . . you want to find me like that?"

"Don't worry about it," said Morales. "Even if Andy *was* murdered because of what he saw in Naples, anything he told you was hearsay and inadmissible in court. You're no threat. If it was a frame, the frame holds—somebody killing you just opens it up again. You're in the clear, Quinn. We should all be so lucky."

"I'm not the lucky one," said Quinn. "Groggins is on Death Row, Odom lost his pension, and me . . . well, we know about me. But you? You made lieutenant and sleep like a baby."

"I was in line for the job," Morales growled.

Quinn shook his head. "Odom was in that line too, right ahead of you. He had seniority, a good arrest record, better test scores—I checked. I'm surprised the grand jury didn't come knocking at *your* door with a subpoena."

"Odom *wouldn't* have had such a good arrest record without perjured testimony."

"He was right about Groggins, though, wasn't he?" insisted

Quinn. "Groggins fooled me—I got him acquitted. He didn't fool Odom."

A blue radio-controlled car crashed into the curb and lost a wheel. One kid rushed the crippled car, lifted a boulder over his head with both hands, and flattened it.

"Did Groggins fool you?" asked Quinn. "Did you know he killed those college girls when we sat down over coffee?"

Morales turned and looked at him.

"What did you tell me at Tod's?" The muscles in Quinn's jaw looked like they were grinding walnuts. "You said if I was going to have such smart friends, I needed to become a better judge of character. How am I doing?"

Morales nodded. "You're doing fine. Better than I remember."

"I'm going to find the guy with the crewcut," said Quinn, "and I want you to help me." There wasn't any hesitation in him anymore. "Get me the last three months of Tod's phone bills, you should be able to do that. Financial records, too— bank accounts, credit cards. Any major shifts in his balance? Was he overdrawn or overextended? I want to see if Tod owed somebody money, somebody who might have sent this guy with the crewcut to make an example of him."

"It might have been a message hit," agreed Morales grudgingly. "An ugly hit like that keeps everybody honest. I'll run those errands for you; that's easy enough. A word of advice, though, since you pay so much attention to the things I say— find out who hated Tod. Nothing in his house was taken. All the man who killed him wanted was Tod. And he wanted him very dead."

Two of the kids were fighting, swinging wildly, stomping each other's cars. One kid was crying, blood trickling from his nose where the other had hit him. What a baby.

Quinn ran over, stepped between the flying fists, and separated them. Always the good citizen. The streetlights came on as Morales calmly watched the kids kick their cars to pieces.

Chapter 17

"**M**r. Stratton? Would you—"

"John. Call me John, honey." He watched the carousel behind her spinning around, the brightly painted horses going up and down to "Raindrops Keep Falling on My Head."

"Uh . . . John, would you please step over here for a moment?" said Erika Maanz, the senior publicist from Koltnow-Hines. "There's someone I'd like you to meet."

John Stratton tugged politely at his pearl-white cowboy hat, walked over, and stuck out his hand toward the nervous man in the gray suit. "Howdy, I'm John Stratton."

"Mr. Stratton, John," said the man, pumping his hand, "I'm William LaCosta, vice president for corporate relations, First Bank of the West. It's an honor to meet you, sir."

"Nice to meet you, Bill." Stratton was wearing his formal duds—white Stetson, western-cut dark blue suit and black ostrich-skin boots. His belt buckle was discreet, the turquoise-and-silver bolo a gift from the president of Mexico. He looked more like a successful oilman than a cowpoke. At sixty-three years old, Stratton was still an imposing figure—six-four, handsome as a lion, with a full head of silver hair and twinkling blue eyes. He inspired confidence, rather than envy.

A cowboy movie star during the 1950s, Stratton had moved to television in the early '60s, starring in *The Lonely Badge*, the story of an upright retired sheriff running a cattle ranch with his three daughters. The critics howled, dubbing it "*Gunsmoke* on the Ponderosa," but the show spent fifteen seasons in the top-ten slot, and was still being rerun in every major market. These days he spent most of his time on his two-thousand-acre ranch on the eastern fringe of Orange County, far from the ocean and freeways and congestion. He was still having the last laugh.

Erika Maanz handed a five-foot blowup of a check to LaCosta, who held it out to Stratton. They grinned at each other as the photographer flashed away. When the still photographer was done, the two of them repeated the process for the camera crews from two local TV stations, LaCosta intoning, "And First Bank of the West is proud to donate one hundred thousand dollars to the California Literacy Program."

The crowd that had gathered at center court of Southcoast Plaza Mall applauded loudly and on cue. Stratton waved good-naturedly to them, excused himself, and sat down at a bench next to one of the potted palms. The publicist's assistant announced over the P.A. that John Stratton would be signing autographs in one hour and giving out a silver dollar to every child with a current library card.

South Coast was one of the largest malls in Southern California, a former beanfield, now the multimillion-dollar centerpiece of Orange County retail—three levels of upscale shops, spacious and clean and safe, soft music floating through the air-conditioning. No outside noise or humidity was allowed to intrude—it was a church of immaculate consumption, stacked with bright, soft luxuries. Japanese tourists might first want to see Disneyland, but they spent most of their vacation at South Coast Plaza, nibbling frozen yogurt as they wandered its vast corriders.

On this warm Saturday afternoon, the escalators were packed with suntanned kids from Newport and Laguna and Huntington Beach, bored kids with their own credit cards, their equally bored parents loaded with shopping bags from Nordstrom and Cartier and Fiorucci. Fresh from aerobics classes and liposuction, the moms had smaller, firmer butts than their daughters, but the fathers still watched the girls from behind their sunglasses.

A year ago, Stratton had been approached by a consortium of backers who encouraged him to seek elective office. They were mostly developers and high-tech entrepreneurs, flush with cash, searching for a candidate who shared their free-market philosophy. Stratton, with his own "bootstraps" success story, his rugged, wholesome image, and nonpartisan background, seemed ideal.

"John," said Erika Maanz, glancing at her notes, "later, I've scheduled some shots with a racially balanced group of kids for possible use in your political campaign. I've also got a reporter from the *Orange County News* here to do a brief interview about the literacy program. He may also want to discuss your gubernatorial plans—the front office is issuing leaks to selected media and—"

"Don't forget upstate radio and TV, Erika, those ranchers and farmers vote too," said Stratton, nodding pleasantly at the mothers holding up their children dressed in cowboy clothes. He took off his hat and waved. "I worry that all you high-priced talent sometimes get too slick for your own good."

She took a deep breath, smoothed the hem of her pale yellow suit. "Koltnow-Hines has a reputation for diligence as well as—"

"Spare me the axle-grease. You get the results of those focus groups?"

"Preliminary research gives you an extremely high Q-rating across most of the demographic." She nodded. "High-recognition, high-approval, but you're a little flat among eighteen-to-thirty-year-old women." She tugged at her pearls as Stratton scowled. "These women were too young to remember your movies," she explained, "and they've only seen your TV series in reruns. The literacy program should help; their children are the target audience. As you can see"—she indicated the crowd waiting around the silver-dollar display—"we've got a lot of young mothers here. We've also discussed the possibility of you doing a couple of safe-sex spots, wearing your sheriff's badge—"

"Nope," said Stratton. "I thought I made myself clear. I'm happy to do public-service spots, but they can't have anything to do with sex or drugs; no AIDS advisories, no just-say-no. People confuse the message with the messenger, so that's out."

She scratched a line through something she had written in her notes.

Even starting out in the movies, Stratton had been careful with his image. When Ronnie Reagan and Gary Cooper, and even the Duke himself, were touting cigarettes from the back covers of *Life* and *Look,* he had steered clear. People needed heroes—and heroes had needs of their own.

Today, he still ran his own career, selecting his appearances for maximum effect—he didn't do variety-show walk-ons, he didn't allow himself to be roasted by has-beens from the Friars Club. Stratton presented a major Emmy every year, *by himself.* He was the official spokesperson for NASA—"the Next Frontier." He limited his commercial work to three long-term clients: an American car company, the California Fruit and Vegetable Growers, and First Bank of the West. He made $5 million a year from those accounts, plus residuals from *The Lonely Badge.*

A political career would end the endorsements, which was why he had hesitated when the consortium first approached him. He liked the sound of Governor Stratton, but he hated the idea of a pay cut. Still, there were other considerations. . . . His candidacy would be formally announced in five weeks, right after the Rose Bowl. He was grand marshal this year.

"The reporter from the *OC News* is here"—the publicist smiled at a dour, unkempt man in a fake-leather jacket—"his name is Jim Bennett," she whispered.

"I'll do the stand-ups with the kids first," said Stratton. "I want to look fresh for the shots; the reporter'll keep." He was gone before the publicist could answer, striding over to where the children were gathered behind a thick red suede rope, holding up their library cards.

For the next half hour, Stratton smiled, held up kids for the camera, handed out silver dollars, and flirted with the moms. The reporter waited nearby, shifting from one foot to the other.

"I'll be back in five minutes," Stratton said to the crowd, then walked over to the reporter.

"Glad you could make time," sniffed Bennett, riffing through his notebook.

Stratton glared at him. "Would you mind moving? You're standing on my mark."

"Huh?"

"My mark." Stratton pointed to the intersecting strips of adhesive tape on the floor. "That's where I stand for my camera shots. You're on my mark."

Bennett sniffed, moved back a bit. "Sorry." He shook his head. "I mean, it's not like the cameras are rolling—"

"It doesn't matter if I'm on-camera," Stratton said tightly, "they're still my marks. Mine. Not yours."

Bennett looked over at the publicist, but she was busy. "Whatever you say." He shrugged. His fake-leather jacket crackled like plastic wrap.

"Property rights are the foundation of this country, the basis of all law," said Stratton, hooking his thumbs in his belt. "Our founding fathers *died* for those rights."

"I'm the rock-music reviewer most days," apologized Bennett, "I don't know shit about rights."

Stratton shook his head sadly, turned away, and watched the kids on the merry-go-round. Poor kids. They thought they were riding the range, but they were just going round in circles.

Chapter 18

"The new receptionist reported that you had a series of rather desperate phone calls Friday night?" said Antonin Napitano, the diminutive publisher of *SLAP* magazine. He poked at the barbecue grill with a long fork. "I do hope there wasn't a family emergency, dear boy?" His voice was a resonant coo—the first time he heard it, Quinn imagined him gargling with warm olive oil.

"Turn those ribs, will you?" said Quinn.

"I feared that your little girl drowned in the bath," said Napitano. "I don't know why. It was an image that came to me as soon as I heard about the phone calls. I pictured fragrant bubbles. A rubber ducky. A woman screaming. It was quite vivid." The breeze sent mesquite smoke from the barbecue into Napitano's jowly face, but he didn't blink. He was a soft little man with a heavy-lidded gaze and eyes hard as pennies.

"Everybody's fine, Nino. You just have an ugly imagination."

"That is true." Napitano stabbed at the rows of ribs and hot-link sausages with the fork. Flames shot up from the grill. "I suppose some would consider that a weakness."

"Never."

It was a broiling Sunday afternoon, the day after Andy's murder, and Quinn would have rather been anywhere else. Instead, like the rest of the staff, he was attending a command performance at Napitano's Brentwood home. The theme: "Classic American Barbecue." Washtubs full of iced Lone Star beer and RC Cola were scattered across the four acres of groomed bluegrass. Sturdy redwood picnic tables groaned under platters of buttered corn on the cob and fried chicken, ceramic bowls of baked beans and jalapeño spoon bread, stacks of peach cobbler and sweet-potato pie—all of the food flown in from a hole-in-the-wall restaurant in Fort Worth that didn't accept checks or credit cards.

Napitano was a recent emigré to Los Angeles, selling off the chain of European tabloids that had earned him critical scorn, a personal fortune estimated at over $100 million, and two fruitless investigations by Interpol as to the source of his initial capitalization. On this muggy day, the publisher was resplendent in creased jeans and a pearl-button shirt embroidered with large red parrots. His purple suede cowboy hat was tilted rakishly back, emphasizing his oversized head.

A dozen Weber grills smoldered around the pool and tennis courts, each one manned by an unhappy editor. To please Napitano, the staff had rented full western regalia: ten-gallon hats and pointy-toed boots, duster coats and rawhide dresses. They sweltered under the midafternoon sun, glancing at Quinn and Napitano chatting away beside the three-hole putting green, wondering why Quinn always got such special treatment from the boss.

The two of them *were* an incongruous match—Napitano imperious in spite of his short stature and dude-ranch finery, shoulders thrown back, jaw thrust forward; Quinn slouched beside him in khaki shorts and a baggy, garishly striped Seminole Indian shirt, his hair wild. The emperor and the barbarian.

Quinn watched the flames, drifting with the steady popping as the meat juices splattered against the coals.

"A friend of mine was murdered yesterday," Quinn said suddenly, then stopped, unsure whether to continue.

Napitano looked up from the grill. He speared a hot link, brought it to his full lips, and blew on it, not taking his eyes off Quinn. "Perhaps that was the source of my vision?" His front teeth cautiously popped the casing—juice ran down the fork, dripped off his chin as he chomped at the sausage. "You think?"

Quinn didn't bother answering. He had gone through Tod's datebook early this morning—the calendar was a jumble of appointments and meetings at the production company, Tod's daily workout regimen, sailing dates, and regattas. Nothing that would get anybody killed. The phone numbers listed were almost all women, beside each name a book title: *Fear of Flying, The Little Prince, Tropic of Cancer* . . . What was it, some kind of erotic code?

He watched Jen dance by herself beside the swimming pool, swaying to some country twang. She waved a bottle of mescal at him, gave him a war whoop, her raven hair glossy in the sunlight. The fringe on her Annie Oakley skirt whipped back and forth.

"Ms. Takamura's photographs of the Samsons were magnifico," Napitano said, following his gaze. "I think she is right though, the portraits of the crazed teenagers in the crowd, these are much more exciting. We shall make the piece a photo-essay, very stark, very minimalist. You need just write an introduction."

"Did you know a man named Tod Bullock?" said Quinn. "He worked for Sissy Mizell."

"Bullock?" Napitano shrugged. "I don't think so."

"I found your name in his datebook. He would have called you a couple of months ago. I can get the exact date. Do you know—"

"*Someone* from her office got in touch with me," said Napitano. "I do not recall the name. There was talk of them doing a show about me, but I broke off discussion when I was told there were to be two other publishers on the panel. Antonin Napitano does not share the stage."

Indeed, Napitano had launched *SLAP* with a full-throttle national media blitz, personally directing the strategy. He was interviewed on the top-rated morning news show and *Entertainment Tonight,* profiled in *Forbes, Barrons,* and *GQ.*

A year later circulation was up, ad revenues were up, and the targets of its exposés were no longer laughing off the charges of "a sensationalist rag." *SLAP* was almost respectable, even if Napitano wasn't.

Napitano stood with his hands on his hips, chin held high, watching the overcooked sausages burst on the grill. Strands of lank hair crept from under his cowboy hat as he inhaled the aroma. "This Tod Bullock . . . he was a friend of yours? I saw on the news that one of Sissy's producers had been murdered. The man who killed him committed suicide. Yes?"

"No." Quinn watched C. Thomas Cavendish, *SLAP*'s film

critic, carry a plate of chicken wings toward the tennis courts. The man who last issue had used the phrase "postmodernist twaddle masquerading as ensemble ennui" in a review of an animated short was wearing sheepskin chaps and a blue cavalry shirt.

"I know you find Cavendish amusing," said Napitano, nodding at the critic, "but submission is a vital lubricant within any organization; it allows individuals to find their rightful place with a minimum of friction."

"Like a baboon troop?" said Quinn. "Maybe that could be the theme to your next party? 'Primate Fever'—we all show up bare-assed, our butts painted bright red?"

"Would it matter to you?" Napitano shook the barbecue fork at Quinn's blousy short-sleeve shirt. "I should be angry. Look at you—the invitation clearly said 'Cowboy Attire' and you show up as an Apache."

"Seminole."

"What's the difference?"

"The Apaches lost. Seminoles never surrendered. They just lay low in the Everglades, waiting for hurricane season to blow the white man away."

Flames shot up around the meat, but Napitano's face remained impassive. "I have been to Miami," he said. "Your proud Seminoles spend the day wrestling alligators for the enjoyment of menopausal tourists from New Jersey."

"Yeah, kemo sabe, but it's *their* alligators."

A stony-faced Hispanic waiter interrupted, gliding between them, his jacket white as frost. He unloaded a pile of fresh steaks onto the butcher's block, heaped his silver platter with blackened ribs from the grill, muttering disapproval at the waste.

"I *told* these men to wear sombreros," Napitano grumbled as the waiter left, "the dressy ones with the little balls on the brim. . . ." He stopped, watching Patterson, *SLAP*'s managing editor, run over the grass toward them.

"Antonin," Patterson panted, holding up one hand, trying to catch his breath. "We need to cut six pages of copy." He checked his watch. "Less than an hour before we go to press. I've had the page flats sent over for your—"

Napitano waved him quiet.

Quinn had seen Napitano like this before, eyes glazed, almost distracted, suddenly reciting verbatim from articles that had appeared months earlier, critiquing the editing, the layout, even noting the typos.

"Carry the Suburban Call Girls feature over to next month," Napitano said, his eyes half-closed, "turn the Spielberg interview into a one-page Q. and A. I'll deal with his people on that. Trim 20 percent from book reviews, music, Hollywood gossip, and the money pro." He looked at Patterson. "And kill the Harrison cartoon."

"He has a contract," Patterson said cautiously.

Napitano's droopy-eyed smile showed rows of tiny white teeth, milk teeth that had developed a taste for finer things. Quinn watched Patterson scamper off, and wondered what Napitano would look like when he attained his full growth.

"Nino, I need a favor." The words tasted sour. "I'd like you to call Sissy Mizell. Ask her if she'll talk with me—at her convenience, of course. The friend of mine who was murdered yesterday . . . he was the one the police think killed her producer, Tod Bullock. I'm making some inquiries on my own, and thought maybe she could give me some background on Tod."

"On your own?" cooed Napitano. "How daring, but then, why depend on the police? What have they ever done for us?" He hummed softly to himself. "Who knows what you will uncover, what dirty little secrets? Hmm? That's what it is all about, yes? The truth is always a little foul, there is an . . . odor to it. I myself rather enjoy the smell, but I thought you had lost your appetite."

"Will you call her?"

"I have an idea," Napitano said innocently, tapping his cheek with a forefinger, "why don't you do a feature on Sissy? That way you can make your inquiries, and do something nice for Nino. Her program picked up five affiliates last week alone. Our magazine should be there, don't you think?" He fanned the coals with his hat, sent smoke curling around his rapacious grin. "Yes, I will make that phone call," his lips puckered, "you go *do* Sissy. Do her good."

"Just make a phone call, Nino"—Quinn glowered—"I'm not asking you to jerk off."

"Now, I've gone and annoyed you," sighed Napitano. "People instinctively dislike me. It has been this way since I was a child . . . but you, Quinn, people like *you*. They invite you into their lives, show you their hearts, share their shabby dreams. Why do you suppose that is?"

"Maybe my dreams are shabby too."

"I do not think so." Napitano pursed his lips. "Not at all."

"Are you going to call her?"

"Of course, dear boy. How could I deny you anything?" Napitano paused, wrinkling his brow. "I have heard some interesting rumors about Sissy Mizell, nasty whispers. She may have appeared in some pornographic films some years ago. I had a couple of people on the story—they turned up nothing, but they didn't have your gifts." He prodded the thick T-bones with the tip of the fork. Juice squirted onto the coals, engulfing the steaks in flame. "Now, someone close to Sissy is murdered. Hmmmm. Yes, dry her tears, Quinn, perhaps she will show you her heart."

"I just want to find the guy who killed my friend."

"Don't impose limitations on yourself," said Napitano. "Haven't I taught you anything? Make sure you talk to her husband, Mr. John Stratton. An interesting man in his own right. He's being groomed for higher office—Senator Stratton, Governor Stratton . . ." He gave a grand shrug, keeping his own counsel. "I met John Stratton at a fund-raiser when I first moved to this country—he has eyes like clear blue glass. Who wouldn't vote for a man with eyes like that? You've seen his movies, of course—I saw *Dodge City Standoff* five times at a tiny theater in Napoli, stole money from my father's pants to do it." He shrugged. "Some preferred Clint Eastwood, but I liked John Stratton best. He never shot a man in the back, not even a bad man."

"Yeah, the Man in White was a real role model for you, I could tell that the first time we met."

"You would be surprised," said Napitano.

Quinn watched Jen dancing with McAdams, the kid who was tearing up the ad department.

"A handsome fellow, this McAdams," mused Napitano, "but too many muscles for my taste. In Italy only laborers have such bodies." He glanced at Quinn's brawny arms. "Pardon."

Jen's throaty laugh rang across the party.

The steaks curled on the grill, burnt black. Quinn put the lid down, so he wouldn't have to look.

"Yes." Napitano rocked on his three-inch bootheels. "Go ahead and start on this Sissy Mizell project, follow it wherever it leads you. Surprise me. I want you to continue working with Ms. Takamura. She has very rigorous standards. I pay her more than you. Were you aware of that? Quite a bit more."

Quinn kept his mouth shut.

Napitano pursed his lips. "Ms. Takamura's journalistic credentials are almost as impressive as yours, and, let us speak frankly, her services were in considerably greater demand when you were both hired."

"I have no problem with that. Jen may be at risk working with me, though. I think the man who killed Sissy's producer, the man who killed my friend . . . he may know I'm looking for him."

"How exciting." Napitano clapped his hands together in delight. "Danger. Death. Sex. Politics. You and Ms. Takamura take all the time you need—she's been lobbying for the magazine to take a harder, more serious edge, and I have a difficult time arguing with a woman when she's right."

"I've never had that problem."

"Are we going to fuck their teeth out on this one?" Napitano leered. "That's what I've been waiting for since I hired you. I knew it was just a matter of time until you got hold of something tasty. Make those inquiries, dear boy, and don't stop for anything." His eyes glittered in his pink face, each shiny iris reflecting fire and smoke. He looked like a murderous infant.

"You know, Nino," Quinn said quietly, "I always knew when opportunity knocked, it would be somebody like you at the door."

Napitano shifted those hard eyes on him. "I knocked, you answered—now here we are."

They stood next to each other, watching the afternoon wind down.

Chapter 19

There were security grates on the windows of the Venice Herbal Bar, ivy curled so thickly around the rusting grillwork that the interior of the storefront was shaded and cool and green as a forest. Quinn stood in the doorway, caught in the glare from outside, giving his eyes a chance to adjust.

Ceiling fans spun lazily overhead; it sounded like there were mosquitoes somewhere in that twilight room. Men and women in business attire sat at the small round tables, drinking; they had their collars undone, drinks in hand, but jabbed at each other with their index fingers as they talked. The shelves along the walls were lined with glass jars filled with gelatinous, unfamiliar shapes—he half expected something inside to stare back at him.

Jen waved him over to her table near the bar, moving her camera bag onto the floor so he could sit next to her. She wore black cotton pants and a simple black blouse that emphasized the starkness of her chopped hair and smooth complexion. It was Monday afternoon, the day after Napitano's barbecue—he had stayed up late, but Jen looked like she had gotten all the beauty sleep she needed.

"Sorry I'm late," he said. "I spent all morning at a taping of Sissy's show, then talked to some of the pages and camera crew afterward—total dud. Not much straight talk from the *Straight Talk* staff. Nobody knew Tod very well, but they all described him as enthusiastic. Not smart. Not talented. 'Enthusiastic.' "

"How was the show?"

"Today's theme was 'Low-Budget Recipes for High-Energy

Romance!' " said Quinn. "If you're nice to me, I'll bake you a mock-cherry turnover."

"I'm not that nice." The bone hoops through Jen's ears bounced as she smiled.

A tall, thin man watched them from behind the teakwood bar, a serene expression on his bony face. He was balding in front, but the mirror behind him showed a dozen wispy braids hanging to his shoulders. Ornate dragons were carved into the bar, fierce, snarling beasts devouring their own tails.

The breeze from the fans carried the scent of cinnamon and licorice and lemon and other things more exotic . . . underlying it all was a faint mushroom smell, the odor of fresh-turned earth.

Quinn pushed his hair back with both hands. "You said on the phone that you got lucky."

"That's not exactly the way I described it," said Jen. "After the barbecue, I called a friend of mine at the network. He put me in touch with a producer, Gillian Winter. She should be here soon. Gillian used to work for Sissy—started out as a researcher, eventually moved up to line producer. About six weeks ago, without any warning, she was fired, and replaced by Tod. Sissy gave her a generous severance, but she's bitter. I thought she might be able to prep us for our interview tomorrow with Sissy."

"I'm more interested in Tod than Sissy. If we find out who had a reason to kill Tod, we find out who killed Andy."

"Gillian worked with Tod," said Jen. "I also think she went out with him for a while."

"Let's find out." Quinn pulled Tod's electronic notebook out of his jacket, turned it on.

Jen acknowledged the wave of a businessman on the other side of the room. "Where did you get that?"

"It was Tod's," said Quinn. He scrolled through the phone numbers. "Here she is: 'Gillian Winter, red tulips, Monday.' " He shook his head. "This guy was popular, with a capital *P* for penis. I've been working my way through his phone numbers alphabetically—almost all women, and all of them in mourning. If I knew what kind of cologne this guy wore, I'd soak in it. What does the adjective 'enthusiastic' mean to you? In reference to a man? Does that mean he rolls over and begs?"

"You sound jealous."

"Curious."

"You live with your ex-wife. You see someone like Tod, a swinging bachelor—"

"I don't live with my ex-wife. I live next door to my daughter. My ex-wife lives with her."

"Whatever you say." Her earrings bounced again. Quinn couldn't tell if she was serious or just teasing. "I know you're not dating anyone at the magazine, I just wonder if you're one of those divorced guys who watches too much TV, sees the bikini girls on the beer ads and feels left out."

"You must really be attracted to me," said Quinn. "That's it, isn't it?"

Jen's cool green eyes were unmoving, slim ellipses in the mask. "I do find you attractive"—that got his attention—"but I never have sex with anyone over twenty-five, and you're about ten years beyond the cutoff point."

He tried not to react.

"Men get weird after twenty-five," she said. "They get distracted in bed—they're either thinking about their career, their ex-wife, or worried about not being King Stud. I prefer the young, hard ones with no ambition and not much upstairs— they pay attention."

Quinn could feel the blood pounding in his ears. "What are you, twenty-four, twenty-five? I've been there. You think being free is better than being tied down, and not eating veal or tuna will make the world a better place. You'll find out."

She just watched him with those cat eyes.

Maybe she was right. He felt old and tired, and for the first time since he had started at *SLAP* he was having trouble sleeping. Every time he closed his eyes he saw clumps of Andy's hair floating on the wind, drifting past on the lazy air currents, just out of reach.

She took his hand, squeezed it. Did he look *that* bad? "I'm just having fun with you," she said. "We started out arguing, and I enjoyed it and thought you did too. I didn't mean to hurt your feelings. We're going to be working together, and I'm glad. I have great respect for your writing."

"Now I feel like your grandfather." He grinned. "I've wanted to work with you for a long time too. Spotting the torn lottery ticket in Andy's van . . . that was impressive. Now, I know why you get paid more than me." She had a beautiful smile. He beckoned to the man behind the bar. "Bartender?"

The man pursed his thin lips but didn't answer.

"I'm sorry, Sandor," Jen said gently, "my . . . associate doesn't understand. Perhaps you could suggest something for him."

Sandor nodded to her and glided over so soundlessly that Quinn glanced at the floor to make sure the guy had feet.

"What do you recommend?" said Jen. "And be nice, Sandor, this one hits back."

"I can see that," said Sandor, checking Quinn out, taking in the boots and jeans, the unruly hair and tight dark blue T-shirt. "Yes," he said, nodding thoughtfully, "much too much yang."

The man's voice was moist and deep; Quinn thought of earthworms twisting through rich black soil. Quinn knew all about yin and yang; he had seen every episode of *Kung Fu*. His yang was just fine. His everything was just fine. He just needed some sleep.

Sandor turned and went back behind the bar, brought down jars, and starting grinding something with a mortar and pestle. He added liquid from a crystal decanter and kept working.

"What *is* this place?" Quinn glanced around. "We've got the Sorcerer's Apprentice behind the bar, and the Armani and Valentino fall collection sitting around getting their auras stretched. Why aren't these people flashing their gold cards at Morton's or Michael's or someplace else with a house mineral water? What are *we* doing here?"

"It was Gillian's suggestion," said Jen. "Sandor is one of the most knowledgeable herbalists in the U.S., and the only one who speaks English. His clientele is mostly high-powered entertainment types who appreciate his concoctions. Larry—the man who waved—is an attorney at Creative Film Associates with a bad back. Sandor will give him something that will relax his lumbar muscles, but keep his mind sharp for the contracts he'll be reviewing this evening. Get it?"

"Hey, no offense. I like it here at the Magic Kingdom." He watched her sitting next to him with her perfect posture, at ease in the hard-backed chairs. Ballet lessons. No, karate. Being with her always made him feel like he needed a shave. "Morales came by my place early this morning . . . unofficial business. He says even if Andy *was* murdered, the guy who did it is long gone. I'm not so sure. I want you to understand that before you—"

"Andy didn't kill himself," said Jen, "I know that. So does Morales. I appreciate you trying to protect me though." She nodded, completely sincere. "It's sweet. Now, what do you want to ask me?"

"Am I that obvious?" He shrugged. "Okay. Morales gave me a copy of Tod's phone calls for the last three months. When we're done with the producer, let's go over it together."

"What are we looking for?"

"A pattern," said Quinn. "I got a log of the Laker games from Channel Eleven, start times to final buzzer. We go through Tod's calls and find what number he phones just before and just after the games. If there's a pattern, if the same number keeps showing up, *that's* Tod's bookie. You get in too deep to those guys—they send out somebody to collect, and they don't say please."

Sandor appeared at the table, set a double shotglass in front of each of them. Quinn's was filled with a cloudy gray liquid. Jen's was clear and golden.

She drank half of hers, held it in her mouth for a moment before swallowing, then licked her lips, smiling at Sandor.

Quinn held the shotglass up to the light.

"It's a peaceful elixir," Sandor explained to him, "to smooth the flow of chi through the body—a blend of astragalus, ginseng, licorice root, and other herbs. I made the drink triple strength"—he glanced at Jen—"in light of the obvious need to harmonize this one's dissonant energy patterns."

Quinn took a tentative sip—a bittersweet taste, with a faint woody undercurrent. Another sip. It wasn't so bad, but it could use a cold beer chaser.

Jen finished hers, smacked her lips. "Wonderful, Sandor."

Sandor gave her a slight bow.

"What's this like?" said Quinn. He took her empty shotglass, held it upside down over his open mouth. A golden drop formed on the lip of the glass, started to fall.

Her finger darted out, stole the drop and put it into her mouth.

"The potion is called Goddess of Beauty," Sandor said to Quinn, "named after Maku, the Chinese goddess of eternal youth. I use deer-antler tips from the Kirin spotted deer, placenta hominis, and royal jelly." He looked at Jen. "For this most beautiful lady I add ground saltwater pearl—and for her . . . *possible* future pleasure, I included live cordyceps to the gentleman's elixir." He lowered his lashes and backed away.

"What did he mean by that?" asked Quinn.

Jen smiled to herself. "Cordyceps is a mushroom—very rare, very potent, very expensive. It's supposed to build mental energy . . . and sexual power."

"Maybe I should order a six-pack to go."

Jen toyed with her empty glass. "Cordyceps is quite distinctive—it's a carnivorous mushroom. Most fungi feed on vegetable hosts, but cordyceps grows only on the heads of certain caterpillars."

Quinn's tongue felt thick; there was barely room for it in his mouth.

Brakes squealed and all heads turned toward the windows. A blue Mercedes with a crumpled bumper had pulled into the handicapped parking space out front, the right tire half on the curb. The car door slammed and a lean, leggy woman got out, reached back in the open window and stuck a HANDICAPPED placard on the dash. She glanced at the curb as she passed, kicked the tire with her high heels, and pushed open the door to the herb bar.

The woman headed right for them. She wore a short blue leather skirt and a tailored blue leather jacket, a clove cigarette bouncing between her lips.

The woman in blue stuck out her hand to Jen. "You're her, right?" she said, smoke pouring from her nostrils. "Harvey's friend? He didn't exaggerate; you *are* a dish. Don't get up, babe," she said to Quinn, who hadn't moved. "Sandor!" she barked, sitting herself down. "Give me whatever the hell Madame Butterfly's drinking! Chop-chop!"

Chapter 20

"**S**o you want some dirt on the bitch?" said Gillian.

"We want information," said Jen.

"I'll take dirt," offered Quinn.

Gillian swiveled between the two of them. She was a tense executive with a casual, tousled Rodeo Drive hairdo that didn't suit her. "This is off-the-record." Her voice was brittle, cracking with every word. "I have a reputation to uphold." The clove cigarette popped as she took a deep drag, exhaled its heady fragrance. She belted her drink. "Sandor!" she hacked, holding up her glass. "Another one of these!"

"If you're looking for anonymity, you chose a strange place to meet," said Jen, glancing at the other tables.

"Oh, I bet Gillian knew just what she was doing." Quinn stared at the producer, a slight smile on his face. "Right? I mean, getting fired must have stung. Such a public humiliation in a business where appearances are everything. You have a reputation to uphold, after all. If people think you're going to just lie there and take it, you might as well move back to Duckburg. How am I doing?"

"Welcome to hardball." Gillian nodded, returning his stare. The blue leather outfit rustled softly as she leaned toward him. "Look, babe, I don't care who knows I spoke with you; I don't want to see my name in print, that's all. The bitch *sues*. She will tie my ass up in court forever, just to make an example of me. I've seen her do it. Shit, I've helped her do it."

"Gillian, I've told you about smoking in here," Sandor said, setting the shotglass in front of her.

She gulped the drink down, took one more drag on the

cigarette, then stubbed it out on the underside of the table. "Happy?"

"I don't think in either-or terms," said Sandor, already on the other side of the room.

"I wish I knew how he does that," said Gillian. "There's plenty of people I'd like to sneak up on."

"Why did Sissy fire you?" said Quinn.

"He gets right to it, doesn't he?" Gillian said to Jen. "Dive on in, huh? Headfirst, that your style?" She picked a bit of tobacco off her front teeth, examined it with a critical expression, then flicked it away. "Sissy got rid of me because she was jealous."

"Her husband was attracted to you?" said Quinn.

Gillian snorted. "From what I've heard, John Stratton's got a cock on him like Trigger's big brother, but Sissy's name is tattooed all over it."

"Tod?" said Quinn. "She was jealous of you and Tod?"

Gillian nodded. "Tod was my assistant before he was Sissy's—I taught him everything he knew. About television, anyway." One corner of her mouth twitched, then fell. "Tod and I decided to stop seeing each other after he began working directly for Sissy. It was a mutual decision. She's very territorial. I agreed with him completely—I didn't want to stand in his way."

"Tod and Sissy were having an affair?" said Jen. "Is that what you're saying?"

"An 'affair'?" Gillian had a bitter laugh. "No, dearie, an affair is something people have in movies with subtitles. What Sissy and Tod had was something else—something that got him my job as compensation for services rendered."

"Do you know that for sure?" said Quinn. "Maybe Sissy decided Tod had ability and wanted to make some changes."

"I'll tell you about Tod's *ability*," said Gillian, lighting another clove cigarette, "and it didn't have anything to do with producing a talk show." She blew smoke at Quinn. "One time I was in the middle of a conference call, talking at the speakerphone to these syndication honchos in New York. Tod's standing behind me rubbing my shoulders, because, believe it or not, I get stressed out sometimes. Anyway, things are going well, the honchos love me, and next thing I know I'm standing up, my hands on the desk, and Tod is behind me, bending me over while he pulls aside my panties."

Gillian ran a finger around the rim of her glass. "Bottom line: For the next half-hour he fucks me so slow and smooth it's like I'm weightless. The honchos are doing all the talking, back and forth, and once in a while I say uh-huh. Every time I start to come, I have to clamp my mouth down on Tod's forearm so New York doesn't hear me."

She looked over at Jen with this sad, lost expression. "The thing I remember most was the gentle way he offered me his arm, like he was feeding me." She shook her head. "By the time I finally hang up, you could have wrung out my panties, and Tod had teethmarks so deep they didn't go away for two weeks."

"Wow," Jen said softly.

"I used to hope . . ." The cigarette bobbed from one side of Gillian's face to the other, until she got her breath back. "Tod's gone. We'll never get back together now."

"You don't know that he and Sissy were lovers," said Quinn. "Maybe Tod got promoted because he had fresh ideas. I heard that he was the one who came up with the new opening for the show—the one where the camera zooms onto the pair of clapping hands."

"Who told you that?" Gillian's teeth were yellowed—the bright red lipstick she wore made them look even dirtier. "What's so brilliant about clapping hands anyway? The old opening was fine." She leaned over the table toward him. " 'Over-the-counter Facelifts.' *That's* brilliant. My concept. 'Babysitters Who Kill.' Also my concept."

"People get fired every day in Hollywood," said Quinn. "They all think it's because they didn't kiss the right ass."

" 'Is Your Husband Bisexual? The Seven Warning Signs.' " recited Gillian. "We blew Donahue out of the water with that one. I lined up the guests, prepped the bitch with questions, even came up with the segment where the studio audience tried to pick out the bisexuals from our onstage lineup." Her voice was so raw it hurt to hear it. "And you want to tell me about *fucking* clapping hands?"

"Let's say Tod and Sissy *were* lovers," said Jen. "Did anyone else know about them?"

Gillian shrugged, noncommittal. "Sissy likes to flirt, so she gets away with murder. I know *I* never discussed it with any-body."

"Did her husband know?" said Quinn.

Gillian shrugged.

"Did Tod have any enemies at the studio?" said Quinn. "Someone who was passed over? Someone who resented him because he was Sissy's favorite?"

Gillian patted her fluffed hair. "Tod was very careful of people's feelings. That's why he had no future in this business."

Sandor stood beside the table, offering Gillian another drink.

"What's this?" said Gillian.

"A female-essence enhancer," said Sandor, "to calm—"

"Save it." Gillian pushed the drink away. "What do I look like, some hippie chick working on a macramé project? Get me something with balls, Sandor, it's a doggy-on-doggy world out there and I need all the help I can get."

Sandor left.

"The police found drugs at Tod's place," said Quinn. "Was he a heavy user?"

Gillian shook her head. "Maybe some coke or pot if there was a party, but he didn't have a problem."

"Was he seeing a doctor, a shrink maybe?" persisted Quinn. "Somebody he might have been getting drugs from? I found several entries in his notebook for a—"

"What do you keep asking about Tod for?" said Gillian. "I thought you wanted to talk about Sissy."

"We're getting to her," said Quinn.

"You don't give a shit about Sissy," said Gillian. "Why are you so interested in Tod? He's . . . gone."

"If you know anything that can help us—" started Quinn.

"I tried to get you on the show," interrupted Gillian. "After What's-his-name killed that black girl at the convenience store. Great video. They couldn't use the whole thing on the air, too messy, but an unedited copy made the rounds. Sissy wanted to do an entire show around you. Everybody hates the news media. Can't blame them."

"Let's talk about Tod," said Quinn.

"Quinn here never got back to me," Gillian said to Jen, "left the state, address unknown. What's-his-name . . . Groggins, that's it, *Groggins* agreed to a live linkup from prison and the D.A. was a definite *go,* no trouble there. Too bad," she murmured, "the ratings would have been through the roof."

Quinn glanced at Jen. "This is going nowhere."

Gillian grabbed his arm, leaning toward him, her voice lowered to a raspy whisper. "You think the cops blew it. Tod's murder. That's what this is all about, isn't it?" She bobbed her head, eagerly. "Sissy could have done it—she's capable of anything. Tod was ready to come back to me, I'm sure of it now. I told him there was plenty of jobs in this town, we didn't need her. It was just a matter of time until he dumped her."

"Did you ever see Tod talking to a man with a crewcut?" asked Quinn. "Older man, large economy size. Maybe he came by the office one day. Tod might have acted nervous . . . ?"

"Sissy was convicted for passing bad checks," said Gillian. "I've seen the arrest ticket, you wouldn't believe the junk she bought."

"That's all in her official bio," said Quinn. "She was twenty years old at the time, a high school dropout with three miscarriages and an abusive husband. That's part of her audience appeal—she's seen it all, and overcome it all. She even got a pardon from the governor. You televised it."

"Don't tell *me,*" said Gillian, "I produced that show. We got a thirty-six share in every major market and the entire staff got a bonus. The governor gave a nice speech, didn't he? What he didn't mention was that his niece was trying to break into TV with a state-college degree in broadcasting—Sissy made one phone call and got the kid a job at the New York affiliate."

"You'd say anything to get back at her," Quinn said. "I don't blame you—I'm a bad loser too."

"That's not it. Not all of it, anyway." Gillian pouted. "I know Sissy better than you do."

"I don't mean to be cruel," said Quinn, "but Tod was seeing lots of women, he had them scheduled like 747s coming into LAX. If jealousy got Tod killed, any one of them could be responsible."

"I know that." Gillian turned away, reached for a cigarette, but her hand was shaking too much. "You think I'm stupid?" she said softly. "It didn't matter." Gillian looked at Jen, her lips quivering. All the hardness in her had melted away. A single tear ran down her cheek, but she made no move to brush it away. "You put up with a lot when you love someone," she whispered.

People at the next table looked over, then went back to their conversations.

"I'm sorry," said Quinn.

Gillian lowered her eyes. "Even after he broke it off . . . he sent me flowers every week. Even after I got fired . . . every Monday morning, a dozen red tulips . . . today was the first Monday I didn't get flowers in a long time."

Jen patted Gillian on the back.

"I've got to go." Gillian dabbed at her eyes, got mascara on the back of her hands.

"Why don't you ask Sandor to mix you a Shen-tonic cock-tail?" said Jen. "It's good for a broken heart."

Quinn looked up at that.

Gillian shook her head, already standing. Her first few steps were shaky, but by the time she reached the door, she was in full stride.

Chapter 21

Liston wished it were raining, a good old Alabama thunderstorm rattling the windows, cooling the rage that boiled inside him. He remembered the exhilaration he had felt Friday night, shoving the gun through Tod's screaming face.

Sissy hadn't called. Not a word. It was as though he no longer existed. He wished it would rain.

It was Monday evening, his living room steeped in twilight, lit only by the floral bisque Italian candelabras that ringed the room—$39.95 each from the Cable Shopping Club, toot-toot. The candlesticks were crusted with glazed pink and yellow roses, hot wax dripping off the ceramic petals.

Shadows from his trophies flickered across the wall, the poised football players bigger than life, seemingly in motion. He sat in the armchair, surrounded by flames, so angry he was afraid to leave the house.

Watching the videotape of his appearance on *Straight Talk* helped. It always had. He zipped through the public-service announcement about the dangers of smoking for pregnant women, right past a thirty-second spot in which a worried college girl and her mother had a conversation about douching that seemed to make them both feel better.

Liston watched Sissy lean forward on the studio sofa, looking directly into the camera. He pulled his bathrobe closed without thinking, as the camera moved closer.

"What happens when you have it all, and then lose it all?" Sissy said. "How do you go on with your life? How do you replace your dreams? Our three guests today will try to answer these questions. Let's give them a *Straight Talk* welcome!" The audience erupted.

Liston was one of her three guests; the other two were a former child sitcom star, derailed by puberty and cocaine, and a woman who had made and lost a fortune as a fashion designer while in her teens.

Liston had sat on the couch right next to Sissy, sitting so close he got whiffs of her perfume every time she tossed her hair. *L'Air de Joie.* He had spent a couple of hours in a perfume store right afterward, sniffing every bottle in the place before he hit that familiar scent. It cost three hundred dollars an ounce—he sent a bottle to her, bought another one for himself.

As always, he found himself not listening to what Sissy said—all he could hear was the rising and falling of her voice, a warm tide tickling the inside of his ears like a kiss. It wasn't what she said, anyway, it was the teasing way her voice pulled you in, like she knew things about you nobody else did, and it didn't bother her at all.

He fast-forwarded through the thirty-year-old child star who was making a comeback doing voice-overs for cartoons, sped through the ex-fashion designer jabbering about her ten-year struggle with anorexia/bulimia.

Sissy crossed her legs toward Liston, who sat there in his blue suit with the buttons pulling across the front. "This here's the man I been waiting to talk to," she said, laying her hand on his thigh. "Don't go 'way now, ladies," she cautioned as the camera cut away.

Even now, sitting in his easychair, Liston could still feel her hot grip on him as the commercials rolled by.

The doorbell interrupted.

Must be the kid with the pizza. Liston freeze-framed the video as the doorbell rang again. "Keep your shirt on!" he yelled, pulling himself up.

He sidled down the hall in his robe and slippers, stopping once to adjust his knee brace. The bell rang again as he jerked open the door.

Sissy stood on the front step, wrapped in a caramel-colored coat, her long hair tucked under a floppy hat. She pushed past him, dropped her coat on the floor, and whipped off the hat.

Her hair fell around her bare shoulders like a torrent of pink champagne.

He checked the street before closing the door, then hurried to pick up her coat—cashmere—and lay it across a chair. "I'm surprised—"

"Surprised is the very least of what you are, Emory Roy," she scolded, the hint of a southern drawl making his upper lip sweat. She stalked the living room, pivoting on the tips of her pink high heels. She had on the same frilly white, low-cut dress she had worn on the show two weeks ago Tuesday, "Middle-Age Porn Stars!" She sat on the edge of his armchair, her breasts rising and falling.

He became aware of his dowdy slippers and the diaphanous kimono with the bleary-eyed Buddha on the back—he knotted the robe around his ample waist and wished he could cut off his feet.

She took in the guttering candelabras with a quizzical expression. "What's going on here, child? You belong to one of those weird end-time churches? I expect you to start dancing with snakes and sermonizing in tongues."

"You didn't call. . . ."

She hardly glanced at the wall of trophies, not even his rookie NFL gum card in the 18-karat gold frame. He absently buffed his battered old helmet with his sleeve as he watched her make a circuit, measuring the room.

"A very polite Hispanic gentleman rang my doorbell very early Saturday morning," said Sissy. "Lieutenant Morales from the Long Beach Police Department. He apologized for waking me up, then told me"—she glared at Liston—"he told me Tod was dead."

Morales—the cop from the news conference Saturday afternoon. Standing there next to the chief when they announced the Naples homicide closed. Liston had cheered from his armchair. Yeah, he remembered Morales—a real Dapper Dan. Wonder how he managed to lose the barrio accent.

Sissy faced him. Her fingernails peeking out from her fists were the pale purple of Jordan almonds.

"Things got out of hand at Tod's," said Liston. "I admit it."

" 'Out of hand?' " exploded Sissy. "That's what you call it? You . . . big . . . dumb . . . damn you!" She slapped at him, but he caught her hands, held them so she couldn't hurt herself, feeling her soft skin strain against his beefy mitts.

"I'm so sorry," he said, over and over until she stopped struggling, "I didn't mean for it to happen like that."

She pushed him away, stood swaying in the center of the room. "What *did* you mean to happen?"

"You didn't call," said Liston, not wanting to get into that. "I haven't left the house in two days, waiting for the phone to ring."

Sissy noticed the freeze-framed TV. On-screen, she and Liston were stopped in midword, heads inclined toward each other. "Whatever are you watching *that* for?" she said. "I declare, sometimes you remind me of my old granny with her scrapbook and memories."

Liston snapped off the set, threw down the remote so hard it shattered against the floor. "Next time you need help, you call your granny," he growled.

Sissy took a step backward.

"You asked *me,*" said Liston. His face felt so hot it was sunblistered. There were tiny red spots at the edges of his vision. "I was happy just to watch you, but you asked me for help."

"Don't you raise your voice to me, Emory Roy Liston," ordered Sissy. She kept her distance though. "You were the one came to me after the show, all stammering and googly-eyed. You said, 'Miss Sissy, I'm big, I'm strong, and I'm not afraid of anything. *Anything.* You ever have a problem no one else can handle, a problem no one wants to touch, you call me.' I didn't know what to say."

"I didn't hear from you for over a year," Liston grumbled. "A month ago you call—you knew what to say then."

"Who else was I supposed to ask?" There was a slight quiver in her voice that made him want to put his arms around her. "You think I should have gone to Studio Security?" she asked. "You think I could trust a rent-a-cop?"

Liston shook his head.

"I never asked you to kill Tod. Did I?"

Liston could feel his heart beating faster as he looked at her. She missed Tod, even after what the little punk had done to her. "No," he said, squaring his enormous shoulders, "you never asked me to kill him."

"There was no need to kill him." She shook her head, trying to make sense of it. "I had already agreed to Tod's terms. All he wanted was to be made a line producer. I did it. I was happy to do it. You were supposed to make sure he kept to the bargain, to convince him, that's all. You were supposed to *scare* him, not kill him."

"I told you I was sorry. What else you want me to do?" The robe was too small for him now—he wanted to rip his skin off to give his heart room. "Try blaming Tod."

"It doesn't do any good for me to blame Tod," she said quietly, "you've seen to that." She shut her eyes for an instant—when she opened them she seemed like her old self, just back from a commercial break and raring to go. "Where are they?"

He bustled over to his desk, picked up a large manila envelope, and brought it to her. "Tod didn't live up to his part of the deal. You let him get away with that, you're going to be paying for the rest of your life."

"Poor Tod never held out on me," said Sissy, opening the envelope. "Never. You just didn't ask him nice. He just wanted some insurance, just like we all do. This world's a hard place."

The tiny red spots danced before Liston's eyes. "Tod tried to make a fool of me," he growled, trying to see her through the lightshow. "I wanted to protect you, you *and* Mr. Stratton— I'm a great believer in the sanctity of marriage."

Sissy pursed her lips. "Don't you talk about my husband, Emory Roy. You hear?" She pulled a sheaf of medical records from the envelope, riffed through them. A few flakes of something shiny drifted down.

"The records are all there," he said, "but one of the X rays is missing. You said there were six in the file, but Tod only had five, so that leaves one unaccounted—"

"I know my arithmetic," said Sissy. She held the crumbling X rays up to a candelabra. "The medical records aren't important, not without the X rays to back them up." Her skin was translucent in the soft light. She flicked the X rays with her nail, dislodged a bit of the brittle acetate. "We don't have to worry about Tod copying these, they're too old and fogged to reproduce, but that missing X ray . . . that could be a problem."

"Not unless somebody knew what it was. With Tod gone . . ." He watched the candlelight flicker across her face. "You're safe now."

Sissy exhaled slowly. "Maybe you're right." She suddenly cocked her head, reconsidering. "What about that boy you left in the van? Did you ask him if he had it?"

"His name was Andy." Liston ran a hand over his brush cut, felt the stiff hairs prick his palm. "He didn't know anything either."

"Well, Emory Roy,"—Sissy stamped her feet—"he was at Tod's. He must know *some*thing!"

Liston shrugged helplessly. "He was just in the wrong place at the wrong time and got blindsided. It happens." His knee was killing him. He wandered over to the trophy case.

"Did this Andy talk with anyone before you caught up with him?"

Liston tenderly laid his big hand on the game ball from the conference championship with Oklahoma. What a day that had been. Four sacks and an interception, he ran back for a TD.

"Well, *did* he?"

"A guy named Quinn." Liston wiped the ball clean with the sleeve of his robe. "Just some guy. Nobody. I've got his license-plate number, I'll check him out."

"Some nobody named Quinn." Sissy shook her head in disgust. "You can check him out tomorrow morning. He's coming by my office to interview me. He's a reporter." She looked like she was going to be sick.

The doorbell rang and Sissy jerked at the sound. Liston reassured her with a whisper and hurried to answer it. He opened the door halfway, gave the kid with a pizza a twenty, and told him to keep it. When he got back to the living room, she was gone. The candles were almost out.

"Sissy?"

The back door was unlocked. He checked every room in the house anyway—the smell of her perfume was so strong he couldn't believe she was really gone.

Andy had lied to him. He said he hadn't told Quinn anything and Liston had believed him, certain he was too scared to lie. It was more than fear. There had been a recognition between them in the van, man to man, a quiet understanding in the stillness just before the gun went off.

The candles were sputtering, going out one after the other, the darkness deepening by the moment, until only one candle was left. Quinn was a reporter. Andy had lied to him. He shook his head sadly as the last candle flared and went out, leaving him completely alone. You think you know somebody, but you don't.

Liston remembered the way Andy and Quinn had lounged around the burger joint, the way they had talked, laughing together, having fun. Whatever Andy had said, it must have been funny.

Liston was going to have to sit down and talk with Quinn. It would be nice to play with somebody who was good size, somebody who knew how to move. Yeah, they'd have their talk, and one way or the other, Quinn would let him in on the joke. He hoped Quinn would make him work for it.

Chapter 22

The wreath of tiny black roses on the outer door of Country Girl Productions swung wildly as Sissy bustled into the waiting room like a galleon in full sail. "Well, aren't you a pretty little thing," she said to Jen, her pink taffeta dress surging around her plump knees. "And *you*,"— she squeezed Quinn's upper arm—"you big hunk, you must be Quinn. I bet you got some ideas in that head of yours about this little gal. I know how men's minds work."

"I've got ideas all right," said Quinn, "but they're not doing me any good."

Sissy laughed, her fleshy throat jiggling like she was drinking warm cream. "Hold all my calls," she ordered the receptionist, then laid a lightly freckled hand across Jen's shoulders. "I love your *SLAP* magazine; y'all're ornery devils, but I read it every single blessed month—it's like a visit from Auntie."

Sissy led the way, sashaying slightly; Jen right next to her in full stride. Quinn followed their giggles down the hall. It was Tuesday morning but they looked like they were on their way to a slumber party.

Sissy's office was on the thirtieth floor, the penthouse suite, so overdecorated with white-pine furniture and medieval-style tapestries that it seemed smaller. There was no executive desk, no computer, no metal, no sharp angles—instead the room was broken into cozy conversational alcoves. There were cheerful, multicolored Early American rag carpets on the floors, pillowy couches draped with crocheted afghans, and vases of fresh-cut flowers. Perched on every coffee table was a sterling-silver candy dish piled with chocolates.

Jen paced the room taking readings on her light meter,

while Quinn instinctively headed to the windows, not for the view, but to get a sense of perspective. If you stayed in the center of the room, you were inevitably drawn into the plump sofas. He imagined himself sinking into their overstuffed contours and never getting out. Sissy's intention might have been to create an atmosphere of feminine charm and intimacy, but it felt like a claustrophobic nest.

"Mr. Napitano said y'all were looking into Tod's murder," said Sissy, her face suddenly serious. "You're working on a piece about violent crime hitting even the beautiful folk?"

Quinn nodded.

"I don't mind telling you, this whole thing's knocked the starch out of me," Sissy said wearily. "It's only been four days since Tod . . ." She swallowed. "I keep expecting him to walk through the door." She patted a spot on the couch beside her. "Come on over, I don't like to raise my voice."

Quinn eased down into the plush wing-back chair beside her, the furniture arranged so that he had to brush past her.

"You find out anything more about that bastard who killed Tod?" said Sissy. "All the police said was he was some kind of dope dealer—must have been higher than a kite to go kill himself."

"He wasn't—" said Quinn.

Sissy clucked sympathetically, her strawberry-blond mane rippling around her shoulders. "I confess there's been times I could commit murder, but, darlin', this girl ain't never been tempted to put a gun to her head."

Quinn picked a chocolate-covered cherry from the candy dish, popped it into his mouth. "Were you and Tod close?"

"Oh my, yes—we're all family here." Sissy bobbed with pleasure watching him chew. "I like a man helps himself." She ran a finger through the candy dish, selected a chocolate-covered cherry for herself. "You feel free, honey," she called to Jen, "put some meat on them bones, give a man something to hang on to." Her teeth bit into the chocolate and sugary juice squirted out. She licked her pale lavender nails.

"Tod started out less than a year ago as a production assistant," said Quinn. "When he died he was a producer. That's pretty astounding. What was it about Tod that allowed him to move up so quickly?"

"Oh, you'd have to knowed him," said Sissy. "Tod was just willing to do whatever it took. Show business isn't like anything else—a body can move as fast as it can, *up or down*, there's no rules against it. I started out as the afternoon *Million-Dollar-Movie* girl at station KFGB in Biloxi; six months later I was anchoring the eleven P.M. news. God bless America."

Jen took Polaroid test shots of Sissy leaning over, talking to Quinn. The camera whirred, spitting out photos.

"Tod was quite a ladies' man, wasn't he?" said Quinn. He saw Jen on the other side of the room, adjusting the drapes so that the light was even. "Jealousy might have been the motive for his murder."

"You think the dope dealer who killed Tod was somebody's husband?" Sissy plucked at the bodice of her dress, fanning herself. The pink taffeta rustled with electricity.

"He wasn't a dope dealer," said Quinn, "and jealousy is just one of the possibilities we're looking into."

"Did Tod ever mention getting threatening phone calls?" said Jen.

"Not that I know of," said Sissy. "Tod did have a way with the ladies," she agreed, "that's why he was such a good producer. Most of my audience is females, and Tod knows what women like. Knew. Tod knew." The tops of her milky breasts were visible in her signature décolletage, faint blue-vein tracery on that soft white skin—a road map that breathed.

The critics had mocked her when *Straight Talk with Sissy* first went national. "Imagine Dolly Parton with an attitude," began one review. THE FIRST REDNECK YENTA, headlined another.

Her second week on the air, Sissy had read the worst reviews to a stunned studio audience, then looked into the camera, and announced, "I ain't about to change my ways to please a bunch a' big-city snobs wouldn't know an honest response if it bit 'em on their knobby butts." The audience jumped to their feet, their frenzied clapping rising and falling, feeding off itself, eleven minutes of sustained applause, a network record.

"This may be reaching," said Quinn, pulling himself forward, a tar baby caught in the stuffed chair, "was Tod seeing a doctor on a regular basis? A psychiatrist, maybe? I was at his house in Naples. There were all these notations on his calendar—"Dr. M."—beginning about four or five months ago. All of the times were at night. Most doctors with regular evening office hours are therapists of one kind or the other."

"Well, Tod never talked to me about seeing some head-shrinker, but then he knew what I think of them."

"Would you ask your Personnel Office to check with your medical carrier? If Tod was going to a therapist it would certainly be covered. I understand the need for confidentiality but—"

"It's a little late to worry about that," said Sissy. "I'll have the office take care of it."

"Thanks," said Quinn. "I appreciate you seeing us on such short notice. I know how busy you must be."

"You got no idea, child." Sissy ticked off the details on her manicured fingers: "I've got conference calls to affiliates all this week, the usual tapings for my show, plus, we start shooting my first network special at the ranch the day after tomorrow—*Sissy's Home Album*. The network wants to celebrate my fortieth birthday"—she winked at Quinn—"and it'll kick ass in its time slot."

"You're going to be forty?" said Jen. "Your skin is flawless—pink marble, that's what I thought when we were introduced."

"You could learn something from this little gal"—Sissy pinched his leg—"butter wouldn't melt in her mouth. Not like you. You act like you wouldn't hurt a fly, but I think you're up to something." She smacked Quinn on the leg. Maybe it was meant to be playful, but the blow stung. She eyed his T-shirt and jeans critically. "Don't they pay you enough at that magazine to afford real clothes? You're a good-lookin' man, you should work on yourself."

"I wouldn't know where to start," Quinn smiled.

"You listen to me," said Sissy, "I used to sell Avon. I did. Door to door. It was after my first divorce—I was the top seller in the tri-state area. You don't book thirty or forty orders a day, every day, without learning what turns people off and what makes them reach for their pocketbook."

Quinn held up his hands in surrender.

Sissy ignored him, and pointed at his engineer boots. "My first husband wore boots like that. He never shined 'em either.

I thought he was the sexiest man I ever met, but I was fresh off the vine." She popped a chocolate in her mouth and chewed, not taking her eyes off him. "I hope to heaven you're worth more in bed than that sorry Georgia cracker." She turned to Jen. "Look, I embarrassed him."

"He's having a rough week," said Jen, examining the row of Polaroids, "you should have seen him in my bathtub a couple of nights ago."

"Oh, my land." Sissy popped another chocolate into her mouth, chewed with delight. "I wish I could have been there. That must have been something."

"You'd be disappointed," said Jen, snapping shots of the office, the furnishings, then moving in on Sissy.

Most photographers Quinn had worked with used motor drives on their cameras, firing bursts of five and ten shots at a time, machine-gun style, hoping to catch something usable. Jen took her time, carefully framed each shot, waiting for the right moment.

He understood now how she had gotten such incredible photographs of those preteen gangbangers last issue—she was patient enough to stand in position, pushing the danger zone until the stone-tuff glare was dropped, and only the child remained. A child with a 9mm handgun for a toy, a child with "Crips Killer" tattooed across his hairless chest, but a child all the same.

Sissy bloomed under Jen's attention, not so much posing as radiating heat. She was fleshy and full, but nothing about her went to waste—she used every inch of herself, every pound, every rounded curve.

Jen stalked her, played to her, moving around the office with a quiet intensity, utterly confident. It wasn't until Jen stopped to change cameras that Quinn realized the hair on his arms was standing straight up.

"Did Tod ever ask for an advance on his salary?" asked Quinn. "Was he having any money problems you knew about?"

"No . . ." said Sissy. "What kind of problems?"

"Gambling problems," said Quinn. "We know he had a bookie."

Sissy blotted her upper lip with a tissue. "He never mentioned it. I don't think Tod cared all that much about money. Besides, if he needed a loan, all he had to do was ask. Like I said, we're family here."

"I know you and Tod were close," Quinn said carefully, "but it's been suggested—"

"Yeah, and I know by who." Sissy crumpled the tissue and threw it onto the floor. "I heard Gillian Winters gave you an earful. That ugly stick is just looking for a reason why she got fired, and not looking in the right places. Gillian got lazy. She wasn't cutting it anymore, and Tod deserved a chance to show he could. That's the God's truth. I cared for Tod a great deal"— she looked at Jen, then back to Quinn—"but I love my husband." She dabbed at her lashes. "Waterproof mascara," she said to Jen, "where would we girls be without it?"

Quinn didn't take his eyes off her.

"I got an idea," Sissy said. "Why don't y'all come out to the ranch Thursday and watch us tape my special? Get to know John and me a little better."

"We'll be there," said Jen.

Through the windows Quinn could see Santa Monica Bay—surfers bobbed like specks in the water, waiting for waves on a glassy blue sea. Catalina Island was dimly visible to the south, its rocky peaks clouded by mist. He and Andy had taken a helicopter ride over the island once—Andy spent the whole time being airsick, but refused to let the pilot turn back, wanting to get his money's worth.

"You're looking down in the mouth for a man just got invited to a shindig," teased Sissy. "Hey, you."

"W-What?" said Quinn. "I'm sorry . . ."

"I must be losing my touch," chided Sissy. "Honey, you look like you could use one of my hot-fudge sundaes." She walked over to the bar. "Don't even *think* of saying no. I got a complete soda fountain here—I treat myself to a hot-fudge sundae every morning for breakfast."

She set three glass sundae dishes on the counter, flipped open the lid to the freezer. "I use coffee-fudge swirl, that's one of my secrets." She effortlessly dredged a stainless-steel scoop through the tub of ice cream, plopping thick balls into the dishes, humming to herself.

Jen snapped away as Sissy bent over the freezer, frozen

vapor rising around her beautiful pale, round face like steam on the moon.

Sissy twirled a ladle in the Crockpot of hot fudge. "You know Lieutenant Morales?" she said, the ladle clanging on the sides of the pot as she stirred. "He offered to appear on *Straight Talk* next time we do a show on crime. Expert-of-the-day. Audiences love experts, even if they don't make a lick of sense, it gives people a comfort. I learned *that* selling door-to-door—always talk up your test labs, your gold seal of approval, whatever."

Quinn could see Morales now, every hair in place, ready with a sound bite to any question. The perfect talk-show cop.

Sissy dropped steaming fudge onto the mounds of ice cream, one ladleful, then two, then three. She gave each sundae a head of whipped cream, dropped a maraschino cherry on top of the first two, laid them on the counter for Quinn and Jen. She put six cherries on her own sundae, winked at Quinn as she bit into another one, holding it by the stem.

Jen put down her camera and dug in, gobbling at the sundae, giggling like she was getting away with something.

"Grab a spoon," Sissy said to Quinn, waiting until he had begun eating before she started. "You're a pretty thing," she told Jen in between bites, "I already told you that, but you'd do better with a slightly darker lip gloss, something with more red in it to bring out your eyes. Other than that, there's nothing wrong with you, girl."

Warm fudge ran out the corner of Sissy's mouth. Her tongue snaked out and retrieved it. "Now *you*"—she shook her head at Quinn—"lose the boots, get a haircut, and work on your interviewing technique—you give a body way too much time to think in between questions. But I do like the way you sat right down next to me." She nodded her approval. "Most men shy away. You're not scared of a thing, are you?"

"You'd be surprised," said Quinn. The hot fudge burned the roof of his mouth.

Chapter 23

"**T**hat can't be right," said Quinn.

Morales didn't even bother responding. He stood there on the edge of the Xavier Park basketball courts, arms crossed on his chest. The noon sun beat down on his dark suit and tie but he didn't seem to notice.

Quinn wiped sweat off his forehead with the back of his hand. The temperature must have risen twenty degrees since they left Sissy's office this morning. "Tod was in hock to a sports book. Way deep. I'm sure of it."

Morales raised one eyebrow.

"Tod was making regular calls to a bookie," Quinn explained. "Every Laker game for the last three months is bracketed by a call to this one number. You need an access code to get past the busy signal, but a guy I know is making inquiries."

"You have such unsavory acquaintances." A smile flirted across Morales's full lips. "If you were on parole, I could run you in just on the basis of your known associates."

"The guy with the crewcut was sent to collect," Quinn insisted. "When Tod couldn't pay, he got killed. Andy was just a bystander."

Morales shook his head. "I told you—"

"That can't be right, Esteban."

Morales straightened his tie, pressed a dimple in his Windsor knot. "You asked me to go over Tod's bank records and I did—he had over four thousand dollars in his checking account, ten thousand in savings and plenty of slack on his credit cards. Even if he was in way past that, he had more than enough money to buy himself some time. *You* got it wrong, not me."

Quinn thought about that while he watched the kids play

basketball, twenty or thirty of them scampering around the blacktop, twisting, grunting in Spanish, calling out to each other—"¡Bola, hombre! ¡La bola!" Everyone wanted their shot, convinced they could make it. No surprise there. It was the nets on the baskets that caught Quinn's attention.

The tiny park was in the worst part of Long Beach: Magnolia and Seventeenth, an area crusted with trash and graffiti. Basketball nets didn't last over*night* in this neighborhood. Bare rims were the rule, maybe chain-nets, but not these white jute ones that swooshed so perfectly.

Morales wasn't paying any attention to the game—he checked the surrounding streets. Only his eyes moved.

"You brought your friend from the airport," said Morales. He didn't bother looking toward where Jen sat in her car, a white Corvette convertible. "It must be nice to be driven around by a woman."

"Don't give me a hard time, will you? She said we have to take turns driving. Today is *her* day. She's right. Fair is fair."

Two priests with whistles around their necks ran up and down the courts, their long black robes flapping against their shins. They didn't call many fouls. One kid tripped another as he was going in for an easy lay-up, stole the ball. The nearest priest tripped him back, sent him flying. It was easier than using his whistle. Besides, these kids had grown up with whistles and sirens blaring, they didn't even hear them anymore.

"When you talked with Sissy Mizell Saturday . . . when you told her Tod was dead . . . how did she seem?" Quinn wasn't sure himself what he was asking.

"I showed up on her doorstep at seven A.M. with my bad news," said Morales. "She taped her show the night before, and hadn't gotten more than a couple hours of sleep, but she was sweet as honey, invited me right in."

Most cops would have just called to inform her of Tod's death, to confirm her whereabouts at the time of the murder. Morales believed in personal contact with the rich and famous.

"I wasn't asking about her manners," said Quinn. "How did she react when you told her about Tod?"

Morales shrugged. "She fell apart. I let her cry, then we had coffee. She made it herself—you'd never guess she's a big star."

"The reason I'm asking," said Quinn, "is that I talked to someone who used to work for Sissy." He remembered the popping of Gillian's clove cigarettes in the herbal bar. "She thought Tod and Sissy were having an affair. Maybe Tod wanted to call things off and Sissy didn't. People get killed that way."

"All the time," agreed Morales, "but not this one. I break a lot of bad news, that's half my job." He shook his head. "Sissy didn't know this was coming. I was looking too. She didn't have any idea."

"What about her husband? How did he take the news?"

"Mr. John Stratton? He was out for his morning ride." Morales snickered. "Myself, I always preferred the Cisco Kid."

"Love or money, that's what you told me murder was all about. If it wasn't love, Esteban, it's got to be the bookie."

"It's not so easy playing policeman, is it?" said Morales. "Nobody confesses anymore, the bad guys refuse to leave clues . . . you might as well go back to writing."

Women had spread ponchos and blankets on the grass near the courts, laid out sliced oranges and bananas and papayas with their black seeds stark against the yellow flesh. They sat there in the shade of the jacaranda trees, watching their children play basketball, rocking their babies, talking to the other mothers. The ground smelled sweet with the purple blossoms that fell from the trees.

The concrete walls bordering the courts had been scrubbed clean and decorated with lush murals: brightly colored scenes of Aztec warriors, an old couple holding a brown baby, Fernando Valenzuela on the mound under an azure sky.

"What did you call me out here for?" said Quinn, watching a lowered green Buick cruise slowly past. Four teenagers rode inside, staring sullenly back at them.

"At five o'clock we give the park back to *them*," said Morales, nodding at the Buick. "Not until then. I come here every day on my lunch break. Other men in the neighborhood take shifts too." He rocked slightly on his heels, following the progress of the Buick. "Jorge Tellez has a garage nearby—he comes at one-thirty with his four mechanics. Ernesto Chavez brings his sons at four o'clock. In the off-season, the football coach comes with a half-dozen of his biggest players. The mothers are here always, of course"—he shook his head at the wonder of it—"they are the bravest."

"You're here by yourself."

Morales smiled, showed his teeth. "No. You're here with me."

"Right." Those *vatos* in the Buick wouldn't hesitate if anyone got in their way. Men, women or children, it wouldn't matter. Even Morales was pushing his luck.

Morales must have seen him working that one through. "It's a matter of respect," said Morales. "Not for the badge, or for me—it's respect for the boundaries that keeps them back. We claim these hours and no more. We leave by five o'clock. No matter what the score is, *we leave by five.*"

A woman on an intricately woven brown blanket held up a peeled orange to Morales. He shook his head politely.

"Sunday, when you came to my house, you asked what had happened to me," Morales said. "I've been a police officer for twelve years, and most of that time was wasted, because I made the job personal. *I* wanted to catch the bad guys. *I* wanted to put them away. The truth is, you don't get ahead in law enforcement by enforcing the law."

Morales's broad brown face was impassive as he spoke; only the way he slightly stretched his bull neck betrayed his bitterness.

"These days I'm a smart cop," explained Morales. "A smart cop parks his cruiser behind a Union-Seventy-six station and crams for the sergeant's exam. Instead of making busts, a smart cop studies how the division commander dresses, what church the chief goes to, maybe who the mayor sees when his wife is out of town. The one thing a smart cop *doesn't* do is waste time fighting crime. Crime is not going to go away—it was here long before us; it will be here long after we're gone."

The green Buick was back, pulled up next to Jen's car. Quinn started forward, knowing he was never going to get there in time, but the Buick drove slowly away, two of the passengers throwing hand signs out the window. Jen waved back at them.

Morales nodded at Jen, impressed. "Pretty *and* smart."

"Okay," said Quinn, "you're not a crimefighter. I'm not either—but I want to find who killed Andy. You wouldn't have

liked Andy . . . but I did. That's not it though. I'm not trying
to bring anybody back from the dead. I'm not even trying to
bring somebody to justice. I just want to be able to sleep at
night, and not wonder if somebody out there is looking for me.
You talk about boundaries, Esteban . . . where is it safe for me?"

Morales glanced over at him. "Good speech," he said, and
went back to patrolling the area with his eyes. "You carrying?"

"I don't have a concealed-weapon permit."

"That's not an answer." Morales showed his teeth again.
"This man with the crewcut—if he's what you say, he knows
the ropes. Big man, that's what your pal Andy told you, right?
I'd carry some firepower. Magnum loads. Go for a head shot,
too—it's difficult, but I've seen a big man take a full clip and
still keep coming. Lot of bad guys wear vests these days. Head
shot, that's what I'd do."

A heavyset woman with a toddler in her arms walked over
and set down her blanket. She put the baby on the blanket,
ordered him not to move, then sat on her haunches, clawing
the grass with a hand rake. Her face hovered intently over the
task.

"Do you know what that woman is doing?" Morales asked
lightly.

"No."

Morales's face hardened. "She's checking the grass for dis-
carded syringes, broken glass crack pipes . . . the baby will crawl
when she is done, but only in the area she has cleared. Even
this young they know to trust their mother."

Quinn didn't say anything. Morales hated pointless expressions of sympathy.

"I played in this park growing up," Morales said softly. He
inclined his head to the heavyset woman who sat back on her
blanket, bouncing her fat baby. "I used to take my sons back
here once a week, so they could understand. We always would
stop at Taco King, listen to the music, watch the people . . . They used to like it, but now they see all the dirt, and
they don't like the menu, the tongue and tripe. The boys don't
speak Spanish, that's part of it. Linda and I decided that we
weren't going to speak it around them. Sometimes I wonder if
we made a mistake."

Quinn watched the kids play basketball, enjoyed their gangly energy. "Is that all you wanted to tell me?" he said at last. "Jen's waiting."

Morales reached into his suit jacket, came out with a small glassine envelope cupped in his palm. "The evidence team vacuumed this up from Tod's living-room rug." He smiled broadly at Quinn, shaking hands.

Quinn looked at the envelope in *his* hand now. There were several hunks of cloudy brown acetate inside. "What is it?"

"Keep that down, will you?" growled Morales. "We don't know exactly. Old film is the best guess. It's brittle, obviously broken off a bigger piece. Some sort of negative. The lab guy thought it was at least twenty years old."

Quinn shook a dime-sized chunk of film out of the envelope, held it gently. It didn't look like much. "Tod's grandmother owns the place in Naples—maybe he was going through one of her old photo albums?"

"That's what I told the lab tech," said Morales, "but then, this is just another case for me. File it and forget it. If I was an eager beaver, fresh out of the academy and ready to rid the streets of evil, I might dig a little more, ask some more questions, because there *wasn't* any old photo album at the scene—I went back and looked. Top to bottom, inside and out. But I'm not really interested. I put the rest of the film bits into the evidence locker—you can keep that piece."

Quinn tucked the envelope into his shirt pocket, where it wouldn't get crushed.

"We're even now," said Morales.

"Thanks, Esteban."

"Don't embarrass me," Morales warned. "You find something, I want to know about it. Maybe you'll get lucky."

Chapter 24

No one answered the door, as usual, so Quinn went around to the backyard, walking through weeds and keeping an eye out for catshit.

Jen had dropped him off at the *SLAP* parking lot to pick up his Jeep after he left Morales. She couldn't identify the film chunks from Tod's rug, but she had taken half the sample to show a retired photographer she knew. Maybe it would take an old expert to recognize old negatives. That's why Quinn was *here*—Cliff wasn't a photographer, but he knew about film.

Cliff was lying in the chaise longue reading *Daily Variety* and cursing, a red plastic cooler and a portable phone beside him on the grass. He had the show-business paper in one hand, holding it at arm's length, blocking the afternoon sun. A five-ounce can of "Martini, extra dry" was balanced on his rounded brown belly, pitching and rolling with every breath the old man took.

The tiny white Speedo swimsuit showed off the crenelations of his skinny, deeply tanned body. Cliff Silver was seventy-four years old and had spent most of it poolside, flakking for the movie studios. Tiny purple veins whorled near the surface of his wrinkled, leathery skin. He had red-rimmed eyes and a beaky, intelligent face topped by a thatch of shiny black hair—Lizard Man meets Grecian Formula.

"Well, Quinn," he said, not turning, "you going to stand there gawking like a tourist, or you going to join me?"

Cliff had been senior entertainment critic at the *Times-Herald* when Quinn started working at the newspaper, the last of the cynical insiders who thought reporters, studios, and stars were all on the same team. He was fired a few years ago for soliciting blocks of tickets from theater owners in exhange for favorable coverage. Cliff had been doing the same thing for fifty years, but six months before retirement, the paper decided he was an affront to its ethical standards.

Quinn had driven him home afterward, the back of the Jeep filled with the contents of Cliff's desk in cardboard boxes. "What are they talking about, *graft?*" Cliff kept saying, "I've been handed broads and booze since I got a byline. What kind of a newsman turns his back on a freebie? Errol Flynn gave me his old Packard convertible once—thing didn't have ten thousand miles on it. I'm supposed to say *no* to Errol Flynn? Jesus, I've accepted things I didn't need, didn't even want, just so's not to alienate a source."

Cliff spit into the center of the *Daily Variety* and tossed it aside—the paper fluttered into the dead grass, a tepee of headlines. "They don't even get the obits right anymore," he said.

Quinn stood next to him. He held out the glassine envelope Morales had given him. "Take a look—"

"Two o'clock is the best sun of the day," said Cliff. "Get out of my light."

Quinn pulled up a lawn chair and sat down, still holding the envelope as he stared out at the view.

The Nichols Canyon estate was in the fourth year of Cliff's total neglect, the rose garden run wild, more thorns than flowers, the hedges overgrown. The back of the lot dropped off into a steep rocky ravine dotted with brown scrub. Downtown L.A. rose in the distance, black-glass highrises shimmering in the heat, the freeways snarled like threads.

To the right and left of the property line, the neighbors' lawns were green and neatly trimmed. Quinn could see clear blue water sparkling in a series of concentric round pools in the distance, colored lanterns hanging overhead. Laughter trickled through the lush trees.

"That's nothing," Cliff said, dismissing the party next door with a toss of his head. "Small-timers having a small time. I went to a bash at Jack Warner's old place that went on for five days straight. Ice sculptures on every table, snow in drifts six feet high, igloos set up on the patio with these big-titted starlets tending bar. Ava Gardner was even drunker than me, tossing snowballs at Cary Grant. Gable was there too, and Carole Lombard, fighting as usual, all of us bundled up in furs from the prop department."

Cliff sipped from the can on his belly. "It was the middle of July and still ninety degrees at midnight, but Jack Warner didn't let that stop him. For five days there was a line of ice trucks backed up on Mulholland Drive waiting to get in. They were giants in those days." He shook his head. "*This* tycoon"— he jerked a thumb at the neighbor's cascading waterfalls— "made his money on a chain of strip-mall muffin shops. A real visionary." He upended the can, burped, and opened the cooler. "Mar-tooni?"

"No, thanks. Look at these." Quinn held out the glassine evidence envelope. "Do you have any idea what type of film this is? It's supposed to be at least twenty years old . . . I thought maybe it was that nitrate movie stock they used a long time ago—"

"You don't know what you're talking about," Cliff cackled. "They haven't used nitrate stock since the 1930s."

"Would you please take a look?"

There was salsa music coming from the party next door, fast and peppery, a sweaty south-of-the-border beat.

Quinn nodded at the portable phone. "Does that work?"

"Probably," said Cliff. "It hasn't rung since you came by for Oscar night." He squinted at the film, felt its thickness.

They watched the Oscars together every year. Quinn brought champagne. Cliff provided an obscene running commentary on the past excesses of the Hollywood old guard, now accepting their Lifetime Achievement awards with solemn humility.

"Remember last year's Oscars?" said Cliff. "The two of us spent half our time trying to adjust the TV. I should get a new set for the next time you come by. I guess there's no hurry."

"I've been really busy," Quinn apologized as he dialed Teddy's number. Teddy was a bookie, an old contact. He had given Teddy the number that appeared on Tod's phone bill every time there was a Lakers game.

"That was good champagne you brought," Cliff said to himself, holding a piece of film toward the sun. "Cristal. That's what they're drinking now, aren't they? In my day it was Dom Pérignon or it was nothing. Everything changes. I don't even know what to order anymore."

"Hey, Quinn," said Teddy. "Got that info you asked about . . . your party *did* have an account with that number."

"How much was Tod down, Teddy?"

"Not down. Up. Nine K."

"He was ahead nine thousand?"

Teddy chuckled. "It happens. Like I told you before, even if your party was down, no book is going to cancel a customer. That's bad business—how they going to pay if you do that? The most you do is break something they don't use to make a living. Ciao."

Quinn set the phone down.

"You done with your phone calls?" said Cliff. "I don't want to interrupt a busy man. What's wrong?"

"You interviewed Sissy Mizell when she first moved her show to L.A., didn't you?" said Quinn. "Did you ever hear anything about her appearing in a porno film?"

"Dirty movies?" Cliff jiggled the glassine envelope. "That's what you thought this was? Forget it. This isn't movie stock." He handed back the envelope. "It's a kind of negative—I thought for a minute it might be thirty-five millimeter reversal, but it's not movie film." He stifled a burp. "The emulsion's all wrong."

"Too bad," said Quinn. "I'm investigating a homicide. The man who was murdered worked for Sissy. He just got a big promotion, and I thought he might have had some leverage on her."

"I don't know anything about Sissy making dirty movies," said Cliff. "Besides, I'm not sure how much leverage that would give anybody these days. Stars today . . . dope and sex and babies without daddies, it doesn't hurt people's careers anymore." He grinned. "Thank God it was different in the old days, I'd have had to work for a living."

"Thanks anyway."

Cliff rooted in the cooler. "I got Vienna sausages if you're hungry?" He held up a frosty jar of tiny gray hot dogs. "Don't give me that look. You don't know what good food is."

"No, but I can recognize it, and I've never seen *that* stuff before in my life."

"You're showing your ignorance," said Cliff. He flexed his right arm, the bicep surprisingly large. "You see if you can do this when you're my age." He jumped up from his chair and snapped off a dozen push-ups, his stringy muscles twisting as they worked. There were indentations from the chaise-longue straps running across his back. Cliff got back to his feet and threw his hands high in triumph. "Ta-da!" He staggered and started to fall.

Quinn barely caught him, lowered him gently. He seemed so light. Cliff lay in his arms for a moment, eyes glazed, panting, before he blinked, and blinked again. The old man scooted back onto his chair, embarrassed. Quinn pretended to examine the grass-stained knee of his jeans.

"Booze makes me dizzy these days," said Cliff. He still didn't look at Quinn. "My mind stays sharp and clear, I remember everything, but . . . the rest of me gets dizzy. When I was younger, it was just the opposite." He shook his head. "I liked it better then."

"You look great," Quinn said innocently. "Except I think your hair turned to shoe polish."

"You get old, you'll find out." Cliff glared at him.

"I know all about it. I stay up all night now, the next day it feels like somebody's been taking batting practice on my spine."

"That's *nothing*," said Cliff. His breathing was back to normal. He popped open another martini, took a swallow, then reached into the cooler and tossed Quinn a carton of orange juice. "Take it. Go on, it's fresh, not reconstituted. I'm particular about my highballs—these canned-cocktail people got the martini down pat, but I can't find a decent screwdriver to save my prostate."

The sun was hot. Quinn shielded his eyes. "You want to go out for some real food?" he said. "My treat. We'll go to Junior's for deli."

Cliff ran a hand over his brown stomach. "I don't digest so well these days. Besides, I don't like going out. People drive too fast, and everything costs too much. You're the only one who visits. Just you and the kid who delivers groceries and cat food . . ." A silky blue Persian cat ambled by, its fluffy tail tickling Cliff's bare leg as it passed. Cliff lunged at it, cursing.

The cat leaped into Quinn's arms. He petted it. "What's this one's name?"

"Garbo," sneered Cliff. "Isn't that a crock? The widow Atwater, the old bat who owned this joint, named all the cats after stars: Garbo, Douglas Fairbanks, Junior and Senior, Myrna Loy, Henry Fonda, Robert Mitchum, Shirley MacLaine . . . all of them fixed. Mickey Rooney would shit if he knew what she did to his namesake," he chuckled.

"The widow was crazy for Hollywood," said Cliff. "She had scrapbooks full of my clippings from *Scandal* and *Photoplay* and the *Hollywood Insider*. That's why she took me in after I got canned from the newspaper. Every night we'd sit on the patio with a couple of pitchers of martinis while I told her stories about the glory days." He shook his head sadly. "That old girl mixed a great drink."

Quinn scratched Garbo behind one ear and she purred. He could see more cats flattened against the grimy windows at the back of the house, dozens of them sleeping in the sun. The widow's will had given Cliff free room and board at the mansion as long as any of her cats were still alive. He nuzzled his neck against Garbo's soft fur and she arched her back. "How many cats are left?"

"Too many," said Cliff. "Drop her, will you? You know how many diseases cats carry?"

"Probably not as many as humans," said Quinn. He rubbed noses with Garbo, then put her down. She scampered past Cliff, brushing against him so that the old man winced. "How many are left?" Quinn repeated. "You going to be out on the street anytime soon?"

"Don't worry, I'll be colder than a mackerel before the last of these mangy bastards is dead; there's still seventy or eighty of them. The executor can't wait for us all to croak; he can get eight million for this dump as a teardown. Screw him. Michael J. Fox is the youngest, a calico barely five years old. The widow found him a week before she died. I tried to tell her Michael J. Fox is no real movie star, but she loved *Family Ties*. What can I say?"

They were so close Quinn could smell the baby oil and iodine mixture that the old man used on his skin as suntan lotion. "Did she name one John Stratton?" he asked.

"Sure," said Cliff. "Pure white Tom got a chunk out of one ear." His bloodshot eyes narrowed. "Why?"

"You knew him, didn't you? In the old days?"

"Sure. I knew them all, partied with them all. It was different then; the studios looked after the press and the press looked after the studios. Now"—he stared at Quinn like there was a bad taste in his mouth—"it's every man for himself."

"Did Stratton have a temper?"

"Who doesn't?" Cliff slicked back his hair. The roots were white. "John Stratton always played a good guy because he *was* a good guy. The honest cop. The fearless sheriff. You've seen his old movies; the camera loved him. Oh, he drank a bit, chippied around on his old lady, but who didn't? After she died, he turned into fucking Father Flannigan. He missed some great times—"

"His wife died?"

"Betty Andaluse. Cute little trick under contract to Universal. She had a couple of decent parts . . . Paul Muni had the hots for her, but she married Stratton and gave it all up."

"How did she die?" Quinn was leaning forward now.

"Fire. Coroner said she must have been smoking in bed." Cliff shuddered. "The whole house went up, beautiful place in Bel-Air. Stratton got some nasty burns trying to save her, kept going back in looking for her. The firemen gave up before he did. He was in the hospital for over a month—received a thousand letters and get-well cards a day, sacks of mail and flowers piled up in his room at L.A. General; it was in all the newsreels."

"So he got a career boost out of her death?"

Cliff shook his head. "The studio tried to milk it, but he didn't want any part of that. He didn't work at all for a year; went horseback riding every day on his ranch and refused all interviews. Stupid bastard. Million dollars' worth of free publicity and he's not talking."

"Maybe he loved her."

"That's no excuse," said Cliff. "Love will ruin you. You remember how I used to brag that I dated Marilyn Monroe when she was first getting started? 'It was like drowning in tits,' that's what I used to say. I lied." His gaze was bleary and distant. "It was Marilyn's stand-in on *The Seven-Year Itch* that I dated— Helen Labeck. God, I was nuts about her. Then one day I found myself standing in Weisberg's pricing engagement rings, thinking about what we were going to name our kids. I dropped her like a hot potato." He shook the martini can, checking. "Funny thing though . . . I watch *The Seven-Year Itch* on TV, I can't stop thinking about how clean Helen's hair used to smell. Like it was always just washed."

"Maybe you should have bought a ring. Name some kids."

"And end up like you? No thanks." Cliff turned his face directly into the sun. "You haven't been right since the divorce."

There was a lump in Quinn's throat too big to talk past. He was glad Cliff had his eyes closed.

"It's not like you're torching for your ex," said Cliff, "it's different than that. When I was *seriously* drinking, I used to drive to the marina after midnight, cut one of the sailboats loose, just to watch it drift out to sea. There was something about the sight of a sailboat bobbing alone on the waves, not a soul aboard . . . It was so sad and beautiful that it made me cry—but then, I was shitfaced at the time. You remind me of one of those sailboats."

Chapter 25

Cliff was dreaming of white-hot sand and making warm, sweaty love with Helen Labeck, when a shadow fell over them. He shivered and opened his eyes, crying out as he felt her slip away from him.

"Easy there, Pops."

Pops? Cliff blinked, trying to focus. The sun was directly behind the man's head, so that he couldn't see his features clearly. Big round face. Dark side of the moon. All spiky.

He blinked again, trying to get beyond the sheer size of the man leaning over him. He thought of that huge actor from the old horror movies . . . ex-wrestler, ugly as a dose of clap . . . what was his name? The man moved and Cliff realized that the spikes were his short, bristly haircut. It looked like a buzz saw on top of his head.

"Sorry to wake you, Pops, but I'm in a hurry."

"Don't call me 'Pops.'" Cliff tilted the chaise longue so the back was upright, but the man didn't move away. He stayed where he was, blocking the sun.

The man smiled, his face shiny with the heat. He had one of those ruddy complexions that never tanned, just burned and peeled. No wonder he was all covered up in one of those nylon jogging suits. Afraid to let his skin breathe.

"What are you doing here?" croaked Cliff. His mouth was dry; he looked around for his martini. "This is private property."

The man flashed a badge. "I'm Sergeant Nagurski," he said, putting the shield back into his pocket. "We've had a complaint from one of the neighbors. Some old bird's been spotted in the bushes waving his weenie."

"Nagurski? That's quite a name. There was a Bronco Na-gurski . . . he played football . . . but that was back in the Dark Ages. He's dead now." Where was that drink?

"I played some football too, Pop. Back in the Dark Ages. I'm not dead, though."

"You're a cop?"

"This old bird could be in real trouble," said the man. "The housekeeper said he made threatening gestures at her with his sexual organ." He looked like he was smiling, but the sun was directly behind him again, and Cliff couldn't be sure.

"What division are you from?" said Cliff. He rubbed his eyes. "I know some of the local dicks. . . ."

"I'm new," smirked the man. "Nobody knows me."

"Would you mind moving?" said Cliff. "You're in my light."

"*Your* light?" laughed the man, sitting down on the chaise so that Cliff had to move his legs or get crushed. The lawnchair groaned under the weight of the man. "I read about the Sun King in a World History class, but I didn't figure he'd look like you."

"You're no cop." Cliff was in direct sunlight now, but he shivered anyway.

"What a coincidence, I think you're lying too," said the man. He tugged at the scraggly hair on Cliff's leg and Cliff gasped. "You're not the Sun King. You're some old bird in a bikini bottom runs around a nice neighborhood exposing himself."

Cliff tried to slow his heart down. It sounded like an alarm clock going off in his chest. "There's . . . people in the house." He nodded toward the widow's broken-down mansion. Cats stretched and preened in the window.

The man didn't even glance at the house. "You're lying again. You're in trouble, Pops, maybe even more than weenie trouble. I saw that young fella talking with you a while ago . . . husky kid."

Cliff cleared his throat, looked away. One of the cats . . . Bette Davis, was up on her hind legs, swatting at something trapped against the window.

"What was the big kid's name?"

"That was Jack. . . . from Jack's Landscaping . . . Officer. He comes by every few weeks to give me an estimate on yardwork. He should be back any minute with his crew if you want to talk with him."

The man shook his head sadly. "Don't try to protect him; protect yourself. The big kid's name is Quinn. I followed him over here—he checked his rearview a few times, but he didn't spot me. That's because I stay way back. You learn that when you play football, Pops. Defense wins the game." He suddenly tore off a patch of gray hair from Cliff's leg and Cliff yelped. "I lost him in traffic after he left here," the man said calmly. "He drives like a maniac. I almost got in an accident." He tore off another patch of hair.

Cliff howled, beat at the man without effect.

The man lay sprawled across Cliff's legs, almost crushing him. One of the chaise's supporting straps had already given way under the weight. His face hovered over Cliff, red and hot as a number two klieg light.

"You're hurting me," said Cliff.

The man ignored him. "What did Quinn ask you?"

When Cliff didn't answer the man tore a tuft of hair off his chest. Cliff screamed and bucked but the man stayed put, smothering him with his enormous bulk. "Don't make me hurt you," he whispered in Cliff's ear, "I don't want to do that."

Cliff almost believed him. He tried to speak, wet his lips. "Give me some room," he gasped. The man backed off a little.

"How much does he know?" said the man. His features seemed pliable—his lips fleshy, his nose thick and bulbous. "He must know something, driving around like a wild man, asking questions. I saw you two through the bushes, but I could only hear a few words."

"Show business, that's all." Cliff had to raise his voice to be heard over the beating of his heart.

The man's face was so close that Cliff could see the exploded capillaries on his cheeks, the ruddy scars darkening while he watched. "You don't tell me what he wanted, I'm going to tear out your tongue—then we'll try charades, you like show business so much."

"You better leave," said Cliff, "I get people dropping in on me all the time, they don't even call beforehand."

"I know you." The man's eyes narrowed as he wagged a finger at Cliff. "I thought you looked familiar, Pops, but I couldn't place you at first. You know show business, all right, *you're* Mr. Hollywood." He pumped Cliff's hand, crushing it in his grip. "You're that geezer who used to host *Tinsel-Town Trivia* on cable. I watched you all the time. You were great. Yeah." He nodded, pleased with himself. "That explains it, right?"

"What are you—?"

"Now, I know why he came here." The man grinned. He was the ugliest jack-o'-lantern Cliff had ever seen. " 'Silver Screen gossip from Hitch to Bacall,' " the man recited, " 'ask Mr. Hollywood, the man who knows *all*.' " He nodded to himself. "That's just what Quinn did. He asked you."

"You want my autograph, mister?" Cliff sneered. "Is that it? You a stage-door Johnny?"

The man leaned closer. He smelled of grape soda. A drop of sweat hung from the tip of his nose. "Did you tell him, Mr. Hollywood?"

Cliff abruptly twisted and the chaise collapsed, sending the two of them tumbling. He was up and moving before the man could get to his feet, but the man tripped him as he dashed past. Cliff scuttled forward on his hands and knees, tearing at the grass as he pulled himself up again. He raced for the house, barefoot and quick, heart pumping, hearing the man's heavy footsteps right behind him.

Cliff leaped onto the back porch, and through the open kitchen door, scattering cats. He heard hissing and screeching, the man cursing, kicking. Just as he reached the winding staircase, he felt a huge hand grab his shoulder—he cried out, but the hand slipped off on the layer of baby oil that covered his body. He took the stairs two at a time, three at a time, feeling them shake as the man crashed after him.

The door to the master bedroom flew open as Cliff pushed through, dived into the security compartment in the closet and slammed the door. He threw the bolts and leaned against the steel door, panting. He hit the light switch—the bulb flared and went out, leaving him in complete darkness.

The eight-by-twelve vault had been installed by the previous owner, a French box-office star who had a two-picture deal with Columbia, and a fear of "ze dangerous love of my pistol-happy American fans." The star's two pictures had bombed, the overzealous fans had never shown up, and the widow had grabbed the house as soon as it hit the market.

The security chamber was bulletproof and fireproof. It had a chemical toilet, a twenty-four-hour air supply, and an outside telephone line.

Cliff stayed huddled in the darkness as thunderous blows beat against the inch-thick steel, reverberating within the tiny room. He pressed his fingers into his ears, shaking, waiting for the storm to pass.

Chapter 26

Liston rapped on the door, tentatively, his battered knuckles barely touching the wood. His hands throbbed from beating on Mr. Hollywood's secret compartment this afternoon—his shoulders ached from hurling himself against the steel door, taking a running start, again and again, until his whole body was a massive bruise. It felt good.

The door swung open and Sissy stood before him. She took in the new blue jogging suit he wore, then ushered him inside, placing her hand on his arm so that her warmth ran through him like hot syrup. He followed her down a short corridor and into her office.

He had called her from a pay phone an hour earlier; she had ordered him over before he could get more than two words out. He found himself talking to a dial tone.

"You're working late," he offered.

"I'm always working."

"No one saw me," he tried again.

" 'Course no one saw you, that's why I told you to use my private elevator." She strode to the couch, sat down in a wave of pale pink ruffles. Pink was her signature color, she always wore at least a bit of it. "I get lots of company I don't want the security cameras to see." She arranged herself on the flowered couch, fluffing her hair out around her bare shoulders, imperiously draping her arms across the back of the sofa. "So?"

His head felt heavy. He could hardly hold it up.

She just stared at him. It was like he had let the whole team down and it was the last game of the season and he was never going to make it right.

"You followed them after they left my office, didn't you?"

"For a while," Liston said carefully, not wanting her to know the extent of his failure. "They went back to the magazine and took separate cars. I stuck with him." He eyed the chocolates piled in the dish on the coffee table between them. "I lost him in the Hollywood Hills. He drives fast and the traffic, everybody cutting each other off. . . ."

She stayed on the sofa, her arms stretched to the sides, long fingers plucking at the rich, brocaded fabric. For a moment he thought she was going to invite him to sit next to her.

He had never been in her office before—it was filled with lace and embroidered pillows and rounded couches, full and female and smelling faintly of her perfume. The room was like a drawer of frilly underwear.

"Things are going from bad to worse, aren't they?" she said.

"What do you want me to do?" said Liston, shifting from one foot to the other. "Just tell me."

Sissy selected a chocolate from the dish, took a bite, grimaced, and tossed it back. "Bad to worse," she repeated.

Liston ground his teeth, holding back his anger. There were times when she used that tone with him. . . ."It's easy for you—*I'm* the one who's out there on the field, taking hits. I don't even get any thanks for it."

Her eyes were cool. "I didn't realize that's what you wanted from me."

"That's not—"

"Thank you, Mr. Liston."

His cheeks burned—before he knew what he was doing he had taken a step toward her, fists clenched. She retreated back into the soft pillows, mouth twisted in fear, and he stopped himself, embarrassed, unsure of what he wanted to do next.

She gathered herself, stronger now, her eyes fastened right on him so he couldn't look away. She patted the sofa next to her, but he shook his head. Seeing her pout made him feel better. He had to refuse her something.

"Don't worry," Liston said, reaching into the candy dish. "I'm going to have a little talk with Quinn. I got his license-plate number. The girl's too. No telling how much she knows." He grabbed a handful of chocolates and pushed them all into his mouth, enjoying her annoyance. "Never met a man yet who could keep a secret from a woman."

Sissy raised one eyebrow. "You're an expert on women?" she said. "I should have you on another one of my TV shows, Emory Roy, you're one of a kind."

"I don't like you making fun of me."

She smiled at him. "I'm just teasing, Emory Roy—what's the matter, don't you like being tickled?" It was hard to stay mad at her.

Liston licked his fingers. "I'm going to have a talk with those two, just as soon as I get their addresses from the DMV. You don't have to know a thing about it. It won't even make the papers, I'll see to that."

"Haven't you done enough?" Sissy glared at him. "Where is it going to end? How many people you going to have to kill before this is over? Look at me. Damn you, look at me! You didn't have to kill Tod. A man your size . . . don't you think Tod would have done anything you asked him to?"

"He took too long to do it," growled Liston. "People think they can make me wait," he said softly, "those people got another *think* coming."

"I should have never sent you for the X rays," she said, voice breaking. "I should have picked them up from Tod myself. He would have handed them over to me. All of them." She picked up a needlepoint pillow and hugged it to her chest. "I *loved* Tod," she said in a little girl's voice, looking directly at Liston. "You didn't have to kill him."

He met her stare, seeing himself in her sad eyes. "Yes, I did." He watched her bosom rise and fall—he didn't know how she managed to cry without making a sound. "Please stop," he said. "Sissy? What do you want me to do?"

"I want you to wait," she said solemnly. It was like she was pronouncing sentence on him. "I've invited both of them out to the ranch the day after tomorrow. Let me spend some more time with them, and I'll find out all I need to."

"What if Quinn's got the missing X ray?" said Liston. "How would you like to see *that* plastered all over the newsstands?"

"There's no rush," insisted Sissy. "If Quinn and Jen had anything solid as that, they wouldn't still be sniffing around asking questions." She shook her head like it was all decided and he was supposed to just shut up and follow orders. "You stay home and let me handle things. I've been dealing with snoopy reporters for years."

Liston dropped his gaze. "I didn't tell you before, but . . . this afternoon, before I lost Quinn, he was talking to Mr. Hollywood." He faced her. "Cliff somebody—he used to have a gossip—"

"I know who he is." Sissy stroked her throat with the back of her nails, her eyes glittering.

"That's why I don't think we should wait," Liston said quietly. "They're getting close. I used to be a cop—you ask enough questions, sooner or later you get the right answer."

"Don't do anything yet," said Sissy. "Cliff Silver isn't God, he just had a TV show. The police have closed out the case—if you do something foolish, they may take a second look."

"If you say so."

"Your hands are bleeding," she said like she just noticed. "What have you been up to?"

"Nothing."

She rose from the chair effortlessly, her frilly dress crinkling against her creamy knees as she came toward him. She picked up his hands, brought them closer. "Oh, child," she clucked, "you really have hurt yourself."

"It's not so bad."

She led him to the ice-cream bar in the corner, took him behind the counter. She filled the stainless-steel sink with ice cubes and cold water, emptying tray after tray, Liston wincing at the clatter, wanting to tell her not to bother but afraid to break her concentration.

He felt her slide the sleeves of his jogging suit up his thick forearms, heard her throaty coo as she felt his muscles. The cold jolted him alert as she plunged his hands and wrists into the ice water. He pulled them out, mainly as a reflex.

She kissed his torn knuckles, eased his hands back into the ice. He had to bend forward. "Shh," she soothed him, "let me take care of you for a change."

He watched her dim the lights.

She pressed a button and a panel in the opposite wall moved, revealing a wide-screen TV. She picked up a remote control and switched on the set.

He looked at her.

"I wanted to surprise you," she said as the VCR started. "Remember when I had you on the show? We used a clip of you from a football-highlights video, a clip of you getting tackled. Remember? Someone in the studio audience actually fainted. It was a great piece of tape."

"I remember."

Football's Greatest Hits! flashed the title, some quick credits, and there was Joe Theismann, quarterback for the Redskins, getting tackled, his leg bending at an impossible angle before snapping. Another career-ender.

She turned up the sound. Bill Harshky was racing downfield when he got speared from the side with a crunch that sent his helmet flying. She stood next to him. He started to straighten up but she pushed his hand back into the ice water. "You have to take care of yourself," she said, not taking her eyes from the screen, "your hands swell up, what good are you?"

No good at all. More thuds and crunches from the television, that skinny end with the Pittsburgh Steelers getting flattened by Bubba Paris. The crowd roared at a series of hits, players cartwheeling headfirst into the turf. The on-field microphone caught every grunt and crunch, while the announcer exuded sympathy.

Sissy's hand slid under the elastic waist of his pants, dipped into his boxer shorts. He felt her hand gently squeeze his remaining testicle, squeeze him again and again, with just enough pressure, just short of pain, pumping the blood through him.

Daryll Thomas from the Packers got sandwiched between two free safetys running full speed, one hitting him high, the other low. It sounded like a jumper kissing the concrete from ten stories up.

"Your husband . . ." Liston choked. "This isn't right."

She squeezed him harder and he bit his lip shut. He heard the ice shifting as he slumped over the sink, the cold moving slowly up his arms. He couldn't feel his hands anymore. The only sensation he had was of her massaging him, slowly increasing the pressure. A single diamond dangled from a gold chain around her neck, nestled in the hollow of her throat—cold fire against her pink skin. He could see the blue veins along the tops of her breasts. She was squeezing him harder, her thumb resting against the base of his stiffening penis.

Her perfume was stronger now. He wished he had put cream rinse on his pubic hair after his shower this morning; the hairs must feel like wire against her soft hands.

The room was filled with grunts, howls of pain, and victory. Her thumb was pressing him harder, her mouth slightly open, her eyes wide. "I won my time slot all last month," she said. "That'll get the network's notice. . . . Every day, every single day. I beat the soaps on Channels Four and Five, Phil on Seven and Oprah on Eleven."

"Oprah had reruns." Liston smiled.

She suddenly squeezed him so hard he cried out. "It wouldn't have mattered," she spit, "I still would have beat her. People love me. They may watch Phil and Oprah and Sally, but they *love* me." The pulse was beating faster at the base of her throat.

Liston moaned, his head dropping forward.

Her cheeks flushed. "You said you'd protect me," she said, the light from the TV reflected in her eyes, "you said you'd do whatever it takes."

"Yes . . ."

"*Whatever* it takes?"

"Yes."

She slowly ran her thumb down the length of his penis, stopping right before the head, circling him with her nail. He couldn't tell if the groan came from the TV or from himself.

"Here you are," she said as Liston rushed across the TV screen, dodged two tacklers, picking up speed as the crowd cheered him on. He broke one tackle, then another, the announcer yelling, cheering him on. Sissy squeezed him harder.

Just as Liston almost made it to open field he got wrapped up around the ankles. He swayed in the man's grasp, almost pulled free, when he was clipped at the knees. The sudden snapping sound quieted the announcer and the crowd. Liston lay on the grass, stunned, then began to writhe and scream, tearing at the grass.

Liston came in a gush that splashed across her wrists. She slapped him hard, right across the face, and he tasted his own sperm. She bent close, kissed him, and the cold spread through his body and he was weightless, floating in her embrace.

Chapter 27

"Careful where you step," warned Quinn as he and Jen made their way to the back of Cliff's house.

There had been a nasty note from the *SLAP* receptionist on his desk this morning when he got to work. Someone—she thought it was the same man—kept calling and asking if Quinn was there. The man refused to leave his name or number. Cliff had called only once, but she wasn't thrilled about that either. She said he sounded hysterical. And drunk. They got cut off in the middle of the conversation, but at least he left his name.

It was 10 A.M., Wednesday, and his turn to drive. On the way over, Jen told him about her meeting last night with her old photography teacher. Quinn still had trouble with what she had found out.

Quinn pushed Cliff's overgrown azalea bushes aside, looked back at Jen. "X rays? Are you sure this . . . Louis knows what he's talking about?"

"No, I went to an incompetent for help." Jen pushed past him, the weeds scratching against her black leggings.

Jen always dressed in some variation of basic black, stylish but allowing full freedom of movement. She never wanted to wear something that prevented her from crawling around to get the best shot. Today she wore a black turtleneck, short skirt, and textured leggings, with black ankle boots.

"What Morales gave you were pieces of old X rays," said Jen, "at least twenty years old, according to Louis. That's why the pieces were so yellowed—there's no way you can wash out all the photochemicals from film stock, and over time—" She stopped, seeing Quinn's face.

Quinn stared at Cliff's overturned lawnchair in the back-yard. He bent to one knee—the cooler was on its side, half-filled with martini cans and melted ice. He glanced back at the house. He could hear cats crying. "Stay here," he ordered, start-ing for the back door.

"Absolutely," said Jen, matching him step for step. "I obey, O mighty alpha-male."

Quinn slowed as they got closer to the house, listening—he heard only cats. The windows were full of cats, lined up two and three deep . . . thick curtains of soft fur. He looked up at Cliff's window, half expecting to see the old man toasting this overcast Wednesday morning.

"Maybe he went out?" said Jen.

Quinn shook his head. He wished he had a gun with him—something in a .357 magnum, extra husky, just like Morales had suggested.

"If you're worried," said Jen, "why don't you just call the police? They're paid to walk into situations like this."

It was a good idea. They moved back to the lawnchairs, where there was plenty of open space, and Quinn picked up Cliff's portable phone from the grass.

The 911 operator answered immediately. It was one of the few times he felt happy about the way his taxes were spent. He described the overturned chairs, the abandoned booze, the des-perate phone message. The operator said they'd send a car out to investigate. He gave her the address and there was silence.

"Just a moment, sir." The operator put him on hold. She came back shortly. "I'm sorry," she breezed, "we have had nu-merous false alarms from that address, so unless you can give us specifics about a crime in progress, you'll have to wait for a regular patrol unit."

"How soon do you expect that to be?" said Quinn, already giving Jen the thumbs-down sign.

"I really couldn't say, sir."

Quinn broke the connection and headed back to the house. The screen door squeeked as he opened it. His hands were shaking. Something brushed against his leg and he yelped, the kitchen echoing with his fear.

It was one of the widow's cats nuzzling his ankle. Then another one. And another. Cats of all sizes, all colors, purring insistently, arching their backs for pats as he walked through the darkened kitchen and pulled a heavy carving knife from one of the drawers.

Jen eyed the eight-inch blade in his hand, then reached into her camera bag and pulled out a stun gun. It crackled as she tested it and he smelled ozone.

"You always carry that?" he whispered.

She smiled.

They went through the bottom floor room by room, moving quietly, their steps sending fur balls floating across the hardwood floors. Jen touched him on the shoulder—he wasn't sure if she was steadying herself or reassuring him, but it felt good. The living room was dim, hazy sunlight filtering in through thick lace curtains and years of dust. The sofas and chairs were draped with gray-white sheets, ghostly hippos grazing on the Oriental carpet. The room smelled of cat piss—it made his eyes itch.

A single blue nightlight lit the main hallway, an orange tabby curled next to it as though for warmth. Quinn listened at the foot of the stairs—the house hummed with the purring of cats, dozens and dozens of throaty voices murmuring their private satisfactions.

Quinn gripped the handle of the knife even tighter, put one foot on the bottom step of the winding staircase. "You sure you don't want to wait outside?"

Jen just stared at him.

Quinn started up the stairs, taking them slow, keeping to the sides where they were least likely to squeak. When he turned to check on Jen, she was close but not too close, watching the rear, covering them both.

He stopped every three or four steps to listen, but heard only the steady purring that seemed to come from the house itself. He crouched near the top of the stair, peering down the long hallway, illuminated only by a line of blue nightlights. The air was acrid with urine, matted cat hair clumped along the worn carpet. No wonder Cliff spent most of his time outside.

Quinn heard a noise in Cliff's room. He eased closer, hugging the wall. The door was open, the room dark. Cliff always kept his door closed. Always. It was the only room in the house that didn't smell like a litter box. A desiccated mouse lay in the hall, just outside the door, a feline offering to the great god Cliff. Another noise from the room.

"What is it?" Jen whispered in his ear.

Quinn shook his head, reached into the room and found the light switch. He flicked it on as he jumped into the room, flailing a swath with the knife, yelling. He blinked in the center of the empty bedroom, feeling ridiculous. The knife fell to his side.

The four-poster bed was rumpled, pillows propped up facing the TV. Heavy curtains blacked out the windows. The walls were covered with photos of movie stars of the thirties, forties and fifties, most of the stars standing next to Cliff, toasting the camera with their martini glasses. A wastebasket was filled with cocktail cans, a jar of jumbo green olives open on the nightstand.

Jen stood in the doorway. She glanced behind her, then back at him, still on guard for any sound from the stairs, from the hallway.

Instead, the sound came from behind a wall.

"Who's there?" yelled Quinn, knife at the ready.

"Quinn?" Cliff's voice was faint. "That you?"

"Cliff! Where are you?"

The wall swung open. Cliff crouched in a small dark cubbyhole, hiding there in his white Speedo, squinting in the bright light of the bedroom. "Is he gone?" he squawked, still hunched over in the corner, black hair sticking out on all sides. "He's gone?" Cliff's eyes darted back and forth, then settled on Quinn. "What *took* you so long?" he wailed.

Quinn went over to Cliff, scooped him up in his arms, and carried him over to the bed. "Are you hurt?" he asked quietly, sitting next to the old man.

"There was no light in there," Cliff mumbled, still blinking, hanging on to him, "I couldn't see a thing. Not a thing. There was a phone, but it took me forever to call your office . . . my hands kept shaking and I couldn't find the right buttons. I was a little drunk too. I got dizzy talking to your receptionist, fell right over and tore out the phone wires. I tried . . . I tried to put them back in, but it was *so* dark."

"Was it a big man? Heavyset? Crewcut?"

"He said he was a cop," sobbed Cliff. "Sergeant Nagurski. I knew he was no cop."

Quinn put his arm around Cliff's thin shoulders, held him until he stopped shaking. He seemed so much more frail than he had yesterday afternoon.

"You brought a gun, didn't you?" Cliff's eyes were off again, bouncing back and forth from one side of his head to the other. "I told your receptionist . . . I think I did . . . you brought a gun, didn't you?" He suddenly noticed Jen, patted down his hair, and thrust out his hand. "Cliff Silver, Silver-not-Gold," he said, his usually smooth patter sounding mechanical and uncertain.

"Hi, Cliff." She smiled. "I'm Jen Takamura." She sat on the other side of Cliff, patted his skinny brown arm. "*Nice* bathing suit."

Cliff puffed out his bare chest for her, sucked in his stomach, then started to cry, turning away, pretending he just had to clear his throat. "The bulb in the vault burned out," he said flatly. "I sat in the dark listening to him beat on the wall, wondering when it was going to give way. Even after he stopped pounding, I was afraid he was out there waiting."

"There's no one—" said Quinn.

"They do that, you know"—Cliff bobbed his head, oblivious—"like in *Back to Bataan:* You think you're safe, but there's Nip snipers hiding in the coconut palms, just waiting for you to stick your face out." He looked at Jen. "No offense, miss." His lower lip quivered, and he dropped his head. "A man can die without light," he said, his voice so faint Quinn and Jen both leaned closer to hear. "Shrivel up and die. I wanted to come out . . . but I was afraid he was still here." His eyes darted toward the door.

Quinn glanced toward the door, wishing he didn't feel the need to check. "You're safe now."

"No I'm not. None of us are." Cliff snickered at the carving knife Quinn still held. "That's not going to stop him. He's *big*. He said he used to play football, and I believe him—he's got shoulders like a Mack truck." He nodded at Jen's stun gun. "Put that away, girlie. You come at this fella with that joy-buzzer, you're just going to make him madder."

"Why debate the point?" said Jen. "Let's get out of here."

"He played football?" said Quinn. "Pro ball? Did he say where?"

"I need a drink," Cliff croaked. He scooted off the bed, went through the wastebasket, shaking cans, draining the last few drops of a daiquiri. He looked at Quinn. "I got to change." He mouthed the words: "I wet myself," grabbed clothes out of his dresser, and ducked into the bathroom. When he came out he was wearing white tennis shorts and a polo shirt with a frayed collar. He had neatly combed back his hair. Smelled like he had thrown on some cologne too.

Jen was examining the yellowed lace that covered the canopy bed.

"Nice, huh?" called Cliff. "That was the widow's pride and joy—it was Bette Davis's bed in *Jezebel*. Wonderful movie. Nobody could play a bitch the way Bette could. Of course, she wasn't really acting."

Jen laughed.

Cliff beamed back at her, but Quinn could see his hands shaking so badly that he had to push them into the pockets of his shorts.

Chapter 28

The empty can of Rob Roy cocktail clattered against the kitchen wall and Cliff reached for another one. He sat on the red tile countertop next to the sink, white tennis shorts billowing across his scrawny legs. An ivory-handled revolver rested in his lap. The noon sun glared through the windows, but Cliff had every light in the house on. He said he wasn't leaving until he finished the six-pack. He held up the remaining four cans. "Rob Roy?"

"No thanks," said Quinn.

"Maybe later," said Jen.

"Health nuts," Cliff said contemptuously, brave after two quick ones. "Afraid of booze, afraid of steak, afraid of sunlight." He belched, thumped his wrinkled brown chest. "How old do you think I am?" he asked Jen. "Go on, take a guess."

"Why wouldn't the police come out here?" Jen said. "Quinn called but they weren't interested."

Cliff snorted. "Me and the widow used to drink pretty heavy"—he took a long swallow from the fresh can—"and sometimes we'd start fighting, throwing the damn cats around, and one or the other of us would call the coppers. By the time they got here, neither of us would press charges, and they'd get on their high horse about wasting the taxpayers' money." He rubbed his belly at the memory. "She was a good old gal." The wind brushed branches against the house and he pointed the revolver at the window. "Who's there?" he shouted, the huge gun wobbling in his hand.

"There's nobody there," said Quinn.

Cliff's face fell, his mouth drooping into a nest of wrinkles. He handed Quinn the gun. "Here, you take it, before I hurt

193

myself." Cliff looked his age now—he had since they found him upstairs a half hour ago—old and lonely and scared that something was going to happen to make him dead a moment sooner than absolutely necessary. People thought the less of a life you had, the less you valued it. Quinn knew better.

"Cliff? Hey, Cliff!" said Quinn. "Let's get out of here. We'll take you to a motel, or you can stay at my place. You take the hide-a-bed, I'll take the reading chair."

"That guy got to me," murmured Cliff, idly rubbing the bare patch on his leg where the hair had been torn off. "Calling himself Sergeant Nagurski . . . he was having a good time with me. Bristly red hair, mean little eyes . . ." He waved his hand in the air like he was erasing something. "A classic heavy, straight from a Central Casting wet dream. You remember Bob Mitchum in *Cape Fear*? The real one, not the remake. This bristly son of a bitch would scare Bob Mitchum."

"I think you handled things beautifully," said Jen. "Hiding in the vault . . . that was intelligent."

Quinn hefted the long-barreled revolver. It had smooth ivory grips and a silver-plated stock, decorative curlicues etched into the metal. He spun the chamber, removed one of the slugs—45-caliber. You could bring down a buffalo with a gun like that. One shot.

"That there pistola was a gift from Desi Arnez," Cliff said proudly. "I had it tucked away in my bottom drawer. Now Desi, *there* was a fellow who could party. Go all night and get to work on time in the morning." It was the highest compliment Cliff could pay to anyone.

"What did this guy want?" said Quinn. "The heavy."

"Goddamned cats saved my life." Cliff shook his head in disbelief. "He tripped over one of them on the stairs, or he'd have caught me for sure. A cat. Glenn Ford, I think. I wish the widow was here—she'd bust a gut."

"Cliff?"

"He kept asking me how much you knew," said Cliff, shaking his head. "How am I supposed to answer that? One minute the heavy talks like he's looped, the next he's plenty savvy. He's sure interested in you, though—you're number one on his Hit Parade. Maybe next time you and him could leave me out of it."

"He must have followed me from the magazine," said Quinn. "Somebody's been calling the office, asking if I'm there." He walked to the window, stared out at the backyard. Now the man with the crewcut knew what he drove and knew where he worked. What else did he know? Seeing Cliff's lawnchair lying broken on the grass made him feel queasy. He had to turn away. "I'm sorry you got dragged into this, Cliff."

"The heavy said he was tailing you," said Cliff, "but he lost you in traffic after you left here. That's when he came back for me." He glanced at the bare patches on his leg where the big man had pulled the hair out. He nodded suddenly, remembering—"He knew me, though." His face was a drunken mixture of pride and embarrassment. "Not at first, but then he recognized me. That's what set him off."

"Recognized you as what?" asked Jen.

"I was in television for a few years," said Cliff, quietly checking his reflection in the chrome stovetop. He smoothed down his jet-black hair before turning back to her. "I was Mr. Hollywood."

Jen stared at him blankly.

"It was just a little one-camera cable show on Hollywood trivia. We showed clips from classic films and I answered phone-in questions . . . I used to wear a tuxedo." Cliff went through the cans scattered across the countertop, shaking them, trying to see if there was anything left inside. "Once the heavy realized who I was . . ." He shuddered, looked at Quinn. "I think he was going to kill me."

Quinn nodded, thinking about how recognizing Cliff had made the heavy snap. He almost had it, but Jen beat him to it.

"Maybe it wasn't you he wanted to kill," said Jen, "maybe he wanted to kill Mr. Hollywood?"

Cliff didn't understand.

"Maybe he was afraid you knew something," explained Quinn. "Something about Hollywood? Secrets of the Silver Screen?"

"I knew plenty," said Cliff, "that's no reason to kill me." He glanced at the window. "Maybe we *should* get out of here? . . ."

"Last Friday night a man was murdered," said Jen, holding up the glassine envelope. "The police found these—"

"Quinn showed me that yesterday," said Cliff. "I already told him, it's not from a porno film."

"They're pieces of an old X ray," said Jen.

"Doesn't look like anything to me," said Cliff, trying to focus on the chunks of cloudy film. "What's the big deal about old X rays, anyway? Doctors used to X-ray you for a chest cold back then, it was supposed to be good for you—there were kid-actors getting dosed to clear up their pimples." He laughed, lost his balance, and had to hang on to the sink.

Jen helped Cliff steady himself. She did it casually, as though it happened all the time. "Tod . . . the man who was murdered last weekend, he started out as a talk-show researcher, confirming the guests' résumés, doing background checks." She smiled at Cliff, trying to keep him interested. "What if Tod struck gold on one of his assignments? What if he dug up something on a big star, something that showed up on an X ray?"

"I dug up plenty in my time," said Cliff, still woozy, "but I hardly ever used it." He pulled Jen toward him. "In the old days," he whispered, "the studios had headbreakers on the payroll to protect their interests. You hurt one of their stars, they hurt you back."

"Did Stratton's studio protect him?" asked Quinn.

"They protected *all* their stars," said Cliff, "that's what the system was there for. But Stratton . . . I never heard anything bad about him. Not compared to others . . ." He burped into his fist. "There were some nasty bastards playing good guys on the screen, but Stratton wasn't one of them."

Quinn bent down and scratched a gray Siamese behind the ear. The cat licked his hand with its raspy tongue. He stood up, brightening. "Yesterday, you told me Stratton's first wife died in a fire. Maybe the X rays were from the wife's autopsy? What if they showed that she died of a broken neck, not from the fire? The studio could have covered it up, if they were as powerful as you say."

"*Mistaken Identity*," recited Cliff, "Nineteen thirty-seven, Warner Brothers, Asa Heydrich directed, Bogart had a walk-on role. Barton MacLane plays a socialite who goes bust, strangles his wife, and fakes her death in a car crash to collect the insurance. In the last reel the cops find—"

"Okay," said Quinn. "What if—"

"You're barking up the wrong tree," said Cliff. "Stratton's house went up like a torch—Betty Andaluse was burnt to toast, but Jensen from the *Times* gave the coroner a C-note to look at the report. Nothing. No broken bones. No trace of poison. No sign of foul play. Dental records matched, so nobody pulled a switcheroo either. A few of the boys went out drinking a week later, and Jensen got snookered worse than usual. He said Betty Andaluse must have been one hot number, he got a hard-on just looking at her medical chart." He glanced at Jen. "I *never* liked Jensen."

"You told me Tod had stacks of old gossip magazines in his bedroom," Jen said to Quinn. "He could have turned up something on any one of a hundred stars."

"It was Sissy who gave Tod the promotion," said Quinn. "Maybe she owed him a favor."

"Then why kill him?" said Jen. "It doesn't make sense. Maybe Tod deserved the promotion—that's what you told Gillian on Monday. Now, you think he blackmailed his way into the job? What's the matter, Quinn, was he too good-looking for you?"

"She's got you there," cackled Cliff, "I've seen it before. It's part of the male animal. I never walked into a gin mill with Gable that half the bar didn't want to beat him up on general principles. Errol Flynn? Forget it, I wouldn't even go out with him after a while."

Quinn watched Cliff's Adam's apple bob. "Cliff," he said suddenly, "you said the studios hired headbreakers to protect their stars. Did they have doctors on the payroll too?"

Cliff was blank for a moment, then nodded. "Sure. Every studio had a Doc Feelgood or two on retainer. You got a tough production schedule or a star needs to kick a habit, you call the doctor. I've seen them get writer's cramp scribbling Benzedrine prescriptions, seen a whole cast and crew higher than kites. Names you'd recognize too. Yeah." He nodded faster, warming to the idea. "These croakers would do anything—you could get an abortion during lunch and be back on the set that afternoon. I used them myself when I got somebody in trouble."

"I'll take as many names as you can remember," said Quinn.

"Let me get my Rolodex," Cliff said, jumping off the sink.

"I never throw anything out," he called behind him as he raced up the stairs.

"Start under the letter *M*," Quinn yelled after him, "as in 'Dr. M.' *That's* who Tod must have linked up with," he explained to Jen, standing so close to her he felt dizzy. "Dr. M.—I found that name written all over Tod's calendar." He wanted to kiss her, he was so pleased with himself. It had been a long time since he worked on a real story—he had forgotten how good it felt.

"Hope I'm not interrupting anything," said Cliff, standing at the bottom of the stairs—a Rolodex in one hand. Quinn stepped away from Jen. Cliff winked at her. "I asked him yesterday if he had a girlfriend, he says no." He gave her a long, admiring look, his eyes warmer than from just the alcohol. "You two look good together, a regular Nick and Nora. If I was thirty years younger, I'd ask if you had a sister. What the hell . . . you have a sister?"

Jen smiled.

Cliff gathered the remaining canned cocktail. "I want to go to a hotel," he said, walking out the back door, "someplace near you, Quinn, with room service, and cable TV so I can watch old movies. None of that colorization crap. That's all I'm asking. Oh yeah, and a heated swimming pool. I brought my suit."

Chapter 29

The house was a ramshackle three-story affair of white brick, with high outer walls and intricate black ironwork—a Mediterranean-style villa, cool and shaded and very private. It had been a popular design in the 1930s among the Hollywood set, before air-conditioning. Most of the original models had been torn down and replaced with something with better plumbing, or completely restored at enormous cost. This one was overgrown with weeds and brambles, the red barrel roof tiles cracked and missing, the ironwork rusted, the once-white brick crumbling. The front gate drooped open, hanging off its hinges. In the gray evening, the house looked like an abandoned fortress.

It was almost 7 P.M. Rush-hour traffic had slowed them, wall-to-wall up and down the 405 freeway. They had driven Cliff to the Bel-Shore Inn, checked him into a suite with a minibar, and put it on Quinn's credit card. There were two studio doctors whose names began with the letter *M*, but Dr. Hugh F. McChesney was the only one still listed with the California Medical League.

Quinn checked the address on the mailbox against the one from Cliff's Rolodex. "This is it." He looked up and down the street, then opened the mailbox. The box was stuffed with circulars for OCCUPANT, a copy of *Golden Years* magazine, and past-due bills—telephone, two Visa cards, water/sewage and electric—all addressed to the doctor.

Dr. McChesney's once-glorious villa was on a dead-end street in Palos Verdes, an exclusive enclave just below Los Angeles. PV was a rugged peninsula that jutted into the Pacific, full of narrow, winding streets and rugged bluffs overlooking the ocean. People didn't put up fences between themselves and their neighbors; they built thick walls, planted impenetrable hedges. Money had gravitated to Palos Verdes for decades—there was a long tradition of minding your own business.

They walked up the cracked flagstone path, one time brushing through a clinging spiderweb. It was a little late to be making a social call, but neither of them wanted to wait until tomorrow. They didn't want to wait five minutes. They were getting closer, they both knew that. Besides, if this really was the doctor Tod had visited, he was used to evening calls.

There were two bell buttons next to the front door. Jen rang the one marked "Office." A minute later she rang it again.

The door swung open and a sallow, pinch-faced young woman peeked out through the chain-latched door. "Talk fast," she said, "I'm busy."

"We're here to see the doctor," said Jen.

"Both of you?" said the woman. She had a nasty, humorless grin. "Who hurts the most?"

"Could you let us in?" said Quinn.

"You have an appointment?"

"Not exactly," said Jen.

"Yes," said Quinn.

The woman wiped her nose with the back of her hand. "You're quite a pair," she said. "Not what I'd call a matched set. What did you want from the doc?"

"We'd rather talk to him directly," said Quinn. This woman was placing entirely too much faith in the strength of that chain latch. "Maybe you could blow your nose on your sleeve, then go get him."

Jen put her hand on his arm, trying to shut him up.

"That's going to cost you, asshole," said the woman. She had tiny rodent eyes and a narrow beaky nose. "I'm out of morphine so you can forget that. The Valium is ten dollars apiece, and the Percodan goes for fifteen dollars. No quantity discount for you." She snapped her fingers, held out her hand. "Take it or leave it."

Jen pulled a twenty-dollar bill out of her jacket and handed it to the woman. "Keep the dope. Please ask the doctor to come to the door. We need to ask him a few questions."

The woman scrunched up her face. "You ain't customers?"

Quinn was so tired of meeting stupid people. Every statement had to be repeated, every request explained in triplicate—you'd think the whole world worked for the government.

"We need to talk with the doctor," said Jen. "We're doing an article for *SLAP* magazine, and hoped he could help us."

"Grandpa? You're shitting me?"

"Your grandfather's Dr. McChesney?" said Jen. "Could you please ask him to come to the door?"

"I'll ask him," brayed the woman, "but he's not a good listener these days." She had lipstick smeared on her front teeth. She looked from Jen to Quinn. "Grandpa's croaked. I'm just taking care of his customers with what's left."

"When did he die?" asked Quinn. He felt like he was swimming and had hit a patch of cold water. You think the Pacific is cold until you hit one of those icy bottom currents, and the chill curls around your heart and starts to tighten. All you can do is keep swimming and hope to get past it.

The woman jabbered on.

"When?" repeated Quinn.

Jen touched him lightly on the wrist. Reassuring. "Could we come in and talk with you?" she said to the woman. "We'll make it worth your while, Ms. . . . ?"

"McChesney. Silly. Call me Randy."

"When did he die, Randy?" Quinn said slowly.

"I don't know," Randy said as she unlatched the door, "a couple of weeks . . . what's today? Wednesday? Yeah, almost two weeks." She was wearing a pair of big macs with no blouse, her tiny breasts peeking out from the baggy overalls. There were bunny slippers on her feet—probably to hide the needle marks. Quinn knew where the morphine had gone: right into the veins of her ankles and feet. She took the other twenty dollars Jen held out, and they followed her as she scuffed through the house in her soft little slippers.

The rooms leading off the corridor were clean and tidy, but it looked like a lot of furniture was missing. Whole rooms were nearly empty, dark, unfaded areas of the rugs indicating where sofas and chairs had once sat.

If McChesney had died two weeks ago, somebody hadn't killed him to cover up Tod's murder. Or Andy's. Assuming McChesney was the "Dr. M." that Tod had been seeing.

The doctor's office looked like it had been vandalized. Diplomas and professional certificates hung crookedly on the walls, some with the glass broken. Pharmaceutical cabinets had been stripped bare, a jar of wooden tongue depressors spilled onto the floor. Books had been pushed off the shelves, and file cabinets hung open, their contents strewn across the room. Cardboard boxes lay stacked haphazardly next to a rolltop desk, their sides bulging and split, reports poking out.

Randy shoved aside a stack of manila folders, lay down on the examining table, and put her bunny slippers into the chrome stirrups, giggling. She fumbled in the pockets of her overalls, came up with a bent joint that had been stubbed out. She relit it and took a deep drag. "My feet are killing me, and I got less than a month to take what I want from this dump before the bank forecloses," she said. "My meter's running— what do you want to know?"

Quinn wrinkled his nose—the office smelled of rubbing alcohol. "First off," he said, "what did Grandpa die of?"

"What kind of an article are you working on? I seen *SLAP*, but I don't buy it." Randy twirled a strand of her ratty brown hair between her thumb and index finger. She leaned toward him so that one of her breasts slipped out of her overalls. "You ever need people to work in the office? I look lots better with makeup. I type real good, make coffee too, I got no problem with that feminist shit."

"Come in and fill out an application," said Quinn. He gave her his best smile. "Randy, how did Grandpa die?"

Randy shrugged. "He was old."

"Were the police called?" asked Quinn.

"He was *old*," said Randy. "What are you, retarded? He was like in his seventies—you get old, you die."

Jen bent down and reached into one of the cardboard boxes, pulled three X rays out of a folder. She bent one edge and it snapped off, crumbling in her hand.

"Everything in this place is like that," said Randy. "Broken down, and falling apart."

Quinn checked the box. He took one folder out, carefully removed the X ray and held it up to the desklight. It looked like there were spots all over Mr. Bruskin's liver. He checked the file. Dr. McChesney had diagnosed cirrhosis, late stages, recommendation . . . Quinn squinted. The ink on the report was too faded.

Randy took another hit off the joint, stubbed it out on the desktop, and dropped the roach into the pocket of her overalls.

Quinn riffed through the manila folders, worked his way through the *Se*s without finding John Stratton's name. Same with the *A*s—no Betty Andaluse, no Elizabeth Andaluse. He did find the name of a perky sitcom actress from the sixties who had maintained a continuing prescription for amphetamine-sulfate, from 1962 to 1974.

Jen photographed the overturned files, the scattered X rays, stepping lightly over the broken glass. Randy covered her eyes from the flash as though she were a mole.

Quinn went back through the loosely stacked boxes, rummaging around until he found the *Ms*. No Sissy Mizell. It was a long shot. Twenty years ago that might not have even been her name. Twenty years ago she wasn't even in show business, barely out of her teens and already on her second marriage. Even if she had been a patient, how could that justify killing Tod? He wished the good Dr. McChesney were here to answer some questions. Such a convenient death . . . for somebody.

"Randy?" Jen had put aside her camera and handed Randy a sheet of paper. "Maybe you can—"

"What a stud," whistled Randy, holding the paper in front of her nose. "I'd fuck him in a second."

"Have you ever seen him before?" said Jen.

Randy stared at the paper. "I wish."

Quinn peered over Randy's shoulder, saw a grainy picture of Tod. "How did you get that?" he asked Jen. He was impressed. A little annoyed, and not sure why—but mostly impressed.

"I had Sissy's office fax it over to *SLAP* this morning, before you got to work," said Jen. "Randy? Do you know if this man ever came by looking for your grandfather?"

"He could come by looking for me anytime he wants," said Randy. "Can I keep this picture? In . . . in case he shows up."

Quinn stared at the wall of old photographs and diplomas. There was an empty place. He looked closer, then picked up some frames that lay on the floor, and tried to fit them into the empty spot. They were all too big. "Randy?" Quinn tapped the bare wall. "What went here? You can see there's a nail hole in the plaster. Something used to be here. You remember what?"

"Junk"—Randy shrugged—"hanging next to the other junk."

"It was a plaque," said a severe old woman standing in the doorway. She wore a dark gray dress, a black mourning ribbon around her upper left arm. "It was an award from a local medical society. Doctor was very respected." She tapped her foot, frowning at Randy. "Miranda, what are these people doing in Doctor's office?"

"None of your damned business," said Randy. "This is my house now. I can do what I want."

"This is not your house," said the old woman. Her hair was gathered in a tight bun. "This is your grandfather's house. His office. His life. You're a looter."

"I'm a relative, his only relative," said Randy. "You're just hired help, Sarah."

Quinn held his hand out to the old woman. "My name is Quinn. This is my associate, Jen Takamura." He kept his hand out, waiting for her. "We work for *SLAP* magazine. We're researching an article and wanted to ask the doctor some questions . . . based on his acknowledged expertise. We had no idea he had passed on. I'm very sorry for your loss."

The old woman shook his hand in a firm, dry grip. "I'm Sarah Cranston," she said simply. "I worked with Doctor."

"You worked *for* Grandpa," sneered Randy.

"Shouldn't you be leaving?" Quinn said to Randy. "You must be late for *something*."

"This is my place," said Randy, "for now, anyway. All this crap is mine—pill samples, furniture, books, and papers—all of it. The bank gets the house, but I can take anything that's in it."

"Why don't you go for a walk?" Quinn said to Randy. His voice didn't change but his eyes did. She stiffened. "Go on. You'll feel better," he said.

Randy looked at Jen, then back to Quinn. She stalked toward the door. Jen grabbed the picture of Tod back from her as she passed.

Chapter 30

Every time Liston thought of Mr. Hollywood slamming the door in his face yesterday he wanted to put his fist through something. Something soft, something that screamed.

Who would have thought that scrawny old coot could run so fast? It was broken-field running, his knee was killing him, and the cats underfoot didn't help either, but Liston still should have caught him. No excuses—he had missed the tackle.

It was just after seven o'clock, the freeways had thinned out, and supper was on the table all over L.A. Liston wasn't hungry. He was sitting behind the wheel of his big Chrysler, the car parked on a dark street one block from the High Five! He could see satellite dishes clustered on the roof of the sports bar—the sign out front flashing RUGBY TONIGHT! and BASKET-BALL TONIGHT!

Liston was supposed to stay home, that's what Sissy had said, stay home and stay out of trouble. He didn't blame her for losing faith in him—he had promised to protect her, to put himself in the way of anyone who threatened her, and instead, it had been one long screwup.

He shook out a handful of aspirin tablets, chewed them as he watched people going into the bar. Killing Tod was an over-reaction, okay, but Tod should have handed over the X rays like he was supposed to. Every one of them. Sissy had told him there were six X rays in the medical file. Six. Not five. It was the principle of the thing.

He licked aspirin off his lips, rubbing his knee so it didn't lock up on him. It was hard to come out of retirement, and that's where Liston had been for all these years. You lose your touch sitting in an easychair, watching the game go on without you. That's why he had been so grateful to Sissy for calling him . . . what was it, two or three weeks ago? She needed someone she could trust, and there was the intimidation factor, she said—Tod wouldn't argue with Liston. Tod *had* argued with him, though. Right to the end.

Tod had surprised him. Then Andy showed up, and that was a surprise too. Then Quinn, and now this Jen Takamura with her camera . . . one surprise after another. Every time he turned around, somebody else was piling on. There was a rhythm to the game, a pattern that you learned to read and anticipate, so you could protect yourself. A player couldn't afford to be surprised. That's how people got hurt.

According to the DMV, Quinn's Jeep was registered in Long Beach and Jen's Corvette belonged in Venice. His address was a phony, a maildrop on Atlantic Boulevard, but hers was legit. He had checked it out this afternoon—there wasn't even a security system for the front entrance to her building. He waited across the street for a couple of hours, in case she came home for dinner. She didn't.

The cool blue neon of the High Five! beckoned, and Liston stifled a groan, remembering the pleasure in Sissy's office last night, hearing her sweet-talk, her hands squeezing him as he bent over the sink, up to the elbows in crushed ice the color of blue neon. He had promised her that he would stay out of trouble. He would have promised her anything, but now . . . Sissy had no idea of the danger she was in.

He left the keys in the ignition, left the car door unlocked, and walked toward the High Five! He was looking for someone at least 250 pounds, someone carrying serious meat and a bad attitude.

The chunky, pimple-faced bouncer checking I.D.'s at the door of the High Five! asked to see his license, laughing, said he wanted to make sure Liston was of legal age. Liston pinned the punk's right wrist down using only his index finger, held it down, watching him squirm, before walking past him.

The High Five! was packed and noisy, big-screen TVs on every wall bringing in three different basketball games. Waitresses in short skirts carried trays of nachos and beer to tables full of screaming fans. They were young, mostly college kids.

The boys were getting bigger all the time, probably steroids or those fancy-pants gyms they all went to. The girls seemed to be getting even skinnier, poor things. He thought of Sissy, the pink fullness of her, and his hands clenched into fists. He had let her down.

Liston cleared a path for himself through the crowd, finding openings, using his chest as a battering ram. He got a few angry looks that faded when he showed interest. Gutless wonders.

Mr. Hollywood hadn't believed he was a cop. Liston shook his head, seeing his reflection in the mirror over the bar—the look on his face so tortured that at first he didn't recognize himself. He *had* been a cop once, right after getting released from the pros, a good one too.

It was a small department outside of Chicago that didn't require a degree in police science, and didn't let a questionable physical stop them from hiring someone as gung-ho as Liston. He enjoyed owning the streets, legal-like, walking into dark alleys as though it was broad daylight. He liked putting on the uniform, buttoning the buttons, cinching the belt—every day was game day.

Liston didn't waste his time on small busts. He let speeders go with a warning, dropped truants off at school with a kick in the ass. "I didn't become a cop for the paperwork," he told his favorite waitress at the greasy spoon. It was the teamwork that attracted him, the sudden shift from dull routine to violent confrontation . . . he liked being a hero.

He calmed domestic disturbances by loosening his tie and ordering the husband to make him coffee while he talked gently with the wife. He arrested armed suspects without drawing his own weapon, just grabbed them by the throat and shook them. He was shot twice, but didn't lose the collar either time. Then one day Clazusky from Internal Affairs called him in and demanded his badge—too many of Liston's busts were suing the city for unnecessary force, and winning. Liston was no longer cost-effective.

He drove to Southern California after his forced resignation, stopping at gin joints along the way when he got too angry to drive. In a cowboy bar outside of Jasper, Wyoming, he almost beat the local bronc-roping champion to death, crushed his windpipe with one blow. The sheriff arrested him, but had to cut him loose; Liston knew enough to always make the other man throw the first punch. Self-defense covered a lot of ground.

Liston wandered through the High Five!, spotting potentials, keeping track—a huge blond kid with a Notre Dame sweatshirt drinking beer straight from the pitcher, a muscle-bound type in a green-striped rugby shirt, a barrel-chested loudmouth with no front teeth. . . .

Liston walked over to the table where the guy in the sweatshirt was chugging away. "Notre Dame?" he said, pointing to the sweatshirt, pretending to be drunk. "That's a girls' school. You got tits under that sweatshirt?"

The blond kid looked confused. He was almost as big as Liston, all arms and shoulders, with hands like oven mitts. The pitcher of beer in his grip looked like a jelly glass. "It's Notre Dame," he said, acting like he hadn't heard right. "It's a university," he smiled nervously. "Sir."

Sir. That really pissed him off. "I know what it is, you douchebag. Do I look stupid to you?"

"Is this a joke?" The blond kid glanced around the table. "I don't get it." He looked at Liston with these puppy-dog eyes; give him a minute and he was going to roll over on the floor and lick himself. "Can I buy you a beer, sir?"

"Can I buy you a beer?" Liston mocked in a high falsetto, leaning right into the kid's face.

The blond kid just stared at him, then picked up the pitcher and drained it. This was it. Liston waited for the kid to come after him.

"Nice talking with you," said the blond kid, going back to his conversation with his friends around the table, seven of them in their sweatshirts and innocence.

Liston stood frozen, not two feet away from the kid, watching them all talk about the team, the game, the score, the girls . . . round and round it went and no one made eye contact with him. It was like he was invisible. He almost lost it. He could start with the blond kid and work his way around the table before they had a chance to call their mommies. No. Someone else had to make the first move. Mr. Hollywood would have given his description to the cops, and Liston didn't want to make it easy for them. He had too much to do first.

The toughguy in the green-striped rugby shirt had his chair tilted back against the wall near the emergency exit, a pretty girl on each side. He looked like he did some serious iron; probably goosed it with a little juice too. His nose was flattened and there was scar tissue layered around his eyes—this one liked to mix it up. Perfect.

The toughguy followed Liston's progress toward him but kept his chair propped back, his hands on the necks of the girls on either side of him.

Liston sat down at the table, right across from him. "Hi," he said cheerfully. "I was hoping you could help me."

"I can believe that," said the toughguy in the rugby shirt.

The girls giggled. They were pretty things, but their hair was weird, sticking out of their heads in tufts, with silvery ribbons tied on the ends.

"We're waiting for somebody." The toughguy flexed his arms. "You're sitting in his spot."

Liston grinned. "Your name's Delbert, isn't it?"

"Sonny," corrected the girl on the right. She had blue peacock-feather earrings that matched her eyeshadow. "His name is Sonny."

"Shut up," said Sonny. He stared at Liston, his expression guarded, the green-striped shirt stretched across his beef.

"You work out, Delbert? You're a real specimen. I guess that's why you got two girls, while some poor bastards got none?"

The legs of Sonny's chair softly touched the floor as he dropped down to face Liston. "Fuck off."

"Watch your language there," said Liston. "I'm sure these ladies deserve more respect than that." He gave each of them a quick bow of the head. "What I wanted to ask you, though," he said earnestly, "I see you got your arms and chest all developed like Superman, but I was wondering why you hadn't bothered building up your dick muscle?"

The girls started to laugh, then stopped.

"Good thing for you I'm on probation," said Sonny. "I'd kick your fat ass from one end of the room to the other."

"I heard these guys across the way talking about you," Liston said, ignoring the threat, "they said you had a dick like a peanut." He spread his thumb and index finger an inch apart, showed the girls. "Delbert's hung like a hamster."

The girl with the peacock earrings giggled and Sonny smacked her with the back of his hand.

Liston's eyes widened.

"I don't want to fight you, fatso. You get a heart attack, I'm the one who's fucked."

The girl was crying, holding her mouth.

All the sounds in the room were contracting, the music and conversations getting fainter as they collapsed into a tight ball around him. Liston couldn't hear anything but Sonny's excuses and the girl with the peacock earrings sobbing.

Liston reached out to comfort her, but Sonny slapped his hand away.

Somebody was bouncing a basketball against the wall . . . it sounded mushy, like the ball wasn't completely inflated, which was an easy way to ruin the equipment. Nobody was cheering though, so it wasn't some slam-dunk halftime competition on TV. Liston slowly became aware that he was breathing hard, gasping, grunting with exertion, so loud that he couldn't hear the basketball anymore. He looked down and blinked at his fists.

Sonny bounced gently from the rear wall, covered in red, still in his seat, the front legs of the chair touching down, sending his head flopping forward onto the table.

The whole room was completely quiet. The music pulled. TVs switched off.

Liston stood over the table. The girl with the peacock earrings was trying to scream—the beer glass shook in her hand, drops of Sonny's blood falling slowly through the golden foam. He pushed through the emergency exit—either an alarm went off or the girl with the peacock earrings had found her voice.

The night was cool and he felt clean and peaceful inside, nothing hurt. He started the car, threw the black Chrysler into gear, seeing a crowd from the bar in his rearview. He gently eased the car away from the curb, glided away with the lights out, his hands resting on the steering wheel. He didn't even bother flooring it.

He felt like a kid again, smelling fresh-cut grass and sweaty shoulder pads and sure he was going to be young forever.

The steering wheel felt sticky—the car passed under a streetlamp and Liston saw that both of his hands were covered in blood. He looked closer. One of Sonny's teeth was embedded between the knuckles of his third and fourth finger. It gleamed in the yellow overhead light like a championship ring.

He was going to drive over to Jen Takamura's place, and wait for her to come home. Let her see what a winner looked like.

Chapter 31

"Thank you," Sarah Cranston said to Quinn, watching Randy stumble down the hall. "That young woman . . ." She shook her head, disgusted. "She turned up the day after Doctor died—I don't know how she found out."

"Would you like to sit down, Ms. Cranston?" said Jen, clearing the old woman a spot on the cracked-leather sofa.

"Miss," Sarah corrected her, "and I'll stand." She held herself stiffly erect, watching them, her head making quick birdlike movements. "Just what is it you wanted to talk to Doctor about?"

Jen placed Tod's picture down on the desk where Sarah could see it. "Were you Dr. McChesney's nurse?"

"Housekeeper. Twenty-four years. Right after his wife divorced him. *She* was his nurse. After the divorce, Doctor made do, but he had trouble keeping people. Most people." Sarah reached out and straightened a sheaf of loose reports on the desk, right next to Tod's picture. "I kept things up—cooked, cleaned, and mended."

"I'm sorry about the doctor," said Quinn, "it must have been a shock."

"You already said that," said Sarah. "I'm old, not feeble-minded." She brushed crumbs from the sofa into the palm of her hand, turned the wastebasket right side up and dumped the crumbs.

"How did the doctor die?" said Quinn. "If you don't mind me asking?"

"Are you from the insurance company?"

"No," said Quinn. "We're doing an article on Hollywood physicians. . . ."

Sarah glared at him with her schoolmarm eyes.

"I'll be honest with you, Miss Cranston," said Quinn. "We're not working on an article, that's not why we're here."

"Good for you." Sarah nodded at him. "The one thing I can *not* abide is a liar."

Quinn picked up Tod's picture and handed it to her. "This man was murdered last Friday night. A friend of mine was murdered a few hours later. We're trying to find the man who killed him, and we don't have much to go on. We were hoping you might be able to help us."

Tod's picture trembled in her blue-veined hands. "This young man . . . he's dead?"

Quinn glanced at Jen and she nodded, moved closer. "Miss Cranston?" he said. "Maybe you better sit down."

"No thank you." She carefully set Tod's picture back down on the desk, smoothed it out. "Women should never sit," she said. "It's a sign of sloth, and one sin leads to another." She looked at Jen. "Dead?" She moistened her pale lips. "That fine young man . . . dead?"

"I'm sorry," said Jen. She took the old woman's hand, clasped it tightly.

"Dead. First Doctor and now . . . Tod." Sarah sighed and squeezed Jen's hand until her knuckles were white as frost. It was as though she had put off saying Tod's name, not wanting to hurt herself.

Quinn waited as long as he could. The lights were on but the dark wood paneling made the room heavy and oppressive. He could taste the dust at the back of his throat. "How did the doctor die?"

Sarah suddenly stepped away from Jen, wiped her hand on her white dress. "I found him, you know," she said brusquely. *"Doctor."* She stared out the office window. There was a huge old weeping willow out back, its branches etched with silver in the moonlight. "I went to see why he wasn't at the table for breakfast and he was at his desk slumped over. He had on his black suit, tie . . . just like always, but I knew he was dead. Doctor was never late for breakfast—I make fresh buttermilk scones every morning."

"Did the doctor have any visitors the night before?" asked

Quinn. "Someone who might have rung the bell after you were asleep?"

"I waited until after breakfast to call the authorities," said Sarah. "If you don't eat scones while they're hot, you might as well throw them out."

"What did the . . . authorities determine to be the cause of death?"

"His heart. It stopped."

"You're sure, Ms.—Miss Cranston?" said Quinn. "The reason I keep asking is that the man who killed my friend . . . the man made it look like suicide. The doctor must have had drugs in the office . . . did the police check for signs of an overdose?"

Sarah stayed where she was, looking out the window. "He had lovely hands," she said. "Doctor was very proud of his hands—always scrubbing them, trimming the nails. Such lovely clean hands. We ate breakfast and dinner together every day. I used to love to watch him hold a coffee cup."

The room felt even darker, her words falling like dry leaves in the dead air. Quinn fought to shake off the sensation that they were drifting apart in the twilight. "Miss Cranston? We need to know," he said.

"It wasn't drugs. I'm not saying that Doctor didn't enjoy his morning shot—he always waited an hour after breakfast, so as not to interfere with his digestion. One shot midmorning, another midafternoon. Never in the evening, never before breakfast." She kept her back to him. "Tod asked me the same thing. He was quite concerned, just the way you are. I told him, as I'm telling you, all the doors and windows in the house were bolted from the inside. Doctor insisted on proper security . . . because of the . . . medicines he kept on premises."

"When was the last time you saw Tod?"

"Over a week ago. I had come back from Doctor's funeral the day before. I didn't have his phone number or I would have called him—I know he would have wanted to attend. Poor Tod, you should have seen his face when I told him Doctor had died. I thought he was going to faint." She sighed, exhaling slowly, the sound like a faint breeze through the willow tree. "When was Tod killed?"

"Last Friday." Quinn could see her reflection in the window, the small wince when he told her.

"These last few months, Doctor was happier than I can remember," said Sarah. "I credit Tod with that. Do you know how Tod found Doctor? He saw his picture in an old magazine and tracked him down, just wanting to meet him. Isn't that amazing? Doctor told me himself. He was so pleased—he didn't think he took a very good picture."

Quinn looked at Jen but she didn't get it either.

"The two of them liked to talk about old movies." That made her smile for an instant. "Doctor didn't much care for the studios or the stars, but he did love the movies they made. Isn't that curious? He said it proved you *could* make a silk purse out of a sow's ear."

"Were you there when they had these conversations?" asked Jen.

"No, dear. Doctor was a very private man. He did tell me that Tod knew a great deal about the old days, 'the Golden Age of Hollywood,' Doctor called it. Before all this nudity and violence and the moral rot. Doctor was very impressed with Tod. We both were. It's very rare to meet a young person with an appreciation for real values."

"Did the doctor have any visitors besides Tod in the last few weeks?" said Quinn. "A big, middle-aged man with a crewcut? Big like a football player. Did *he* ever come by?"

Sarah turned away from the window and faced Quinn. "No one like that ever came to the door. Did he kill Tod?"

"Yes."

"I hope you find him," Sarah said somberly, her eyes bright.

"I hope so, too, Miss Cranston," said Quinn.

"I want him to die in the gas chamber," she said. "Screaming. Strangling on his own scalding vomit."

Quinn stared back at her. It was an effort to keep her in focus—her dark gray dress was part of the shadows in the room.

"Is it possible the man with the crewcut might have made an appointment with the doctor without you knowing?" Jen said. "As a patient?"

Sarah shook her head. "Doctor didn't have many patients. None, really. The studio didn't need him anymore, and he never built a regular practice. He did abortions for a while, but then the courts made it legal, and he didn't even have that. I think Doctor liked it better in the old days, the patients sneaking in to see him, the fear, the silence. He didn't have a bedside manner, none at all."

"The doctor was having money troubles, wasn't he?" said Quinn. "Overdue bills . . . taxes . . . he must have been anxious."

She patted her bun, reassuring herself that it was in place. "Some time ago he put most of his money into those junk bonds . . . he liked investments, but they didn't like him. Then last year his insurance company went belly-up. Can you imagine that? Who ever heard of an insurance company going broke?" She smoothed her skirt, as though reassuring herself. "First the banks, then the insurance companies. All gone."

"Was Tod giving Dr. McChesney money?" said Jen.

"I didn't ask."

"Miss Cranston . . ." said Quinn, "I don't mean to pry, but what happens to you?"

"How very kind of you to ask." Sarah had a resolute Yankee jawline. She looked at Jen, indicating Quinn with a nod. *"This one has a good bedside manner, not at all like Doctor. I could tell that the first time I saw him, before he said a word. I'm a very good judge of character."* Her thin mouth puckered, but it was nothing like a kiss. "I can't tell about you," she said to Jen.

"I know that Tod and the doctor became friends," Quinn said gently, "but I think the reason Tod first sought the doctor out was because of something the doctor knew. A patient he had a long time ago. Someone from the golden days. Is there anything you can tell us that might help?"

Sarah smoothed her gray hair, patted it in place. "All I know is that Doctor had been sad for a long time, and Tod made him happy. The two of them would stay up half the night watching television. . . ." She pointed to an empty place on the bookcase. "That's where Doctor kept his TV set," she said. "Miranda took it two days after he died." She shook her head. "You should have heard the way Doctor and Tod laughed. . . . like a couple of schoolboys. Such beautiful laughter, I could hear it right through the door."

"The doctor was in love with him, wasn't he?" said Jen.

The room was so still that Quinn lost track of the time. Jen's question hung in the air like perfume.

"That's not something he and I ever discussed," Sarah said at last. "There was no need to. I just know that it had been a long time since I heard Doctor laugh . . . and Tod changed that. He was a wonderful young man. He brought me flowers. That very first day he showed up at the door asking to see Doctor, he brought white roses. So polite. Even after Tod knew he was welcome here and didn't need my approval, he still brought white roses. Now . . ." She turned away, back toward the weeping willow, her yellowed nails digging into the palms of her hands. "Now, they're both dead."

Chapter 32

Quinn drove through the winding streets of Palos Verdes, Jen beside him, not speaking, both of them happy to be out of Dr. McChesney's office. He felt like he had been breathing bad air for the last two hours, the exhalation of a dusty life. He pushed down the accelerator and the Jeep surged forward, the night wind rushing past, carrying the scent of eucalyptus and saltwater.

He offered to put the top up, but Jen waved away the offer. She sat straight up, combing her hair out with her fingers, shaking her head, letting the wind blow through her. Beyond the trees, Quinn could see helicopters crisscrossing the sky over East L.A., searchlights flickering in the distance—nine o'clock and nothing's well. He wished the two of them could keep driving and never stop.

Instead, they went straight to Belmont Shore to check on Cliff, see if the Bel-Shore Inn was living up to his high standards. When they dropped him off at the hotel that afternoon, he was calling room service for a sunlamp and a pitcher of martinis.

Cliff was barricaded in his room—he made Quinn slip his press pass under the door before letting them in. They stayed longer than they intended but Cliff still got annoyed when they got up to go. They left him stretched out in his swimsuit on the bed, blinking under the ultraviolet glare, a martini glass balanced precariously on his chest as he watched a Marx Brothers comedy. *La Dolce Vita*, 80-proof. Quinn heard the locks clicking into place before they reached the elevator.

He headed toward the freeway by the ocean route, pointing

out the offshore oil platforms to Jen, the artificial islands illuminated like birthday cakes. The platforms were four-story
geometric structures, neat rectangles painted in soft pastels
of blue and yellow, all heavy equipment out of sight. David
Hockney would have loved the view, even if the Sierra Club
didn't.

Quinn drove slowly along the shore, unwilling to let the
evening end. Sand blew across the road. There were no other
cars. Something had happened between them in these last few
days. . . . Love was at the heart of Tod's murder, love in all its
forms. Love was at the heart of the mystery, and as they drew
closer to that mystery, the intimacy between them grew.

The two of them had walked through Cliff's dark house
together, walked on tiptoe, every sense alert. He had smelled
her clean sweat as she edged past him, dust motes sparkling
around her in the dim light, so aroused by her that he could
hardly breathe. Sharing fear was more intimate than sex. Sometimes.

They watched the flickering lights on the offshore rigs,
neither of them speaking, the night alive with stars, clusters
and constellations like a storm over the Pacific. He didn't need
to see the Cheshire moon. He could feel that icy grin looking
over his shoulder. The realization of danger came a moment
later—he shivered in the warm air, knowing how close he had
come to taking Jen back to her apartment.

He leaned toward her. "You can't go home," he said. "I
don't know what I was thinking. The man with the crewcut, he
followed me to Cliff's from *SLAP*. He might have seen you
drop me off in the parking lot." She moved closer to him. "My
home address isn't listed with the Department of Motor Ve-
hicles, but if he saw your license plate, he can find out where
you live. He could be waiting for you."

Her eyes were wide but she didn't waver.

"I'll drive you home tomorrow, when there's light," said
Quinn. "Let me take you to the Bel-Shore Inn now."

Jen shook her head no.

"Do you have a friend you can stay with tonight? Someone
you can trust?"

She nodded.

"Good. Give me directions," he said.

"Oh," she said, her eyes half-closed, letting the wind rush through her hair, "I think you know the way."

He could barely hear her over the noise of the engine. Sand swirled across the street like stinging rain. He drove to his place, speeding all the way.

Chapter 33

Quinn opened the front door to the cottage, looked around before walking in. These days he left a light on when he went out. He wished he had also started picking up after himself. He made a quick survey, gathering socks, T-shirts, pants, a half-eaten sandwich, and a stack of newspapers. It was almost midnight.

Jen sat at his desk—the only organized area in the room—enjoying his discomfort. The desk filled one whole side of the cottage, eight feet of burled walnut, one clean slab of wood, burnished to a dark luster. Rachel had bought it for him shortly after they were married, paid for it out of her own account, and refused to tell him how much it cost. He knew even before he asked that it was too good for him. He loved that desk. Jen sat there, her long fingers resting lightly on the rich grain.

Quinn walked over to the desk, unlocked the bottom drawer, and took out the .357 magnum revolver. He checked to make sure it was loaded, then stuck it between the cushions of the leather reading chair. Out of sight, within easy reach. "Guns don't bother you, do they?"

"Not for a long time," Jen said quietly. "Even if they did, I saw your friend Andy's van, remember? I've got the eight-by-tens hanging in my darkroom."

He heard Katie cough, turned, and looked up at her open window, waiting. Silence. Good.

Katie got croup easily, a dry, barking cough that made her sound like a seal. If she started in her sleep, sometimes the unfamiliarity of her own voice would wake her in a panic. When she was a baby, Quinn would get up in the middle of the night with her. Her attacks were less frequent now, but Katie still kept her window open—the moist air helped.

He saw Jen watching him, and walked into the kitchen and got out the popcorn popper. The perfect host. "I've got beer? Juice? Kool-Aid with real sugar?"

"Tea?"

"Sure." He put two mugs of water into the microwave, peeked back into the room. She sat in the swivel chair, checking out his neat stacks of yellow legal-size pads on the desk, the calendar with his interviews scheduled. She had the chair tilted back, her legs swaying.

"I like your antenna," she called, pointing to the gold-lamé brassiere draped over the rabbit ears of the TV.

Quinn turned off the overhead light, left the room illuminated by the bare bulb in the kitchen. "I was doing a piece on Madonna impersonators. You want to borrow it?" He brought her the tea, took a sip from his own.

Jen wrinkled her nose over the mug, sniffing.

"Sassafras," he confirmed. "Tastes like root beer. My daughter . . . it's the only kind of tea I've got."

She took a sip, raised an eyebrow.

He went back to the kitchen and threw a handful of popcorn into the hot-air popper. He stayed in the kitchen, watching the kernels bounce against the plastic housing of the popper. He wanted to join her, but the room was so small he wasn't sure there was room for the both of them in there.

When he brought in the bowl of popcorn, she was sitting on the sofa with her legs tucked under her. The black tank top showed off her shoulders, her collarbone a delicate curve. The baggy black trousers showed nothing. Her boots were on the floor, laces undone, socks sticking out of them. He wished he could see her bare feet.

His sheets were hanging out the sides of the sofa bed, a queen-size geometric print by that Italian designer, a pattern of contrasting grids—it looked like the couch had sprung a leak into Mathemagic Land. Crossing the room he had a choice of sitting on the sofa or in the reading chair. He chose the sofa, kicking off his boots too, putting the bowl of popcorn between them.

"You don't have women over very often, do you?"

"Hey, this is Casa del Love Nest."

She glanced around. "You should get a small lamp for atmosphere, maybe some candles. You might think about putting a screen or curtain in front of the kitchen to hide the stove and sink—*that* doesn't put anybody in the mood. The hardwood floors are elegant but too stark; you should have a rug to break it up, add some texture."

"Don't stop now. I'm taking notes."

"I think living behind your ex and your kid is kinky. Either that or you still want to be married."

"I *do* still want to be married," he snapped. "I just don't want to be married to Rachel."

"I'm only trying to help."

"How's the popcorn, Ms. Takamura? Did I do that right? Too much salt? Not enough? A little to the left? A little harder? Faster?"

"I knew it." Jen shook her head. "You come to my place and snoop through *my* personal things, but I make a few harmless observations and you get all huffy." She dug into the popcorn. She ate each kernel individually, probably chewed it twenty times before swallowing. "We're working together now—we should be comfortable with each other."

He reached into the bowl, grazed her hand, and retreated.

"Do I make you nervous?"

"Absolutely."

"No, really?"

"Really."

"You're honest." She smiled, nibbling her popcorn. "Just like Miss Cranston said."

"She said I had a good bedside manner too."

"I wouldn't know."

They sat on the couch, listening to each other crunch popcorn, slouched in opposite corners, their knees brushing as they shifted position.

She watched him over the rim of her mug, half her face illuminated by the kitchen light, the other half in shadow. He had no idea what she was thinking. Jen was close enough to touch, but utterly beyond reach.

You forget the things you missed the most—you had to, or go mad with longing. Jen reminded him of all that he had lost since Groggins killed Doreen at the minimart, killed her right in front of him, making sure that Quinn was part of it. Blood enough to go around.

There's a certain innocence that we all keep—no matter what evil we do, we believe in our own good intentions. Groggins had taken that away from him. Shown him the true value of such intentions.

Looking at Jen made him miss a part of himself that had died, lost that afternoon while the cameras rolled.

Jen leaned toward him. "What is it?" She took his hand. "You look so sad."

"I'm fine."

She shook her head.

"I'm tired." He laid his head back against the sofa. He wished he was alone so he could cry. "I've been going full blast since Andy called Friday night . . . so much has happened, and it's catching up with me."

"He was a good friend, wasn't he?"

"Yes." Quinn thought of Andy's impenetrable speed-rap tutorials on particle physics and non-Euclidian geometry, Andy interrupting himself only long enough to offer Quinn a piece of his lastest scam. Something on the ground floor. "You'd have liked him; he was a Mensa member too. He passed the entrance test, anyway, but I'm sure he never paid his dues." Except for maybe at the end.

Jen plucked at the end of the sheet that trailed out of the sofa bed. "The man who killed Andy . . . did you really think I was in danger tonight? In my own apartment?"

"I don't know." Quinn watched the sheet slide back and forth between her slender fingers. "He's out there, though, circling, waiting for an opening. I'm sure of it." His eyes strayed to the revolver poking from the leather chair. Two steps away. He pushed his hair back with both hands. "Yesterday he followed me from the magazine parking lot to Cliff's house." He sighed. "I didn't see a thing. We're not getting any closer to him—he's getting closer to us."

She smoothed out the sheet, flattened it against her leg,

watching him. "So what do we do now? Tell Morales about Dr.
McChesney? Maybe he'll reopen the investigation."

"We're on our own," said Quinn. "I can't ask Morales for
any more favors. I called him last night to find out if Tod's
movie magazines had been inventoried. I wanted to go through
them, see if I could spot what caught Tod's attention."

"Good idea. When do we start?"

"We don't. Morales said Draveki brought the magazines
back to the station and left them for the uniforms. They're all
over the precinct by now, pages tacked up on bulletin
boards . . . Morales didn't even sound mad. He said it was a
closed case, and what did I expect?—'Boys will be boys.' "

"We should ask Sissy about the magazines," said Jen. "Tod
would have told her if he found anything—he would have been
proud of himself. Talk shows are always looking for celebrity
scandal, even if it's twenty years old. That's the kind of hustle
that would have impressed Sissy enough to give him a promotion."

"I still don't trust her," said Quinn.

"Strong women scare you." Jen smiled. "I like her. I can't
wait to go out to her ranch tomorrow." She yawned, demurely
covered it with her palm. The delicacy of her movements never
ceased to get to him, the way she scratched her earlobe with
the backs of her nails, not pulling roughly on herself. He felt
bulky and awkward next to her. She stretched and winced,
rubbing her neck.

"What's the matter?"

"I need to see my chiropractor," she groaned, rolling her
shoulders in the tank top, her skin the color of warm amber.
"Lugging around cameras all day throws me out."

"Let me help." Quinn slid directly behind her on the couch,
turned her around so that she faced directly away from him.
"Relax," he said, kneading her bare shoulders, gently working
the heel of his hand into her trapezius muscles at the base of
her neck. He sat cross-legged behind her, his knees pressed
against her hips.

She sighed, and let her head droop forward—his thumbs
made small circles along her spine. She smelled like honey. He
could see delicate black hairs along the nape of her neck. He

squeezed harder and she gave a soft cry—"Sorry," he whispered, lightly rubbing the sensitive spot until she relaxed, deep-breathing.

He imagined what it would be like to feel her breathing against him, their arms wrapped around each other, mouths pressed together. . . . He softly kissed the back of her neck before he realized what he had done. "I'm sorry," he said, pulling away. "That wasn't right. I'm sorry, Jen. I shouldn't have done that."

She stayed nestled against his kneecaps. "It was a nice kiss. Don't apologize." She slowly rolled her neck from side to side. "That's much better now. Thanks." She swiveled around on the couch and faced him. She placed her hands on his cheeks and slowly kissed him, the tip of her tongue sliding into his mouth, tasting him for one long, sweet moment and then she was staring into his eyes. "That was also a nice kiss." She smiled and he knew that was as far as things were going. "We should get some rest."

Quinn didn't say anything, he just nodded—he wanted to keep the sensation of her inside his mouth for as long as possible.

He got extra blankets from the closet, turned around, and saw that she had pulled open the sofa bed. He watched as she turned her back to him and started unbuttoning her clothes, then tossed her a blanket.

Jen nodded in the dim light, wriggling under the covers. He sat in the leather chair, the blanket over his shoulders, trying not to look. She brushed her hair off her cheek. The sheets rustled as she shifted position, one leg peeking out from the covers.

He felt himself stiffen, but couldn't turn away. He pulled the blanket around him, wanting to say something, but not trusting his instincts, the moment ebbing away with every beat of his heart.

He was too old for her—she had already made that clear. He had an ex-wife and a child and responsibilities . . . she was free of guilt, free of everything, free in a way he would never be again. He closed his eyes, listening to her breathing, lulled by the soothing rhythm, drifting with her, sinking deeper now, barely conscious, the blanket warm around him—it was like she was right next to him. He reached for her as he fell asleep.

O

Quinn jerked awake, the blanket damp with sweat. He picked up the revolver, listening. The only sound in the room was the clock ticking. Two-thirty. Jen lay curled up on the couch in one of his T-shirts, the sheet twisted around her.

He pushed his covers off, got up from the chair, and walked quietly through the room, wearing only the jeans he had gone to sleep in.

The door creaked as he scampered out onto the porch. Cricket sounds in the grass, wind in the trees. He checked Katie's window, pulled himself up the tree to make sure. She slept peacefully, two fingers in her mouth. He climbed down and started a circuit of the house.

The night had grown overcast—that sliver of moon was hidden behind clouds now, the stars barely visible. The fog was rolling in from the sea, hanging heavy in the air. He and Rachel should have installed security lights for the yard, floodlit the whole area.

He squinted, trying to see, as he checked the doors and ground-floor windows, still listening. He squeezed the grip of the revolver so hard that his hand ached, and he had to keep wiping his sweaty palm on his jeans.

The fog was even thicker on this side of the house, where the ground sloped down and held the moisture—a pool of deeper darkness where the streetlights couldn't reach. He moved slowly across the grass, straining to hear.

He heard movement at his elbow, whirled, and shouted "Freeze" as he pointed the gun into the shadows.

Two yellow eyes stared back at him. Blinked. The Barrys' neutered tom jumped down from the windowsill and padded off.

Quinn exhaled. Freeze? Great. Book 'em, Danno. He tried to laugh, but his teeth were chattering. It wasn't cold.

Chapter 34

"Ummm," said Sissy, under the touch of John Stratton's powerful hands. She closed her eyes, her cheek pressed into the sheared sheepskin as he kneaded her full hips, digging in. She smelled lanolin and the vanilla massage oil.

A fire blazed in one corner of the bedroom, throwing off waves of heat so that the room felt like a hothouse. Sissy was a great pink orchid, blooming in the crackling warmth. "Ummm."

It was almost 3 A.M. They had gone to bed early tonight, but she had awakened out of a sound sleep, terrified. John tried to quiet her, but her muscles were cramping so painfully she couldn't bear to be held. He knew what to do—he got out the massage oil and built a fire.

"It's all my fault," he said softly, his voice so sad that she was glad she couldn't see his face.

"No," she said. "I only got myself to blame." She tried to relax as he worked on her, thinking of the way the studio audience had cheered for John when he appeared at the end of the show last weekend. "Governor Stratton!" they had cheered. She purred, feeling John's strong hands sliding across her back. She imagined the inauguration party at the governor's mansion, elegant gowns spinning across the floor, then Liston crashing through the French doors, covered in blood, falling at her feet. Every head in the room turned toward her, the air filled with their buzzing voices as Detective Morales snapped rusty handcuffs on her white wrists and led her away.

"You're thinking about it again, aren't you?" John's hands stopped. "I should have never suggested calling this Liston fella. I should have—"

"Hush."

Liston *was* out of control, a danger to everyone around him. She was going to have to keep him away from Quinn and Jen—she didn't want anybody else killed. Liston was a wild one, for certain. Last night . . . jacking him off behind the soda fountain . . . "Ummm." She smiled into the warm sheepskin. She should have picked up the X rays herself, but John said it was best to send someone like Liston, someone who wouldn't take no for an answer. What made Tod think he could get away with it? She groaned out loud.

"Am I hurting you?"

Two months ago Tod had walked into her office, all nervous-like, and said that he had uncovered something "highly embarrassing," and if she wanted it to *stay* covered, he wanted to be more than her lover. He wanted an executive position. She slapped him so hard her hand hurt. Then they fucked their way across the office, messed up the sofa pillows good—fucked all morning until the overnight ratings arrived. God, she loved a greedy man.

Stratton's fingers ground into her constricted muscles, releasing pain and fear—she could taste it at the back of her throat like sour vomit. Okay, Sissy girl, she told herself, you've been scared before and you've never let it stop you. Twenty years ago she had been arrested for passing bad checks, taken to the New Orleans lockup, and deloused like a common whore. She had wet her pants and the booking matron cursed her, and wouldn't let her change. *That* was scared.

By the time Sissy finished her thirty-day sentence, the warden was writing her letters of reference, even bought her a new dress for her interview at a local radio station. The booking matron still sent birthday cards—last year she had started a *Straight Talk with Sissy* fan club at the jail.

Liston was the only thing connecting her to Tod's murder, and he wouldn't go to the cops—he was too much in love with her for that. She thought of Liston's face last night, the way he snarled as he came, like it hurt.

Stratton leaned into the backs of her thighs, massaging her plump flesh with the heels of his hands. More oil, still warm from the microwave. He basted her like a Thanksgiving turkey.

"Ummm, that's the spot."

Stratton laughed at her pleasure, a low, easy chuckle as his hands walked across her skin. The fire crackled, embers smacking against the screen.

People would be arriving at the ranch tomorrow for the beginning of the four-day shoot, a prime-time party for Sissy and her friends—the best guests from the last three seasons, celebrities and stars and just-folks, all there to help her celebrate her fortieth birthday.

It seemed like only last week she'd turned sixteen. She was still married to Talbert then, but already knew it was a mistake—she was taking a secretarial correspondence course, having the lessons sent to a girlfriend's house because Talbert didn't hold with women getting an education.

She wondered what that ol' boy was doing. Probably still driving a truck with a six-pack under the seat. Still slicking back his pompadour with Wildroot cream oil. She thought of the first time they made butt love . . . the way Talbert ran a hand through his greasy hair, lubricated her with Wildroot . . . He told her that's what Elvis did, honest-ta-God, he heard it from his cousin in Nashville. He probably believed it, but she didn't. Talbert was lots older, had been in the army and married twice before, but even then, she was smarter than he was.

Talbert most likely didn't even have hair anymore—that was twenty years ago. If he still had hair, he was still combing it into a pompadour, still using Wildroot and Elvis to get where he wanted to go. If he'd been smarter he'd have knowed he didn't need Elvis.

John was massaging her feet now, taking each toe in his big hands, starting at the foot and working toward each pink tip. Slowly. One by one. "Ummm." Each time a toe cracked he chuckled again. When he was done with her toes he started on the feet themselves. She was proud of her feet, they were tiny and well shaped, soft and pedicured. Not a callus or a rough edge on them.

She would have liked to run for governor herself, but the pollsters said she was too flamboyant, too outspoken. She had been pardoned for the bad-check charge, but some people would never forgive nor forget. To hell with them.

Every day for as far back as she could remember she had made lists of things to do to improve herself. She practiced grammar in the mirror and French kissing on her hand. She had coffee with the supervisor who talked to her boobs—that got her from the secretarial pool to *Million-Dollar-Movie* gal. She left breathy, anonymous messages on the anchorman's home-phone machine—that got him divorced and her promoted to late-night news.

Keep climbing, girl, because it's a long way down. That was her motto.

Warm oil squirted across her broad back, ran down her spine, and puddled along her tailbone. John leaned over her, using both hands, making wide, sweeping motions, her skin warming from the friction and the glow of the fire.

She hid her face in the soft fleecy wool as John entered her. She imagined herself dancing across the polished parquet floor of the governor's mansion. Barefoot.

Chapter 35

"**Y**our daughter hates me."

"Don't start on that again, will you?" said Quinn. It was late morning, Thursday, as he balanced the Thomas brothers' mapbook on his knees, and made the turnoff onto the narrow backroad to the Big J Ranch. "She doesn't hate you. She's just . . . cautious around strangers. She didn't expect to see you in my bed."

"What was I supposed to do? She walks into your place this morning, no knock—"

"She has a key," said Quinn. "She doesn't have to knock." The road wound through walls of trees, dry brown underbrush on both sides.

"Daddy's little girl," Jen teased him, "I can hear her wrangling a Porsche out of you for a graduation present, a baby-blue convertible. You'll be snapping away with an Instamatic and telling everyone in earshot, 'That's my kitten.' "

They looked at each other and burst out laughing. It felt good. For the last half hour Quinn had felt a growing uneasiness, a foreboding that deepened as they neared the Stratton ranch. They had picked up clothes and camera equipment that morning at Jen's apartment, Quinn talking loudly to nonexistent cops as he opened the door, the .357 magnum resting in his hand.

The apartment was empty, no sign of a visitor—he and Jen had joked about it driving toward the ranch, even as he kept a steady watch in the rearview mirror.

They left the freeway for progressively smaller roads, the conversation dwindling, until they stared at the eroding landscape, and kept their thoughts to themselves. It was only when he announced that there hadn't been another car behind them for the last twenty miles that they relaxed. She held a camera at arm's length, snapping shots of the two of them mugging, cheek-to-cheek on the open road.

John Stratton's Big J was a two-thousand-acre spread at the eastern edge of Orange County, rugged terrain dotted with steep ravines and dense scrub—canyon country, butted up against the Cleveland National Forest. Stratton had bought the range for ten dollars an acre when he got the part of U.S. Marshal Chance Tyrone in *Dodge City Standoff*. The property was fifty miles from the ocean and fifty years behind—no subdivisions, no strip malls, no string bikinis. Most of the locals thought the country had gone steadily downhill ever since Ike.

"Slow down," said Jen, putting aside her camera.

The Jeep came to a stop at the wooden gate blocking the road. Two uniformed security guards flanked the way, one of them holding a clipboard.

"*SLAP* magazine," said Quinn.

The guard stared at the guest list, ran a black-leather-gloved finger down the clipboard. His lips moved as he silently read the names. Quinn could see his own impatient reflection in the guard's mirrored shades. "You ain't here," the man grunted.

"Check again," said Quinn.

The other, smaller guard walked over and stood directly in front of the Jeep, laid his hand on the butt of his holstered pistol. Same plain blue uniform as the one who stood alongside, same jackboots and mirrored shades—Terminator, Jr.

The guard with the clipboard leaned against Quinn's door. "You deaf? I said you ain't here. This is a private road, so turn around!"

"Try looking again." Jen smiled sweetly at him from the passenger side. "Please, Officer?"

The guard came slightly to attention, nodded at her, and started down the list again.

"You two must be hot, standing out here in the sun all day," Jen said.

"This ain't nothing, ma'am," said the guard with the clipboard, jutting out his chin. "We're trained for anything." His finger jabbed the list of names. "Whattaya know." He swung open the gate.

Three hot-air balloons drifted in the distance, red, white, and blue above the ranch house.

As they got closer Quinn could see a large, rambling two-story hacienda, an imposing structure of adobe brick and pine logs, red-tile roof. This was what the Santa Fe–style crap that was crawling all over Newport Beach was trying to imitate, but the hacienda was the real thing, already old when Stratton bought the land.

According to *TV Guide,* in the five years since he had married Sissy, Stratton had poured over $9 million into extensive renovations and new construction on the ranch. Quinn counted one, two, three large outbuildings surrounding the ranch house, a couple of barns, corrals, and a man-made lake.

There was a parking lot off to one side of the road, half-filled with media vans and expensive cars. Another uniformed security guard directed them to the parking entrance like he was parting the Red Sea. Quinn eased in next to a white Rolls with smoked windows and a flat tire.

A young woman in a long, frilly gingham dress hurried over with a clipboard. She had a nametag that said, "Howdy, my name is PENNY." "You're . . . ?" She looked from Quinn to Jen.

"Jen Takamura, *SLAP* magazine."

The woman glanced at the clipboard, said, "You're in the West Bunkhouse, rooms Hopalong Cassidy and Roy Rogers."

"Pardon me?" said Quinn.

Penny handed him a schedule of events and a photocopied map of the grounds, and pointed out the West Bunkhouse. "It's right over there, rooms one and two. Keys in the door." She spotted a blue news van pulling into the lot. "Cocktail party at three, poolside!" she chirped, and hurried off.

They carried their bags to the West Bunkhouse, a four-unit log cabin, each with its own bathroom. He left Jen on her doorstep, then went into his room next door, closed the blinds, and turned up the air conditioner. He bounced on the double bed, listening to the shower running in Jen's room.

He tried to pretend that the two of them were on vacation, but it didn't work. Something bad was coming. He knew it. He sat there on the bed with the air conditioner humming away, and waited for the man with the crewcut to kick in the door. Quinn hoped the man would try it. He'd put six bullets into his head before he stepped across the threshold. A nice tight pattern. Just like Esteban had taught him so many years ago.

No. He didn't want to meet the man with the crewcut. He wanted to bang on the wall, tell Jen to grab her things, and pile into the Jeep. The two of them would go someplace where they didn't have to check the rearview mirror.

He didn't knock. She wouldn't leave, anyway. Instead, he got out a small gray box and swept the room for bugs, methodically pacing off the floor, the walls, the ceiling. Nothing. Nobody was listening. He smiled. Andy put the gray boxes together in his spare time—said they were better than anything he could buy commercially. The Hopalong Cassidy Room was clean. Thanks, pal.

He peeled off the shirt he was wearing, put on the oversized sports shirt with the dinosaur heads printed all over it. He looked in the mirror; Tyrannosaurus Rex roared from his chest. Katie had given it to him last Christmas—his lucky shirt. It couldn't hurt. He stayed with the jeans. He lay back on the bed and stared at the oil painting of Hoppy on his white stallion . . . what was that horse's name? He wished Napitano were here to see the bunkhouse with its split-log walls and wagon-wheel light fixture—the Littlest Buckeroo would be in cowboy heaven.

From the bed he could see out a large picture window: There was nothing out there but thousands of acres of raw acreage, trees and more trees, the beginning of the national forest that bordered Stratton's Big J Ranch. It made Quinn miss the beach.

There was a knock and Quinn turned, noticed the door to the adjoining room, and cautiously unlocked it. Jen stood there, hands on her hips, hair wet. She had changed into baggy black-checked shorts and a white silk blouse, the same black combat boots polished to a high shine. She was using the darker lip gloss that Sissy had suggested. It *did* bring out the green of her eyes.

She checked out the dinosaurs snarling across his chest. "*Nice* shirt." She was serious.

"Thanks." He looked into her room. It was much like his: white-pine desk and dresser, telephone, minirefrigerator, a couple of raw-wood chairs. Rustic, except for the color TV—Sissy probably couldn't stand the idea of one of her guests not being able to watch her show.

He walked through her room with the bug-detector. She didn't say a thing until he told her it was all clear.

"Did you get a decoder ring with that?" she asked.

"You have any heavy tape?" He was still jumpy.

She popped open one of her camera cases, handed him a roll of duct tape, then followed him back to his room.

He got on the floor, tore off a strip of tape, and attached his gun to the underside of the desk chair. "Just in case," he said, pushing the chair back into place. "I wanted you to know where the gun was. It's loaded. You should be able to pull it free in one motion—"

The phone rang and Quinn jumped. He picked it up, listened. "Nino, I was just thinking of you," he said, watching Jen roll her eyes.

"Of course you were, dear boy," gushed Napitano. "I did that favor you asked me."

"That was fast." Quinn had spoken to him only that morning.

"Always eat dessert first," said Napitano, "you never know when you may drop dead."

"You saw the coroner's report?" said Quinn. Cliff had been certain, but Quinn wasn't convinced.

"It took some doing," said Napitano. "After twenty years the records are put on microfiche, and are not so readily available. I have some standing in local government—"

"I get it, Nino. *Molto grazie.* Now could you tell me what the report showed?"

"My good friend the county clerk sent me a fax. The report was very clear, very complete—Elizabeth 'Betty' Andaluse died from injuries sustained in a fire. No indication of foul play." Napitano's breathing was audible over the phone. "Quinn?"

"I'm still here."

"Yes," said Napitano, "I too am disappointed. Stratton was my boyhood hero, but I would have loved nothing more than proof that he murdered his first wife . . . and perhaps these others last week. Ah well, we must take what fate gives us. You have the rumor of Sissy's infidelity from this ex-producer of hers . . . why not follow that? Murder is good, but adultery is better. Talk to people who work for Sissy—let them know we will pay handsomely for information. Reliable. I do not like being sued. Reliable. Find me a fucking, a *good* fucking, and we will put Sissy's picture on the cover."

"No thanks, Nino. I don't sniff out bedrooms."

Nino clucked into the receiver. "Oh, dear boy, you are missing one of life's great pleasures."

Quinn heard the dial tone, and hung up the receiver. He wanted to take a scrub brush to his ear. Scrub out Nino's mind too.

"Well?" said Jen.

"Cliff was right," said Quinn. "Stratton didn't kill Betty Andaluse. So it wasn't her X rays Tod got from the doctor. If Tod was blackmailing Sissy, that's not what he was using."

"Maybe he wasn't blackmailing her at all," said Jen, exasperated. "There were plenty of people who had reason to kill Tod. Boyfriends. Husbands. Women he used once and threw away. So he sent flowers, big deal. There was probably a waiting list to kill him."

Quinn nodded wearily. "We might as well go back to the city. This is a waste of time now."

"So what?" said Jen. "What's wrong with having a little fun while we can? It's been almost a week since your friend was murdered, and neither of us has had a break. The man with the crewcut will still be out there when we get back. We'll find him."

She put her arms around his neck—more tender than passionate. "The ranch is sealed off and crawling with security, why not take advantage of it, relax and enjoy ourselves? Eat, drink, and take pictures, and we hit Napitano up for overtime. In a couple days we'll start in again. We'll get back Tod's movie mags from the cops, page by page if we have to. I don't intend to walk away—let's just take a break. I've spent more time in war zones than you have, Quinn. You *need* R and R. Rest and Relaxation." She smiled at him. "Is that so bad?"

Chapter 36

Q uinn and Jen didn't need
the diagram that Penny in the gingham dress had given them
to find the cocktail party—all they had to do was follow the
laughter, the tinkle of toasting glassware. The pool was behind
the hacienda, Olympic size, surrounded by umbrella tables and
vaguely familiar faces. There was that young, hot comedian,
two or three soap-opera stars, and the singer who won a
country-music Grammy last year.

Three different camera crews covered the festivities, their
steady cams tracking the guests like mosquitoes. The buoyant
host of *Entertainment Now!* stood in the corner with his sound
man; he kept flubbing his voice-overs, muttering shit-shit-shit.
His toupee was crooked too.

Sissy and John Stratton held court at the far end of the
pool, Sissy in a pink sundress and a floppy pink straw hat.
Stratton wore faded jeans and cowboy boots, a denim shirt with
what must be pearl buttons flashing in the sunlight. Trademark
white cowboy hat. Sissy waved at Quinn and Jen—they waved
back.

Someone was calling Jen's name. Some guy in a ratty black
suit and a Dodgers cap. A cigarette holder? Oh yeah, Christian
Smith, the wunderkind of the Cannes Film Festival, the ultra-
low-budget director whose overuse of the wide-angle lens had
supposedly reinvented the slasher film. Quel genius!

Jen took Smith's photo. "I'm going to make the rounds,"
she said to Quinn, moving off, a couple of cameras slung around
her neck, rolls of film in her pockets. She liked to work light—
a couple of cameras, no tripod, no reflectors. Smith ran up to
her, kissed her on both cheeks. She winked at Quinn, and

headed toward the middle of the pool where a bunch of young guys were playing water polo at a hundred decibels.

Quinn strolled along the edges of the party, nodding to everybody. He was trying to take Jen's advice to kick back and enjoy himself, but it was impossible. He kept turning things over, trying to see if he had missed something. A waiter pointed out one of Sissy's production assistants, a short, stocky woman in a pink satin STRAIGHT TALK WITH SISSY! jacket.

"You're Press, yeah?" she said as he walked up to her, before he could say a word.

"Uh . . . yes."

"I thought so." She beamed behind her round glasses. "You're not good-looking enough to be on-air, and you're not dressed well enough to be a studio exec. You might be a roadie, you have the build for it, but you look too intelligent. Had to be a reporter." She was proud of herself, swaying next to him. "Am I talking too much? I'm a little bombed . . . it's hot and I asked the bartender for a rum-and-diet-Coke, easy on the rum, but I think he . . . am I talking too much?"

"No, you're talking just right. My name's Quinn; I'm writing a feature on Sissy for *SLAP*."

"I *love* that magazine!" She caught herself, checking him out more closely. "You staff or just freelancing?"

"Staff."

"Great!" She shook his hand, harder this time. "I'm Rita Burke; I'm . . . in production." Her face fell for a moment. "I'm not sure I should be talking with you. I mean, I should clear it with the boss."

Quinn grabbed a couple of pâté things from a waiter, offered her one.

She shook her head. "I didn't mean anything negative, when I said you weren't good-looking enough for on-air. Gosh, who is? You're not going to put that in your article, are you? I wouldn't want to get in trouble."

"Don't worry about it, Rita." Quinn patted her arm. "I'm looking for somebody . . . I'm not sure if he's here—middle-aged guy, very big, powerful. He's got reddish hair he wears in this bristly crewcut like a college jock. You seen him?"

"What's his name?"

"Now I'm the one who's embarrassed." Quinn smiled. "I

lost my notes and can't remember. He might have been a football star at one time."

"Was he a guest on one of her shows?" Rita scrunched her face up, thinking. "Sissy likes athletes—she has lots of them on as guests. She says they fill the screen *emotionally*. Is that too technical for your article?"

"Do you remember this man? Bristly red crewcut?"

"Nope." Rita shook her head. "I can ask around, though. Sissy would know. She's got a photographic mind."

"Thanks anyway."

"You sure he's going to be here? I've seen the guest list, but she keeps adding people. Which is great, don't get me wrong. You hear about the latest numbers? Donahue must be crapping his pants." She fanned herself with her hand. "I *am* talking too much."

"I do it all the time," said Quinn. "Nice meeting you." He passed through four or five clusters of conversation, then spotted Jen sitting on the side of the pool, her bare feet splashing in the water, talking to two of the water-polo players.

"Quinn!" Sissy called, beckoning him over. Nancy Tyler-Tuck from Channel 6 had joined her and Stratton, each of them balancing a plate full of jumbo shrimp. "You having a good time, darlin'?" asked Sissy. She dunked Shamu in cocktail sauce and bit it in half, smiling as she chewed. "Where are my manners? You know Nancy, I'm sure"—Nancy Tyler-Tuck waved a shrimp at him rather than shake his hand—"and this is my husband, John Stratton. John, this here's Quinn, the magazine writer I told you about."

Stratton had a firm grip but he wasn't trying to prove anything. He was tall, six-four, six-five maybe, with a handsome, weather-beaten face and a full head of gray hair. He was in his mid-sixties, but looked like he could still do his own stunts. Honest eyes, clear and direct—you could trust him with anything. No wonder the biggest bank in the state paid him seven figures annually to be their spokesman.

Nancy Tyler-Tuck nibbled at the shrimp like she was afraid to smudge her lipstick, put down her barely touched plate. "That was so delicious, Sissy"—she preened—"I think I'm going to burst. How I envy your healthy appetite."

Sissy restrained herself. "You better clean your plate now,

Nancy," she said sweetly, "or I'm going to give them shrimps to you tomorrow morning in an enema."

Nancy Tyler-Tuck blanched. She glanced from Sissy to Stratton to Quinn, waiting for someone to laugh. "Well, uh . . . Is that the mayor I saw just walk in?" She spritzed her mouth with breath spray. "Duty calls. Ta-ta."

Sissy watched her click off in her high heels. "God, I hate a dainty eater." She gobbled down another shrimp in one bite. "Everything good in life gets you messy, you might as well dig in and go for seconds—that's my philosophy." She licked dark red cocktail sauce off her upper lip. "Never trust a bony-assed woman," she said to Quinn, "they don't know how to enjoy themselves."

"It's a bony-assed world," said Quinn.

"See, John," laughed Sissy. "I told you I liked him. He's nasty." She glanced beyond him. "I see your pretty little gal-friend is meeting the swim team. You better watch yourself," she teased. "You two should come on the show, sometime. You like that? We'll do a show on 'odd couples'—I'm just joking, don't take offense. You two would be good. Multicultural, that's what they call it, right?"

"That's what we always call it."

"You hurt his feelings, Sissy." John Stratton laid a big hand on Quinn's shoulder. "She doesn't mean any harm. She's too honest for her own good."

"That sounds funny coming from you," said Quinn. " 'The Man in the White Hat.' "

"You had a chance to look around the ranch?" said Stratton. "You should blow some of that city stink off. I stay out here as much as I can—too much traffic and craziness on the Coast. You know one of Sissy's producers was killed last week. Murdered. Terrible thing."

"There's a real crime spree going on," said Quinn. "A friend of mine was murdered just after Tod was killed. Then the other day an old pal of mine was attacked in his own home. Big ugly son of a bitch threatened his life."

Sissy shook her head. "Oh, my."

"This old pal of mine," said Quinn, "I think you know him, John. Cliff Silver."

"Cliff?" Stratton looked startled.

"Who?" asked Sissy.

"Cliff Silver," said Stratton, voice booming with pleasure. "Silver-not-Gold. I didn't know he was still alive. Damn, that's good news. You said he was attacked? He's all right, though? Good." He turned to Sissy. "Cliff was an old drinking buddy, back when I was still big box office. I'd meet him at the Brown Derby after a day's shoot and he'd be on his second pitcher of martinis, and charming the pants off the cigarette girl. Jeez, the stories he could tell, I don't know how any of us kept out of jail. He still flakking for the studios? No, what am I saying; he must be retired."

"He's retired from flakking, but he's still drinking full time."

Stratton had a good solid laugh. He stood with his thumbs hooked in his belt. The buckle was a chunk of turquoise the size of a baseball. "Give Cliff my best and tell him to give me a call."

Quinn nodded, watching Stratton's clear blue eyes.

"I'm gonna leave you two boys to talk your men-talk," said Sissy. "I got a party full of people just *waiting* to kiss my sweet butt, and I don't think I should make 'em wait a minute longer." She turned on her heel and sashayed toward the producer of *Entertainment Now!*

"She's something, isn't she?" Stratton said admiringly, watching her walk. "I never met anyone like her. Love at first sight—you hear about it, but I'm telling you, it happens."

"I believe it."

"You should have brought Cliff to the party," said Stratton. "Wouldn't that bring back memories. . . . "

"I hear rumors that you're going to announce for governor in the next few weeks," said Quinn. "Maybe you could give me an interview?"

"Who told you that?" Stratton grinned. "I'm thinking about it. Bunch of folks been after me to do it, but I haven't decided yet. It's hard to leave the ranch."

"It is pretty."

"*Pretty?* You don't know the half of it," said Stratton. "I got an idea. How 'bout I give you a personal tour of the ranch, just the two of us? What do you say? I'll pick out the most gentle horse in the barn for you." He hitched up his jeans. "You could get a head start on interviewing me. I bet you got some ideas about politics. I know I'd sure be interested in hearing 'em."

"You're talking like a politician already, John."

"That mean you'll go riding with me?"

"I'd like that," said Quinn. "First let me tell Jen where I'm going. She worries about me when I disappear."

"I know what you mean. Sissy keeps me on a short tether too."

Quinn walked over to the pool. The water-polo players were still playing footsie with Jen, and she was playing back, splashing this blond hunk with flat abdominals and eyes like glazed ham. Quinn was going to have to start working out more when this was over—he could still do one-handed push-ups, but he was starting to get thick around the middle.

"Hi," said Jen. "Sit down and keep me company."

"I can't—I'm going off with Stratton. We were talking a few minutes ago, and when I mentioned Cliff, he tensed up. Not much. A little. Maybe it was nothing."

"Why don't you stay here with me?" said Jen. "Stay out of the woods."

He ran his hand over her hair, gently squeezed her neck. She half closed her eyes. "I've got to go," he said quickly, before he wouldn't be able to leave. "I'm going to call Morales, let him know where we are. I don't want to take any chances."

"The man with the crewcut," Jen said softly. "He may have been a guest once on Sissy's show."

Quinn stared at her.

"Davis"—she nodded at the blond hunk—"he's a big fan of Sissy's, watches *Straight Talk* every day. He even arranged his classes at USC so he wouldn't miss her. I described the man Cliff told us about, and he thinks he remembers him."

"He thinks?"

"He's not sure."

"Does he remember the man's name?"

Jen shook her head. "He remembers the red hair though, and that the man was a professional football player once."

"Doesn't mean anything," he said. "I talked to one of the production assistants—she said Sissy has jocks on the show all the time. They fill the screen. *Emotionally*. I think Davis will tell you anything to keep you splashing in the pool with him."

Jen's eyes could cut glass.

He wanted to apologize. "I'm going to call Morales," said Quinn. "Then I'm going to go for a ride with Stratton. Just to be on the safe side, why don't you stay with the group—it doesn't matter which group, just don't be alone. Be part of a crowd. I'll meet you back at the bunkhouse." He'd apologize later.

She had already turned away.

Chapter 37

"Y ou doing all right back there?"
Stratton turned in the saddle. He stifled a laugh, seeing Quinn bouncing atop the gray mare as they made their way up the steep trail through the forest.

"Too many trees," grunted Quinn. "Reminds me of *Deliverance*."

The trail wound through thick stands of poplars and pines, the late-afternoon sun trickling through the branches. Buster, Stratton's golden palomino stallion, led the way, his polished hooves kicking up pinecones as they climbed.

Quinn glanced behind him but the trail was clear. There was no telling what was in the trees surrounding them.

"What are you looking for?" called Stratton. "You expecting someone?"

"You tell me."

Stratton urged Buster into a fast trot with a squeeze of his knees, riding low, as they broke free of the woods and raced to the crest of the hill. He reined Buster back onto his hind legs, wheeled around, the two of them caught in a flash of sunlight.

Quinn stared at them, mouth open at the sheer beauty of the pose. Stratton and the golden stallion had used the identical pirouette in the opening credits of his TV show, *The Lonely Badge*, but familiarity didn't lessen its impact.

They had ridden onto a high plateau midway up the mountain, the hills around them dappled with yellow and purple wildflowers—the last explosion of color before the Santa Ana winds howled in from the desert, sucking the life from everything. Stratton stretched his arms wide as Quinn rode up. "Well, what do you think?"

Quinn stiffly got down from his horse. "I think I'm going to walk back," he said, rubbing his thighs.

Stratton grinned. It was a wide-open grin, strikingly boyish in that rugged face—so perfect Quinn knew it was phony. He had interviewed actors before and the good ones always played to the camera, even when they were alone. Stratton was so good nobody thought he was acting for most of his career. A few years ago, the Academy had wised up and presented him with its Lifetime Achievement Award.

Yeah, Stratton had a great grin and a way of standing around doing nothing that made women melt. He had been watching himself on-screen for forty years—he knew what his every expression looked like, every movement, as self-aware and poised as a ballet dancer. To John Stratton the world was one vast mirror.

"What are we doing here, John?"

"It's good to get away from the womenfolk once in a while."

"Womenfolk? Yeah, circle the wagons, John."

Stratton shrugged and walked Buster across the clearing. Quinn took another look back at the trail, then followed, listening to the horse's labored breathing as they walked toward the sound of rushing water.

"Buster's over twenty years old," said Stratton. "I try to get him to slow down, but he's got the heart of a champion." He patted Buster's heaving flanks. The horse nuzzled him as he dropped the reins to let him graze. "If there's a God in heaven, Buster's going to die in full gallop."

The stream sprang from a source higher up the mountain, cutting its way down the plateau in a loud, icy rush. Stratton picked his way down the smooth rocks, jumping agilely from one to another, until he sat on a flattened boulder at the very edge of the water. He stretched out, propped his bootheels up, and beckoned to Quinn.

Quinn eased himself down the streambed, almost slipping on the wet rocks. The .357 magnum was tucked in the inside pocket of his blue nylon flight jacket, his whole left side bruised from the heavy gun bouncing against his ribs.

He had thought about leaving the gun in the room, but took it at the last minute. If he had been able to talk with Morales he might have felt better, but according to his son, Esteban and Linda had gone out for dinner. Quinn left the number at the bunkhouse. He asked the kid to read it back, but he had already hung up.

A hawk flapped from its perch atop a nearby tree and Quinn whipped around, listening for something that might have spooked the bird. The woods were quiet. He turned back to see Stratton watching him with bemused interest.

Quinn wouldn't have felt quite so jumpy, but Jen's latest information kept nagging at him—even though it did come from the water-polo player. There might be a long list of people who wanted Tod dead, but if the man with the crewcut had really been a guest on Sissy's show, she was back at the top of that list.

"Come on down here," called Stratton from the water's edge, "I don't want to have to shout."

Through the trees they could see the sun setting beyond the hills, the dry land smoldering in the rosy light. New houses were going up in the distance, rows and rows of them.

"The ticky-tacky gets closer every year," said Stratton, nodding at the houses. He spit into the bubbling water. "I'm sixty-four years old—I'm glad I'll be long gone before the bulldozers reach here. I hate suburban life. I hate the PTA and carpools and turkey-necked accountants riding lawnmowers across their quarter-acre spreads."

"John, let me give you some advice," Quinn said, enjoying Stratton's forthrightness, unable to stop himself from liking him. "If you're serious about a political career, keep those thoughts to yourself."

Stratton tugged at his white Stetson. "Much obliged." He listened to the water bubbling over the rocks for a few minutes, then looked up as though he had decided something. "I brought you out here so we could talk privately." He aimed those clear blue eyes right at Quinn. "I take quite an interest in my little girl."

"You have a child?" Quinn was surprised.

"No," chuckled Stratton. "I call Sissy my little girl." He fanned himself with the hat. "We've got our fifth anniversary coming up. At my age, the years run by too fast." He waved at a fat green fly. "I know what you're thinking. You look at Sissy and see a big star, tough as gristle—I see past that."

"What do you see?"

"Right to the point"—Stratton nodded his approval—"that's just how Sissy described you." It was just as well that Quinn hadn't brought a recorder—the rushing water made too much noise to have picked up anything. "She said you were working on a story about Tod's murder. I don't know what there is to write, that's your business, but you best go easy on my little girl, because she took his death hard."

Stratton looked away and Quinn saw his features in profile, his gaze far beyond the distant hills. "When someone you care about dies, dies so sudden you don't have a chance to say good-bye . . . it takes a while to get over that." He turned his head, and Quinn could see the sunset reflected in his eyes, a firestorm racing across the earth.

"I know what you mean."

"Sissy's no hothouse flower," Stratton said, "but I wouldn't want you to do or say anything that might hurt her." Stratton skipped rocks into the water—one of them landed close enough to Quinn to splash his pants. "She's the only person on this earth who matters to me."

"What about Tod? Did he matter?"

Stratton deftly threw the rock, got five skips straight down the creek. "I didn't know the boy well."

"I guess Sissy made up for that," said Quinn. Stratton reached for fresh rocks. "I talked with a woman earlier this week . . . she said Tod and Sissy were having an affair."

Stratton stopped in midthrow, bounced the rock in his hand. "I've heard that story before," he said evenly.

"Did you believe it?"

Stratton took a deep breath, sighed with pleasure. Quinn did the same. The breeze smelled of sage. "I got over two thousand acres," he said, "but this is one of my favorite spots." He had his hat off and the breeze lifted his fine, elegant gray hair. "I come here every evening Sissy works late."

"A friend of mine told me almost every homicide comes down to love or money. Love or money—I can't decide which one got Tod killed. What do you think, John?"

Stratton looked over at Quinn, perplexed. "I thought the police already settled that?"

"They got it wrong," said Quinn. "The man who murdered Tod is still walking around—two days ago he walked into Cliff Silver's backyard and almost killed him too. Cliff got a good look at this guy. He could pick him out of a lineup in a second." Quinn watched Stratton carefully, the languid way he stretched out on the rocks, comfortable, staring at the running water, his boots rocking to the rhythm. "The killer shouldn't be hard to locate—we think he might have been a guest on *Straight Talk.*"

Stratton stopped. The wind died but the water kept moving past him. He slowly sagged, bit by bit right in front of Quinn— it was as if he was hollow inside and all his supports were giving way, one after the other. He put his face into his hands, not making a sound. There was a curious frontier bravery to him at that moment, a sense of making do, making the best of a hopeless situation—it was Custer's Last Stand and the Alamo about to be overrun and no one leaving.

Quinn reached out for him. "John?"

Stratton took his hands away, straightening up, filling out again. "I had a bad feeling when I heard Tod was dead. . . ." he said. "But I figured, let sleeping dogs lie." He swallowed. "This man you're looking for . . ." The words must have jagged edges, the way he grimaced. "Is he a big man? Got a butch haircut like a red pinecone?"

Quinn shook his head. He felt numb—utterly surprised at Stratton's question. The best he could do was nod his head.

The sunset showed every crease in Stratton's leathery face, the crow's-feet at the corners of his eyes, the furrows alongside his mouth. "It's my fault," he said. "I take complete responsibility."

"I don't understand."

"It's my fault," said Stratton. "I told Sissy to call him. This man you want . . . his name is Liston. Emory Roy Liston. He was a guest on the show, just like you said. Liston told Sissy that if she ever needed anything . . . *anything,* to just say the word. She has that effect on men. You know that." He shook his head, angry at himself. "When Sissy had this . . . trouble with Tod, I was the one told her to call Liston. I had seen him that time on the show, and just *knew* he was one bad hombre."

"This trouble . . . Tod was blackmailing her?"

"You were right about them . . . seeing each other." Stratton's gnarled hands clenched into fists. "She had broken it off and Tod was threatening to go to the tabloids."

"What about the X rays?"

Stratton shook his head. "I don't know about any X rays. Tod said he was going to sell his story to the highest bidder. He said the other talk shows would fall all over themselves to interview him. I didn't want her to pay him, but she insisted." He gritted his teeth. "That little shit's kiss'n'tell wouldn't have hurt Sissy's career a bit—there's no such thing as bad publicity, not for her." He clamped his jaws shut. "She was worried about me." He shook his head. "You believe that? She knew that kind of scandal would finish any political ideas I might have."

"Your wife fooling around behind your back," said Quinn, "it must have made you mad."

Stratton squinted into the sun. "Young people overestimate the power of jealousy," he said softly, then turned and looked directly at Quinn. "Once you get to be my age, you learn to forgive people almost anything."

"You didn't care about Sissy and Tod?"

"I didn't say that." Stratton tried to smile but it broke apart on him. He took off his pearl-white hat and smoothed the felt with his fingers. "Maybe that's why I told Sissy to send Liston to talk with him. We used to do that in the old days—ask Cliff. We were always getting hit up by sharpies who thought movie stars were walking dollar signs. We'd send somebody like Liston to talk to the sharpie. That's all it took in the old days."

The brim of the cowboy hat went round and round through Stratton's fingers. "Sissy told Liston about Tod, but decided not to use him. She said he was crazy in love with her, but unreliable. Maybe she was a little scared of him too." The edges of his hair looked ablaze in the fading sunset as he looked up at Quinn. "There's some people, they just won't take direction."

"You don't know *anything* about X rays?" Quinn sounded uncertain. "You never heard of a Dr. Hugh McChesney?"

Stratton cocked his head. "McChesney? You're going way back with that one. He was one of the studio docs—I never went to him, but Jimmy Joe Kincaid used to see him when he got himself a dirty dose."

Quinn felt a cold wind at his back and looked over his shoulder. "Do you know where Liston is now?"

"Don't blame Sissy for what's happened. She still liked Tod even when he threatened to spill the beans—she said a boy like that could run a network someday." He shook his head. "No, if anyone's to blame, it's me."

"I want to find Liston," said Quinn.

"I never met the man myself," said Stratton, "but I should be able to get you a phone number. You're welcome to him, but I want Sissy kept out of it. You try to drag her in, I've got some heavy-duty lawyers who'll tie you up in knots. That's no brag, that's a promise." A pine bough had washed up next to his boots. Stratton reached down, pulled off some pine needles, and put them in the corner of his mouth. "Sissy's not the only one who likes straight talk, so let me make it clear: A year from now, I may be the governor of the state. I can be the best friend or the worst enemy you ever had. It's up to you."

Chapter 38

Quinn couldn't find Jen anywhere. He had been looking for her for the last half hour. She wasn't poolside, or at the dinner party in the hacienda. She wasn't in her room.

He had checked her room as soon as he got off that damned horse, ran right over. He wanted to talk with her about what Stratton had said, see what she thought.

There was no answer at her door, and when he went inside his own room, he found a note from her on the bed. The note said she was going on a picnic and wouldn't be late. It sounded like she was talking to her father. Don't be out past midnight, princess!

He taped the gun back under the desk chair, then lay on the bed, finishing the roast-beef sandwiches he had grabbed from the buffet at the party.

He was going to have to wise up about women. That was his next big project. Then he was going to hit Nino up for a raise, and move into his own apartment. He'd still see Katie every day, but he needed some privacy. He was going to slow down, stop reading too much into things, imagining there was chemistry when there wasn't. After he nailed Liston.

He called Morales again, but he and Linda were still not home.

Morales should be able to run down Liston's address fast, particularly if Stratton came up with a phone number for the man. Bringing Liston in for questioning was one thing, getting him charged with murder, let alone *convicted,* was going to be considerably more difficult.

Quinn had followed enough trials to know how often the guilty walked away laughing, freed on a technicality, a defense attorney's skill, or a jury's stupidity. Then there was always the eager reporter who handed somebody like Groggins a Get Out of Jail Free card.

He looked up and saw the painting of Hopalong Cassidy smiling down on him, the lawman's six-shooters drawn. Fuck you, Hoppy. There was a point where you said you were truly sorry, then went on with your life.

The TV was off, but he stared at the blank screen anyway. Without Sissy's cooperation, there was a good chance that Liston would beat a murder charge. Quinn didn't have any hard evidence. Cliff could I.D. Liston, but that was just an assault charge, and Cliff wasn't the most credible witness.

Maybe Forensics had found one of Liston's hairs at Tod's. Maybe he spit on the carpet or left a spot of blood in Andy's van . . . anything that Morales could use to get a search warrant, see what Liston kept under his pillow.

He picked up the phone and called home. Rachel's line rang and rang. He checked his watch. Eight-thirty, still early; she had probably taken Katie to Grandma's Sugarplum for cherry cheesecake. Bring me a slice. He hung up.

The best thing to do was find out all he could on Liston. Get a copy of his appearance on Sissy's show, see what he looked like. Talk to Sissy off-the-record.

He heard Jen's voice in the next room, jumped up, so relieved he wanted to shout for joy. He couldn't help worrying about her. It wasn't that she wasn't able to protect herself. His hand was on the connecting door before he realized that she was talking to someone else. He pressed his ear against the door—the voices were muffled, but it was her and she seemed to be having a good time. He crept back to his bed, switched on the TV. Jen laughed and he spilled his beer.

O

Jen's jaw ached from laughing. She lay on the bed, propped up on her elbows, watching Davis act out his coach's manic peptalks. For the last three hours he had kept her giggling—he had just turned twenty, an All-American water-polo goalie

260

at USC who vacationed on his dad's Goldcard, and bragged about never reading newspapers.

Davis's world was frat parties and throw-up contests and long-legged homecoming queens. It sounded silly and unreal . . . and fun. The kind of mindless exuberance she never had the chance for.

Jen had dropped out of high school in her junior year, said good-bye to her mother, and hitchhiked to New York City with her carefully wrapped portfolio and her battered Nikons, taking pictures all the way. She got work almost immediately; art directors were awed by this gutsy kid with the elegant aesthetic, a teenager who could turn a Bed-Stuy shooting gallery into a Hogarth lithograph.

That June, when her former classmates were pinning on their prom-night corsages, she was in a field hospital in Afghanistan, holding a flashlight in a cave outside of Kabul while Hassan removed cluster-bomb fragments from the back of a twelve-year-old boy. The boy didn't make a sound, just stared at Jen, ashamed to cry in front of a woman.

Hassan was a Mujahedeen veteran, barely seventeen, a righteous warrior in defense of Islam who slung his dented Kalashnikov over his shoulder with a bright red sash, and layered his eyelids with indigo mascara. He was the most beautiful man-child she had ever met, fearless and utterly devoted. The two of them had scrambled across the craggy landscape for months, dodging government patrols, taking photographs of cease-fire violations. They made love on the frozen mountaintops, left melting angels in the snow.

The last evening before she was to cross back into Pakistan, Hassan took her hand and asked her to convert to the one true religion and marry him, asked her while they lay out under the stars, their bodies steaming in the night chill. She didn't answer; she didn't have to. He knew. The reality of her leaving, the permanence of it, hung in the air like frost. She watched him start to weep, so innocent that he was unashamed, not able to turn away from her. She had seen the same fierce innocence in Quinn last night—too sad to sleep, too tenacious to quit.

"Whatcha thinking about, babe?" said Davis, flopping down next to her on the bed.

"Just how different we are."

"Hey"—he squeezed her bare knee—"I don't care."

"What does that mean?"

He played with the hem of her baggy black shorts. "Why don't we . . . get comfortable?"

Jen could hear the buzz of the TV coming from Quinn's room. She was still mad at him for leaving her to go riding off with Stratton, too proud to admit *she* had found out something about the killer. Davis thought he remembered seeing the man with the crewcut on *Straight Talk*. Even if Davis was wrong, it was worth sitting down with Cliff and watching tapes of Sissy's show. What else did they have to go on? You'd think last night meant nothing to Quinn. She had felt a connection between them last night, an intimacy. She liked being in that small room with him, the sheets carrying his smell. . . .

She wondered how clearly Quinn could hear them. She could put on MTV, let the music mask the noise she made. She didn't usually care—she had lived with roommates before, you got used to the idea of somebody listening in. Amanda, the ballet dancer she roomed with for a while in New York . . . Jen used to enjoy listening to her and her boyfriend going at it on the other side of the wall. She probably had a better time than Amanda.

"How 'bout it, babe?" Davis plucked at the tiny buttons on her black silk blouse.

"Not right now." She took his hand away. He had a beautiful body, lean and muscular, not a mark on it. His hair was sun-bleached blond, short in the front, with a single rat-tail braid hanging to his shoulder in the back. Everyone on the team wore it that way, he said. She tugged at his braid, smiling. Male bonding always cracked her up. If there was a club or a team or a pack, boys would set themselves on fire to join, and not think twice about it.

Davis picked up the remote, turned on the TV, pouting as he switched through the channels.

O

Quinn heard her TV go on. Great. That was really going to prevent him from hearing them. He and Jen should be going over their notes right now, sharing ideas. Stratton had made a lot of sense—not that he was telling the whole truth. No one did that.

Jen should be here with him. If she wanted to work together, they should be together. He was tempted to bang on the wall, tell them to knock it off, he was trying to sleep.

He stared out the picture window at the dark forest beyond. He got up and stood before the window, rested his hands on the sill, not wanting to have anything in between himself and the night. The wind had cleared away the cloud cover—dense sheets of stars twisted across the sky. He felt small and naked standing there in front of the universe.

O

She let Davis fumble with her blouse while she played with his hair. It felt good to relax, just let herself be carried along with the sensations. Ever since she started working with Quinn there had been this . . . intensity. They were too close, too fast. Her work was challenge enough; when it came to sex, she wanted it simple and easy. With Quinn, everything counted, everything was complicated.

The only light in the room was the glow from the TV. She hummed along with the song on MTV as Davis kissed her and missed.

She remembered her first conversation with Quinn, not even a week ago. She had teased him about his Jeep, said it made her feel like she was swimming in testosterone. He had told her to keep her mouth shut so she didn't swallow any. Then he got embarrassed. He tried to cover it up, but she could tell. It was one of the most attractive things about him.

She must have laughed out loud thinking of Quinn's nervousness, because Davis stopped for a moment, then went back to her blouse. She made intelligent men uncomfortable—the dumb ones didn't have enough sense to be nervous.

The TV needed adjusting, the image rolling over and over in a blur of colors. It reminded her of Quinn's Seminole Indian shirt at Napitano's barbecue. Damn.

She sat up. Davis looked surprised. "I'm sorry," she said, "I'm just not in the mood. I don't know what's wrong with me."

"You want me to do something?" He was searching. "I can . . . um . . ."

"It's not you, it's me. I had a lot of fun at the picnic, and I thought we'd have an even better time back here, but . . . it's not happening."

He helped her button back her blouse, which was so sweet she kissed him, and then he got the wrong idea and she couldn't blame him. "Let's just say goodnight," she said.

Davis got up quickly, opened the door, and stopped, his outline silhouetted against the stars. Maybe he was waiting for her to change her mind. He slammed the door so hard the TV picture fixed itself.

O

Quinn winced at the sound of her door slamming, then heard their connecting door open. He didn't turn around. "That was pretty quick," he said, staring out the window. "I guess that's part of the appeal of young guys. They go in, they get the job done, then they leave, and you can get back to more important things."

"Why don't you look at me? There's nothing out there."

"Quit ordering me around," he said, turning. She stood there in the dim light, barefoot, her hair messed up. She was so beautiful it felt like somebody had punched him in the heart. "Your blouse isn't buttoned evenly," he said. "First time for him, huh?"

She smiled with her eyes. Started to redo the buttons, but they were tiny and her hands were trembling. Good to know that he wasn't the only one less confident than he made out to be.

He walked over to her, calmly buttoned her up, not looking down into those green cat eyes. All he needed was to get the shakes now, he'd never hear the end of it. His fingers slid against the thin fabric as he worked, careful not to touch her. "Better?" He stepped back to admire his handiwork.

"Perfect," she said, watching him as she slowly unbuttoned her blouse. He swallowed but it didn't ease the pressure in his throat. She kept going, staring directly at him, and he couldn't take his eyes off her.

The room was getting warmer. He should open a window. Her blouse slid off her shoulders and onto the floor in a silken

heap. Then her shorts. Her skin was smooth in the soft light—
gold that breathed. Her nipples hardened as he watched. He
pulled at his collar. If he was so hot, how could she be cold?

"You're overdressed," she said.

He wondered, not for the first time, if she could read his
mind.

Chapter 39

"A little more hot," said Jen, turning her bare back to the spray. "Please."

Quinn turned the handle until the water warmed up a few more degrees, almost too hot for him. He cracked the bathroom window, the cool air from outside filling the room with steam.

"That's better." She stretched in the small shower stall, brushed against his knees, his chest—skin to skin as she wrapped her arms around him, her body even warmer than the water. She seemed smaller without her clothes, nestling her cheek into his chest, tiny kisses in the mist. He felt himself harden against her belly.

Such an abrupt shift between them. All the sharp edges had disappeared, no words, no resistance. They were together.

He held her close, felt her strength, lithe and taut as a wild animal. He felt bulky and awkward next to her—the Japanese word for foreigner translated as "big, hairy barbarian." Now, he understood.

He rocked her in his arms, turning slowly in the shower spray, water running down between them, tickling as it trickled between their pressed-together bodies. She giggled, and so did he—all caution between them gone, dropped with their clothes back in the other room.

The bathroom was lit only by the yellow hall light. The blue tile made it seem like they were under the sea, beyond the reach of sunlight, warmed only by their beating hearts.

He bit her ears, ran his tongue inside each pink shell, water running down his chin. Her neck smelled like clove and cinnamon. Fine hairs drifted across the peak of her jaw, and this hint of the primitive made her even more alluring. He wanted to lick every inch of her, mark her, define her with kisses, know every hill and valley of her body, every muscle, every hair, every bump and bone.

It couldn't last. He was going to lose her and he wanted to remember everything about her.

He kissed her eyebrows, reveling in their thick sensuality, kissed the graceful ellipses of her eyes, caressed her eyelids with his lips, soft cries coming from deep inside him. You'd have thought he was falling, the way he reached out for her.

Her breasts were tiny, not even filling his hands, but her nipples were long and thick between his teeth. She gasped, tearing at his hair. He wanted to swallow her whole.

She placed the palms of her hands against his chest, holding him off. Her finger pressed against his lips stopped his unspoken question. She picked up the bar of soap, lathered it in her hand, the sound making him even harder. She cupped the head of his penis in her fist, squeezed him until he cried out, then let go. She gently pushed him against the wall, the tile cold against his back. He shivered, moved away, but she was insistent, not speaking, her eyes dancing with pleasure as she pressed him back. The hot spray beat against his chest.

She stroked his face with her fingertips, spreading the soap. He closed his eyes, as she gently outlined his lips, then worked her way down his body, slowly, gliding over his neck, soaping his arms, his fingers. She tugged at the hair on his chest, rough now. He peeked through the soapy spray, eyes burning, glimpsed her on her knees in front of him, water coursing down her spine. He closed his eyes.

She lathered first one leg, then the other, ran her hands down his thighs, her fingers scratching him. He wondered for a moment if she was angry at him, then she cupped his balls in her warm, soapy hands.

He bit his lips shut, arched his back against the cool tile, the spray beating directly against his face, down his chest, and onto her upturned face.

She massaged his balls with both hands, gently rolling them between her palms. He felt his stiff penis slide against her cheek, tightened his buttocks reflexively as she pressed her index finger against his rectum. Her tongue licked the slit of his penis as her mouth closed over him.

Just as he started to come, he pulled away from her, groaning. He lifted her to her feet, held her close, and kissed her, sliding into her warm, sweet mouth.

She sucked gently on his lips, whispered in his ear, the water pounding so loudly against the tile he couldn't hear what she was saying.

The shower was filled with steam, perfumed clouds rising toward the stars. She reached up, gripped the shower head, and hung on, the spray hitting her hair as she bent forward. He got behind her, put his hands on her slim waist, kissed the base of her spine, the full curve of her hips, overwhelmed by the ripe femaleness of her, kissing her cheeks, water running down her smooth skin as he licked his way up her backbone.

He put his hands on her shoulders and she laid her head back, still hanging on to the fixture. She turned and looked at him as he slowly entered her. She drew him in deeper, and he groaned with her, grinding his teeth, as they stared into each other's eyes.

They stood pressed together, perfectly fit, his arms clasped around her belly, nuzzling her neck as she squeezed him in her own hot embrace, tightening around him, a secret kiss as they swayed in the steam.

Her hands slid down the tile as she pushed her hips against him, head thrown back, crying out, and he joined her, splashing his heart inside her, gasping, hanging on to her, as they sank to the floor, crying, holding each other, laughing as the water beat down on them.

Someone was applauding. They both looked up, blinking in the spray.

A huge man with a crewcut stood outside the open door, clapping his hands as the steam rolled around him. He pulled a pistol from his brown three-piece suit, flashed a badge—"Sergeant Nagurski," he announced—then smiled. "Just kidding. You know who I am. Those security guards, though"—he shook his head—"send them back to night school." His face glistened in the mist. "A gal in a gingham dress told me where you two were staying," he mocked, staring at their nakedness, "but I didn't expect to get *this* lucky." He touched his necktie. "I'm glad I dressed up special for the occasion." His voice was rough, the edges soft with a faint southern drawl.

Quinn couldn't take his eyes off Liston, overwhelmed with the sheer solidity of the man. For the last week, he had chased a vague description, a nightmare made tangible only by the blood left in his wake—now here he was introducing himself, big and ugly as a mudslide.

Liston rocked on his heels in front of the picture window, eyes bright with anticipation.

Through the wisps of steam, Quinn could see the last sliver of the Cheshire moon grinning at him over the treetops.

Chapter 40

J en stood up and faced Liston. "I'm going to get dressed," she said. "If you're going to kill us, I don't want to be found naked."

Liston kept the pistol pointed at her belly button, those little eyes of his darting across her body like wasps.

Quinn stepped in front of her, hands raised in surrender, acutely conscious of the vulnerability of external genitals. "Why *not* let us get dressed? You worried?"

Liston nodded, then backed out of the bathroom, beckoning them to follow. He dead-bolted the front door and pocketed the key, watching them step into their underwear. He held the gun at waist height, close to his body, waiting for them to finish, a dreamy smile on his face.

Jen ran her fingers through her wet hair, mumbling as she combed the black strands away from her face.

Quinn glanced at her, not sure what she was up to. "You and I should go for a walk," he said to Liston, "it's hot in here, somebody your size must be uncomfortable."

"I like it hot."

"*I'm* burning up," said Jen, peeling off her top, the one she had just put back on. "Do you mind?"

"Be my guest," said Liston.

Jen undid her baggy shorts, put a hand in one pocket. She tripped taking off her pants, staggered close to Liston while he guffawed. Her hand whipped out of the pocket and she touched him with the stun gun. There was a crackle and he was thrown back against the door, mouth twisted in pain.

Quinn raced for the desk chair with his .357 magnum taped under the seat.

Jen jabbed Liston once, twice, three times, with the stun gun.

Liston howled with rage, the air smelling of ozone and burnt hair as he rushed her, ignoring the jolts. He backhanded Jen against the wall and turned on Quinn.

There wasn't enough time for Quinn to reach the gun—he swung the chair against Liston's chest, shattering it, the revolver sliding across the wood floor.

Liston barely reacted. He tucked his pistol inside his brown suit, giggling, dropped into a three-point stance, and charged, slamming Quinn into the desk.

Quinn got to his feet, still reeling with the impact. He batted at Liston with the broken chair leg, caught him on the ear, continuing to beat at his face as hard as he could. He felt a shock run up his arm with each blow, but Liston didn't seem to feel a thing—he crowded in, taking the hits, enjoying himself.

Liston grabbed the chair leg, tore it from his grasp. Quinn kneed him as they grappled, but Liston only grunted, arms around him in a bear hug, slowly tightening his grip, squeezing, their faces pressed so close it was like they were dancing cheek-to-cheek.

Quinn could hear popping sounds, champagne corks—what was there to celebrate? Someone using his voice was screaming. Liston dropped him, then watched as Quinn staggered up, his body twisted like a corkscrew, trying to fight. Liston laughed, grabbed him by the back of the neck, and drove him facefirst into the mirror. Quinn saw his own dazed expression racing toward him in the glass—then blood splattered across his reflection.

He felt himself sail through the air—185 pounds and Liston was tossing him around like a beach ball. He landed on the bed, bounced three times before he stopped. He could see Jen crumpled against the opposite wall, head gashed, blood dripping off her earlobe. He crawled toward her, but Liston grabbed him, heaved him back on the bed.

Liston picked the stun gun up off the floor, staring right at Quinn as he pressed it against his own chest. He jerked, clenched his teeth, hot sparks in his eyes as the current crackled through him. Again. And again. His eyes never left Quinn. He tossed the stun gun into the corner, then flopped down on the mattress.

The bed groaned. Maybe Quinn did. He couldn't feel his right shoulder.

Liston stripped the pillowcase off the pillow, turned Quinn over on his back, and gently wiped his face, dabbing carefully at the cuts. He slowly pulled a long sliver of glass out of Quinn's cheek, holding him down with one hand while Quinn shrieked. "What are you complaining about?" Liston said good-naturedly. "Look at *me*." He gingerly touched the side of his head, already puffing up. "That was some thumping you gave me."

Quinn held himself rigid, tensing at the slightest touch—Liston's concern was even more terrifying than his fury. He could see Jen. She hadn't moved.

Liston turned around to follow Quinn's gaze. "Let her sleep," he advised. "She'll be okay, don't worry. Women are tougher than we are. Don't let them kid you."

Hopalong Cassidy stared back at Quinn from the opposite wall. Where were the good guys when you needed them?

Liston was so heavy that the mattress buckled, rolling them right next to each other. His wide necktie flopped out of his suit jacket, a flutter of beige fabric dotted with footballs. "Some fun, huh?" said Liston. "We've had some good times, haven't we? Me chasing you, you chasing me . . . now here we are, two peas in a pod."

Through the window, Quinn could see the Cheshire moon grinning through the trees, an evil cat sitting up there in the branches, watching him, enjoying every minute of it. He thought of Katie, and how she always hated that moon, scared as much for him as for herself. He wanted to call her. Tell her that he loved her.

"Killing us isn't going to help you, *Liston*," Quinn said softly. "Yeah, I know your name. So do the cops," he lied.

Liston basked in some inner glow, some private knowledge he was bursting to share. "You've got that last X ray, don't you? Once I recognized Mr. Hollywood, I knew what you were up to. Did you show him the X ray? Did you give him a peek? Well, it's not going to do you any good—it's too late."

Quinn's ears were still ringing. The X rays again?

Liston dabbed at Quinn's nose again, tossed the bloody pillowcase onto the floor. "You're not hurt so bad"—he patted Quinn and Quinn flinched—"I think I snapped your collarbone, maybe some ribs . . . your nose was broke before, so don't blame that on me."

"I'm willing to let bygones be bygones." Quinn coughed up blood.

Liston laughed. "Cool customer, I like that. Andy was the same way. Were you buddies, or partners?"

"He was my friend."

"I liked him myself—real soft hair . . ." He lifted a wet strand of Quinn's hair, dropped it back on his face.

"These X rays you—"

Liston punched him in the stomach. Quinn grunted, doubled up on the bed. "Don't start with me. I don't even *want* the X ray. You keep it. Show it to Tod in hell."

"I don't have—"

Liston punched him again. "Sure. Tod doesn't have it. Andy doesn't have it. You don't have it either. Nobody's got it. The X ray doesn't exist. I made it up." Liston slapped him across the face. *"Wrong."* Liston slapped him again and again, spraying the sheets with red.

"Give me some room," gasped Quinn. "You're crushing me."

Liston rolled away an inch. One of his eyes was puffed almost shut, the other one watched Quinn. "Sissy said you'd back off, but you're no quitter. I could see that."

"Sissy wouldn't want you to do this," said Quinn. "You're ruining things for her."

Liston leaned toward him, his face bruised and swollen from being beaten with the chair leg—his head looked like a bag of beets. Quinn shrank from him, but Liston kept closing in. "Don't you think I know the spot I've put Sissy in?" whispered Liston. His breath smelled of grape soda. "Don't you think I know? Well, you're going to help me make things right. Killing you wouldn't help—it's too late for that." He smiled. "You're going to have to kill me."

Quinn wet his lips.

"I'm giving you a chance to be a hero—when are *you* going to get another chance like that?" He flopped back on the pillow next to Quinn. "I'm not afraid of dying. I'm *ready*—you have no idea how ready I am. Sometimes I catch a glimpse of myself . . . I see what I am now, and I know what I used to be. Oh, I can still give a good hit, still take a good hit"—he idly punched Quinn, made him cry out—"but it's not the same."

"Liston—"

"I remember Sunday afternoons," Liston said distantly, "and the smell of grass. . . ." His face twisted. There was a blackened patch of raw skin on his neck where Jen had tagged him with the stun gun. "I tell you, Quinn. I *miss* it."

"Why don't you get some rest?" Quinn said, painfully sitting up. "I'll take care of Jen. You can stay here."

Liston's face grew purple with anger, sweat beading across his forehead. "I asked you to kill me," he raged, drawing back his fist, "not patronize me!" His fist trembled, knuckles bulging. The room was so quiet Quinn could hear the shower dripping.

Liston suddenly wiped his face on his sleeve. "You just help me"—he glowered—"and all is forgiven." He hung his head. "I tried to kill myself this afternoon. I wrote my note, sat there in my easychair . . . and couldn't pull the trigger. It's no fun by myself."

"Go ahead then," said Quinn. "Do it, but leave me out."

Quinn didn't want to kill Liston even if he was serious. There had been more than enough killing already. He wanted Liston to *talk*. Wanted him to tell the truth about those X rays. That's what all the dying had been about.

"You should read my suicide note," said Liston. "I'm no writer, but it's pretty good. I don't make any apologies for killing Tod—he brought that on himself. Nobody holds out on Emory Roy Liston." He jabbed his finger right between Quinn's eyes. "Nobody."

Quinn waited until Liston stopped poking him. "Did you kill Dr. McChesney?" Liston furrowed his brow and Quinn flinched. "Why keep secrets at this stage of the game? Did you kill him?"

"I don't know any Dr. McChesney," said Liston. He sat cross-legged, a pillow in his lap, pulling feathers out one by one. "What are you trying to blame me for now?" One eye was swollen shut, the other glared at Quinn, bulging with hate. "You think I'm some kind of monster. I resent that."

"Resent it all you want," said Quinn. He was exhausted. He could barely stay awake. "You're going to kill me anyway. Why don't you and I go off by ourselves, and settle this thing in private?"

Liston laid down the pillow. "You don't get it." He whipped out the revolver, jabbed Quinn with the barrel. He glanced over to where Jen lay sprawled on her side, and aimed the gun at her.

"Please, don't," said Quinn.

Liston pulled back the hammer.

"Please," Quinn begged, "please don't."

"Love changes things, doesn't it?" Liston shook his head in disgust. "You think you're tough, but you'll beg to save her. You think you're good, but you'll do anything to keep her safe. *Anything*." He jammed the gun into the mattress between the two of them and fired. The shot was muffled—feathers floated in the air.

Quinn choked at the gunpowder stink.

Liston opened the fingers of Quinn's right hand, wrapped them around the pistol butt. "Do it," he said.

The gun wobbled in Quinn's grasp as he sat up on one elbow—it wasn't heavy; his whole right arm was numb.

Liston lay back on the pillow, peacefully folded his hands on his chest. "Do you believe in reincarnation?"

Quinn felt like he was falling through the bed, falling through the earth; Liston's voice was the only thing he had to pull himself back up with, but it was thin and sharp as piano wire. Just listening to him was cutting Quinn to pieces.

"Me, I believe it. I think we come back. Over and over." Quinn could see the Cheshire moon over Liston's shoulder— they both had the same leering grin. Liston picked up Quinn's arm, placed the gun under his own chin. "Kill me."

Quinn thought he heard Jen stir, but he couldn't see her. He tried to hold the gun steady . . . using both hands. It hurt to breathe—something important was broken inside him. He fumbled for the trigger, but his fingers were stiff and wouldn't bend.

"You want to hear something funny?" Liston said. "When I got hurt . . . when the Bears cut me . . . the guy who replaced me on special teams was Jim Jamulka. Last year he was inducted into the Hall of Fame." He shook his head. "I was bigger, quicker, and could fake him out on my worst day hung over. He makes the Hall of Fame, and I'm lying here with you. That's something, isn't it? I mean, that's funny."

Quinn's index finger found the trigger. He could feel Liston watching him, pain flooding the room, his pain, Liston's . . . Jen's. His finger wouldn't move. He kept trying to bend it . . . pointing the barrel right at the center of Liston's silly little smile.

"Do it."

He thought of Andy alone with Liston in the van, Andy holding a gun to his own head while Liston watched. He wondered if Andy's hand shook as much as his was shaking now.

Liston's eye was drooping, a soft-boiled egg with blood in the yolk. "Kill me!"

He made a hard fist, squeezing . . . and the hammer dropped.

Liston stuck a thick finger in between the hammer and the cylinder, preventing the gun from firing. "Ouch." He smiled. "That was close." He took the pistol from Quinn's grasp, let the hammer down gently. "I thought you'd have more trouble with it," he said, impressed. "You got a real aptitude for killing, you know that?"

"You make it easy," said Quinn. He watched Liston twirl the gun around his finger, round and round she goes. . . .

"You're no better than I am." Liston slapped him across the face. "You're just like me."

"No I'm not."

Liston slapped him harder this time. "You pulled the trigger. We're the same—no better, no worse."

Quinn grabbed for the gun, but he wasn't even close. Liston pushed him away, climbed on top of him, straddling him. Quinn tried to scream but Liston's enormous bulk squeezed the voice out of him.

"Who needs you?" Liston loomed over him, the pistol pointed at Quinn's head. "I don't." He lurched suddenly, then touched his brown suit jacket, surprised. There was a bright spot on his necktie, his fingertips smeared with red.

Quinn could see Jen leaning against the wall, his magnum unsteady in her hand, trying to get off another shot before she passed out. A piece of silvery duct tape was stuck to the barrel—it looked festive.

As Liston started to get off him, Quinn tore the gun away, pressed it into Liston's smothering belly and fired once, twice. Liston jerked, then looked down at him, wide-eyed. It was raining in the room. A hot, drenching rain, and none of them had an umbrella.

Liston lunged at him and Quinn fired again and again, Liston grunting with each shot. The gun clicked, empty now, but Quinn kept pulling the trigger as Liston reached down for him. He felt the big man's hand gently pat his cheek, then Liston sagged and toppled across him.

Quinn gasped for breath, pinned beneath the man's weight, cheek-to-cheek again. He felt Liston's lips move but heard nothing, just felt a warm bubble burst against his ear. Jen was trying to help roll Liston off him, but it was no use. There was an echo bouncing from wall to wall, howling from every bone in his skull as Quinn drowned in flesh.

Chapter 41

"I'm disappointed in you, John. Here I thought you were the Man in the White Hat." Quinn had to raise his voice to be heard over the merry-go-round at the South Coast Plaza mall, children screaming happily as they whirled to an instrumental version of "My Way." Quinn had surprised Stratton in the middle of reshooting ads for his upcoming gubernatorial campaign.

It was late Saturday afternoon, almost a month since that evening at the bunkhouse, and when he closed his eyes, Quinn could still hear the wet sound of gunshots muffled in Liston's belly.

"It took me a while to figure it out," Quinn said evenly, pacing himself, "but there's not much else to do in the hospital."

"You had quite a shock," offered Stratton. "I hear you're held together with steel pins and baling wire. Looks like they fixed your nose—too bad, I liked it the way it was." He smiled at Quinn, signing autographs with a practiced scrawl. "Don't rush things. No one expects you to be a hundred percent after what you been through. Why don't you stick around? I'll buy you a soft drink."

Stratton wore his signature string tie with a conservative blue suit today. No cowboy hat. No boots. A statesman with a hint of the prairie. In less than two hours he would address a crowd of thousand-dollar-a-plate supporters in the Grand Ballroom to officially announce his candidacy for governor. Law-and-order was expected to be a major campaign theme, particularly in light of the recent murders that had struck so close to his family.

"Liston kept talking about X rays at the bunkhouse," said

Quinn. "Those first couple of days, flat on my back, doped-up with painkillers—I still thought it was *Sissy* that Tod was blackmailing. You told me you didn't know anything about any X rays, and I believed you. Gut reaction, I believed you." He shook his head. "You never got enough credit as an actor, John. Lifetime Achievement Award, bullshit—you deserve the real thing."

"That's it for now, folks," Stratton apologized to the remaining autograph seekers. He took Quinn by the arm, walked him a few paces away. "You don't look so good. You best be careful you don't tire yourself out." He didn't sound sympathetic.

"I asked Napitano to go over Betty Andaluse's autopsy report," said Quinn. "Nino said it all checked out, but I had to see for myself. Even before he brought the report to the hospital, I knew what I was going to find." He was breathing harder, giddy, watching Stratton's handsome features tighten as he spoke. "It was a lousy copy, but the signature was legible: 'Hugh F. McChesney, M.D., Coroner.' "

Stratton didn't move. "That was a painful period of my life. I don't have to discuss it with you or anybody else."

"What did Dr. McChesney find when he X-rayed the remains of Betty Andaluse?" The children's cries undulated as the merry-go-round spun. "Did she have a broken neck? A crushed skull? Maybe a couple of bullets melted against her rib cage? She didn't die in the fire. She was dead already."

Stratton didn't move.

"McChesney must have been starstruck by you," said Quinn, "all that money and power and good looks. Here you were a Cinemascope hero, and he was just an L.A. County coroner making fourteen thousand a year—I looked it up. Hooray for Hollywood. He probably jumped at the chance to help you."

Stratton waved off the production assistant who hovered nearby.

"If I went back through the newspaper files for the week Betty died, I bet I'd find *another* woman who was killed in a fire. Someone about Betty's size, a Jane Doe nobody cared about. McChesney just had to switch the X rays and phony up the dental charts. McChesney gets a cushy job with the studios, and you got to keep on riding the range."

Stratton led Quinn closer to the merry-go-round, the brightly colored horses whirling past, the music so loud it was impossible to record their conversation.

"It was McChesney's idea to switch the X rays," said Stratton, his lips tight. "He told me he destroyed Betty's X rays, he said no one would ever know. Then forty years later, Tod shows up. . . ." His eyes flashed. "If Doc needed money he should have asked me. I'd have taken care of him."

"Like you took care of Betty Andaluse?"

"Betty . . . that was an accident." Stratton took his time. He had to keep swallowing. "I drank some in those days, Betty did too. . . . I was young, hot-blooded, and I couldn't stand anybody even looking at her. She was so beautiful . . . I never touched her face, never—I'd cut my arm off first." He cleared his throat, looking away. "That night . . . I pushed her, and she fell funny. . . . It was an accident." He shrugged helplessly. "I burned the house to the ground. . . . I thought it would do some good. The newspapers wouldn't understand—"

"It didn't fool McChesney though, did it?"

"No." Stratton snorted at the memory. "He knew right away. It didn't bother him though—'No sense crying over spilt milk,' that's what he said. Doc was a cold fish but he was crazy for the pictures. I got him put on contract at one of the other studios, and over the years we lost touch. It was a long time ago."

"Not long enough."

Stratton nodded. "Tod saw a photo of McChesney in an old scandal sheet. Doc had been arrested for botching an abortion on some extra from *The Birds,* and the magazine made a big deal of it. Tod recognized him from my scrapbooks . . ." Stratton's face darkened. "I keep my scrapbooks in the bedroom at the ranch . . . *our* bedroom," he said bitterly. "Tod must have gone through them when . . . when he was . . . visiting, must have spotted a photo of me and McChesney. I used to run into Doc at parties in the old days. I didn't care—there was nothing to hide. Not really."

"Who are you trying to convince?" asked Quinn.

The production assistant stayed a healthy distance away, holding up a cellular phone to Stratton. He ignored her.

"I never hit a woman after Betty died," said Stratton. "I swear to God. You ask Sissy. Her first husband used to beat her, and she said he was the last man who'd ever raise a hand to her. I never even raised my *voice* to Sissy. Ask her."

"I did ask her. About an hour ago." Quinn savored the panic on Stratton's face. It was there just for an instant; then he got control of himself. "She told me you're a perfect gentleman." He let Stratton relax. "Liston was a gentleman too. A real conversationalist. I thought he was going to talk me to death."

"I'm sorry about that. Sorry about your friend too, but there was no way I could have predicted Liston would go crazy."

"I don't think Liston was crazy," Quinn said. The wooden horses on the merry-go-round were wild-eyed, nostrils flared. "Liston was just someone who took on a job and couldn't rest until he finished it. He thought by protecting you, he was protecting Sissy. Liston didn't believe Tod had turned over all the X rays, that's why he kept asking me if I had 'the last one.' It made him angry thinking he had let Sissy down. Did you ever see Liston angry?"

"You don't scare me," said Stratton. "I asked around about you. You don't have any credibility with the cops, and you *sure* don't have any proof." He put his thumb against his forehead, pushing back a pearl-white Stetson that wasn't there. "Let me ask you something. Did you ever hear about a movie called *Badman from Durango?*"

"No."

Stratton barked laughter. "Neither did anybody else. It was my best performance and it died in a week. Critics loved it—ask Cliff. It came out in June 1957. I was number three at the box office that year and people stayed away in droves."

Quinn watched him.

"I played a ruthless outlaw," said Stratton, "a desperado who shot a cattle rancher in the back and left his partner to die. Great part, but I wasn't right for it. The public didn't want to see me play a bad man. I'm just not believable in that role. So, you think anything you want, but in life and in the movies, there's good guys and bad guys, and I'm one of the good guys."

The production assistant waved frantically at Stratton. She held up the phone and mouthed the name "Sissy." Stratton glanced at Quinn, then hurried to the phone.

Stratton was right—he was one of the good guys. Nobody could touch him.

Morales had visited Quinn every day in the hospital. Just before he was released, Esteban told him the department had concluded that Liston was a psychotic fan who acted alone. All Quinn had was circumstantial evidence of Stratton's or Sissy's involvement with Liston, and that wasn't enough for the police, or for *SLAP*. Napitano said that a libel judgment against the magazine could cost tens of millions of dollars, and he wanted to keep his art collection, and perhaps, dear boy, it was best to fuck someone who couldn't fuck back so hard.

Stratton's handsome face was eroding as he listened to Sissy on the phone, his strong features crumbling like a sandcastle as the tide raced in. Quinn imagined the Cheshire moon purring overhead as the water rushed the beach, its vast, hungry yellow grin spreading across the stars. The moon was going to have to settle for Stratton this time. It was going to have to wait for Quinn.

Stratton dropped the phone onto the floor, then slowly walked back over. "You bastard," he said, "you didn't have to do that. We could have worked something out."

"I kept wondering what would have made Tod hold out on Liston," said Quinn. "Who in their right mind would refuse Liston anything? So I took another look at the autopsy report, and it said there were five X rays. It was a switched report, but five X rays were standard at the time. Sissy didn't say much when I called a little while ago, but I got the idea you told her that there were six X rays in Betty's autopsy file. That's what Liston must have thought too." He chastened Stratton with a forefinger. "Sissy seemed very upset with you, John. I think she was willing to forgive your little 'accident' forty years ago, but killing Tod . . . that was different."

"Sissy's leaving me." Stratton sounded like an old black-and-white soundtrack, cracked and fading.

"You should have played it straight with Tod. All he wanted was to be a big shot, have some fancy business cards printed up and sleep with starlets. Tod was no threat to you. You didn't have to turn Liston loose on him. He kept his part of the deal."

"I don't make deals with trash like him," snapped Stratton. "What's mine is mine. People today have no respect for private property; that's what's wrong with this country. People waltz right into your house, into your bedroom, take what they want. . . ."

"Did you kill Dr. McChesney?"

"No one cares about right or wrong anymore." Stratton tugged at his collar, trying to catch his breath. "Gimmee, gimmee, gimmee," he snarled, "that's all people are interested in— well, somebody's got to stop them."

Quinn walked to the up escalator.

"Sissy was supposed to be onstage with me when I make my announcement," Stratton shouted after him. Heads turned. "Now what do I do?"

Quinn didn't answer. He rode the escalator, watching Stratton get smaller and smaller below.

Traffic was light along the coast. Quinn drove slowly, watching the waves roll in. He thought of Andy as he passed Belmont Shore, hoped he was someplace where there were free coffee refills and everything was on sale.

Jen was waiting for him at the restaurant. For the last week, Quinn had been staying with her, ever since he got out of the hospital. He was too banged up to take care of himself, and Rachel was busy and . . . he wanted to be with Jen. Katie hadn't talked to him for the first three or four days, but yesterday she had told him about her science project, so maybe things were going to be okay.

The hostess at the restaurant smiled as he walked through the door a couple of hours later, then took his arm and brought him to a table overlooking the pier. Before he sat down, he spotted Jen on the other side of the dining room.

Jen waved and started toward him, wearing a floral-print crepe dress, the red and yellow hibiscus blossoms shimmering as she walked across the room. It was the first time he had seen her when she wasn't wearing basic black.

"You look a lot better," said Jen, hugging him.

"I am better." He brushed his lips against her neck, kissed her softly. "Now."

She did a slow turn so that he could appreciate the new

dress. "Have you been getting into trouble again?" she said playfully.

"Just like I promised." Over Jen's shoulder he could see the wide-screen TV in the bar. Stratton and Sissy were standing onstage at the Grand Ballroom, holding hands as thousands of red, white, and blue balloons floated down onto the cheering crowd.

Quinn stared at the screen as Sissy and Stratton raised their hands overhead and the crowd roared their approval. Stratton seemed almost embarrassed, but Sissy was radiant, flushed with the applause. Quinn grimaced.

"What is it?" Jen said.

"Nothing."

Jen glanced at the set, took in the happy couple. "You're surprised?"

"No. Yes." He wanted to kick in the picture tube. "You should have heard Sissy's voice when I told her what Stratton had done. She was going to divorce him."

"And you thought that she wasn't going to change her mind?" Jen shook her head. "You thought Sissy was going to turn down the key to the governor's mansion?" She slipped her arms around his waist. "You don't understand women. Some women," she corrected herself.

He turned away from the set. "It's not over."

"I know that." Her fingertips stroked the angry lines out of his forehead. "I know you." She stood on tiptoe, kissed him tenderly on the mouth, and he closed his eyes and gave in, holding her close as the dining room sounds faded into silence. There were just the two of them, dancing to the music.